J.T. HOWELL

Deviant

Contents

1	A Precarious Procession	1
2	Migrants	10
3	Sacred Carnage	24
4	An Unexpected Kindness	36
5	Under the Brazen Leaf	47
6	Through the Canopy	62
7	The Best Day	74
8	The Temple of the Peacock	91
9	A New Arrival	101
10	Quiet the Mind	117
11	Infernos and Pies	131
12	An Overdue Revelation	145
13	Feeding Time	157
14	In the Mind Palace	172
15	A Short Tour	186
16	The More They Stay the Same	200
17	The More Things Change	216
18	Broken Promises	228
19	Mourning the Dead	240
20	A Lover Scorned	252
21	The Nature of Spirits	265
22	A New Defense	278
23	Under Siege	291
24	The Last Tal'Rach	307

1

A Precarious Procession

The Undergrowth was dark this time of year, and the dense canopy above completely eclipsed the morning sun's light. The lowest reaches of Tabulrossa were illuminated solely by a handful of ambling spirits, commonly known as rach. Their ghostly bodies cast an eerie glow as they snaked their way wistfully around the thick trunk of the giant tree upon which the city was built. Hundreds of citizens packed the winding streets built upon the massive roots spiderwebbed across the forest floor. Their excited voices echoed in the cavernous expanse around them. The awaiting masses gathered on the sidewalks, jostling for a better view of the procession, expectantly peering toward the city's center. The typically vacant streets of the Undergrowth would have been overrun by the waves of onlookers if not for the armored wardens who held the eager tide at bay.

Alistair smiled at the crowd's varying expressions of awe as he strode down the center of a wide boulevard flanked by two wardens on either side. He understood the citizens' joy, even if he did not share their sentiments. Today was the only chance most people would have to glimpse the masters of Tabulrossa—the day of the Calling. When the Tal'Rach's song would echo across the countryside, beckoning humans and rach alike to the great city, soon, the Undergrowth would be flooded with light as hundreds of rach filled the metropolis to the brim, compelled by the ancient song. One day a year, pilgrims across the land were allowed through the otherwise closed gates. It was a joyous day for most, but Alistair dreaded it.

Wrinkling his nose at the musky, rotted smell the Undergrowth was famous for, Alistair led his elite squad off the busy streets and entered a dark, vacant road. As Archwarden of Tabulrossa, it was his duty to protect every human and rach in the great tree. No day was more treacherous for the public's safety than today. The gates would be thrown open in a few hours, and thousands of strangers across the land would flood into the city to make it their new home. Any one of them could be a Deviant. Alistair shuddered to think what would happen if one of those monsters managed to sneak past the gates. Not only was the city at its most vulnerable during the Calling but so were the Tal'Rach. The great spirits created the mighty tree of Tabulrossa and presided over the city built in its branches, trunks, and roots. There would be no life without them, and the Deviants knew that.

The graying archwarden clenched his jaw resolutely and followed the winding path, ignoring the mossy, abandoned buildings on either side. It was his twentieth Calling since joining the wardens and his fifth as archwarden. Each year was more harrowing than the last and added decades onto his life, but Alistair took it all in stride, being a consummate professional who dealt with stress efficiently. He had earned the reputation of having ice in his veins, though he did not enjoy how freely his subordinates talked about him when they thought there were no ears around to listen.

Today was worse than any previous Calling Alistair had experienced. His heart pounded with fear since the disturbing report earlier that morning—the same report he was on his way to verify. If the story was true, then the entire city was in peril.

A faint melody floated into his ears, and Alistair stopped dead in his tracks. In horror, he peered towards the city's center, towards the great trunk. The Tal'Rach's song had already begun, and they had undoubtedly started their procession, using their avatars to promenade through the city.

"Faster, we haven't much farther to go." Alistair deepened his voice, hoping his sternness would mask his terror.

They had run out of time.

The five wardens jogged behind, armored boots stamping the mossy forest floor, passing dozens of empty, dilapidated buildings. The Undergrowth was not a suitable place to live since the area depended on the rach to provide light. The number of rach who dwelt in the city had recently declined. As an entire year had passed since the previous Calling, the city was almost devoid of rach. Most citizens had abandoned the lower reaches decades ago in favor of the sunny and warm streets in the canopy. What was once a glorious, sprawling garden in Alistair's youth was now a dark, moss-ridden waste filled with burial grounds and unsavory figures.

The archwarden led his patrol off the root path, around an ancient burial ground towards a cluster of half-collapsed buildings. He examined the young wardens as they neared their destination. They were not upset like Alistair, though confusion was evident on their faces as they followed their superior. They had not heard the same report the archwarden had. If the harrowing account proved true, they would be terrified like him soon enough.

Dread seeped into Alistair's troubled mind as he neared the cluster of vacant homes. The putrid smell ahead already confirmed the unsettling account one of his scouts reported only an hour earlier. The patrol turned the corner of a long-abandoned storehouse, and one of Alistair's wardens vomited in disgust. A metallic taste in his mouth threatened the archwarden with the same fate, but he breathed through his nose methodically, compelling his body to remain respectable in front of his unit. Projecting strength was his duty as their leader. He hesitantly stepped into the alleyway, his knees trembling with fear, and his wardens trailed behind. Dried blood caked the ground below, and body parts covered the alley like fallen leaves. Something crunched beneath his boot; he raised it to reveal a severed hand. His tongue was dry, and the metallic taste grew stronger, once again threatening to empty his stomach.

Counting the number of casualties in the narrow alleyway proved impossible, but Alistair recognized each one as a warden by their distinctive armor. Nevertheless, searching for signs of struggle, he estimated roughly thirty bodies strewn about the mossy ground.

All the evidence suggested that this was a slaughter. Alistair had received reports of missing patrols earlier that morning and sent scouts to investigate the outer reaches of the Undergrowth. Only one returned. The terrified survivor who retold the account could barely speak upon her arrival.

Another warden retched as they inspected the grizzly scene,

and Alistair did not blame her. He would have thrown up by now if every cell in his body was not fighting the visceral reaction to the horror surrounding him. Alistair did not have the luxury of allowing his body to show weakness as the Archwarden of Tabulrossa. He ignored his bodily urges, fixating on the end of the alleyway, at the scorched wall. Burned into the mossy, ancient wood was a rough insignia depicting a ram's head, a pair of horns curved menacingly.

"Veremund," the warden to his right hissed, causing a wave of terrified whispers to wash over the group.

The name of the rogue Tal'Rach filled each of them with dread, and rightfully so. Only one of the great spirits could massacre thirty armed wardens, and only the Ram spirit would commit such an atrocity.

The chaotic Tal'Rach was the youngest of the great spirits that ruled Tabulrossa. Recently, he had neglected his sacred duty and terrorized the city instead of protecting it. This abrupt shift created a schism between him and his nobler brothers and sisters. Alistair was close enough to the Tal'Rach to know they feared that Veremund's current path would result in him turning into a Deviant.

Throughout history, certain rach became corrupted by the darkness, tainted, and twisted into Deviants, also known as Ae'Rach in the old tongue or dark spirits. They would possess ordinary humans, hundreds at once, killing the host and creating a monster focused only on destruction and chaos. For years, the Deviant forces ravaged villages and towns across the land. It had been ages since a great spirit succumbed to the darkness, and that was the father of Deviants himself. Lucian. It had been centuries since the Tal'Rach destroyed him and rid Tabulrossa of his wrath, but his stain on the world endured with the Deviant menace. Alistair's sacred duty was to safeguard the realm from such a threat. For years, they were winning, but then the Ram spirit began to turn.

He started by protecting the Deviant scum, constructing havens for them across the city, then attacking wardens outright. The great spirits were benevolent beings of such enormous power as to create Tabulrossa, and there was no telling what a corrupt Tal'Rach would be capable of. Today, Veremund was making his final play. This slaughter was proof enough.

Alistair had decreased his patrols at the eastern gate to compensate for the missing wardens. This diversion had drawn him away from his rightful place by the Tal'Rach's side, leaving them vulnerable. The ram was planning a frontal assault.

"Talia," Alistair snapped at the nearest warden, forcing himself to focus on the present. "Run as fast as you can, gather every warden between here and the eastern gate, and search the pilgrims thoroughly. Deviants will attempt to infiltrate the city to aid Veremund. Make sure you execute any you discover. Take Jaron with you."

Talia and Jaron saluted obediently and took off into the dark. To Alistair's dismay, the abandoned streets were significantly brighter than before. Dozens of rach floated above him in all shapes and sizes. An enormous whale radiating blue light passed above the rooftops while a flock of blazing red eagles soared toward the canopy. More and more rach streamed in from the countryside, meaning the Tal'Rach were well into their procession. They would be an easy target for the wrathful ram.

"The rest of you, with me," Alistair bellowed, sprinting out of the alley, the remaining wardens trailing behind. "Straight to the Tal'Rach, we must defend them at all costs."

They ran through the empty streets, breathing laboriously as dozens of rach floated above them. A scrawny rabbit sprinted next to Alistair, then disappeared behind a wall of an abandoned house. The sweet song of the Tal'Rach echoed through the entire city. Alistair scanned the air above as they arrived at the main road they had used earlier that day. The Tal'Rach were powerful beings, their song intoxicating to the lesser rach, so hopefully, they could lead Alistair to the procession.

There. Towards the left, a swarm of rach floated in the air, dancing in circles above the rooftops. The procession had passed Alistair's position and was almost halfway to the eastern gate. That was where Veremund would strike. The archwarden barreled past the dispersing crowds. Luckily, the road had cleared considerably since the Tal'Rach passed, and the onlookers returned to their homes above. Alistair charged through the loitering remnants, almost colliding with an elderly gentleman as he drew closer to the Tal'Rach.

Alistair shouted at each warden that he passed, ordering them to follow. The green-armored guardians were quick to obey once they recognized their commander. Soon, Alistair had at least a dozen wardens on his heels as he approached the grand procession. He hoped that it would be enough to defend against Veremund's onslaught.

The Tal'Rach continued their song, and the rach flowed into the city like a great river of light. After sprinting across half of the Undergrowth, the archwarden and his followers finally caught up with the grand procession of the Tal'Rach, which had almost reached the eastern gate. Alistair let out a low sigh. They were not too late.

Hundreds of robed figures pranced gleefully in concentric circles. The Tal'Rach resided in the center of the glorious dance. The illustrious spirits strode proudly in the boulevard's center, smiling and waving at the sea of revelers who basked in their presence. They were larger than most humans, over a head taller, and seemed to radiate light. Each had the characteristics of a different animal. Wolf. Lion. Snake. Bull. Spider. Raven. Ocelot. Boar. Fourteen in total. Ancient beings older than the foundations of the earth. Even the run-down street of the Undergrowth seemed regal in their light.

Hundreds of women robed in white accompanied the Tal'Rach, the priestesses. The women sang to the glowing rach flying above their heads, and the ghostly figures mimicked the dancing women below. Alistair couldn't help but smile at the beautiful display, but it did not slow him. Only a handful of wardens were part of the parade, and his meager force may not be strong enough to repel the impending attack.

He needed to be closer. One minute more, and he would be within reach. He could not fail.

Someone screamed.

The crowd broke and flooded the street, slamming into Alistair and his wardens. Halting, he ordered his patrol to follow suit and tighten ranks. The building beyond the crowd exploded in fire. Children screeched in fear as their parents carried them from the carnage. Alistair pushed determinedly against the tide toward the inferno.

As the crowd thinned, he beheld a towering figure bathed in azure flames. Long, curved horns sprouted from his midnight-black hair. His skin shone brightly in the firelight, made taut by massive muscles protruding from his tunic. His eyes were dark, full of hatred, narrowing as the wardens came into view.

Veremund. The dark ram spirit.

He smiled viciously. Balls of fire sprouted from his palms. He hurled one directly at Alistair.

2

Migrants

The road to Tabulrossa wound across great plains near the foothills of the Dragon's Teeth. The sun had recently risen above their jagged peaks, lighting the broad thoroughfare's dewy grass and worn dirt. The most powerful city in the world was also the most remote, built in the shadows of the infamous mountain range. The nearest village lay more than a day's walk southward. A horde of migrants trod sluggishly northward along the edge of the mountains, ragged after such a grueling journey.

Their spirits were bright, however, for today was the day of the Calling. The lustrous city was known worldwide as the most prosperous and peaceful place on earth. Life in the outside world, however, was not so idyllic. A war raged in the western marshes, a drought decimated storehouses in the southern plains, and pillaging was commonplace across the land. Tabulrossa seemed to be the only safe place left, and today was the only chance for poor, desperate souls to secure a better life for themselves and their families.

However, it was the most dangerous destination for Sarina

and her friends.

She stood on a rocky outcrop, leaning against her thick wooden staff, examining the steady flow of pilgrims approaching the city. The canopy of the great tree was not yet visible across the horizon, but she knew it was near. Sarina was in her middle years, though most people assumed her older by her steely and severe demeanor. She cut her auburn hair short, barely reaching her shoulders. She wasn't known for frivolity, even in her past life.

Sarina glanced at the mountain pass behind her, which led into the treacherous range that marked the world's edge. Swallowing hard, she turned from the dangerous route, hoping she hadn't made a terrible mistake. Sarina forced the doubts out of her head. How would her companions accept her leadership if she didn't trust her instincts?

Climbing down the rocky outcrop, Sarina joined the others in the shaded hollow below. Most were crouched on the ground, hiding from wandering eyes on the nearby road. They perked up at her arrival, eager to hear her decision. Her ragged and dirt-stained companions resembled the masses trudging toward Tabulrossa, tired and travel-worn. Stoic Laithe kept his watch at the hollow's entrance, mousy Benjin glued to his side, as usual.

Kez sat in the center, staring sightlessly at the cavern wall. Callandra and Beriane had fallen asleep, their arms intertwined. It was dangerous to lower their guards so close to Tabulrossa, but Sarina could hardly blame them. It had been an arduous journey and an even more challenging year. She could count the nights they spent with a roof over their heads on one hand.

They numbered six in total, including Sarina, though there

had been over twenty at the start of their journey. The wardens had grown more aggressive, more bloodthirsty. One by one, the monsters clad in green armor hunted her friends like animals. Each of their faces still haunted her. She felt she had failed all of them, though she was rational enough to know better.

Deviants did not survive for long in the wild. It was only natural.

Two years ago, Sarina met the others shortly after the Tal'Rach proclaimed the Ninth Edict. The group of outcast Deviants had numbered over thirty. They found her only days after her village drove her out with shovels and pitchforks. Either the mob or the warden patrols would have captured and executed her if she hadn't stumbled upon the other Deviants. Most were kind and hospitable, though a few were particularly bristly. Having no home and no prospects elsewhere, Sarina decided to join the band of Deviants and remained with them ever since. They were an eclectic bunch from all nations and different walks of life but tethered together in their oppression. Dark spirits, the world labeled them. But Sarina had never met an Ae'rach, much less been one herself. None of the Deviants she had met in the past two years were possessed.

They met various groups in safe houses across the land, but the encounters were always treacherous. Sharing safe havens for a group of their size was unpleasant, and resources were slim and difficult to acquire with wardens constantly on the hunt—Sarina and her companions' survival depended on trusting one another. A few months after she joined, a deadly warden ambush killed the group's original leader. Eventually, the others relied on her and expected her to make decisions. It was an annoying pattern in her life, finding others following her lead when she only wanted to fade into the background. Sarina had no idea what they saw in her. Maybe it was her calmness in challenging situations, her penchant for constant questioning, or her stern demeanor; regardless, she begrudgingly accepted her role. After being hunted across the world, only six remained, and Lucian damn her if she allowed another to fall to the butchers who called themselves wardens.

The forces of Tabulrossa routed out the Deviants' havens one by one. It had been months since Sarina had seen a safe house untouched by the wardens. It seemed as if no safe place remained in the world, and their options were practically nonexistent.

Now, she only saw two paths before them. Cross the Dragon's Teeth and venture into the unknown, or enter the most dangerous place on earth for a Deviant. The city of Tabulrossa. Home of the wardens and their masters. The Tal'Rach. The authors of the Edicts.

"What did you decide? Where are we headed?" Benjin asked expectantly. The wide-eyed youth was the first to pop up as Sarina entered their makeshift hideout. He was the youngest and the most excitable; Sarina was surprised that he had survived this long. Benjin had been a part of the group longer than Sarina, as had the other survivors. The Fourteenth Edict marked him as a Deviant, a man who loved men.

"The pass through the Dragon's Teeth is too dangerous. Our rations will only last two more days, and there is no way of telling how long the journey will take. The pass rises above the tree line, and we lost our last blanket weeks ago. We would probably freeze to death on the first night." She gestured towards the tiny sack of their remaining supplies that Callandra and Beriane used as a pillow.

The two women awakened at the sound of Benjin's questioning, trepidation replacing their dreamy expressions. Like Sarina, they were Fifteens, marked as Deviants in the Fifteenth Edict as women who loved women. They joined the band of refugees only days before her. Frankly, she was jealous of their love. Sarina had not been so lucky in matters of the heart. The Fifteenth Edict complicated such affairs.

"So our fate lies in Tabulrossa. How fitting," Kez spoke in a low, hoarse rasp. The older woman remained on the ground, resting her legs, blindly gazing in the distance. She had been in the group the longest; her strength and resolute heart had kept them all sane these past years. She was born blind and moved with as much ease as any person Sarina had met. The Eighth Edict marked Kez, and all sight-impaired people, as a Deviant.

"W-we can't, Sarina," Benjin pleaded frantically. "They will slaughter us before we reach the gates. I'd rather freeze to death."

"Calm yourself, Benjin," Sarina reassured him. "Tabulrossa is the last place a warden would look for a group of our size. And frankly, there is nowhere else to run or hide. I spoke with a grizzled Deviant at the last safe house. According to her, a Tal'Rach has become friendly to our kind. They call him Veremund. He has helped almost a hundred Deviants into the city over the years and offers constant protection."

"But how can you be sure?" Benjin began, but a soft pat on his shoulder silenced him.

Kez silently crossed the hollow and sat next to the anxious Deviant. "Do not let your fear cloud your judgment, boy," the elderly woman drawled. "Tabulrossa is our best option. I, too, have heard stories of this Veremund. I overheard a tale about a man sneaking into the city with his lover. They called Veremund's name, and within ten heartbeats, the great spirit appeared and carried them to safety. They left the city the next day and returned with ten more Deviants, and the Ram spirit saved them all. According to the stories, hundreds of our kind live within the great tree."

"There was a similar story a Fourteen told to me when we ran into that group headed south, last year," Beriane chimed in; she beamed brightly as hope returned to her delicate features. She glanced at her wife, Callandra. The tall woman smiled at her lover approvingly.

Sarina breathed a welcome sigh of relief. She thought the mere mention of Tabulrossa would have sent the others running into the Dragon's Teeth to their inevitable doom. But yet again, Kez's calming words saved them from sheer panic.

"No time to waste, then," Laithe said flatly. The rough man with sun-darkened, bronze skin and raven hair tightly gripped a pair of worn axes in his burly hands. He hid his weapons expertly underneath his dirt-stained cloak, lifting his heavy hood to obscure his features, and exited the hollow. Benjin was close on his heels; the young man had an obvious crush on the hardened mercenary, though Sarina was sure Laithe would never reciprocate his feelings.

Sarina gathered her friends and departed the hollow hastily, surprised that Laithe had spoken at all, being the most standoffish Deviant in the group. However prickly his disposition, the mercenary, and his axes were the only reason the remaining six survived the journey. Most in the group were not skilled warriors, though each was armed to the teeth.

Sarina was reasonably competent with her quarterstaff, and Kez was remarkably talented with hand-to-hand combat for a wizened woman without sight. She concealed a dozen daggers beneath her cloak and was in a state of constant vigilance, relying on her other heightened senses.

Laithe's ferocity was essential in a fight, however. He had been a Deviant his entire life and only survived as long as he had by being an efficient killer. Laithe's bright yellow eyes distinguished him as part of the Roursche Clan. The amber-eyed clan far to the south was labeled Deviants in the Second Edict. To Sarina's knowledge, Laithe was the last surviving Roursche in the world.

They snuck towards the road in pairs, Laithe and Benjin leading the way, then Callandra and Beriane, with Sarina and Kez close behind. Keeping their heads down, the six Deviants quietly joined the stream of dust-covered travelers; the blind woman and the Roursche kept their deep hoods drawn to conceal their identities. Any man, woman, or child would rat them out to the wardens if they became suspicious of their true nature. Physical Deviant attributes were challenging to disguise, but Kez and Laithe managed effortlessly after years of deception.

Within an hour, the mid-morning sky grew full of rach. At first, only a smattering dotted the blue expanse, but hundreds of spectral creatures soon snaked across the sky, shining bright in the morning sun. Children gasped, and elders laughed in joy at the sight. Rach were not especially rare; Sarina had encountered her fair share, but never before had she seen a gathering of this magnitude. She couldn't help but smile as she stared upward at the great migration. The rach mimicked the humans on the muddy path below, a sickly sweet melody floating across the plains called both groups northward towards Tabulrossa. For most pilgrims, this journey would end in their salvation from the wild world, but for Sarina and her friends, it could result in death. Sarina was thankful for the rach above, for they distracted the pilgrims around her. They were too focused on the glowing rach above to notice a group of Deviants in their midst.

The city finally came into view along the grassy horizon. At first, Sarina thought it was a mountain. The green dome was neither stone nor rock but a sprawling canopy. A crown of brilliant green sparkled against the late morning sun, hundreds of thousands of leaves rustling in an emerald sea. The enormous canopy stretched for leagues, supported by countless thick trunks.

"It's an entire forest," Beriane breathed quietly. "The stories said it was only one tree."

"It is only one," Benjin said brightly, full of wonder and excitement. "That monstrous plant grew from one seed. Fueled by the Tal'Rach's power. But the thinner trunks you see are called drop roots. Each one thicker than any tree back home in the south. But they are roots; the great trunk lies deep within and is larger than you can imagine. I hear they all have platforms and bridges connecting them. Some people even live in hollows carved in the wood. Maybe we can find one of our own!"

"I wasn't aware you knew so much about Tabulrossa, Benjin, much less anything else," Kez said dryly.

"Don't let my handsome face fool you...you know what I mean, Kez," Benjin said ruefully. "I was a scholar back in Ralsford, and there were plenty of books about Tabulrossa and the Tal'Rach. They are more entertaining than the ancient histories."

"Thank you for the lesson, Benjin," Sarina said warmly. Her tone grew firm as they approached the city wall. "But we will have to wait for more. Ready yourselves. The gate is drawing near."

After a grueling period of silent marching, they crossed the city's actual perimeter; the canopy loomed over them, blotting out the sun. Thousands of massive roots breached the earth and wove together in a tight, intricate formation that grew thirty paces above the grassy plains. The great road fed into a gaping, circular opening in the wall. The masses of migrants pushed and shoved their way into the city entrance. A company of wardens in their sickly green armor assembled lazily on either side, reluctantly allowing the crowds to surge inside to the city beyond.

A pair of rough, manufactured doors were flung open, their craftsmanship appearing juvenile in contrast to the beautiful, natural design of the city wall. The construction of humans paled compared to the sheer splendor of the Tal'Rach's creation. They were close enough to the great tree to behold the countless structures built along its immense branches; Sarina could see people on the streets above. Spiral staircases were cut into the drop roots, interrupted now and then by enormous platforms, as Benjin had described earlier. The sheer magnitude of the city frightened Sarina. But not as much as what happened next.

The crowd around her tightened as the pilgrims ahead abruptly halted. What was a free-flowing surge into the city was now a stagnant queue in front of the gates. Sarina jostled around for a better vantage point. Her heart sank. The half dozen wardens guarding the gate had been bolstered by at least thirty more, blocking the entire entrance. One by one, the green-clad brutes roughly searched each migrant, emptying their belongings on the ground and interrogating them thoroughly. Something was wrong. They were hunting for Deviants among the rabble. And they were about to discover six.

The crowd forced Sarina and her companions forward. She breathed deeply to calm herself. As she pushed her emotions aside, her mind raced, thinking of solutions. There was no turning back now; they were too close to the gate, and the wardens would easily detect their retreat. They had to deceive the wardens.

"Keep calm, everyone. I will do the talking." Sarina said. "Kez, keep your eyes closed. Pretend to be exhausted and dehydrated. Beriane and Callandra, act as if you are carrying her. Laithe—"

The burly man had already knelt on the road and covered his rugged features with dirt. Laithe pulled a long, blood-stained strip of cloth from his pocket and tied it around his forehead, the rough fabric hung low along his brow. Clever; hopefully, the wardens wouldn't look too closely at his eyes underneath the fake bandage.

If they did, they were all dead.

"Everyone stay calm," she repeated, hoping to reassure the others. She could sense the terror in them, except for Laithe. "They can't check us too thoroughly with a crowd this size. Answer their questions, but only if they speak to you directly. We have all been through this before."

Her companions silently acknowledged her as they marched resolutely toward the gate until there were only a few migrants between them and the warden checkpoint.

So far, the wardens hadn't arrested or killed anyone in the crowd ahead of them, which would make the wardens more eager to rout out Deviants. Finally, they reached the front of the line, and a pair of wardens stepped forward to examine them. Sarina slowed her breathing, ensuring her demeanor was relaxed.

"How many in your party," the warden on the left demanded.

"Six," Sarina replied, unblinking. Only someone who had a secret to hide avoided eye contact. That or someone terrified. Sarina wouldn't dare show weakness. Not now.

"Forward. Move!" the warden snapped. His companion shoved Benjin toward the opened gate, who yelped at the violent push.

Sarina laid a calming hand on Benjin and led him to another pair of wardens near the gate. They simply had to answer their questions and clear the checkpoint. One of the wardens grabbed the bag from Beriane and tossed its meager contents onto a pile of belongings left behind by the migrants before them.

"Where are you traveling from," the second warden asked gruffly.

"We are—" Sarina began.

"Not you," he spat and pointed at Benjin, who was visibly shaking. "I want him to answer."

"We….uh….we are…from the south," Benjin stammered. Fuck. Sarina kicked herself. She should have acted more hysterical. This warden was clever and sought to exploit the weakest link.

"Where in the south, boy? It's a big place," the warden demanded.

"Um…G-grainsport. Yes. We came from Grainsport,"

Benjin replied slowly, fabricating a story, though his delivery was far from believable.

"When did you leave your homes?" the warden asked, narrowing his eyes. The young man's stammering had raised his suspicions.

"J-just a month ago," Benjin said, finally composing himself. There was hope for them yet. "We wanted to be here for the Calling. The crops died on the farm, and we had nowhere else to go."

"Funny, last I heard, Grainsport burned to the ground by a wildfire six months ago. Hard to farm burned soil in an abandoned town," the warden drawled, drawing his sword.

Fuck. Fuck. Fuck.

"I…I meant outside of the town…in a village…leagues away," Benjin stammered, backtracking. But the damage was done.

"Where are you from, boy? Do not lie to me now," the warden growled and stepped towards Benjin, pointing the tip of his sword at the young man's neck. Before he could reach him, Laithe moved between the two with lightning speed, one hand on the warden's blade, the other in his cloak, gripping one of his axes.

The warden balked at Laithe and sneered, both men mere inches from one another. The warden inhaled sharply, his skin white as a ghost. He noticed Laithe's yellow irises from underneath the false bandage. The Second Edict was a couple of decades old, but every warden knew each Edict by heart.

If the man cried out, every soldier at the checkpoint would descend upon them. Only one option remained: one final gambit.

"Veremund!" Sarina cried. She felt foolish, but the rumors of the ram were all she had left—one heartbeat. The warden was agape in shock. Two heartbeats. The nearby pilgrims shrieked in terror and fled the muddy road. Three heartbeats. The second warden stopped her search with their bag and drew her sword. Four heartbeats.

Instead of calling for reinforcements, the two wardens remained silent, eyeing the Deviants warily with an odd expression. Sheer terror. The very name of the ram spirit seemed to chill their bones. They understood what was about to happen. Five heartbeats. Six. Maybe their fear would prevent them from attacking before Veremund came to the rescue. Seven heartbeats. The wardens within earshot surrounded them but maintained their distance—a dozen wardens.

"What did you say?" the first warden breathed, wildly scanning the crowd. Eight heartbeats. "What did you do?"

Sarina smirked, waiting for Veremund to appear beyond the gate. Nine heartbeats. The rumors must have been true if the wardens feared speaking his name. Ten heartbeats.

Eleven heartbeats. Sarina desperately scanned her surroundings. Twelve heartbeats. There was no ram. Veremund had not answered the call. The warden smiled nastily, lunged forward, and plunged his sword deep into Benjin's neck.

Beriane screamed as Benjin fell to the ground, coughing blood, trembling hands grasping his ruined throat. Before Benjin hit the dirt road, Laithe drew his first ax and buried it deep in the warden's skull. Tearing it out with a sickening crunch, he expertly pivoted and decapitated the dead man's companion with his second ax.

In a flash, Kez charged the nearest warden, her daggers drawn, stabbing with lightning speed. The first three strikes bounced off emerald armor, but the fourth buried itself into the man's neck. He barely hit the ground before she descended upon another victim. Sarina marveled at her prowess. Kez explained that wardens had a particular stench that allowed her to locate them effortlessly on a battlefield.

Sarina cried out in fury and cracked the skull of the nearest warden with her quarterstaff and pushed the weeping Beriane towards the gate.

"Go! Now!" Sarina shouted, sprinting toward the line of armed wardens. She desperately wanted to look back at Benjin's body. There was a chance he was still alive and needed comfort. But it would be a futile, foolish act. If she remained, they would all lose their lives.

The five Deviants barreled into the shocked wardens and the great city of Tabulrossa. If Veremund wouldn't rescue them, then they would save themselves.

3

Sacred Carnage

Laithe pulled his ax out of the fallen warden's chest and buried it into the neck of another. Citizens and pilgrims fled the plaza beyond the gate in a panic.

Good. Laithe would show them something to fear. He slashed his way past another pair of wardens. The green-clad warriors inside the city were softer than their brethren in the outlying lands and proved surprisingly easy to kill. They must not have had much experience with combat tucked safely behind the city walls. Both axes dripping in blood, Laithe stalked further into Tabulrossa, blinded by rage. His companions were nowhere in sight, and he didn't bother searching for them in the turbulent crowd. They were probably already dead, like Benjin.

The young man had harbored feelings for Laithe for quite a while, hanging on him like a lost puppy. He thought it cute but had no energy for a pet. Laithe probably would have obliged Benjin's advances if he hadn't learned better. Sex came with attachment, and everyone died sooner or later. In Laithe's experience, it was always sooner. And poor Benjin was no different.

The fewer attachments Laithe had, the better he was for it. He had been labeled a Deviant for most of his life and learned how to survive, unlike his family, clan, and any friend he ever made. He met several men he fancied enough to share a bed with, but they all fell to the blade, especially after the Fourteenth Edict made him a Deviant twice over. Laithe was lucky that way.

He could search for the others, but his life was about to end, so he decided to kill the greatest number of the blasted wardens as he could before it happened.

Charging through the city, covered in sweat and blood, Laithe tore into the wardens; the fools were stupid enough to challenge him only in pairs. As if two would be enough to stop his onslaught. Pitiful. His rampage took him deeper into the moss-covered city, and he gradually experienced less resistance. Wardens here were preoccupied with quelling the stampeding citizens. It didn't take the blood-soaked Deviant long to realize the people in this part of the city were no longer running from him. On the contrary, they were running toward him.

The road ahead exploded in fire.

A strange group gathered in the center of the road, where the root angled upward into a bridge that arched over the mossy ground far below. A score of heavily armed wardens surrounded the odd, robed figures who towered above their guard. One had a lion's head, another with a bird's wings, and a third sat on a serpentine tail. Despite their imposing size, the creatures were huddled together behind their warden defenders, clearly terrified. But Laithe was not the source of their fear, for they faced the opposite direction toward the burning root bridge. The figures opened their mouths in unison. Oddly, no sound emerged.

A massive ball of light erupted from each, pouring out into the air above, taking the form of a different animal. Raven. Lion. Snake. They were all enormous rach, blazing brighter than the sun. They flew upwards into the canopy in a flurry of light, escaping the unrest of the street. A group of robed humans huddled in their place, crying and screaming in terror. The wardens ushered them down the bridge, away from the flames, and into the alley. Not a single one noticed Laithe and his bloody axes.

Another figure came into view.

He was similar to the creatures who had fled, tall and regal, imposing, curved horns sprouting from his short black hair, but he was somehow different. The giant man was feral, ferocious, and covered in blood. Hot blue flames danced in his palms. He loomed over the bridge's apex with dozens of wardens lying dead at his feet, eyes filled with a glorious rage. His tunic lay tattered on his tight, muscular body, exposing an impressive physique. He angrily hurled a ball of flame at a charging pair of wardens. He spun violently and slashed the throat of a third assailant, who crumpled into a gurgling bloody heap. Laithe knew he was gazing upon Veremund by the sight of his horns, not to mention the sizable contingent of wardens he had slain.

He was the most beautiful creature Laithe had ever seen.

Battle cries filled the root bridge as scores of heavily armed wardens poured out from the alleyways on either end and rushed the raging Tal'Rach. Their armor was more worn, dented, and scratched than the previous wardens Laithe had fought within the city walls. These men and women were veterans, experts at slaughtering Deviants. They passed by Laithe as if he didn't exist, their attention set only on Veremund. The wardens swarmed the ram spirit like a cloud of green wasps. All-consuming fury flooded into Laithe once more. He roared, charging the flanks of the new attackers, eager to bury his axes into more scalps. The green-clad monsters had taken so much and killed countless innocents. They deserved to endure the same pain they inflicted on everyone Laithe had ever known.

Laithe had the advantage of surprise when he descended upon the veteran flanks, who were preoccupied with the rogue Tal'Rach, desperately dodging the massive creature's deadly blows. They pressed in on either side, overwhelming Veremund. Bright red blood flowed from the ram spirit from a dozen deep cuts. He was undoubtedly powerful but already weary from battle and outnumbered by his enemies. It wouldn't be long until Veremund fell. Laithe would not allow that to happen.

Using the momentum of his charge, Laithe barreled into the nearest pair of wardens, hacking at their necks with intense savagery. Three more fell by his blades before the others noticed his arrival. They pivoted to face him. Good. He wanted them to resist so he could make them suffer. Laithe withdrew a dozen paces, allowing several veteran wardens to stalk toward him, holding their swords warily in a defensive manner. The more he could lure from the ram spirit's orbit, the better. He would certainly die in the process, but at least Veremund would have a chance to wipe out the survivors.

The veterans advanced cautiously, keeping outside of Laithe's striking radius until they fully surrounded him. They were expert Deviant slayers, and each had probably claimed countless lives. But Laithe had killed more. And he would make these bastards pay for their crimes.

Standing still as a statue, axes raised at eye level, he barely breathed, sneering at the wardens. Whoever made the first strike would lose, and Laithe would not be so foolish to move before his opponents. Twenty heartbeats passed as the tense battle of wills raged, and Veremund's roars echoed across the Undergrowth. Four more wardens joined the deadly circle that enclosed the ax-wielding Deviant. Laithe was happy to keep them waiting. The screams of their brethren could be heard over his shoulder, slain indiscriminately by Veremund. Finally, after what seemed a lifetime, the wardens' resolve broke. The eldest warden, standing on Laithe's right, a woman with long, graying hair flowing from underneath her helmet, gestured, and the entire circle attacked, lunging at him in unison.

Laithe smiled. He thought the veterans would be more intelligent than this, but he was wrong. He waited until they were close enough to smell their breath. Laithe only moved when their sword tips were inches from his skin, dropping to his stomach with blurring speed. A blade cut into his shoulder as he hit the ground, but not before he swept his axes in a deadly arc, severing feet from their owner's legs. The carnage below was nothing compared to what transpired above. Without their target in his original place, the wardens' blades plunged deep into their companions' chests. Laithe hit the wooden bridge on his stomach, which knocked the wind out of him. He immediately rolled to the side, avoiding the falling corpses of the unfortunate wardens.

The survivors slashed at him, cutting deep into his arms and shoulders. A survivor leaped on Laithe savagely, and his head bounced roughly on the wooden road below. Infuriated, Laithe ignored the incredible pain wracking his body. He snarled—a broken and guttural sound—and slammed his bloodied axeheads deep into his assailant's neck.

Shoving the mangled corpse aside, he attempted to stand, but three more veterans pounced on him before he could get to his knees. Slashing ferociously, he drove them backward, allowing him the space to regain his footing. He leaped sideways, out of the surviving wardens' reach, in a desperate attempt to assess the situation.

Only five wardens lay dead around him; two were screaming on the ground without feet. Nine remained. Each one enraged, rushing Laithe with bloodied swords, covered with his blood. He was about to die, but he would make sure none would survive to tell the tale. Screaming in defiance, he slashed at his assailants.

The skull of the nearest warden exploded between two massive hands. A brutal swipe sent another one flying. Her ear-splitting screams faded as she plummeted from the bridge. Laithe lifted his chin, and he met Veremund's devastating gaze. Hatred, fury, and pain filled the ram spirit's brown eyes as he carefully regarded Laithe, curiosity seeping into his expression. Glancing behind the massive form, Laithe only saw bloodied corpses where the Tal'Rach once stood. He had decimated his attackers in less than a minute. It was more than a little impressive.

"Such beautiful savagery you possess, small one. I admire it," Veremund said, his voice deep like thunder, teeth bared in a vicious smile. "Are you interested in seeing who can slay the most of these wretches?"

Ignoring his wounds, Laithe grinned wickedly at the

Tal'Rach. His heart raced excitedly as he confronted the remaining wardens. What happened next was not a fight nor a slaughter but a dance. They slayed their enemies, Deviant and Tal'Rach fighting in perfect unison. Although they had only met moments ago, each could predict the other's next move and compliment it perfectly. Laithe had never witnessed another who mastered violence in such a glorious way. He loved it.

Unfortunately, the dance was fleeting, and soon the last warden fell to the ground, dead. They leaned against the waist-high railing at the edge of the root bridge, gasping for air, dripping in blood. Adrenaline prevented him from feeling pain, but Laithe knew his wounds were severe. He would probably die on that bridge.

Veremund smiled once more. The Tal'Rach's gaze caused Laithe's chest to swell with pride.

A sizable arrow slammed into Veremund's chest. The Tal'Rach grunted in pain, eyes filled with confusion, then rage.

A graying man in gilded green armor stood on the opposite end of the bridge. Flanked by a dozen archers, he swiftly reloaded the longbow he had recently fired. How many of the green devils were in this city?

"Alistair!" Veremund bellowed, his expression distorted with fury, his hands filled with blue flames.

Laithe moved without thinking. The Tal'Rach was severely wounded, and neither would survive a volley of arrows at such a close range. Laithe threw his whole weight at Veremund, ignoring the fire the Tal'Rach held. Though the ram spirit was thicker than a bull, Laithe's tackle was enough to send them careening off the edge of the bridge.

Laithe wouldn't survive, but Veremund would. That glorious creature must live so that more wardens would fall. Closing his eyes, he accepted his death, wrapping his arms tightly around Veremund.

But the impact and the following darkness did not come. Laithe opened his eyes. Veremund held him in his arms, standing on the mossy ground beneath the root bridge. He scowled at the Deviant angrily.

"Why did you do that?" Veremund spat. "I was so close. Years of planning led me to that bridge."

"Those arrows would have killed you before you took two steps," Laithe said between ragged breaths. "I've seen one slay a fully grown elephant. You need to live."

Veremund furrowed his brow in curiosity. An arrow embedded itself in the ground inches from the Tal'Rach's giant foot. Three more arrows peppered the moss beneath them. The archers lined the railing above, notching their bows and taking aim.

"You may be right," Veremund sighed, eyeing the arrows. "But you have no idea what you prevented today."

"Your death," Laithe said as more arrows rained around them. "I prevented your death."

Veremund chortled. In one fluid motion, he launched himself into the air and breathed a jet of blue fire upwards, scorching the wardens along the railing. They roughly landed on a root fifty paces away, Laithe wrapped in the Tal'Rach's arms. Veremund glanced longingly at the fiery bridge.

"You are probably right, little one," Veremund said somberly. "Maybe you stopped it, or perhaps you offered me another chance. Either way, we are done here."

Then the Tal'Rach leaped forward again, jarring Laithe's

exhausted body on the landing, another fifty paces. Countless arrows flew around them, none close enough to be a threat. Another leap and the deadly projectiles ceased. Laithe's vision blurred as the pain of his wounds invaded his thoughts. He focused on Veremund as they traversed the Undergrowth: strong jaw, arched nose, and piercing eyes. Only then did the pain subside.

There was no way of telling how long they journeyed, and Laithe was too dazed to care. Eventually, the jumps subsided, and he sprawled on soft grass underneath a wooden ceiling. Water touched his lips, and a firm hand lifted his head as he regained lucidity. He was in a hollow underneath one of the trees Benjin had called a drop root. He lay next to a shallow pool of water, and Veremund crouched over him, covered in blood. As he regained his senses, the pain gradually returned to the dozen deep gashes that crisscrossed his body. Laithe examined his savior, shocked to realize the ram's bloodied skin was free of any wound. The arrow once lodged in his chest was gone.

The power of the Tal'Rach was miraculous.

Veremund submerged his hand into the murky depths of the pool beside them. As he pulled his arm out, the water clung to him like a large ball of jelly. He guided the cold liquid upward and gently poured it on Laithe's heaving body. The water enveloped Laithe in a cool embrace, tingling his entire body with a strange vibration. Its tide cleaned the sweat, dirt, and blood from his skin and removed his tattered shirt from his torso. Laithe's pain ebbed as the water subsided and fell into the moss below. He gasped and inspected his chest. His skin was unmarked, free of any blemish. The magical water had even healed old scars from past battles. He regarded

Veremund in awe, who merely smiled in return.

The Tal'Rach pulled more water from the nearby pool and doused himself in it, freeing his perfect skin from the refuse of battle.

"You're lucky that your wounds were not more severe," Veremund said. "I can mend flesh and bone, but I can't replace your head or save you from the brink of death."

"Thank you," Laithe said. "You did not have to do that."

"Consider it an investment," Veremund said. "You may have saved my life but you have also accrued a debt."

"How do I owe you?" Laithe was confused. He was grateful for his life but wasn't sure what he took from the Tal'Rach by saving him from a losing battle.

"Do not concern yourself with talk of debts. We have earned some rest," Veremund replied, his dismal demeanor suddenly brightening. He grinned. Removing his clothes, he lowered his impressive frame into the pool. The Tal'Rach was completely naked save for a necklace draped around his neck. The water bubbled as he waded into its center. Laithe was relieved to see that the only animalistic trait about Veremund's body was his horns. The rest was human and quite impressive.

Failing to quell his primal excitement, Laithe stripped off his soaked trousers and gingerly eased into the pool. To his surprise, the water was now soothingly warm, heated by Veremund's touch. Laithe smiled and waded into the pool's center.

The closer he was to the Tal'Rach, the hotter his body felt—and not from the steaming water. He had relied on himself his entire life, and no one had ever protected him, let alone save him. No one had been strong enough until now. He had always been the savior, pursuing and providing for the men he fancied. But now he felt something he never had before. He felt safe and protected. Laithe waded closer to Veremund, whose chest was well above the surface. It was difficult not to admire his perfect body. The pair continued in silence, washing the grisly refuse of battle from their bodies.

"With those amber Roursche eyes, you are clearly a Two," Veremund flashed a coy smile. "I think you might also be a Fourteen from the way your eyes are fucking me. Am I right?"

Fourteen. The name used to identify men marked by the Fourteenth Edict: a gay man. Laithe nodded. Veremund was right. Was the ram spirit a Fourteen as well?

The ram regarded Laithe lustfully, smirking. Laithe had seen that expression before. It was an invitation. He waded closer to Veremund, drawing his lips closer to his, heart pounding with frantic excitement.

Closing his eyes, he rose to the tips of his toes, waiting for the Tal'Rach to lower his mouth onto his. Instead of feeling the soft touch of lips, Laithe was shoved forcefully backward. He almost fell over into the water, but he regained his balance. Veremund glared at him; a burning rage replaced the Tal'Rach's lust and longing. The sudden change of mood gave Laithe whiplash as he stood awkwardly in the water, unsure how to respond.

"I said you owed me a debt. And sex was not what I was referring to." Veremund snapped. The ram spirit chastised Laithe like an impertinent schoolboy.

"I..." Laithe stammered, but Veremund raised a hand, ordering his silence.

"Regardless of your intentions, you stole something extraordinarily precious from me. I intend to get what I desire, and you will help me. You have shown me your various skills today. These talents will aid me in fulfilling my goal. Understood?"

Laithe impulsively bobbed his head in agreement but was confused by Veremund's cryptic statement. "Actually...could you explain?" He thought he helped the ram spirit and had assumed that the Tal'Rach would be grateful to him for saving his life. But the ram's demeanor had soured. What did Laithe do that made him so furious?

"Answers to all your questions will come in due time. I have more important matters to sort out in the meantime," Veremund said. The Tal'Rach lifted himself out of the pool and padded across the moss towards an old chest concealed under a set of hanging roots. He pulled out an oversized shirt and trousers and dressed himself. "Wait here for a couple of days. This safe house has plenty of food and a fresh set of clothes that should fit you. Meet me at the Brazen Leaf, a pub near the top of the Bole. Ask for Pellum. He will be expecting your arrival. Then you can repay the debt you owe."

Laithe sprung out of the pool and approached Veremund, but the ram spirit smiled and leaped out of the hollow in a flurry of motion. The Deviant was left alone, standing naked on the moss. As confused as he was with incurring a debt by saving the Tal'Rach's life, it was not his place to understand. A wise man should not take the wrath of a Tal'Rach lightly.

Regardless of Veremund's harsh words and disapproving glance, Laithe was only concerned with seeing Tal'Rach again.

4

An Unexpected Kindness

The wide, wooden staircase wrapped delicately around the drop root, rising toward the Canopy high above. The broad, worn steps and intricate railing grew from the wood as if the thick vertical root had formed that way naturally. Occasionally, the stairs emptied onto a broad platform filled with beautifully carved structures. Each balcony seemed like a self-contained village, hanging off the drop root like an oversized fungi. Rope bridges shot out like spokes from a wagon wheel, leading to terraces on nearby roots. Dozens of rach flitted between the buildings, casting the light of every hue imaginable. Tabulrossa was more magnificent than any story could hope to capture. However, the thousands of people fleeing from the Undergrowth seemed unfazed by its beauty.

A terrified man pushed against Sarina from behind, sobbing and urging her to climb faster. Ahead, a young girl clung to her mother's coat as they struggled to keep up with the rest of their family above. Dire their broadness, the stairs were not designed for six people walking abreast simultaneously.

The crowd jostled Sarina as the torrent forced her higher.

Pandemonium struck whenever she entered a new platform, the tide pushing and pulling in every direction. She had already crossed two rope bridges and was on her third vertical root by the time she was halfway to the Canopy. She was unsure where the stairway led, but still, she diligently followed the urgent masses, if only to avoid being trampled.

The glow of the blue flames danced across the dense web of roots below. Screams echoed across the city. The crowd sporadically halted when wardens shoved against the current, descending towards the chaotic Undergrowth. She kept her head lowered as they passed, but luckily they were too preoccupied to notice. She was simply another migrant who sought refuge within the city—one of thousands.

The chaos immediately scattered Sarina and her companions when they entered Tabulrossa. Laithe was the first to depart. Instead of defending the weaker members of the group, the mercenary, consumed with rage, launched an assault on the nearest squad wardens. He rampaged into them like a bull through a herd of sheep. He disappeared into a storm of green armor, steel, and blood, one man against hundreds. No one could survive such odds, even a warrior as skilled as Laithe. Fortunately, he had drawn the wardens' attention with his onslaught, allowing the others to flee further into the city unharmed.

At first, Sarina was confused by the sheer panic their arrival in the city caused. The horrific tales of Deviants instilled fear in every human at an early age, but she couldn't comprehend how such an insignificant group of Deviants elicited such a reaction. As they moved farther into the Undergrowth, the unrest grew, and frightened masses fled the city's center. News of their arrival couldn't have spread that rapidly, and people were running as if chased from the opposite direction. It wasn't Sarina and her group that had them terrified. Something else lurked within the city.

Sarina overheard half a dozen scared citizens relaying accounts of demons and Deviants via scared shouts, and soon, the only name Sarina could hear was Veremund. As blue flame erupted throughout the Undergrowth, the reality of the situation finally dawned on her. Veremund hadn't answered her call because he was preoccupied with attacking the city.

The broiling sea of flailing limbs and stampeding feet divided the group again as the crowds consumed them; she lost sight of Kez and Callandra after a herd of children barreled between them. The crowd urged her and Beriane towards the nearest stair. Luckily, Beriane clung to Sarina's bloodied arm. Sarina had suffered the most injuries during the attack at the gate, except for Laithe and poor, poor Benjin.

They blended in as a simple pair of pilgrims as they ascended the drop root. Sarina lost her quarterstaff during the shuffle, which was for the best. A weapon would make her appear more suspicious, but its absence made her feel vulnerable.

Disaster struck once more as they arrived on the first platform. A scared older man pushed Sarina, and she fell to her knees. When she recovered, Beriane had already climbed too far and vanished around the corner.

Beriane's expression of horror was still seared into Sarina's mind. Now, she had lost all of them. The people she had sworn to protect and guide to safety.

But she would not fail—not now. She would find Beriane, Callandra, and Kez, too, and defend them. No one else would, and Veremund made it incredibly clear where his priorities lay. Before she could do that, however, she must escape the crowds, and only then could she start searching for her friends.

She climbed towards the bright Canopy, focusing on her first objective. Sarina was fortunate that her status as a Deviant was concealable, like all Fourteens and Fifteens. They did not have red hair like Tens, blind like Eights, or come from a specific clan like Deviants from Ones to Sevens. Sarina often wondered what her life would have been if she had not joined a band of Deviants but settled in another village far from her home. She could have married a man, raised a family, and masqueraded as a different person. Her life would undoubtedly be less dangerous and longer. But her heart soured whenever her mind wandered to this fantasy. Such a way of living was no life at all. She would rather have a short, eventful one as herself than a long, arduous one pretending to be someone else. Even now, when she had lost everyone she had ever known or loved.

The long spiral steps emptied onto a wide street. The branch was thicker than any of the roots below. Big enough for a wide boulevard and a row of buildings on either side. Sarina blinked, her vision adjusting to the warm green glow. She hadn't realized how dark the Undergrowth had been. The murky depths of Tabulrossa were illuminated solely by the erratic light of the dancing rach. The lower Canopy seemed as crowded as the drop roots below, though the people around Sarina were considerably calmer now that they bathed in the emerald light of the sun shining through the sea of leaves above.

The current swept Sarina down the street until it forked

in two, one massive branch continuing to the right and the other ascending slightly to the left. The crowd forced her to the left, and she slowly climbed into the Canopy. The road split off into countless additional branches. Thinner branches rose intermittently in the middle of the road or between buildings. These columns of wood were the size of regular trees, their green leaves swaying gently in the wind and covered in purple fruit the size of Sarina's head. Yellow Sylvania flowers bloomed from these branches, emitting a soft glow similar to the rach, who danced between the rustling leaves. They seemed to congregate in greater numbers here than in the Undergrowth.

She was surprised that the leaves in the Canopy were similar in size to those of a typical tree, though she did spot several that were the size of a horse. The complex network of wooden sky bridges spread high above her head and in every direction. The higher she climbed into the Canopy, the calmer the streets became. Children played in manicured yards between beautifully sculpted wooden homes. Pub and restaurant patios bustled with scores of patrons, all of who seemed blissfully unaware of Veremund's attack. A handful of workers climbed the miniature trees, harvesting the strange purple fruit. Crisp, clean water flowed freely in waist-high troughs on the side of the road, collecting in stone wells at every intersection. Sarina had never seen a city quite like it.

Finally, the crowd thinned out, and Sarina regained her autonomy, though she was too distracted with marveling at the city to pay much attention. Her vision was a bit blurry, probably due to the adrenaline. She was dripping with sweat.

Her shoulder stung. Her right arm wasn't sweaty. It was dripping in the blood that flowed freely from a deep gash on her shoulder. She had been bleeding ever since the front gate. How much blood had she lost?

Frantically, she tore off her bloody sleeve and attempted to dress the wound. It proved impossible with one functioning hand. She panicked, and the world spun around her. Her vision became fuzzy. The last thing she remembered before the darkness consumed her was the dull pain of her body hitting the road.

# # #

Sarina's dreams were chaotic, dark, and disjointed. Benjin's corpse lying at her feet, Laithe impaled by a warden's sword, and Beriane crying out for help. Thick vines wrapped around her wrists and ankles. She struggled against them, desperate to help her friends, but the restraints held tight, cutting into her flesh. Sarina bellowed in frustration. She refused to surrender.

A gentle voice edged its way into Sarina's consciousness. "Dear, are you alright?"

Something gently touched her forehead, pulling her into the waking world. She was lying in a bed; it had been years since she had the opportunity to sleep in one, but the soft sensation was unmistakable. She was in a cozy bedroom. Half a dozen yellow Sylvania flowers bloomed on the domed wooden ceiling, bathing her in soft light. Her shoulder was sore, but a quick assessment told her someone had wrapped it in fresh bandages.

A woman nearing her twilight years sat by the bedside. Long, white hair neatly tied in a braid cascaded down her shoulder. She had a kind demeanor and smiled sweetly at Sarina, though her brow furrowed with a familiar grand-motherly concern. The expression reminded Sarina of her grandmother, before the Fifteenth Edict when she had a family to worry about her.

"Seems like you had quite the ordeal, you poor thing. Here, drink some water to calm your nerves." The woman gingerly placed a wooden cup against Sarina's chapped lips. She inhaled the refreshingly cool water, which soothed her sore throat. "How does that feel?"

"Amazing, thank you," Sarina rasped. "I'm sorry to ask, but who are you?"

"Oh, me? I'm the one whose yard you collapsed in two days ago, sweet girl," she chuckled sweetly, refilling the cup from the pitcher on the table. Sarina gratefully accepted another long drink, and her thirst finally quelled. "You can call me Mags. And your name?"

"Florence," Sarina said. It was one of the aliases she used during her travels. It was an old habit, but using the same name could lead to a trail for wardens to track.

"Nice to meet you, Florence. It is a pleasure to have you in my home," Mags said. "Such a terrible business, and during the Calling, no less. Was it your first day in the city, I suspect? What a terrible welcome."

"Yes, it was," Sarina said. Brevity was the best friend of safety. Divulge no more than necessary. Answer confidently, but not too quickly.

"Were you separated from your family?" Mags asked.

"My sisters, Talisa and Gara, and my mother," Sarina said, ensuring pained desperation was evident in her tone. Mags needed to know that she had companions and family members. Most Deviants traveled alone, and Sarina needed to dispel any suspicions Mags might hold for the wounded stranger lying in her bed. "Did you see them?"

"Oh no, you were alone when I found you. You must have separated from your family during the attack. That wretched Veremund. I fear he's the second coming of Lucian." Mags spat the last name with venom. The father of the Deviants was not one to trifle with, though the Tal'Rach defeated him a lifetime ago. "We are in for harrowing days ahead, and it seems like there are more migrants this year than ever before. I hope there's enough room in the boarding houses. Where are you girls from?"

"We are from Fairgut, out in the marshes," Sarina said truthfully. It was improbable that Mags or anyone she knew had heard of the tiny village in the backwaters of the western marshes. Sarina hadn't known anyone to journey to Tabulrossa in her entire life, though that could have changed in recent years. And she wasn't about to risk saying another random city like poor Benjin had.

"Ah, I'm not sure if I've heard of it," Mags mused. Sarina hoped that her gambit paid off; it would be worse if the woman thought the village was fake than if it was a town she had known intimately. "You were in such poor shape. What happened to your shoulder?"

Sarina's hair stood on end. Mags was suspicious. A young woman lying unconscious on her doorstep, bleeding from a sword wound, would make anyone think twice. She was lucky Mags hadn't called the wardens immediately. Sarina twisted her expression, feigning fear and confusion, carefully selecting her following words.

"It...it is all a blur," Sarina started. The best lie was sticking as close to the truth as possible. "We had just entered the city when the explosion happened, blue fire everywhere. The crowd pushed us onward. One moment, Gara was there. The next, she was gone. Then we were on the stairs. We passed a group of wardens, and I didn't see them fast enough. They ran right into me. I was already in the Canopy when I realized the extent of my injuries. And Gara was gone. Then I passed out."

The older woman bowed her head somberly as if satisfied with the story. Mags wasn't an idiot; it was clear that a warden's blade caused Sarina's wound. Mags needed to believe it was an accident rather than the only other logical option.

"Thank you so much, Mags. For helping me," Sarina wanted to change the focus from her past. Mags was curious, and Sarina didn't want her asking any more dangerous questions. She gestured to her bandaged shoulder. "You have an expert touch. Are you a healer?"

"I have three daughters, a bit older than you," Mags explained, chuckling heartily. "So I have plenty of experience dressing wounds. Young girls have the penchant for getting into all sorts of scrapes."

"They are lucky to have you," Sarina said sweetly, pleased. She successfully directed the conversation at Mags. Older people loved to hear themselves talk. One more question and Mags would go on for hours. "Do they live with you now?"

"Aw, thank you, sweetheart," Mags sighed wistfully. "They have all left the house. My eldest became a priestess about ten years ago, and the younger two soon joined the wardens. My Herb died soon after, leaving me all alone."

Sarina caught herself before gasping audibly. Mags was a mother of wardens. Two wardens. No wonder she was suspicious. That would prove to be a challenge. Sarina had to leave this house as soon as possible. There was no telling when her daughters would visit, and they wouldn't be as friendly as their wizened mother.

"I am so sorry to hear about your loss," Sarina said. "You must be so proud of your daughters. All in service to the great Tal'Rach."

"Oh, I am," Mags said before launching into a long story about how she met her late husband. It was overly sentimental and filled with logical gaps, but Sarina was grateful for the older woman's rambling tale. The fewer questions she asked of Sarina, the better.

The day dragged on, and Mags helped Sarina out of bed and into the kitchen. Her home was cozy and charming but much more spacious than one woman needed. They sat around a family-sized table, and Sarina hoped one of the daughters wouldn't swing by for dinner.

Her body was sore, but her legs worked fine—a good start. She would make for the front door the instant Mags left her alone. Thankfully, she had prepared a stew, and Sarina devoured it hungrily. It had been months since her last hot meal, and the broth was delicious, filled with the strange purple fruit she had seen outside. Mags mentioned it was called Tabul fruit. It was oddly both sweet and savory.

"Hopefully, we can find your sisters at the boarding houses," Mags said while Sarina devoured the remaining bits of stew. "They are a bit north of here. I can take you to them first thing tomorrow morning. You should be ready for the journey by then."

Sarina's heart soared. She couldn't believe her luck. Maybe the people of Tabulrossa were kinder and more hospitable than the outside world. Hopefully, Beriane, Kez, and Callandra were as lucky and found asylum in these boarding houses.

But she wouldn't wait for tomorrow. When Mags turned, Sarina would be out the door.

"I have no way of repaying you. Thank you so—" The words caught in Sarina's throat. Her tongue had grown fuzzy, and her vision blurred. Her stomach gurgled, and her head bobbed, losing her equilibrium. Confused, she squinted at Mags, who shot up and rounded the table with lightning speed. Gone was the mask of a kindly grandmother. Instead, an angry banshee. When did she get a rope? In a blink of an eye, Mags lashed Sarina's wrists together behind the chair. Her shoulder lanced with sharp pain. The stew was drugged. She had been drugged.

"I know a stab wound when I see one. You think I'm an idiot?" Mags spat, slapping Sarina brutally, causing the world to spin again. "That was no accident, you Deviant bitch!"

"Why…" Sarina choked, and the effects of the stew gradually began wearing off. Luckily, it was not poisonous. But why drug her? "Why did you help me?"

"I wanted to see if you were dumb enough to betray your friends," Mags said. "My daughters joined the wardens because of me, following the family trade. I knew what you were the second you fell on my lawn, you scum. No matter. My daughters will be here shortly. They won't be as kind as me. The Sanctum teaches such creative ways to interrogate these days."

Sarina examined her captor in horror. Of course. Mags used to be a warden herself. She had awoken in a trap.

5

Under the Brazen Leaf

Laithe waited restlessly in the hollow beneath the drop root with only his questions as a companion. He never considered himself particularly social; as a child, he preferred solitude, and life as a Deviant granted him precisely that. Most of his adult life consisted of evading the wardens in the vast wilderness. He occasionally stumbled across a band of Deviants, who would graciously feed and shelter him in return for his protection. He quickly proved himself an efficient killer, a skill coveted by every Deviant.

It was easy for Laithe to be accepted into any roving band, but he found it impossible to remain in any group for long. Laithe soon discovered that most Deviants lacked his survival instincts and would constantly make terrible decisions, which walked them right into warden blades. Most didn't survive, and Laithe abandoned most groups whose leaders showed themselves to be useless. Thus, he was alone most of his life.

Sarina, however, was different. She was whip-smart, calculating, and ever-vigilant. He had followed her longer than any other. Her exceptional leadership did not prevent death, but such was life for Deviants. After a month with Sarina's group, Laithe realized how much he missed human connection. Not that he liked participating in conversations. He had never been good with words. Laithe was comfortable being on the edge of the conversation, listening to others enjoy themselves. It kept him free of the dark depths of his mind.

But now he was alone with those thoughts, and his encounter with Veremund did nothing but ignite the torrent of emotions he had suppressed for a lifetime. He was confused by the Tal'Rach's behavior, how he first seemed to flirt with Laithe, then looked at him with such disdain afterward. On top of it, he accused Laithe of being a thief. What did he take? He had no earthly possessions to his name, lost his axes during the battle, and even the clothes on his back belonged to Veremund. What could the debt possibly be? Thousands of possibilities arose, each more nonsensical than the last.

Laithe did not enjoy riddles or games. He preferred to allow others to think for him. Sarina would point his axes in the right direction, and he would take it from there.

However, what surprised Laithe the most was the guilt he felt for disappointing Veremund. The pair had only been together briefly, but Veremund haunted his every thought since. He dreamed of their night together and fantasized about what could have transpired in the pool if the Tal'Rach hadn't left so abruptly.

Laithe prided himself on his apathy, and it made him stronger. Scores of men had propositioned him throughout the years, and he bedded those he deemed attractive. But he drew the line whenever his heart was involved. Something odd was happening in the silence of the hollow. Laithe was developing feelings. He had affection for an all-powerful creature that loathed him and was forcing him into an undisclosed service.

Obediently, Laithe waited for the two days as instructed, keeping his mind blank as best he could, then headed out into the deserted streets of the Undergrowth. He was thankful for the low lighting of the city's depths and the deep-hooded cloak Veremund provided him to conceal his identity. He also tore a strip of fabric from a clean shirt to tie around his brow for good measure.

Laithe trekked for almost an hour before he saw another human. The drop roots near his hideout were too thin to hold the spiral staircases he noticed on his first day in the city. But the longer he ambled along, the thicker the roots and the busier the streets became.

He kept his hood drawn, bowing his head. Laithe had spent a lifetime hiding in the shadows, perfecting the art of going unnoticed—no eye contact. No hesitations. Act as if you belong, and no one will think twice. Always know where the light is coming from so you can cloak your face in shadow. The false bandage always helped to keep attention from the amber orbs that marked him a Deviant.

His muscular, intimidating frame and permanent scowl prevented unwanted small talk. The trick was to act menacing enough to avoid encounters but not too threatening to the point of being memorable. Another benefit of his stealth was how freely people spoke when they did not think anyone was listening. Understanding one's environment was vital to survival. Laithe had traveled far, and it was essential to learn the lay of the land quickly. When entering a new city, he sought to ascertain the names of neighborhoods, which areas to avoid, and remote locations where he could hide. He had years of experience, and he hadn't died yet, unfortunately.

He picked his way through the dank, moss-filled expanse of roots and dilapidated buildings of the Undergrowth. The vast district was primarily vacant, save for a few boarding houses filled with new arrivals and burial grounds drawing mourners from above. It was the perfect place to hide. Save for the heavily armed warden patrols he nearly encountered every five minutes. Veremund's attack had drawn out the green bastards in full force.

Laithe learned that the drop roots were called the Aerials after overhearing a conversation between a group of migrants standing outside a boarding house. Thousands of vertical shafts connected the city's depths to the Canopy above.

Laithe departed the sparse Undergrowth and navigated across the rope bridges in the Aerials to avoid detection. Unlike the forest floor, a surprising amount of people lived on the platforms built upon the Aerials. Laithe was pleased by the crowds here. It was easier to blend in when more people were present. It was also brighter, closer to the Canopy, more populated with rach, and illuminated by hundreds of tiny Sylvania flowers. The Canopy was the most expansive section of the city and where the majority of citizens resided, but that was not Laithe's destination. He was searching for the Bole.

It wasn't long until the Deviant gathered enough information on the Bole's location; it was a busy district at the city's heart. Unlike previous places he had visited, Tabulrossa's streets were nameless. Navigation was nearly impossible without the sun guiding him in cardinal directions. It was a mystery how Tabulrossans traveled so deftly around the great tree. They merely relied on simple directions and pub or shop names. It seemed that the citizens of Tabulrossa enjoyed an abundance of leisure, and efficiency was not a concern. Hours passed before Laithe came across the Bole. At first sight, Laithe thought it was a tight grouping of a hundred drop roots, but it was the colossal tree's central trunk. Almost as thick as it was tall, the great tree loomed among the drop roots like a giant among ants.

A vast, ramp-like staircase gradually wound around the irregular trunk. Occasionally, a gigantic platform protruded from the Bole, like a massive wooden toadstool. Each great semicircle held enough buildings to host an entire town. Laithe wondered if more people lived in Tabulrossa than in the lands beyond.

Laithe navigated across the labyrinth of rope bridges to the nearest wooden toadstool, which he suspected was the third or fourth from the forest floor. The streets here were narrower than in the Undergrowth and much busier, which was a relief for someone who wanted to disappear among the crowd.

He immediately headed for the grand stairs and began his ascension toward the Canopy, relying on Veremund's rudimentary instructions to guide him. According to the Tal'Rach, the Brazen Leaf was near the top of the Bole.

Over a dozen semicircular platforms clung to the sides of the immense trunk, each harder to navigate than the last. The streets were irregular, and though Laithe kept as close to the great trunk as possible, the winding roads took him along the platform's edges more often than not before he located the next section of stairs.

The people of Tabulrossa casually wandered the streets. Besides the shopkeepers and pub staff, it didn't seem like anyone in the city worked. It was an odd sight.

Though it was the strangest city he had ever visited, Tabulrossa had one major similarity with every town Laithe had journeyed. At the center of every square and plaza was a tall wooden pillar. Deep grooves separated the column into eighteen sections, each carved deeply with writing. The bottom cylinders were weathered with age, the words barely legible, while the pieces near the top were fresh and bright with newness. These were the great Edicts. Each disc on the pole represented a unique divine law.

For Laithe's entire lifetime, the Tal'Rach decreed a new Edict every few years. Recently, they passed down a new Edict every six months or so. The Tal'Rach had declared four new Edicts since the Fourteenth tainted men who loved men. Four. In two years. Every soul knew them, for they were warnings from the Tal'Rach. The evil spirits, Ae'Rach, would possess groups of people simultaneously, killing the host and assuming control of their body. Deviants. It was utter nonsense. The only spirits that possessed humans were the Tal'Rach themselves.

He ignored the pole and diligently conducted his search. The day grew long as Laithe made his painstaking ascent up the Bole. He regretted not climbing the nearest Aerial to gain height and continuing his search near the top. The higher he rose, however, the more warden patrols he passed. The green-clad troops guarded the top of the Bole more aggressively than the wild Undergrowth. It was undoubtedly more defensible.

According to a passerby, the pinnacle of the Bole held the city's true heart, called the Precipice, which held the temples of the Tal'Rach. No wonder the warden's presence was more substantial here. It was an odd place for Veremund to have a safe house so close to his mortal enemies.

Since the Tabulrossans used pub names as markers, Laithe located the Brazen Leaf expeditiously once he was closer to the Canopy. It nestled at the end of a quiet road along the cliff-like side of the trunk on what must have been the third or second-highest platform. The derelict pub leaned against the rough wooden wall, nestled between a storehouse and an apothecary. It was a seedy little bar with dirty windows. Unlike other pubs in the neighborhood, it had no patio or patrons milling outside. Before Laithe reached the front door, a pair of older men stumbled out, drunkenly singing an incomprehensible tune. Passing them swiftly, he ducked inside.

The Brazen Leaf was as derelict inside as it was outside. Only a few Sylvania flowers clung to the ceiling of the gloomy bar. Patrons occupied less than half the tables, some somberly drunk alone, while others conversed loudly with slurred voices. The Brazen Leaf, it seemed, was a place where people came to lose their minds with liquor. Clever. Drunk men hardly asked questions; no one would believe them in their stupor if they had seen anything of note.

A grizzled man stooped behind the bar, pouring deep purple liquid into a glass mug. He scowled as Laithe approached.

"What do you want?" the bartender asked.

"I'm looking for Pellum," Laithe said, concealing himself under his hood. He still did not know if he could trust the man. And for all he knew, Veremund had been so angry with him that he was guiding Laithe into a trap.

"Ah yes," the man said, his features immediately softened, falling to a whisper. "Our mutual friend told me to keep an eye out for you. You should do a better job hiding your eyes, boy. I am old enough to recognize a member of the Roursche clan."

Laithe bristled at the name of his extinct tribe. The patrons sitting along the bar were well within earshot. He reached towards his belt out of habit for axes that were no longer there. He felt vulnerable without them, weak.

"Easy now," Pellum whispered. "Those drunken bastards are too blasted to notice anything. They wouldn't flinch if I hit them aside the head. I know that because I do it every night at bar close to force the fuckers to leave. They won't hear us. But we should get you somewhere safe. Isam!"

Hardly comforted by the bartender's words, Laithe tensed as a form emerged from the doorway behind the bar. He relaxed a bit when the figure was revealed to be a young man, not much younger than Laithe. Isam was relatively thin, though a bit taller, with olive skin, green eyes, and boyish charm. He smiled sweetly at Laithe, then turned dutifully toward the barkeep.

"What do you need, Pellum?" the tavern boy asked. His voice was high, melodic, and relaxed as if there wasn't a single worry in his head. Laithe was jealous of such naivety.

"Isam, this is the friend we have been expecting," the barkeep said quietly. Isam raised an eyebrow, now regarding Laithe more carefully. "Could you please take him to the back?"

"My pleasure," Isam replied.

Laithe ducked around the bar and followed the barboy to the backrooms. They were musty, with roughly hewn walls carved into the great tree itself—by men, not by the power of the Tal'Rach. Three doors led into a cramped office, kitchen, and closet. Isam passed them and continued down a dimly lit hallway.

The young man was cute, though he reminded Laithe too much of Benjin. May his soul rest in peace. The slender barboy was the type of man Laithe typically bedded in the past. Isam was undoubtedly a Fourteen; Laithe had enough experience to know another gay man at first glance. If circumstances were different, he would have propositioned Isam for some fun, but now he couldn't imagine being with anyone apart from Veremund. The mere thought of the ram spirit excited Laithe.

"This way," Isam called, grabbing a lamp with a glowing Sylvania flower trapped inside and led Laithe into a musty storeroom.

Laithe eyed the lantern with curiosity. He hadn't seen an open flame once since entering the city, except for the blue blaze generated by Veremund. Only rach and these strange flowers illuminated the depths of Tabulrossa. He didn't blame the citizens for avoiding the use of fire, especially after witnessing the damage the ram spirit wrought upon the great tree.

Dozens of wooden kegs lined the walls of the room beyond. The purple liquid that the patrons inhaled in the bar leaked from the spout on the nearest barrel.

The young man sauntered across the storeroom to the last tower of kegs. He reached behind the highest one, and there was a metallic click. In one fluid motion, the stack of barrels split in half and swung in either direction, revealing a secret doorway beyond. Isam grinned and disappeared into the darkness. Laithe growled in annoyance. He did not like surprises. A feeling of vulnerability overcame him once he remembered he no longer carried his axes, but he calmed himself. He could break the barboy in half if Isam decided to ambush him.

The tunnel beyond was pitch dark, save for Isam's lantern. The passage walls were uneven, like the storeroom. It ended abruptly in a spiral stair, plunging into the depths. The pair descended through the gloom until arriving abruptly at a heavy door. Isam pulled out a key from his pocket and unlocked it. The room beyond was shadowy and cavernous, and the lantern light danced off countless boxes and parcels arranged in neat rows. It was like a storehouse, but the contents were a random assortment.

"Smugglers," Laithe said, realizing what the room was.

"Correct. Anything and everything the Tal'Rach have deemed unholy—books, artifacts, a weapon or two, rare animal parts, you name it—is under the noses of the 'great spirits.' It keeps the tavern afloat when business slows. We even have a few wardens as clients."

Isam walked over to a wall and pressed a section, resulting in another metallic click. A door opened along the far wall, another tunnel.

"A second one?" Laithe asked ruefully. "You like your secrets, I take it."

"Just one secret that conceals another. A more important secret." Isam said. "If the wardens ever discover this place, they wouldn't think to delve deeper."

"Smart," Laithe said, but he wasn't sure where the barboy led him. What was more illicit than a smuggler's hold? And what was more important to hide?

Isam guided him into the second tunnel, which twisted back and forth. Laithe and Isam encountered several forks, but the barboy strode ahead with confidence. It was a labyrinth deep inside the Bole; even if the wardens discovered it, they surely would be lost for days before they escaped.

If they escaped.

Laithe attempted to memorize the path, but he became lost and at Isam's mercy after a dozen turns. Gritting his teeth, he suppressed his anger. He instinctively grasped his hips where his axes once hung for the umpteenth time that day. He hated being powerless, and trusting others was not something he was comfortable with. After an eternity of navigating the murky maze, Isam finally stopped.

Laithe wrinkled his nose in confusion. They had arrived at a dead end. Isam smiled knowingly, kneeling by the far wall of the incomplete tunnel. He pressed yet another hidden button. There was a sharp click in response, and the wall shuddered and opened, revealing what was worth protecting.

Laithe's mouth opened in awe.

It was a city.

With the secret wall open, the two men were now on the edge of a vast cavern, at least triple the size of the storeroom above. The hollow was naturally made, with smooth wooden walls covered in moss and hundreds of luminous Sylvania flowers that bathed the secret city in a beautiful, warm light.

A city might have been an exaggeration; a tight cluster of houses on the cavern floor, a fresh well at their center. Three stories of balconies ringed the massive space, each containing scores of doors where men milled between. Men. Only men bustled to and from these entries. In a clearing between the houses on the cavern floor, a dozen sat around tables, laughing, drinking, and eating while one played the lute. A pair strolled around the upper balconies, holding hands—a small group of naked men bathed in a steaming pool of water on the cavern's edge.

"What is this place?" Laithe breathed, feeling his cheeks grow warm.

"A haven for Fourteens," Isam said proudly. "Pellum, Veremund, and I built this place after the Fourteenth Edict. We have sheltered men like us ever since. It is the one place in the world we can live without fear of execution. Welcome to the true Brazen Leaf."

There were no words. There was nothing like this village anywhere. And Laithe had journeyed across half the known world. He had traveled with plenty of Fourteens throughout his life, but every group he was a part of had Deviants from every Edict. Safe houses were for all Deviants, but they were bonded only by trauma, a family of pure happenstance. This place, however, was designed for people like Laithe. For men who loved men.

He was the last Roursche alive, the sole survivor of the Second Edict, and that reality made him feel perpetually alone. He studied the men below and thought that maybe, for the first time since his yellow eyes labeled him a Deviant, he could be part of something bigger. Perhaps he could belong here.

"It is…" Laithe said, but the words escaped him.

"Wonderful?" Isam finished the sentence, brimming with joy. "It never gets old to see newcomers' expressions. Let's get you settled before Veremund arrives. I've heard he had something important to discuss with you. Hopefully, you can help."

Laithe now understood Veremund's anger a bit more. The stories were correct; Veremund had something to protect. But it wasn't Deviants; it was a city of Fourteens. Laithe was now confident he would be more than happy to pay the debt the Tal'Rach mentioned. Isam led Laithe down the nearby stairs to the lowest balcony. Most of the men smiled as they passed by. Some ogled Laithe, admiring his physique. Despite his current obsession with Veremund, the Deviant blushed at the attention.

Isam led him into a door halfway down the balcony, revealing a cozy bedroom with a washroom off to the side. A short table filled with fresh fruit sat beside a plush bed.

"Here we are. What is your name?" Isam asked. "I apologize for not asking sooner. Our mutual…friend failed to tell me."

"I did not give it to him when we met," Laithe replied simply. "We had more pressing matters, like survival, to distract us. You can call me Laithe."

"Well, it is nice to meet you, Laithe," Isam said brightly. "I am Isam, but you already know that. Feel free to rest here. This room is yours. I've already laid out some food and water for you, though we have a mess hall downstairs. It would be best to avoid the others before Veremund speaks with you. He will come by shortly."

"Thank you," Laithe said.

"Not much of a conversationalist, I see," Isam smiled playfully. Was he flirting? The barboy waited for Laithe to reply, but when none came, he chuckled and left the bedroom.

Laithe fervently devoured the meal Isam had prepared for him. It was a cold sandwich and some potatoes, but it was better than the strange purple fruit. Tabul fruit was the only food Veremund stored in the Undergrowth hideout. Laithe didn't realize how starved he was until he licked the plate clean. He could hardly remember the last time he had such a substantial meal.

Once his stomach was satisfied, he lay on the soft bed, legs sore from the long climb, still struggling to fully comprehend the hidden village beneath the Brazen Leaf. It was magnificent. He almost drifted off to sleep when the door opened.

Veremund ducked in, his horns scraping against the top of the door frame. He set a worn leather bag down next to the bed. Laithe's heart leaped in his chest as the Tal'Rach closed the door. Being so close to him was exhilarating.

"Good evening, little one," Veremund said. "Happy to see you found your way here without much trouble."

"I did," Laithe said, unsure what else to say. He was too distracted to think clearly.

"I said you owed me a debt," Veremund said brusquely. Laithe had hoped for more pleasantries, maybe a kiss. Or better, his cock. He craved Veremund's touch. But the Tal'Rach continued matter-of-factly. "Let me explain. Do you remember the warden officer who shot me with the arrow? Yes? His name is Alistair, the archwarden of Tabulrossa. He has been the leader of the order for years, and ever since he took power, the wardens have become more vicious. More Edicts have been decreed than ever, though I'm sure you know that. He is the one responsible. He was the target of my attack. If I can kill him, I can save thousands of Deviants from a horrible death. He rarely leaves the temple of the wardens and is always heavily guarded. The Calling was my best chance to kill him and to end this madness. And you stopped me."

"I see," Laithe's heart sank. His transgression was worse than he could have ever imagined. "I must pay with my life."

"Don't be ridiculous, Laithe," the edges of Veremund's voice softened. "Isam told me your name. I quite like it. I was harsh on you earlier. But I do think that you can rectify your mistake."

"How?"

"I sense that you crave revenge against the wardens as much as I. And I saw you can slay them quite efficiently. So, I brought you a gift to help repay your debt," Veremund said. He opened the pouch at his feet, revealing two battle axes with shining, crescent blades. "Will you help me kill Alistair and end the tyranny of the wardens?"

"I will," Laithe eagerly snatched the weapons from the sack and gripped the ax handles. They weren't his old ones but a new pair. The metal was sharp and free of chips or scratches—perfect instruments of violence.

He smiled viciously. When he arrived in Tabulrossa, murdering wardens was all Laithe wanted. After meeting Veremund, his deepest desire was to please the Tal'Rach. To make him proud.

Luckily, killing wardens is what Veremund needed from him.

"Good, get some rest," the Tal'Rach said. "Our fun begins tomorrow."

6

Through the Canopy

Sarina regained her senses as the effects of the mysterious drug dissipated. Luckily, she hadn't entirely lost consciousness, which was more a curse than a blessing. She was powerless as Mags bound her tightly, but she could feel, see, and hear everything underneath the fog of the medication.

Mags loomed above her, sneering. She brandished a kitchen knife menacingly, inches from her neck. The room stopped spinning, and her mind was sharp again, but her arms were still tied behind her back, her wrists bloodied by the rope. She lolled her tongue to the side and bobbed her head intermittently, feigning a stupor. The old crone must not deduce that she was lucid. Not yet. She had to act quickly; Mags' daughters could burst through the door anytime. Then, there would be no escape.

The knife would present a bigger problem than the ropes that bound her. Adjusting her limbs slowly, Sarina tested the restraints. She froze.

Mags had failed to tie her legs.

She hadn't even gagged her. The old veteran had lost her

touch, relying too much on drugs to subdue her prey. But she wasn't dealing with an ordinary Deviant.

A plan formulated in her mind; there was still hope. Sarina coughed loudly and mumbled, her unintelligible words growing louder and louder. She wanted Mags to focus on her ability to scream, not her unbound feet. She adopted an expression of faux panic, too concentrated on escape to be truly scared. Sarina cried out for help, silenced by a savage smack from Mags.

"Quiet, you pig," Mags spat, threatening Sarina with the kitchen knife. "Do you think my neighbors would help you if they heard?"

She wasn't wrong; hopefully, no one heard Sarina's cries, for they would most certainly aid her captor. But her plan demanded she continue to yell. Defiantly, she called for help once more. The old lady grunted in desperation and hurried to the kitchen counter without taking her eyes off her captive. Mags returned with a dirty dish towel, hunched over to gag the Deviant.

Sarina waited until Mags was close, brandishing the rag and her knife.

Sarina struck.

Grunting, she lashed out savagely with her left leg. She heard a crack as her boot connected with a wrist. Mags dropped the knife and staggered back, crying in surprise and pain. Without hesitation, Sarina brought her left foot down and leaped into the air, chair and all. She pivoted and tackled the old warden, slamming the chair into Mag's frail frame.

They tumbled to the ground in a tangle of bruised limbs and splintered wood. Thankfully, the impact destroyed the chair, releasing Sarina, though the thick rope still bound her hands behind her. She began the struggle to her feet, but a swift kick to her chest sent her sprawling to the floor.

Mags pounced on her with surprising ferocity. The chair should have incapacitated her, but there she was, wrestling Sarina with incredible strength. Although Sarina was much stronger than Mags, it was difficult to subdue her without either arm. The ropes loosened considerably during the struggle but still held tight. As the pair grappled on the floor, Sarina worked her wrists, striving to free herself. Mags was no stranger to combat and assaulted Sarina with a fury of blows. She was about to lose to the retired warden yet again.

Then it came to her, the final option—the knife.

The kitchen knife had fallen under the table, just out of reach. It was only four inches long, but it would be enough. With her remaining strength, Sarina shoved Mags and lunged toward the dull blade. Mags shrieked, finally noticing the weapon.

She dove for it. But Sarina was quicker.

Landing next to the knife, Sarina twisted herself to snatch the blade with her bound hands. Grunting, she rotated to lay her stomach. Angling the knife upward, she arched her spine. It happened so fast that Mags was unable to stop her momentum.

The knife punctured the retired warden's chest, impaled by the weight of her own body. Mags collapsed on top of Sarina, gasping for breath and lashing out in panic.

It was too late. The knife had done its damage. Sarina waited a painful minute, pinned down by the dying woman, until, finally, the movements ceased. With a beleaguered sigh, the old warden breathed her last and lay still.

Sarina grunted and pushed the corpse off. She wearily

climbed to her feet, winded. The knife remained firmly in her grasp. Assessing her body, she was relieved to discover no serious wounds—only scrapes and bruises.

Mags sightlessly stared at her. Sarina briefly regarded the evil old hag, then spit on her. It didn't have to be this way. But people like Mags chose fear over logic. There was nothing to fear about Sarina or any Deviant. It disgusted her. She wasn't the monster; they were.

The door handle turned.

Fuck. Sarina heard half a dozen voices as the door creaked open.

Clear-minded, she focused on the task before her: to escape as fast as possible.

The wardens hadn't heard the tussle; otherwise, they would have broken the door down. They still believed Mags had Sarina detained.

She darted silently across the room and down the hallway, entering the bedroom while simultaneously sawing at the rope with the bloody knife. If only she'd had one more minute to free herself. But Sarina did not deal with hypothetical situations. Only reality. She was still bound, nearly defenseless, trapped in a house with at least six wardens.

She closed the door behind her softly, and she could hear heavy boots on the wooden floor. A woman screamed. Most likely one of Mags' daughters.

The footsteps became erratic. They were frantically searching the rest of the house.

Sarina rushed to the window. Every warden had entered the house, which was convenient for an escape. She lifted the window, but it was bolted shut. With her arms bound behind her, she didn't have the dexterity to unlatch it.

The footsteps grew louder.

Sarina backed toward the door, grimaced, and sprinted at the window. She threw her body forward and cursed as the broken wood and glass cut her body. Her rough landing knocked the wind out of her, and the knife bounced across the yard. Unfortunately, the ropes remained intact.

She heard shouting inside the house. A warden glared from behind the shattered window. Fuck.

She grabbed the largest shard of glass, ignoring the pain as it cut into her palm, and lifted herself off the ground. In her two years as a Deviant, she had been captured and tortured by wardens half a dozen times. She had plenty of experience with bondage.

Bolting toward the street, Sarina sawed the rope with the glass shard, running as fast as her legs would carry her.

Two wardens emerged from the front door as she rounded the corner of Mags' home. They drew their swords, but neither carried a bow. That was good.

Sarina pivoted and dashed down the street. The sound of metal boots hit the road behind her, but she did not turn around. Instead, Sarina focused on weaving her way through the quiet residential street. Without bows, the wardens would have to tackle her, and she was too fast to catch.

The people she passed on the street were terrified when they saw her. Most jumped out of the way, but others attempted to stop her. Anyone with common sense who witnessed the chase would immediately deduce she was a Deviant.

As good citizens of the realm, it was their duty to help the wardens cleanse the world of the Deviant threat. Idiots. She hated civilians who aided wardens almost as much as the green bastards themselves.

Sarina ducked to avoid a purple Tabul fruit launched at her head by a child on a porch, then leveled a man who was attempting to tackle her. All the while methodically sawing the shard of glass against the fraying ropes, ignoring the sting of the tiny cuts it carved on her fingers, wrists, and palms.

The metal footsteps were getting closer. Sarina cursed. She was the fastest person in her old village, winning every footrace during their harvest festival since she was old enough to compete. That particular skill was essential in her life as a Deviant. Evading her pursuers was easy, but she couldn't fight off the entire city while she fled the wardens. Sarina had to blend in somehow.

The road split in two, and Sarina veered right, choosing the path with a steep decline. Using the force of gravity, she barreled into the crowd before her, catching them by surprise. Hopefully, the fallen citizens she left behind would impede those chasing her.

Sarina turned left, right, and left again, sprinting through the labyrinth of suspended roads and bridges to escape the wardens and leaving chaos in her wake. Rach the size of sparrows flew around her head, mocking her with their graceful dance.

She glanced at the road behind her and cursed. Four wardens pursued her. She must have passed a patrol at some point. Luckily, she hadn't run into a warden yet.

Right on cue, she spotted a pair of wardens in the intersection ahead of her, their backs to her.

Shit.

The wardens strolled across the street, unaware of the Deviant rushing towards them, only twenty paces away.

The wardens behind her shouted a warning, their voices

cutting above the din of the busy road. The newest pair stopped in surprise and spun around. They scowled as they spotted Sarina. Ten paces.

Sarina let out a primal scream and charged the wardens in her path, pulling her wrists apart with all her strength. The knotted rope groaned as more fibers snapped.

Five paces.

They clutched their sword hilts. Sarina pulled at her restraints, her wrists screaming in pain. Then the rope snapped.

Two paces.

Metal glinted in the sunlight as the wardens unsheathed their weapons. Sarina raised her newly freed left hand and lunged at the nearest warden. She planted the bloody glass shard deep into his neck.

His sword clattered to the ground as he clutched his throat, choking on his own blood. Sarina shoved him into his companion, leaving the shard lodged deep in his neck and kept running. The four wardens on her heels were gaining ground.

But now she was unbound.

Casting the torn rope aside, Sarina surged forward; this road was more crowded than the others, providing more obstacles for her and her pursuers. She upturned a fruit stand in the middle of the road and punched a random man, who toppled to the ground. Sarina smiled savagely as the trailing wardens struggled to overcome her diversions. Without the restraints, she could now control the chaos in her wake.

The chase continued across the Canopy. The farther she ran, the more wardens were alerted to her escape. Nevertheless, she endured.

She stole a towel from a pub's railing, wiping the blood from her skin, tackled a man, and stole his long, brown cloak. Making a sharp turn, she threw the heavy robe around her shoulders and padded into the crowd. Hopefully, the new disguise would allow her to blend into her surroundings.

Sarina dodged the crowds, taking last-minute turns, and stealing a second cloak for a quick wardrobe change. Keeping the hood drawn to hide her identity, she ducked behind a house and waited. She counted to ten. No wardens passed. Twenty. Nothing. Peering around the corner, she studied the street and breathed a sigh of relief. She lost them.

With her mind still razor sharp, Sarina jogged down the road with a brisk but casual gait. The chase was not over yet; Tabulrossa still crawled with the green bastards, and by now, the entire city was aware of a Deviant loose in the Canopy. The Undergrowth was her best option now; the city's lower depths seemed a better hiding place than the sunbathed streets above.

The layout of the Canopy was complex and confusing, and Sarina tried her best to avoid warden patrols. However, she encountered countless guards as she journeyed across the treetop. Makeshift barricades blocked off entire streets with armed checkpoints. Whenever she dared to venture downwards, the blockades forced her upwards. Anytime she turned right, the blockades pushed her left. All she needed was a staircase to whisk her down the Aerials to the Undergrowth below. But none came.

Her breath became more ragged, exhausted from the chase; her wrists were raw from the bloody rope burn, and dozens of tiny pricks along her body alerted her of the smaller injuries inflicted by broken wood and glass. None of them, however, compared to the lancing pain in her shoulder. Blood soaked her newly acquired cloak. The wound Mags had bandaged must have reopened during the chase.

How much blood had she lost? Her vision blurred once more. Sarina would pass out again if she did not find somewhere to rest. And this time, it wouldn't be a retired warden who would greet her when she awoke.

People around her began to notice the blood stain seeping through her cloak; citizens gasped as she passed by, and some shouted for help. She hurried along, keeping her head down, searching for escape, but there was no sign of a staircase.

"Stop, scum!"

A warden squad spotted her from across a plaza. They drew their swords, and the chase began once more.

Sarina darted down the nearest road, the only one free of warden blockades. It was much broader than the previous avenues and less busy, an odd contradiction. The larger branches held more buildings and, thus, more people. This branch, however, was impossibly broad, and structures sparsely lined the edges.

Panting, Sarina proceeded onward as the road sloped slightly upward. Her weak legs slowed, and the sounds of the wardens grew louder. The road evened out, and she saw what lay beyond. She gasped.

The road widened and descended until it joined with other bridges. Almost a score of gigantic branches met here, forming a bowl-like depression. This was the top of the Bole—the Precipice—the center of Tabulrossa. Over a dozen colossal, intricately crafted buildings filled the clearing, reaching to the heavens. Almost no one dared enter this hallowed ground.

Only priestesses and wardens walked between the buildings. A colossal statue guarded each. One had a raven's head, the other a serpent's tail—representing a different Tal'Rach. The temples formed three tight, concentric circles surrounding the tallest building Sarina had ever seen. The ancient tower loomed over the temples. Thousands of beautifully sculpted arched windows dotted the majestic structure. The building was a vertical branch from the tree itself. There were no offshoots, fruit, flowers, or leaves on the enormous structure. Sarina had heard of such a place. It was where the Tal'Rach created the Edicts and where the wardens trained—the Sanctum.

The wardens had corralled her here, forced her to this very place. She was running directly into the heart of their power.

Her arm tingled, and a bright blue rach brushed against her. It took the form of a tabby cat, its little paws treading as if propelling itself through water. It yawned lazily and blinked at her, floating alongside her as she darted towards the Sanctum. She slapped it in annoyance, but her hand went right through it. The rach regarded her with a lucid curiosity.

She had seen countless rach in her lifetime, but none had ever interacted with humans. They merely floated around as if they existed on another plane. This one, however, was alert.

A shout rang from behind, and the rach swiveled its little head towards the wardens chasing her. It bared its teeth, flattening its ears. It dove to the ground in front of Sarina, forcing her to stop immediately. It winked at her, then bounded into an alleyway between the nearest temples.

The wardens were only thirty paces behind. The rach stopped abruptly, sitting at the end of the alley, staring at her.

It was waiting for her to follow.

Sarina currently had three options: stay and fight the wardens, which would result in a quick death; turn and run towards the Sanctum, which would result in her capture, interrogation, and a long, painful death; or follow this odd rach into the alleyway, which would probably result in her inevitable capture and death.

She chose the alleyway. Her death was inevitable, but she was intrigued by the creature before her. The rach's ears perked up as she approached it and bounded down the alley.

Sarina willed herself to keep up with the small rach, whose luminescent body cast blue light on the alley walls. She spun around, expecting to see the wardens on her tail, but she was alone. They didn't dare enter this sacred space. Clever little rach. However, Sarina wasn't sure what kept the wardens at bay. Were they afraid of the temples? That couldn't be it. They existed to protect them. No matter, she focused on following the rach.

The glowing creature leaped out of the alleyway and into another wide avenue leading to the Sanctum. All roads joined at the looming tower, like a spoke of an enormous wheel. The cat scampered to the right, and Sarina followed. Luckily, this road was vacant, and no one saw the rach and the Deviant cross into another alley between temples.

In the second alleyway, however, the rach dove into a basement window, disappearing into the temple. Sarina waited apprehensively, briefly inspecting the opening. She now wondered if she had chosen the worst death of the three. The sound of wardens echoed from the avenue outside, so Sarina dove in after the rach.

She fell a short distance and landed on something soft, though the drop was high enough that the wind flew out of her lungs. Sarina lay still, too exhausted to stand, staring at the basement ceiling, barely conscious. She had lost too much blood, and the room spun. The soft object that broke her landing was a pile of worn and dirty robes. She was in a laundry room. Two dark shapes towered over her—a pair of women. One was in her middle years, with raven hair and a sour expression, while the other was much younger, almost a child. They examined her with strange expressions. Sarina could not quite put her finger on it.

"Go fetch Marikae," the stern woman said to the younger. "Tell her there is another one."

The darkness took Sarina before she could comprehend anymore.

7

The Best Day

Two days had passed since Laithe first arrived at the Brazen Leaf, and his services to Veremund officially began. He slept the better part of the first day, as it was his first time in an actual bed in years. His body was exhausted beyond his comprehension, and it relished the comfortable confines of his new room.

Once his stomach growled voraciously, he ventured out into the secret village, searching for food. As Isam mentioned, there was a mess hall on the lowest level. Half a dozen men lounged around on picnic tables, casually eating. The residents of the Brazen Leaf were kind enough, but most kept their distance, only speaking to him when necessary. Laithe did not mind it. He was unaccustomed to people showing him kindness. He wasn't used to being kind either. So, he decided to remain separate from the village men. He would protect them but did not need to befriend them. Laithe observed from the edge of the dining area, eating his dinner peacefully in silence.

The first and only conversation Laithe had that day was

with Veremund himself. In the late hours of the day, the Tal'Rach entered the village after dinner, greeted by the Fourteens like he was their king. Every last one, including Laithe, owed their life to the ram spirit.

After mingling with the others, Veremund finally joined Laithe's table. Everyone else promptly vacated the dining area, understanding that the ram needed privacy, leaving the two alone to discuss important matters.

The Tal'Rach was direct, which Laithe was thankful for. Regardless of his feelings, the Deviant was not skilled with small talk. They stayed up late into the night discussing strategy. Veremund laid out a detailed plan, and Laithe sporadically asked clarifying questions when needed.

The goal was simple. Assassinate Archwarden Alistair. What complicated matters, however, was that Alistair never left the most fortified building in the city. Veremund called it the Sanctum.

It was another year until the next Calling, and the Tal'Rach, under Alistair's direction, would undoubtedly deliver at least two more Edicts before then. If they couldn't draw out the archwarden, Veremund and Laithe would weaken his defenses. The Undergrowth was the perfect target. The vast expanse of roots and moss was almost impossible to defend. After Veremund's last attack, the wardens had already increased their presence there. Alistair had to believe that the ram spirit endeavored to reclaim the Undergrowth. They would slaughter as many wardens as possible, forcing the archwarden to send the maximum amount of his troops to the lowest reaches of the city.

The warden order was vast and formidable, but they were not infinite in number. Not only did Alistair have to maintain control of the city, but he also commanded the troops stationed throughout the land. It was an easy deduction, even for Laithe. The more wardens Veremund and Laithe killed, the less there would be to protect Alistair in the Sanctum.

Once the attacks depleted his defenses, they could strike.

The next day, Veremund led Laithe into the labyrinth of tunnels outside the village, but they did not exit through the Brazen Leaf. To Laithe's surprise, one of the tunnels opened into a quiet alley.

Veremund explained they were on another platform farther down the Bole. It was the rear entrance, only used for an escape if the wardens ever discovered the village. He must never use this entrance again. Laithe asked if there were additional entrances in the labyrinth, but Veremund ignored him.

The Tal'Rach instructed Laithe to meet him at the drop root hollow where they had previously sought refuge. Before he could object, the ram spirit disappeared into the labyrinth. Laithe was excellent with directions, but that was in the outside world. Navigating the complex root system of Tabulrossa was a different story entirely.

Laithe spent hours locating the hollow. The ram spirit had already arrived, waiting impatiently for him. Laithe apologized, but the ram spirit wouldn't hear it. Veremund was stern and irritable, almost impossible to please.

They snuck through the Undergrowth and ambushed a patrol of almost two dozen wardens. They hid in the shadows, waiting until their prey was on the apex of a root bridge. It arched high above the mossy forest floor, too high to jump safely. There was no escape.

Veremund appeared at one end of the bridge, assaulting

them from the front, while Laithe attacked from the rear, hacking at the wardens who fled. The Deviant's role was to ensure no one escaped Veremund's wrath. The Tal'Rach wanted no survivors. The fewer witnesses, the quicker the fear would spread. Like a virus, they would methodically erode the wardens' ranks and morale.

The battle ended in less than a minute. Laithe was sure he was superfluous; the Tal'Rach could have dispatched every soldier single-handedly. He had seen him slay triple that number during the Calling. Laithe reckoned that Veremund wanted someone to observe his bloody handiwork; it was apparent that he relished the attention. Whether it was Laithe, the wardens, or the men under the Brazen Leaf, the Tal'Rach craved adoration from others. In the case of the wardens, intense hatred.

They left the bodies in the middle of the bridge and stalked through the city, hunting for more patrols. They encountered three, each only four wardens strong. Laithe barely landed a hit during these attacks before Veremund tore the screaming wardens apart.

Each assault was random, far from the Bole and Veremund's Undergrowth hideout. The Tal'Rach only used his flames at the end of each battle after the last warden had fallen. In some sort of ritual, Veremund burned a rough image of a ram's skull on the nearest wall or in the street at the center of the bodies. He wanted Alistair to know it was him. The entire mission lasted under an hour before the pair returned to the drop root hollow, covered in blood and filled with adrenaline.

"That was an impressive display, little one," Veremund smiled, filling Laithe with unbridled pride. "Haven't seen a warrior like you in ages."

The great ram discarded his clothes and lowered himself into the pool; Laithe's cheeks flushed as he admired Veremund's nakedness. A singular, carnal desire consumed Laithe since he first beheld the Tal'Rach. He fantasized about it. Dreamed of it. Desired it with every fiber of his being. But Veremund did not want him in that way; he had already said so; he merely required Laithe to slay wardens for him, which he was more than happy to do. But he yearned for the Tal'Rach's touch.

"There you go, staring again," Veremund chuckled and beckoned Laithe to join him.

Laithe hastily disrobed and plunged into the pool. Despite the chilly waters, his skin felt hot with embarrassment and longing. Laithe had attempted to steal a kiss from Veremund when they were last naked together but the Tal'Rach firmly rebuffed him. The ram only required Laithe for his skills in battle, not for the bedroom. He was clear about that despite the mixed signals.

"It won't happen again," Laithe assured Veremund. The last thing he sought was to incur the Tal'Rach's wrath.

"I didn't say I wanted you to stop," Veremund said. He waded closer until their bodies nearly touched. "I enjoy admiring your body as well, little one. And since you performed your duties so well, I believe you deserve a reward."

Laithe smiled and returned Veremund's lustful stare, his body shaking with anticipation and excitement. All he wanted was for the ram to take him.

As if reading his mind, the Tal'Rach pulled Laithe close. He leaned over so that his tight stomach was pressed against Laithe's naked chest, staring at him primally. Laithe's whole body felt as if it were on fire. He felt himself growing underneath the surface. Something hard pressed against his stomach. Veremund grew, as well. He could hear the strong heartbeat as the Tal'Rach drew closer, their lips almost touching.

Laithe felt Veremund's chest, the smooth, taut skin against immense muscles. He plunged his hands under the water, caressing impossibly defined abs, moving downward until he grabbed his prize. He was experienced enough to know what to do with his hands once they were in the right place. Laithe pawed at Veremund eagerly, exploring every inch. The Tal'Rach groaned, overcome with lust, panting, growing. Massive hands groped Laithe's body under the water, feeling every inch.

Veremund smiled.

"Not so small, I see," the Tal'Rach breathed. "Good."

Veremund lifted Laithe partially out of the water and into his chest. Their lips finally touched. The Deviant grabbed the Tal'Rach's horns and kissed him passionately, losing himself in the aggressive, lustful kiss. Veremund tasted like bark, sweat, and ash. Laithe savored the flavor, pushing his tongue deeper, eager for more.

After years of depriving himself of physical touch, Laithe allowed his urges to consume him. Veremund responded in kind, grunting softly, as he took control. Laithe's body erupted in pleasure as Veremund deftly worked his sweet spots. Moans escaped his lips, muffled by Veremund's expert tongue.

The Tal'Rach's hands moved lower, hoisting him up so only his bottom was in the water; Laithe wrapped his legs around Veremund's robust chest as powerful hands massaged his cheeks. He was under the Tal'Rach's complete control. It was intoxicating despite being completely new territory for Laithe, who was typically the aggressive partner. He was always stronger, always the one pursuing.

He shuddered as Veremund's finger entered him, and his body tensed. Veremund pulled out of Laithe and nibbled on his neck. The Deviant exhaled, and his body relaxed. The Tal'Rach eased his index finger inside. Laithe let out a primal moan of ecstasy. Once acclimated, Laithe thrust himself onto Veremund's digit, greedily satisfying himself. Only then did the Tal'Rach remove his finger. Smiling devilishly, Veremund roughly grabbed him by the hips, angled his body, and slowly entered him.

It was a pleasure Laithe had never experienced. He panted as the titan thrust into him, leisurely to start, rapidly increasing fervor and intensity. Deviant and Tal'Rach became one underneath the water. The louder Laithe moaned, the harder Veremund's thrusts became. The Deviant wanted it that way. He practically screamed, begging for more. Laithe clung to Veremund, his vision blurred with bliss, tongues twisting around one another. Maintaining his rhythm, Veremund casually waded to the pool's edge and tossed Laithe onto the shore. He wasn't gentle, and Laithe did not care. He wanted Veremund to be inside him again. The Tal'Rach promptly obliged.

Hours passed as the two played on the mossy bank, wrestling around roughly, pleasing one another with wild passion. Laithe lost himself to the dance. They fucked in total unison. Each knew what the other wanted and anticipated his moves, similar to the battlefield. Laithe had never experienced anything like it, never felt connected to another person in the way he and the Tal'Rach had become.

The pair finished several times before they fell in a heap.

"Well, little one, you are quite impressive," Veremund chuckled, leaning on his elbow, assessing Laithe intently. "On the battlefield and in bed—er, the moss."

Laithe smiled, brimming with pride, his chest heaving, his body physically spent. He smiled and rolled onto Veremund, laying his head on an enormous shoulder. He ran his fingertips softly across the sweaty chest, resting it on the cool metal of his necklace. A heavy silver teardrop hung at the end, a dazzling amethyst set in its center. The purple jewel gleamed underneath the metal veins. Laithe held the precious stone, feeling its edges with his thumb.

"Admiring my jewelry, little one?" Veremund asked, smirking.

"Sort of," Laithe replied. "Just always wondered why you wear it."

"It is precious to me," Veremund said wistfully.

Surprised by the vulnerability, Laithe leaned over for another kiss. "Is it—?"

The ram spirit pushed him away, his expression soured. "That is all you need to know."

Laithe's smile faded. Veremund rose from the moss and retrieved his clothes from the far side of the hideout.

Laithe admired Veremund's naked body. The sight almost aroused him enough to want another round. Almost. He was beyond exhausted. Laithe would be surprised if he could walk straight.

Still, he'd loved every second of it. Nothing felt better after a fight than rolling around the moss with Veremund, pounding away the pent-up stress and emotion. The pleasure was indescribable. Killing a dozen wardens and having sex with Veremund, Laithe could not have asked for a better day.

"Wait here a while, then return to the Brazen Leaf," Veremund instructed once fully dressed. "It is best if we travel separately. Be safe. You did well today, little one."

Laithe beamed with pride as the Tal'Rach departed, leaving the Deviant alone in the hidden Undergrowth hollow. Traveling individually to and from the Brazen Leaf was the sensible course of action to avoid attracting attention. Though Laithe doubted Veremund traversed the city on foot. He probably left his avatar, the human he used to take physical form.

It was perfectly reasonable; Veremund avoided traveling with Laithe to protect his avatar's identity.

It stung Laithe that the ram did not trust him with that vital secret. He vowed to earn that trust.

The Tal'Rach could enter and exit their host at will, changing their features. Laithe witnessed great spirits vacate their avatars on his first day in Tabulrossa, though he did not understand what it was.

He had asked Veremund about it later and he reluctantly provided a vague explanation, though Laithe wasn't sure if he would ever fully comprehend the nature of the Tal'Rach. According to the ram, the great spirits couldn't maintain their true form for long and needed a human host, an avatar, or an important object called a vessel. Laithe inquired what his vessel was and Veremund angrily ended the conversation.

Laithe decided not to dwell upon such complex matters and dipped into the pool, which was now quite cold. He lingered in the cool waters, washing off the muck of battle and sex. Per the Tal'Rach's instructions, he waited a long while before stalking through the Undergrowth towards the Bole.

The city's underbelly crawled with wardens, undoubtedly

searching for the culprits of the attacks. Laithe narrowly evaded six separate patrols before he climbed into the Aerials. He doubted they would cease their search for the foreseeable future. They were desperate to find the ram and his Deviants in the Undergrowth.

But their investigations would be fruitless.

The wardens' reaction already proved Veremund's theory: the ram's mark would gradually draw the wardens into the Undergrowth, stretching them wafer thin.

Soon, the archwarden would be vulnerable.

Laithe returned to the Brazen Leaf a bit faster on his second attempt; he had always excelled with directions and was slowly acclimating to the tangled, chaotic streets of Tabulrossa. Pellum greeted him roughly as he entered. The patrons didn't notice him sneaking behind the counter and into the backrooms. Isam, however, was nowhere to be found, so Laithe ventured into the bowels of the Bole on his own.

Using the key Isam had given him the night before, he entered the smuggler's hold. The barboy had been stern when relinquishing the tiny metal tool. Only Veremund, Pellum, and Isam had the privilege, and the other men wouldn't dare leave the village's safety. Laithe understood why Isam would be wary of him, as he had arrived only days ago. But Veremund entrusted him with great power. He only hoped that Isam wouldn't succumb to jealousy.

The longest part of the journey was the labyrinth. He had only traveled its twisting passages twice, once upon his arrival and the second earlier that day. Struggling to remember Veremund's directions, Laithe lost himself in the shadowy maze.

After a while, he thought he might die in those tunnels

unless Isam or Veremund retrieved him. But eventually, he located the familiar dead end with the secret panel. He breathed a sigh of relief as the tunnel wall rumbled open, allowing sweet air to flow in the musky passageway.

Something else wafted through the opening. The joyous sound of soft music echoed against the tunnel walls. Delicate strings and the loveliest voice Laithe had ever heard. He hurried through the doorway and into the village.

The hard life of a Deviant did not allow for trivial pleasures. Hot meals, beds, sleep, laughter, and music were all luxuries. Singing was difficult while the wardens were hunting you, and carrying an instrument was foolish. It had been years since Laithe had last heard music aside from the haunting song the Tal'Rach and their minions sang during the Calling. That dirge filled Laithe with dread.

This song, however, transported Laithe to his childhood, before the Second Edict shattered his world.

His parents had been exceptionally talented musicians, as was common in the Roursche clan. His father played the fiddle and accompanied his mother, who possessed the most beautiful singing voice in the clan. After every dinner, his family would sing great songs of adventure, romance, and tragedy. Laithe fondly remembered falling asleep with this brother and sister to the perfectly orchestrated melodies. His father would carry them to bed in the small hours, making sure not to wake them.

Laithe had nearly forgotten what they looked like: his hulking father, mousy sister, petulant younger brother, and radiant mother. Their faces blurred in his mind's eye, lost in the fog of time. But now, on the balcony above the village, listening to that gorgeous melody, Laithe could see them again.

Tears streamed forth.

Laithe shook himself out of his trance, shocked by his tears. He hadn't cried since childhood, not even when the wardens destroyed his village. Not even after he watched his father decapitated and his mother impaled by a warden's sword. He did not allow himself to despair, and he was too angry for an emotion so cumbersome. So weak. He frantically raised the wall in his heart, forcing himself to forget his family once more.

His stomach growled. The recent fighting and fucking had worked up a voracious appetite, and he hadn't eaten since earlier that morning. Though he wasn't sure how long that had been, time did not seem to exist in this gloomy city. He descended to the dining area, thankful they were still serving dinner.

Almost the entire village was gathered at the tables, finishing their food and watching the young performer play from the makeshift stage in the corner.

It was Isam.

The barboy played a lute while he sang. He had started another tune, this one more upbeat than the first. It seemed popular with the audience. They clapped to the beat and sang along, most of their faces red from the purple alcohol in their mugs. Laithe's cheeks matched their crimson tone when he understood the lyrics. It was an explicit tale about two men on their wedding night. And what they did with the priest. Laithe almost laughed, clapping along as he sat to the side with his meal.

The evening wore on, and Isam barely took any breaks, entertaining the men late into the night. Laithe surprised himself by staying after he finished his meal. Usually, his reclusive nature would compel him to retire early. He was not a fan of loud gatherings like this. But instead, he was lost in the joy of the music. He caught himself smiling.

What was happening to him? Is this how ordinary people felt?

Before he knew it, only a handful of men remained. The rest had returned to their homes, but Laithe was too invested in the music. Isam sang his final song, a nostalgic tale about two lovers meeting in school and falling madly in love. Once he finished, he packed his lute and approached Laithe, smiling broadly.

"Welcome back," Isam chirped, his body shaking from the adrenaline of the performance. He was practically glowing. "Did you enjoy the show?"

"It was good," Laithe said. "I liked the part with the sex."

Isam laughed and slapped the bigger man on the shoulder. "Good. I'm glad you're as filthy as me. Now tell me about the mission. I'm sorry it wasn't fruitful. It was only your first. You'll have better luck in the future, I'm sure."

"It went well, actually," Laithe said. "Just as Veremund planned."

"I don't understand," Isam said, wrinkling his brow. "A successful mission usually ends with leading Fourteens to the village. If it went well, you would have returned with at least a few men. Did you leave them in one of the safe houses in the Undergrowth?"

"We weren't escorting Fourteens," Laithe said, equally perplexed. "It was a raid."

"I see," Isam said, growing dark; when he glanced at Laithe, all joy had vanished, his tone icy and sharp. "Very well. I seemed to be mistaken. Have a good night."

Laithe watched Isam storm off, unsure of what he said to upset him. Pellum operated the bar, Veremund governed the village, and Isam helped the two. But why would the barboy be so concerned with Veremund's actions? Why wouldn't he be happy that Veremund defeated the Fourteens' enemies? Laithe was sure the ram would find lost Fourteens soon enough; he was their protector, after all.

He returned to his bed and flopped down, exhausted and content; Isam's odd behavior did little to affect his mood. By all measures, it was probably the best day of his entire adult life—a great battle, fantastic sex, and good music. He closed his eyes and smiled for the second time in one day. Rare. He could not wait for the next.

# # #

Archwarden Alistair lingered by the circular window of his study, observing the Precipice below. Dozens of wardens and priestesses walked the streets, some casually strolling into the Canopy, others dutifully patrolling the temples. He envied both their freedom and their blissful ignorance.

Unfortunately for him, he did not have such luxuries. The entire security of the city rested on his shoulders. Rumors surfaced regarding the archwarden's competence after Veremund's attack. Only a week had passed since the Calling, and Alistair's rivals within the Sanctum were already conspiring against him.

He smirked. His enemies could plot as much as they like, but their machinations would prove fruitless and self-sabotaging. Their ruthlessness paled in comparison to Alistair's cutthroat disposition, and anyone foolish enough to test him would soon find that out. A warden did not simply reach the highest office in the land by hopes and wishes alone. One had to break a few eggs, and Alistair shattered his fair share.

The whispers of the Tal'Rach, however, were what concerned him. Veremund threatened the lives of the other great spirits under Alistair's watch, a mistake the rulers of Tabulrossa would not soon forget. Losing their favor would be fatal, so the archwarden's next move would be imperative. He had much more to lose than his life where the Tal'Rach was concerned. Especially after the promise they made him when they granted him the title of archwarden. Nothing in this world would prevent him from making their promise a reality, not even a rogue Tal'Rach.

Veremund perplexed Alistair. He had barely spoken to the ram since the Tal'Rach first appeared in the city, soon after the archwarden ascended to his station. His arrival was shocking since all the known Tal'Rach had lived in Tabulrossa for centuries. At first, Alistair assumed there may be more Tal'Rach like Veremund who wandered the edges of the known world. But soon into his tenure as archwarden, he discovered the truth.

Nevertheless, something about their confrontation on the Undergrowth's bridge plagued Alistair. The way the ram spirit uttered his name with such vitriol.

The archwarden wondered if he was the target of Veremund's assault.

The ram barely paid the other Tal'Rach any heed, especially when Alistair appeared. The archwarden had survived enough assassination attempts to know when someone desired to kill him. His intuition told him the ram wanted him dead. But why?

He regarded his desk and the pile of reports from his

officers in the Undergrowth. After losing scores of soldiers during the Calling, Veremund attacked the lower reaches of the city yet again, slaying more wardens. Alistair's forces were already stretched thin, and if he did not secure the unwieldy Undergrowth, the Deviant menace would fester and grow until Tabulrossa succumbed to rebellion. He had no choice but to reinforce his troops. The only reserves he could pull from was from the Precipice itself. But that would be a foolish error. His better judgment warned of such an action. Veremund had been active in the Undergrowth for years, aiding refugee Deviants, but he had never acted like this before.

These attacks were an obvious ploy. Veremund wanted Alistair to send reinforcements to the Undergrowth, leaving the Precipice vulnerable.

"Lieutenant Derrara," Alistair quietly addressed the pale woman sitting on the opposite side of the desk, ensuring no unwanted ears would hear the following conversation. "Please write a letter to our generals in every outpost. Request a full battalion from each. I want reinforcements dispatched to Tabulrossa within the week. Our hold on the Undergrowth is crumbling. Their numbers are essential to rebuff the Deviant threat."

"Such a move will weaken our influence in the outlying regions, sir. Do you think such a drastic course of action is wise?" Derrara asked calmly.

The question shocked Alistair. His lieutenant never second-guessed his choices, which made her an efficient subordinate. The fact that she questioned his tactics was enough to tell Alistair he was playing a perilous game. He must tread carefully.

"I would rather weaken the outlying generals than the protection of the Tal'Rach," Alistair lied. The archwarden still believed Veremund was targeting him. But he would keep that a secret until he uncovered the ram's motivations. "Allude to a threat in your message, but do not offer any specifics."

"And if any of them ask about the upcoming Edicts?" Derrara's professional cadence wavered ever so slightly. She knew she was on dangerous ground, however necessary the question was.

"You can tell them I will announce the Nineteenth imminently," Alistair lied. He knew as much about the next Edict as his Lieutenant. "Remain as vague as possible and stress the importance of securing Tabulrossa. Understood?"

Derrara saluted and left the study; she had worked with Alistair long enough to know when to refrain. She had seen too many people make that mistake to replicate it. Alistair watched her leave. If the ram wanted a war in the Undergrowth, he would have it. But it would not come at the cost of Alistair's security. He had enough to deal with, and a chaotic Tal'Rach was not his biggest concern, not by a long shot.

Alistair gazed out onto the Precipice and contemplated his next move.

8

The Temple of the Peacock

Sarina awoke in an unknown room for the second time in one week. She lay on a strange bed, wearing unfamiliar clothes. This disorienting routine was becoming an unwelcome pattern. She preferred to maintain control of situations, no matter how dire. Helplessness was not a feeling she greatly appreciated.

Once she fully recovered her senses, Sarina gingerly climbed to her feet. Fresh bandages covered her body, expertly applied. She felt no pain, but her head was a bit fuzzy. Drugs. Again. Whoever bandaged her wounds had also taken off her old clothes. In their place, she wore a flowing white robe like the ones in the laundry pile. Knowing someone undressed her while she was unconscious made her feel violated.

The room was stark, less cozy than Mags' cottage. There were no windows, decorations, or furniture apart from a cot and bedside table.

It was a cell.

Sarina took a series of deep breaths to center herself and

avoid panic. A full water pitcher and a wooden cup rested on the narrow tabletop. Despite a sore throat, she refrained from drinking. Whoever held her captive could have laced the water with the same drug that currently flowed in her veins. Against her better judgment, Sarina turned the door handle. It was locked tight. There was only one course of action she could take: wait for her captor to appear.

Someone was taking care of her—her bandaged wounds and the water pitcher were proof of that—but that didn't mean they were benevolent. Mags tended to her injuries as well. Whoever held her captive would return soon.

She calmly sat on the cot, facing the worn wooden door, steadying her breathing and assessing her situation. A strange rach had guided Sarina into the bowels of a temple, but her captors could have as easily taken her to the Sanctum. She remembered lying in a pile of laundry as two priestesses leaned over her before she lost consciousness. They would have undoubtedly alerted the wardens when they discovered her.

The minutes slipped into hours, and she waited patiently, legs crossed, leaning against the wall. She could have hidden behind the door, ambushing her captor when they entered. But she was too exhausted and in no condition to fight. Instead, she prepared herself for intense interrogation. She had killed a veteran, who was also the mother of two wardens. Her daughters would relish in Sarina's suffering.

Eventually, the door opened, and a pair of women entered the cell. Neither of them was Mags' daughter; they were priestesses. Sarina recognized them as the same two from the laundry. Neither seemed frightened of Sarina; they must not know she was Deviant.

Their presence meant that she was still in the temple. Odd. The younger priestess held a tray of hot food, head bowed sheepishly. She stood awkwardly in the center of the tiny room, peeking at Sarina with great curiosity.

"On the bedside table, Minora. Fool girl," the elder barked. She had a thin nose and a square jaw. A golden ribbon pulled her raven-black hair tightly in a bun. The younger woman awkwardly set the dinner tray on the table and waited dutifully by the door. "Now go and fetch Marikae. She will want to speak to our newest stray."

"Yes, mistress Alma," Minora squeaked and scampered down the hallway.

"You survived your wounds at least," Alma said, shutting the door behind her. "We don't have a corpse to dispose of, but now we have to deal with you. What is your name, child?"

"Florence," she replied, using the same pseudonym she gave Mags.

"Liar," Alma retorted. "Give me your real name, stray. No aliases. I like to know who I am talking to."

"How did you—" Sarina began, but the priestess scoffed, interrupting her.

"Because I am no fool, obviously," Alma said. "Now, what is your name? Or I'll be forced to call you stray."

"Sarina," she said, bristling. She was not used to being talked to in such a disrespectful manner. Alma was making an enemy.

"Well, Sarina," Alma sighed, gesturing to the steaming plate Minora had left. "Your dinner isn't getting any warmer."

Sarina glared at the priestess defiantly. How could Alma speak to her with such rudeness? She wouldn't allow anyone to bully her, much less an aging priestess. When she last ate a stranger's food, she was drugged and almost murdered.

Though Sarina was currently drugged, it seemed whatever was in her system was for the pain.

Her stomach growled.

Alma smirked.

Sarina winced.

Reluctantly, Sarina grabbed the bowl and ate the steaming soup. It was delicious. She didn't want to allow Alma the satisfaction, so Sarina grimaced while she ate.

Alma smugly sat in the corner as Sarina devoured her meal, slurping the delicious broth. Its warmth soothed her sore throat, and the spices danced on her tongue. If it did contain drugs, it was better than Mags' stew—small victories. Before she could finish, the door opened, and a third priestess entered the room.

"Thank you, Alma," the new arrival said. "You may leave us."

"Yes, mistress Marikae," Alma bowed graciously. Sarina's jaw would have dropped if it wasn't full of soup. Despite only knowing the severe-looking priestess for a short while, Sarina could hardly believe how submissive she was to this Marikae. Who was this woman who commanded so much respect?

Marikae was tall and slender, with coarse obsidian hair braided into a hive that rose almost a pace above her head. She was one of the most beautiful women Sarina had ever encountered. Although she was younger than Alma, it was easy to see how the older woman groveled at this woman's feet. She had broad shoulders and a long neck, possessing a regal air that commanded respect. Marikae regarded Sarina silently. Her gaze wasn't as harsh as Alma's, but it was by no means softer. Sarina returned the stare, and the two women sat in a silent match of wills.

"You are full of questions," Marikae asserted, finally breaking the silence. Her tone was low and smooth. "I can see them all behind your eyes. Ask me anything, and I will answer you truthfully."

"Truly?" Sarina asked.

"Of course." Something about Marikae's smile disarmed Sarina, her intuition told her to trust the austere priestess. Hopefully, her instincts were correct.

"Am I your prisoner?" It was essential to establish the dynamics of her current situation.

"No," Marikae replied simply. Sarina waited, but no elaboration came. The priestess was playing a game with her. She had to ask the right questions.

"Then why was the door locked?" Sarina asked, taking the bait.

"For your protection." It was the wrong question. Sarina cursed silently. She had to be more strategic.

"You already know that I am a Deviant. My entrance was not subtle," Sarina said, hoping her gambit would pay off. "Why have you not reported my presence to the wardens?"

Marikae smiled brightly. It was the right question. "Because we wouldn't readily betray one of our own."

Sarina nearly coughed, almost spilling her soup onto the bed. What Marikae was suggesting was impossible. The most faithful servants of the Tal'Rach were secretly all Deviants.

"That's impossible," Sarina objected, dumbfounded. "If you were Deviants, the wardens would have razed this temple to the ground years ago."

"The wardens know better than to meddle in our affairs," Marikae assured her. "You are safe within these walls."

"Wardens kill Deviants," Sarina pressed, still unconvinced by the outlandish statement. "That is the way of the world. What makes you different?"

"Our utility to the Tal'Rach," Marikae explained, as patient as ever. "Over half of the women in this temple are Fifteens, including Alma, Minora, and myself. Most of the temples are similar. It has been this way for centuries. Phymeria, my mistress, and the other Tal'Rach decided not to lose their servants after the Fifteenth. Not even for the Edicts. We are more important to the great spirits than you could imagine."

A thousand more questions sprouted in her mind, each giving birth to ten more. If the Tal'Rach spared their servants, did they know that evil spirits did not possess Deviants? If so, then what was the purpose of the Edicts? Were the priestesses conspiring with Veremund? Why had the ram spirit not answered her call?

She had more questions, but the thought of Veremund jerked her back into reality. She neglected her curiosity and focused on the present. She was safe now. And in a position to honor her promises and find her friends.

"There were others with me. Those whom I swore to protect," Sarina explained. "They might be dead, but I need to locate them."

"You need to rest," Marikae said firmly. "We are searching for your friends as we speak."

"I appreciate your help, but I know what they look like," Sarina said. "You may know the city better than I do, but you do not know them."

"There are four of them," Marikae said. "Your fifth friend sadly did not make it into the city. Kez, a short Eight with flowing gray hair. Beriane and Callandra, a pair of Fifteens.

And Laithe, a Roursche Fourteen. We have been watching them ever since the Calling."

"They are all alive?" Sarina breathed, unsure whether to be impressed or afraid of Marikae's knowledge.

"We found Beriane the day after the Calling. She is safe," the priestess explained. "She also informed us about your friends. I assure you they are all still alive, and we will find them."

"Beriane is here?" Sarina rose to her feet, heart racing. She needed to see her friend to apologize for her failures. "Can I go talk to her now?"

"I see that diligence is a key trait of yours." Marikae firmly held Sarina's shoulder, forcing her to sit on the cot. "You have trouble staying still; you need rest. Beriane is in one of our safe houses in the Canopy with the others who aren't priestesses. We cannot house every Deviant in the temples, only the ones with the gift."

"You said the others are alive." Sarina ignored the cryptic statement. Beriane may be safe, but if Marikae was truthful, the others were still in danger. "How can you be so sure?"

"Our spies are everywhere," Marikae assured. "We haven't discovered any bodies yet. The locations of Kez and Callandra remain unknown, but we have learned that the Roursche joined Veremund in his little village for Fourteens."

"So you are working with the ram spirit," Sarina deduced.

"Past tense," Marikae said bitterly. "Veremund and the Deviants of Tabulrossa worked together for years; he saved countless Deviants of every Edict until this year's Calling. Scores of migrants died that day because he was not there to protect them, too busy burning half the Undergrowth. Did you call for his aid as well?"

"Yes," Sarina replied. She did not dwell on the incident at

the gate, but images of Benjin's body still haunted her mind. "Why did he not come?"

"I do not know, I'm afraid," Marikae said. "He has ignored our messages and remains secluded in his village. Instead of aiding our efforts, he and your old friend, Laithe, have been slaughtering wardens in the Undergrowth, drawing archwarden Alistair's attention, and flooding the streets with his legions."

"Is that not good?" Sarina asked. Any Deviant would be happy to hear of such an attack against the wardens. "Are you more lenient with the green bastards since you live so close?"

"The death of wardens means little to me," Marikae said, as hard and immovable as iron. "However, I am concerned about our safe houses in the Undergrowth. It has always been the safest place to hide Deviants, but now Veremund is drawing attention, and it is only a matter of time before the wardens discover our havens. Only this morning, I was alerted that a patrol ransacked a storehouse. They confiscated months of provisions, and now the wardens are motivated to uncover more."

"I apologize for Laithe." She was not surprised that the Roursche was involved in such a plot. "He is more wolfhound than man. I'm sure he's eager to split as many skulls as possible."

"Charming." Marikae raised an eyebrow. "The hour is getting late, and other matters require my attention. Please rest and regain your strength, Sarina."

"I have one final question," Sarina said hastily. The priestess paused in the doorway. "You spoke earlier of a gift that only priestesses have. What were you speaking of?"

"Ah, yes," Marikae said brightly. "I underestimated your

attention to detail. Why don't I show you?"

She cleared her throat and chanted softly. The hairs on the back of Sarina's neck stood on end. She did not understand the words, which sounded like the old tongue, but she recognized the tune. It was the same song she had heard during the Calling. Then it dawned on her.

The Tal'Rach weren't singing that day; it was the priestesses.

A serpent emerged from the ceiling. The emerald rach slithered and danced around Marikae like a sentient ribbon. A tiny rabbit with a pink hue bounded through the door and hopped over the priestess's head. The rach moved of their own volition, but it was clear that Marikae guided them. Whatever ancient words she spoke, they listened.

Sarina gasped. A blue cat phased through the cot and landed on her lap, her skin tingling at its ethereal touch. It was the same rach who had led her to the temple.

"It was you," Sarina whispered to Marikae. "You are the one who guided me here."

"Oh no, on the contrary," Marikae said. "I have never seen this rach before. Your communion with it led you here, not me. Your connection with this peculiar rach is how I know you possess the gift."

Sarina stared at the cat, who stretched lazily on her lap. It let out a silent yawn and curled up contentedly. "What exactly is this gift?"

"We do not control the rach, but commune with them, and harness their power. The power they possess is beyond human comprehension," Marikae said. "If you promise to keep it a secret, I can show you a glimpse of it."

Sarina nodded vigorously. Marikae grinned and chanted again, holding her palm to the sky. The hare on her shoulder sparkled, and suddenly, a ball of amber fire appeared in Marikae's hand. She sustained her chanting, and the serpent glowed. A gust of wind snuffed the flame out. Sarina could only stare in wonder. If this was only a hint of the rach's power, then Sarina couldn't imagine what the women who commune with rach were truly capable of.

"Allow me to introduce myself fully. I am Marikae, high priestess to Phymeria, lady of the dawn, the peacock spirit. Welcome to her temple," she said formally. "You have proven yourself worthy to train with the other prospective priestesses and to harness your gift. I invite you to stay."

"As long as it will help our people," Sarina said, unsure of exactly what she was getting herself into, but too curious to decline the offer. What secrets did this temple contain? She would be happy if she could leverage only one of them to help her friends and other Deviants. "And only if you promise me you will find Kez and Callandra."

"Perfect," Marikae said. "You have my word. But in turn, you must promise to trust me and focus your full attention on your training. Can you do that?"

"Yes," Sarina was surprised at how hastily she answered. Something about this place excited her, and something about this woman piqued her interest, unlike anyone she had ever met.

So Sarina did the impossible, and for the first time in years, she relaxed and blocked out the noise of her duties. Her friends would be fine. Marikae would see to that. It was now her duty, her primary goal, to learn the secrets of the rach.

9

A New Arrival

Laithe ripped his ax from the dead warden's chest, ignoring the sickening crunch of the metal breaking from the shattered rib cage. Wiping off the gristle and blood from the blade, he scanned the battle for his next opponent. But only Veremund remained, standing over his most recent victims. Seven fresh bodies littered the mossy street.

They smiled at one another, adrenaline flowing through them. If they weren't careful, their blood lust would lead to sex in the murky Undergrowth alleyway. Such a dalliance was a common occurrence after a victory.

The smell of the carnage jostled Laithe into reality. He would have to wait until after the mission to taste the Tal'Rach again.

Over a month passed since he joined Veremund, and the pair had fallen into a gruesome, primal cycle. They would travel to the Undergrowth every few days and ambush any patrol unlucky enough to stumble upon them. The warden patrols had grown in number and size since they began their assaults. The wardens were now more prepared and heavily armed, harder to kill. Laithe enjoyed the challenge; he did not fear defeat while fighting alongside Veremund. On the contrary, he relished proving his value to the ram spirit. After their missions, they would find a safe place to regroup and make rough, passionate love.

Laithe was in love with Veremund. He was sure of it.

Two weeks into their bloody campaign, a warden patrol raided their usual safe house, forcing them to find shelter wherever they could manage. An alleyway, an abandoned house, another drop root cave—the location didn't matter to Laithe as long as he was with Veremund.

Occasionally, their battles were too numerous and draining, forcing them to bypass sex altogether before retreating to the Aerials above.

Whether or not they fucked, Veremund would always end the missions without a word, disappearing into the shadows. Laithe had still not caught a glimpse of the ram's avatar, and he resigned himself to the fact that he never would. The ram showed no intention of confiding in Laithe, which didn't bother him. He had everything he could dream of, so why ask for more?

Left to his own devices, Laithe would make the long, arduous return journey to the Brazen Leaf. He would take a unique, convoluted route and steal a new cloak to hide any signs of a battle. He couldn't allow a warden scout to follow him home.

He hated the days of rest between raids. Veremund hardly appeared, and Laithe assumed it was to allow his avatar, whoever he may be, some rest. That left Laithe alone in his room, helplessly idle with nothing to do but eat and sleep. The villagers avoided him like a disease, whispering to themselves in hushed tones when they passed by.

No one was outwardly rude or nasty to him, but they weren't courteous or friendly either. Laithe didn't mind; he was used to such treatment. He didn't blame them; he often returned covered in blood. Laithe was aware of how others perceived him. He was naturally intimidating and effortlessly menacing. He had grown accustomed to such a response.

Word of his exploits spread throughout the village. How the other Fourteens acted around him confirmed this. They were terrified of him.

Pellum never visited the village, so Isam was the only man Laithe knew under the Brazen Leaf. Like the others, the young musician avoided him, but he was the only one who did not hide his disdain for the mercenary. The slender barboy would sneer and stare daggers at Laithe as he passed.

Laithe understood their fear, but their unbridled anger toward him was confusing. He and Veremund protected the Brazen Leaf. They should show a modicum of gratitude.

Perhaps these men had enjoyed peace for so long that they forgot the first law of nature: kill or be killed. Each warden's life threatened this beautiful place, and Laithe would ensure to snuff out any possible threat.

Due to his growing infamy, he spent most of these days in the windowless bedroom, eagerly awaiting the next mission. He only dared to venture into the village to eat and listen to Isam perform. Laithe didn't care if Isam hated him; that wasn't important. What mattered was how much he loved the music.

Apart from his days with Veremund, it was only during Isam's performances that he felt any substantial emotion. Fighting and fucking with the Tal'Rach revealed the lustful heat buried deep within, but Isam's music elicited a contrasting reaction. It calmed Laithe and provoked introspection. The melodious sound reminded him of his past and his family.

He had always repressed his emotions far beneath the surface; it was second nature. It was as simple as breathing. But now Laithe was pursuing these raw experiences daily. He had never felt more alive.

The battle in the alleyway was over, and Laithe's chest heaved with exertion. The kinetic energy from the fight still coursed through his veins, Laithe surveyed the gruesome scene before him. Twenty wardens lay dead, only five by his doing. Veremund blocked the end of the alley, covered in blood, his deep wounds rapidly healing. The pair accidentally encountered this party after they ambushed another near the western gate. They had been searching for a spot to fuck before returning home when these wardens materialized out of the alley.

This area of the Undergrowth was situated in the northern reaches of Tabulrossa, far from any main road. It was composed primarily of ancient burial grounds. The people who rested here died centuries ago, so mourners were uncommon. It was a difficult place for wardens to canvas, even with reinforcements arriving every day.

It was a perfect place to hide.

Laithe and Veremund were shocked when the wardens appeared from the darkened alley. The element of surprise nearly killed them, but the pair managed to repel the wardens and dealt with them swiftly.

"Odd place for a group so large," Laithe observed, wiping the remaining blood from his blades with his shirtsleeve. "This is more remote than we usually find them."

"Looks like a raid to me," Veremund gestured to the broken door halfway down the alley. The door was ancient, but the splinters protruding from its jagged edges were fresh. It had recently broken. "Probably found a Deviant storehouse."

"That's the third one we've seen this week," Laithe shook his head.

"Nothing we can do, little one, we need to focus—" Veremund's mouth snapped shut, eyes narrowed, blue flames sprouting from his palms. "I hear something inside. There could be reinforcements. Careful now."

Laithe drew his freshly cleaned axes and followed Veremund cautiously through the broken doorway. The room inside was cavernous and dank, filled with rotting Tabul fruit and rusting tools along the far wall. It was an old storehouse for fruit harvesters; Laithe had seen dozens of similar structures during their raids. Whoever used this space abandoned it long ago. The cool light of Veremund's flames illuminated a door along the far wall, shattered and hanging off its hinges.

The Tal'Rach stalked towards the doorway, drawn by a sound too quiet for Laithe's human ears to hear. He flanked Veremund closely, gripping his weapons tightly, ready to fight whatever was on the other side of the door.

The room beyond was tiny and putrid, even to Laithe's standards. It was bare, save for a broken table and a pile of leaves in the corner. Laithe dropped his axes as he entered. Flies buzzed around two corpses lying atop the leaf pile. His throat tightened as he drew closer. Laithe recognized the bodies.

It was Callandra and Kez.

They lay in the corner, wrapped together. Two pairs of

sightless eyes staring at the ceiling. Blood poured from a savage wound on the younger woman's throat. Laithe now understood why so many wardens were this far out in the wilds of the Undergrowth; they had located a Deviant hiding place. Laithe kept the wall around his heart erect, not allowing the loss of two more companions to affect him.

"The old one is still alive, but barely." Veremund crouched near the bodies. "Let me spare her from more pain."

The Tal'Rach raised his hand in a tight fist, hovering over Kez's fragile skull. His muscles tensed, ready to strike.

"No!" Laithe yelled and grabbed the Tal'Rach's wrist. Veremund gaped at Laithe with surprise; the Deviant had never been so bold with the ram.

"She is my…" He was about to say friend, but that didn't fully explain his relationship with Kez. She was surprisingly skilled in combat and had saved his life on occasion. He did not like her, but he respected her. "She is one of my old companions. The other woman, too. We all journeyed here together."

"I am sorry you lost them, little one," Veremund's stony features softened slightly. Laithe hoped the Tal'Rach's sympathy meant he was starting to care for him. "But this one will be dead within the day; if we do not treat her wounds immediately, her lifeblood will flow. And neither of us are professional healers. Better to give her a painless death."

"You healed me," Laithe said. "The day we met, I almost died. But you fixed me. Do the same for her."

"I need water for that, little one, and lots of it. We cannot return to our pool, and it would be foolish to search for another." Veremund sounded exasperated, but his gaze briefly flitted upwards. He was lying.

"You can heal her, can't you?" Laithe breathed. "But you

don't want to. Why?"

Veremund growled, face twisted in anger and frustration. "This woman isn't a Fourteen. She is not my responsibility!"

"What is the difference?" Laithe shouted. His rage outweighed his deference to the Tal'Rach. "Fourteens. Fifteens. Eights. The wardens don't seem to care about the specifics. They slaughter us regardless."

"But we are different, little one, can't you see? I am not Lucian, father of Deviants. I am simply the protector of Fourteens. I cannot protect them all."

"Is that why you didn't heed Sarina's call? Because she was a Fifteen?" Laithe seethed. It was all coming together. The day of the Calling. The raids. The icy glares Isam and the others shot at him. It wasn't about protecting Deviants—or even Fourteens, for that matter. Veremund only craved death and destruction. "A Fourteen died that day. He was a good lad. His name was Benjin. While you were preoccupied with your crusade to kill Alistair, he took a warden's sword to the neck. He was waiting for you to save him."

"I cannot save everyone," Veremund repeated, deathly quiet. Laithe waited for an explanation. But none came.

Laithe had enough. He pushed past the Tal'Rach and inspected Kez for himself. The ram lied. Her wounds weren't fatal. Yet. He could stop the bleeding with some cloth. Veremund had spoken at least one truth: she would need the help of a trained doctor.

"Calvin is a healer," Laithe said, recalling the name of the portly man who provided remedies at the Brazen Leaf. "If I can get her home, he can save her."

"It is too late for that, Laithe," Veremund said firmly. He never called the Deviant by his name. "I know what she means to you, but she is already gone."

"I will not let her die, Veremund," Laithe said stubbornly.

"She cannot return to the Brazen Leaf! This woman is not a Fourteen! I will not allow it!" The ram's bellow shook the ancient walls of the storehouse. Blue flames sprouted from his palms as he loomed over him menacingly. But Laithe was unfazed.

Laithe never allowed a soul to order him around as the Tal'Rach had. He had always acted independently, regardless of what anyone else thought. His feelings for Veremund had clouded his judgment, making him subservient. He wouldn't allow it any longer, not after this revelation. "I am bringing her to the Brazen Leaf with your help or not. Otherwise, I will stay here until the next warden patrol. Then you will have no one left on your side."

He wanted his words to sting. They both knew Veremund was losing the favor of the villagers. He hadn't saved a single Deviant since the Calling, and word spread of how vicious the ram's attacks had been. Veremund needed him. He needed an ally. Laithe had always offered his support freely. He had now named a price—Kez's life.

"Very well, little one," Veremund spat, tone filled with a hardened rage. "Have your old friend. Let her be a burden on us all. But know this: if you compromise the safety of our haven, I will personally tear you apart."

"Fine," Laithe said.

Veremund scoffed and stormed off, his horns scraping the rotted door frame, leaving Laithe in the shadows with Kez. He watched Veremund depart, almost regretting his words.

Almost.

Instead, he shifted his focus to the dying woman before

him. Laithe worked expeditiously, relying on the slivers of light streaming from the holes in the old wall. He had dressed hundreds of wounds before, half of them were more severe than this. He tore his shirt, using it as a makeshift bandage. The pressure eased the bleeding, and her breathing gradually strengthened, though it was still pained and ragged.

He would need to carry the unconscious woman to the Brazen Leaf, but the wardens would detect him as soon as he stepped foot in an inhabited part of the city. He would need a way to be inconspicuous.

An absurd idea sprung into his mind. He smiled triumphantly.

Laithe rushed into the main room; his heart soared when he found his prize—a fruit basket discarded on the floor, woven from tree bark. He had seen harvesters use these big packs to carry Tabul fruit across the city, and a few harvesters even delivered to the Brazen Leaf on occasion. It was the perfect disguise.

He inspected the pack. There were no holes, and the two back straps were still intact—perfect. There was even a lid to keep the fruit from flying out; in this case, it would conceal a wounded woman.

Hauling the basket into the backroom, Laithe worked swiftly but gingerly. If the makeshift dressings came undone, she would bleed to death in minutes. There was no telling how long the haphazard bandages would hold.

Laithe nestled Kez inside the container alongside his axes, covering her with a moldy blanket from the corner. He grunted as he hoisted the basket and secured the straps around his broad shoulders. He was grateful she was so light; he could carry her without much effort.

He threw the deep hood over his head, securing the fake bandages low on his forehead. The yellow eyes of a Roursche would expose his identity in a heartbeat, negating any effect the harvester disguise would have.

His journey took hours to complete. Patrols had recently tripled, and the wardens established strongholds throughout the dank city depths. Harvesters typically avoided the Undergrowth, so his disguise would only be effective once they reached the Aerials. He slinked through the shadows, doubling back whenever he encountered a battalion of green-clad soldiers.

After a few hours, the twisting staircase of an Aerial came into view, and Laithe's heart soared. He peered out of the shadows to ensure no warden patrolled the quiet street between them and their escape. The gloomy avenue was devoid of life. His blood froze in his veins.

The street was free of wardens, but it wasn't empty.

Ten bodies hung in a row, dangling from ropes tied to a root bridge. Blood dripped down their pale forms from a gruesome hook that impaled each by the shoulder. The moss below them was dark and wet. Eyes open in shock, teeth bared in pain, the haunted victims swayed slightly, illuminated by the rach above. The poor souls had been left there to bleed out. They must have been there for less than a day. They reminded Laithe of bait swinging on a fishing line. He almost vomited on the spot.

A jagged shape was carved into the chest of each fresh corpse. Laithe paled. It was a letter: "D" for Deviant. It was not an execution but a message from the wardens. For them.

Laithe grunted, his gaze transfixed on the dead, reminded

of Callandra's corpse, which he left behind only hours ago. He had seen plenty of horrors during his life as a Deviant, but nothing at this scale. He couldn't help but feel responsible. He shuddered at the thought and departed the Undergrowth for the safety of the Aerials above.

The journey to the Brazen Leaf was relatively uneventful, for no one looked twice at a harvester. It was the perfect cover. He passed real harvesters who casually waved, barely giving him any notice. By the time he entered the Bole, Laithe had already decided to use this disguise in the future.

He took the most direct route possible but remained cautious to avoid tails. Veremund meant what he said if the wardens followed Laithe home. That was not the way Laithe wanted to be ravaged by the Tal'Rach. Adrenaline was still racing through his veins—fear of being caught, fear of the ram spirit's wrath, fear that Kez would bleed out before he carried her to safety. Life was so much easier when Laithe did not care.

Finally, he arrived at the Brazen Leaf. Pellum didn't recognize him until he was already behind the bar. He narrowly avoided being smacked in the head by the grizzled man, who clucked his tongue with curiosity once he recognized Laithe. Unconcerned with answering the barkeep's questions, he brushed by him silently, entering the bowels of the Bole. The labyrinth proved to be easy today, and Laithe made no missteps.

As the secret village door closed behind him, he cried out for help. The men in the dining hall below observed him warily, and one yelped in fright. Laithe cursed his recklessness; for all they knew, he was the first wave of a warden assault.

"It is Laithe!" he announced, hoping it would quell the

mayhem below. He set his precious cargo next to him. "I need Calvin! I need a healer!"

"You heard him," Isam's clear voice cut above the rabble. "Move!"

Laithe opened the basket and lifted Kez out before Isam, Calvin, and a group of burly men joined him on the highest balcony. The bandages were soaked red with her blood; he was lucky the blanket prevented the crimson liquid from seeping into the basket. Her breathing was hoarse, but she was still alive.

The healer was the first to the scene, his eyebrows raised in surprise when he saw a woman in Laithe's arms. It was still strange to Laithe that the village solely harbored Fourteens. After his argument with Veremund, the absence of other Deviants only fueled his rage. It wasn't right, but he had more pressing issues to deal with.

Once Calvin recovered from his initial shock, he carefully examined Kez. The two burly men behind him efficiently took the injured woman from Laithe's arms. They had done this before. Laithe assumed it was common for those Veremund saved to arrive at the Brazen Leaf wounded, when the Tal'Rach cared to save Deviants.

"To my room," Calvin said, directing the burly men. "Lars, fetch a bucket of water. She's fading fast!"

Laithe moved to follow the men, but Isam blocked his path. He almost pushed him aside, but Isam raised a hand, placing it gently on Laithe's shoulder.

"Calvin will take care of her. You needn't worry about that. It would be best if you rested," Isam said, tranquil and soothing. He smiled at Laithe with a strange expression. "Who is that woman?"

"Kez," Laithe said. "An Eight. I traveled with her before I came to Tabulrossa. Found her bleeding out in the Undergrowth."

"And Veremund allowed you to bring her here?" Isam asked, incredulous. "He's never allowed anyone but Fourteens in the village."

"Not exactly," Laithe said. "I told him I was bringing her or not returning. Nearly decapitated me, but he didn't refuse."

"Interesting," Isam mused, lost in thought until his attention returned to Laithe. "Let's get you something to eat. You must be hungry enough to devour a whole goat."

Isam wasn't wrong, though Laithe hadn't had meat his entire stay at the Brazen Leaf. It was too difficult to acquire in Tabulrossa. Nodding in agreement, he followed Isam to the dining hall.

Laithe slumped onto his regular spot on the edge of the clearing, utterly exhausted. Isam came by with a bowl of hot stew and two mugs of wine. Always stew in Tabulrossa. And always that purple wine.

Isam sat across the table and nursed his glass. He had avoided Laithe for weeks, so his willingness to sit with him was surprising. Laithe began eating silently, unsure how to start a conversation, occasionally glancing at the door where Calvin had taken Kez.

"You care about her, don't you?" Isam asked softly. "You risked a lot bringing her here."

"We've traveled together for a while," Laithe explained. "I'm not in the habit of leaving Deviants behind."

"Noble, but I'm curious," Isam said, leaning in intently. "You have had plenty of chances to help stranded Deviants since you arrived, but you always return bloodied. Why was she the first you rescued?"

"I don't call the shots. Veremund points my blades, and I kill. I'm happy to do it; it keeps them from killing innocents. Most of the time," Laithe winced, remembering Callandra's lifeless body. And the swinging corpses in the Undergrowth. This place was making him soft, making him care.

"Has he told you his reasons?" It was apparent that Isam barely spoke with the Tal'Rach. "Why has he decided to stop helping Fourteens like he once promised?"

"He thinks killing the archwarden is the best way to save us all," Laithe said. He did not care about revealing Veremund's secrets. He no longer respected the ram enough to do so. And with the incident with Kez, he had already destroyed any trust the Tal'Rach had in him. "But I have a question for you. Why are only Fourteens allowed in the Brazen Leaf? Why did Pellum and Veremund decide only to help men like us and forsake the others?"

"It is not like that," Isam said, bristling. Laithe had struck a chord. "At least that's not how it started. We sheltered Deviants around the Fourteenth Edict's declaration, and the men we rescued all happened to be Fourteens. Deviants from other Edicts initially settled in the village but deemed the different safe houses more suitable. Before you arrived, Veremund agreed to shepherd Fourteens here, and other Deviants to the safe houses run by the priestesses. And it wasn't Pellum who made a deal with Veremund. I did."

"Pellum allowed you to use his pub as a front?" Laithe asked.

"No," Isam said, grinning mischievously. "He didn't have to. Because the pub is mine."

"I'm impressed," was all Laithe could say.

"Well, I'm not the savvy businessman you think I am. I

inherited it," Isam said. "From my fathers."

"Fathers?" Laithe asked.

"Yes," Isam said. "It was common in Tabulrossa for gay men to have children before the Fourteenth Edict. My fathers were the original owners of the Brazen Leaf. They opened it before I was born. This hollow and tunnel were always here, though Veremund expanded the labyrinth as a final defense for the village. I used to play here as a child. I hated the idea of owning the pub. I wanted to be a musician, but my fathers told me that it was a fool's errand. I used to sneak down here at night and practice my lute."

"Sounds like a nice childhood," Laithe said, feeling an odd kinship with Isam. "My parents were musicians, too, and wanted me to practice to be an artist, not a farmer like them."

"Sounded like your parents loved you immensely," Isam said. "To bring music into the home like that. My dads wanted me to follow in their footsteps. To become a miniature version of them."

"Well, my parents' love didn't amount to much. They're dead now," Laithe said bitterly. "The Second Edict took them. Like the Fourteenth took yours."

"Yes." Isam stared sadly into his mug.

"So you built this all yourself." Laithe gestured to the village around them.

"It was mostly my fathers', actually," Isam explained. "They had connections with the wardens and heard rumblings of the Fourteenth Edict before it was declared. They spent months preparing and smuggling their friends here. A dozen men already lived here before the Fourteenth was officially declared. My fathers, however, refused to hide. Someone needed to smuggle refugees to the village, and neither would abandon the other. They died three days after the declaration. I saw them murdered myself. The wardens spared me; I was too young to be marked as a Fourteen. After they died, the pub passed to me, but I never wanted to step foot in the cursed place again. Pellum was a close friend of my parents; he took over the pub, and I concentrated on maintaining this village. Then Veremund appeared."

"And he promised to help you protect the Deviants," Laithe said.

"Yes," Isam said. "He arrived a few months after the Fourteenth. He had already begun helping the priestesses create havens around the city, but something drew him here. He vowed to protect all Deviants, especially the Fourteens. When the Fifteenth Edict was declared, the priestesses were overwhelmed, and we helped one another as much as possible."

"Until now, that is," Laithe said.

"Yes, until now," Isam repeated darkly, his expression softened as his green eyes rested on Laithe. "I wanted to thank you for saving that woman. I thought you were the one who corrupted Veremund and convinced him to abandon the Deviants. Now I know I was wrong."

"I'm sorry that he's failed you," Laithe said. "I don't take promises lightly. Though I'm not sure how much help I can be. Veremund nearly tore my throat out because of Kez."

"Don't worry about it," Isam slapped Laithe on the shoulder. "It's good to know you have a heart."

Isam leaned over and kissed Laithe on the cheek. Smiling, he stood and sauntered off, leaving Laithe alone with his thoughts and flushed cheeks.

10

Quiet the Mind

Adaptability was paramount to surviving in the wilds, and Sarina considered herself a fast learner. The demanding routine of the temple consumed her within two short weeks. The rigid structure was refreshing compared to the chaotic life of a Deviant. Each day came with calming predictability, which she fully appreciated after two years of being hunted.

A noisy gong awoke her every morning, pulling her from her restless sleep. She followed the other novices from their communal sleeping quarters into an open-air dining hall overlooking the courtyard, where the women ate their light breakfast in silence.

After breakfast, a senior priestess assigned the girls various chores around the temple, like laundry, sweeping, and cooking. The laundry chemicals stained Sarina's skin, and her muscles cramped after five hours of peeling and chopping potatoes, so she preferred the days she was assigned to sweep the halls. She enjoyed being on her feet, able to move about the temple.

After morning chores, the novices returned to the dining

hall for a simple lunch, usually a meatless stew. Sarina could go the rest of her life without eating stew ever again. Once they finished their meal, the novices were assigned to their afternoon chores, followed by quick lessons with the senior priestesses.

Dinner was the most substantial meal of the day, and Sarina always yearned for it, though she was often too exhausted to enjoy it fully. Afterward, the novices returned to their communal bed chamber for an early bedtime.

The regimen reminded Sarina of her old life before the Fifteen Edict. When she served as her village's mayor, those days were scheduled to the minute, filled with meetings, paperwork, more meetings, and the occasional appearance at festivals. She hadn't sought the office, but she would win every election. Responsibility always seemed to find her. Thankfully, the presence of a routine was where the similarities ended; for the first time since she was a child, she had no one relying on her. It was oddly refreshing.

There was no clear hierarchy in the temple of the peacock, and most priestesses had their own private rooms. They were tiny and barren, like the room Sarina first awoke in. The temple women went about the city as they wished, had similar chores, laughed, and relaxed together in the baths. There were nearly a hundred altogether, all equal. Two groups, however, were distinguished from the majority.

The first was the novices, about twenty altogether, including Minora and Sarina. They were awake earlier, ate separately, worked harder, and were the only ones with required lessons. They slept in one room, using stiff mats on the floor. The senior priestesses prohibited the novices from leaving the temple or interacting with Phymeria, the mistress of the temple.

It was difficult, at first, for Sarina to be submissive. Even before the Fifteenth Edict, she was used to being in charge, as people naturally gravitated to her orbit; asking a senior priestess for permission to use the bathroom was foreign to her. After a week, the freedom from responsibility revitalized Sarina. She slept easier and felt less stressed. She had never desired leadership; it was always thrust upon her. She relished the lack of pressure that came with power.

The second distinctive group within the temple was the senior priestesses, like Marikae and Alma. They were about half a dozen of all ages and dispositions. Nothing distinguished them besides the visible deference they received and their unfettered access to Phymeria's private chambers.

The peacock spirit resided on the upper floors. The temple rules strictly forbade novices from entering them, even for cleaning. Full-fledged priestesses performed those tasks but only upon request and supervision of a senior. Only Marikae and her senior priestesses moved freely without restriction.

Sarina was limited to the basements and the main floor, which contained lavish gardens, chapels, libraries, and a magnificent entryway. When her duties did not confine her to the kitchen or laundry, she was assigned a particular section to sweep. That was the only occasion she caught a glimpse of the Tal'Rach.

Phymeria was the most elegant woman Sarina had ever seen, besides Marikae. She glided across the polished floors, skin pale as the moon, hair black as night, and towered above her servants. Delicate features defined a kind and lovely face. Her only inhuman feature besides her height was the radiant peacock tail that protruded from the hem of her silk dress.

Whenever she passed, the priestesses sank to their knees in a respectful bow until she was out of sight. It was the first set of rules Sarina learned in the temple: bow in Phymeria's presence, do not look her in the eyes, and never speak to her unless she called upon you. The Tal'Rach expelled dozens of girls who failed to follow these simple instructions, throwing them out on the street with nothing to their name.

Phymeria rarely left the temple; if she did, it was only to visit her Tal'Rach brethren. The peacock spirit also frequently hosted her brethren. Her protocol of respect applied to all Tal'Rach, but Sarina could catch a glimpse of most of them.

Lykos. A broad-shouldered man with a lion's head.

Ducarix. A serious woman who slithered on a snake's tail.

Behemoth. A brutish, hairy man with short bull horns.

Ylvara. A woman with the ears of a wolf and claws to match.

These four visited most frequently and Sarina already knew their names. Sarina grew up hearing outlandish stories of the mighty Tal'Rach, but they all failed to capture the splendor and might of the great spirits fully. They filled Sarina with wonder, excitement, and fear. There was no questioning that they were the most powerful beings in existence.

Phymeria and her priestesses were not the only inhabitants of the temple, for rach filled the halls. They gathered around the Precipice temples in greater numbers than anywhere else in the city. Every day, hundreds of ghostly rach flew about the elegant halls; it seemed as if she never saw the same rach twice.

Except for Tavo.

That was the name she gave the little blue cat who led her to safety. She awoke every morning with him curled on her chest. Throughout the day, Tavo would follow at her heels as she completed her daily chores. When she attempted to pet him, she would phase through his body as if he consisted of mist. Not a single rach interacted with humans like Tavo. The spirits only noticed when the priestesses chanted, compelled by the ancient tongue.

The novices were nice enough, but their rigid schedule made it difficult for Sarina to connect with any of them. They ate their meals silently and conducted their chores in solitude. The senior priestesses even taught their nightly lessons individually. By the end of the day, they were too tired to chat as they bathed, falling asleep quickly on their firm floor mats. It was fine enough for Sarina, for they were mostly Minora's age, much too young for her to bond with. She didn't mind that much. Building friendships was not the reason she joined the temple. Her training was.

Every evening before dinner, she would sit down with a different priestess. Occasionally, they were seniors like Alma. To Sarina's disappointment, these early sessions only involved meditating. Each woman used different words and a different technique to lead Sarina into a calm state. Clear her mind. Focus on her inner flame. Release herself from all thoughts and feelings.

At first, she had assumed her instructors would teach histories, the ancient tongue, or the anatomy of the rach. But it was only meditation. And Sarina struggled with such a serene activity. Her overactive mind was one of the essential traits that kept her alive. Her sessions would end with her instructor departing in an exasperated huff. It wasn't their fault; Sarina couldn't forget her duty to those she brought to Tabulrossa. She often wondered what would have happened if she had decided to cross the Dragon's Teeth instead. It was easy to imagine how wonderful the world beyond the mountains would be, where wardens did not hunt her daily.

Those earlier sessions were the worst part of her day. Only when she focused on nothing did the torrent of thoughts flood in.

She had failed her friends.

Beriane was only safe because of Marikae.

Veremund had forgotten them all and had seduced Laithe into helping him.

Callandra and Kez were still out there, waiting for someone to save them.

And she simply sat there, striving to meditate.

Gradually, Sarina's lack of leadership and the rigorous rhythm of her chores allowed her to empty her mind. Her sessions grew longer, and her instructors stopped leaving in frustration. Even Alma had little to criticize. So, two months into her stay in the temple of Phymeria, she finally earned the honor of Marikae as her tutor.

The tall, self-assured woman strode into the study and sat across from Sarina on a plush cushion. She regarded Tavo curiously, who sprawled in his favorite spot in the corner, watching the woman lazily. Sarina hadn't spoken with the high priestess since her first day, which saddened her. Something about Marikae felt familiar, and there was a quality about her that made Sarina feel a kinship. Maybe it was how well she led her subordinates, how they seemed to respect and love her. Her gorgeous features weren't a negative either. Whatever it was, Sarina desired to know her more and to become close to her.

"I'm glad you are doing well in your studies," Marikae broke the silence, smiling serenely.

"Thank you, Marikae," Sarina said. The senior priestesses did not possess any honorific; the women earned their respect. "Though I wasn't expecting it to be just meditation."

"Every novice says the same," Marikae chuckled. The entire room seemed to brighten at the cheerful sound. "Each one of you believes you can make the rach dance on the ceiling on the first day."

"One could only hope," Sarina said slyly.

"You should count yourself lucky," the high priestess said. "Alma was ready to throw you out after your first week. I knew you would struggle at first, but it was clear after one conversation with you that you tend to overthink. But I see the rigor of the temple has eased that issue. You have surpassed the other novices in remarkable time and are ready for the next lesson."

"Wonderful," Sarina sighed. She was one step closer to her goal but did not celebrate for long.

She hadn't heard anything about Kez or Callandra.

Marikae promised to report to Sarina when her network found them. She hadn't received a single word. They were still out there. Sarina hoped the priestesses could locate them before the wardens, but her optimism was rapidly fading. She pushed her worries aside, for she could do nothing for her friends. It was her responsibility to learn the secrets of the rach and find them herself. "But why meditation?"

"Excellent question," Marikae said. "To commune with the rach, you must have a clear heart and mind. They are sensitive creatures easily affected by our thoughts and emotions. Which is why they tend to avoid humans outside of Tabulrossa."

"Then why do they act differently here?" Sarina asked, her

curiosity piqued. The rach inside Tabulrossa may be aloof, but she hadn't noticed an aversion to humans.

"Our Call binds them to the city," Marikae explained. "Without us, the rach's nature would lead them to scatter across the plains."

"This is why you chant daily?" Sarina asked. She recalled the early morning gatherings, where priestesses met in the courtyard and chanted together. It was the same song she heard during the Calling.

"Yes, now back to the lesson," Marikae said patiently. "Once your mind is clear, it is easier to commune with the rach. Only then will they listen to you."

"When you say commune," Sarina chose her words carefully. "Do you mean by chanting?"

"In a way, yes," Marikae said. The answer was oddly cryptic. "If you are ready, we can begin. First, tell me which technique you successfully used to meditate."

"It was Alma's, actually," Sarina admitted. "I imagine a candle in my mind, then light it and think of nothing but the flame. Let everything fade into oblivion until only the candle remains."

"Perfect, that one usually does the trick. Alma may be harsh, but she's quite the brilliant instructor," Marikae mused. "We will do the same exercise tonight, but once the flame is fully focused, I want you to repeat these words: Pyorae mento gara latt hai."

"Pyorae mento gara latt hai," Sarina dutifully repeated, stumbling over the strange words.

"Good, again," Marikae bade. Sarina obeyed and spoke the strange words a second time. "Once you have the flame, repeat the phrase."

"What do they mean?" Sarina asked. "Is it something in the ancient tongue?"

"Oh no," Marikae chuckled. "Nothing that grand. It's gibberish."

"I'm not sure I follow." Sarina felt her cheeks flush in embarrassment. She had assumed the women were using a long-forgotten language. "If they don't mean anything, how do the rach know what I want?"

"Words are not important to them, only intentions," Marikae explained. "The sound of your voice attracts the rach, as does your clear mind; together, they draw them in like a moth to a flame. We chant nonsense words to focus on our intentions rather than their meaning."

"If the words mean nothing, then could I say anything?" Sarina asked.

"You could," Marikae conceded. "But it is easier to access a phrase lodged deep in your memory, so your mind isn't focused on creating new words, simply repeating ones without meaning."

Marikae proved to be a tolerant and patient teacher, much more so than Alma, who allowed no more than one question per session.

"What happens when I draw them in?"

"Great question," Marikae said. She hesitated, clenching her jaw. "I am pleased that you kept what I showed you the first day we met a secret, but you must promise me what I say next stays within the walls of this study."

"Yes, Marikae."

"Once you harness the rach. You simply imagine what you want them to do. And they will oblige."

"Anything?"

"Within reason," Marikae clarified. "The rach are pure, unbridled energy. By harnessing them, you can use that energy to move objects, summon fire, or create gusts of wind. But the rach are limited, like us, though in different ways. A single rach can lift a stone, but not a mountain."

"So if I call a hundred rach, could I lift a mountain then?" Sarina asked, her mind filled with possibilities.

"Let us focus on something simpler," Marikae chuckled. "It has been a while since I have had a pupil as inquisitive as you."

"Apologies, Marikae," Sarina said, blushing.

"Oh, I quite enjoy it," Marikae smiled. "It's rather refreshing. If you don't have any lingering questions, we can begin. Good. We will start by calling the rach to your side. You won't be able to do much else in the first hundred tries. Are you ready?"

"Yes."

Closing her eyes, Sarina imagined a candle. Lighting it, she focused on the flame, how it danced and flickered. Everything vanished, save for the light. Nothing existed but the light. It was only her and the fire. Then she remembered the words Marikae had taught her and began chanting. She repeated the words softly over and over. She grew louder with each repetition until she finally opened her eyes. Three balls of light, the size of her fist, floated in the air inches from her. She smiled, elated.

The rach had answered her call.

Ignoring Marikae's surprised expression, she proceeded to chant. The rach listened to her on her first attempt, but she would not allow the joy of success to tear her out of her trance. Not yet. She wanted to try something else to push herself and to impress the high priestess further.

The rach remained in the air before her, entranced by her

meaningless words. They were waiting attentively. Ready to be directed. She remembered the serpent rach from her first day in the temple and how it danced around Marikae. She brought the image into her mind, replacing the flaming candle. The tiny rach darted across the study and circled Marikae with the same speed and rhythm the serpent had.

The high priestess laughed delightedly as the three balls floated around her in perfect harmony. Sarina changed the image in her mind, switching Marikae for herself. Immediately, the balls flew towards the novice and resumed their spirals around her. She let out a laugh, exhilarated. The rach retreated in response to her laughter, their connection to Sarina now broken.

"You take to this quite easily," Marikae said. "Be proud of yourself; most women take months to summon their rach. Given your blue friend licking himself in the corner, I shouldn't be surprised."

Sarina smiled, then turned to Tavo. The cat's ears twitched as he yawned. "He is different somehow. He doesn't listen to me like the others, like he has a mind of his own."

"Maybe your subconscious is directing him without your knowledge. Sometimes, unique rach behave differently toward certain women with the gift, though the exact reason remains a mystery," Marikae mused. "The rach have roamed the earth since its creation, and we still know almost nothing about them. Though people like us have been studying them and harnessing their power for over a thousand years."

"So, I could get him to dance around me?"

"With some practice, yes. You can connect with any rach," Marikae said. "The more experienced you are, the bigger the rach you can attract. The older the rach, the more it grows and, thus, the more powerful it can be. Let's continue."

Sarina summoned the candle and chanted again. The lesson progressed as she summoned more balls of light. They were never larger than Tavo and she could barely command them to move a few paces before her connection faltered. But it was a start.

By the time Marikae ended the lesson, the sun had set, and Sarina was famished. The high priestess rose to leave, but Sarina grabbed her forearm. There was one final matter to discuss.

"Have you found them yet?" Sarina asked. "It has been two months since you promised to find Callandra and Kez. And you've told me nothing."

"Unfortunately not," Marikae sighed.

"Why?" Sarina asked, not content with the answer. "How hard could it be to find two women in this city? I thought you had the resources."

"It is not that simple, Sarina," Marikae's tone regained its usual strength. "The Undergrowth is in disarray. There are more wardens than ever and almost daily raids by Veremund. I've had trouble protecting our existing havens and storehouses, let alone rescuing rogue Deviants."

"Fuck this training," Sarina said, standing. "I need to find them. I promised I would keep them safe. You obviously can't manage it on your own."

"There is nothing you can do," Marikae said, patting her shoulder in a poor attempt to placate her.

"You promised me that you would find them two months ago. Every day you fail to rescue them is another day where the wardens could murder them. If they haven't already," Sarina spat. The sadness soon dissipated, replaced by rage.

"I am sorry we have not located them yet," Marikae bristled, her voice stern. Sarina had struck a nerve. "But if you leave now, you will not be permitted to return. The wardens will hunt you, and you will be useless to your friends. Only women with Phymeria's favor can leave the temple of their own volition."

"Then let me meet Phymeria. Tonight," Sarina said.

"She will want to test your abilities," Marikae said. "And you just learned a simple summon. If I took her to you now, you would fail, and she would cast you out. Please have patience and trust the process. I will do my best to find your friends."

"But you cannot promise their safety," Sarina spat. "With all your power and promises, they remain in danger."

"I have failed you, Sarina," Marikae admitted. "I have failed many people throughout the years who fell to the wardens' blades despite my best efforts. I want to save someone tonight—you. Do not let me fail you again. Stay here and train. Obtain Phymeria's approval and, therefore, access to the city. Then we can find your friends. Together. And save others in the process."

Sarina's jaw dropped in disbelief. She hadn't expected such vulnerability from Marikae, which made it difficult to hate her as much as she wanted to. The high priestess's speech had an odd effect on her anger. It dispelled it, empowered it, and shaped it into something more.

Resolve.

A fiery determination welled inside her to find Kez and Callandra and save as many Deviants as possible, like Marikae. She had spent two years leading a ragtag crew of Deviants, most of whom were now dead. But Marikae had hundreds of their kind hidden throughout the city, protecting them and growing to their ranks. She did it with the power of the rach. Sarina needed that power.

She made her decision.

"I will stay."

11

Infernos and Pies

Night had long fallen on Tabulrossa; the twisting roots and rotted buildings were barely visible in the murk. Only a few rach remained in the Undergrowth, casting sporadic light and ghostly shadows. The city was deathly quiet, with vacant streets devoid of movement, light, or sound.

There was only one exception.

A monstrous building shone like a beacon among the mossy darkness. Unlike the surrounding abandoned warehouses, the structure was new, free of rot and moss. Hundreds of Sylvania flowers lined the high walls of the keep, where wardens patrolled from its parapets. A pair of green-clad soldiers guarded either side of a great gate, swords drawn menacingly. Eight bodies hung from the battlement. Each corpse was gutted by a rusty hook and branded with a gruesome D on its chest.

It was one of numerous newly constructed warden strongholds. Each housed an entire battalion. Alistair recalled legions of his wardens from the far-reaching lands and funneled them into the Undergrowth. They constructed strongholds throughout the forest floor, routing out most Deviant safe houses. The Tal'Rach themselves had sung the structure into being. It was odd to behold such a beautiful building among the ramshackle waste of the Undergrowth.

A warden squad materialized from a nearby alleyway, Sylvania lamps lighting their path. Two figures trailed behind, ropes tied around their necks—a pair of freshly caught Deviants. The great, heavy doors of the keep opened for them, and they marched dutifully inside.

Laithe watched it all unfold from his perch underneath a root bridge, observing the enemy from the safety of the shadows. He gripped the worn wood of his ax handles tight in anticipation. Blood would soon spill.

It had been six weeks since Laithe returned Kez to the Brazen Leaf. About three months had passed since the Calling, though time was hard to measure, and the days blurred together. Laithe exclusively frequented the Undergrowth or the cave deep within the Bole; he couldn't remember when he last saw the sun.

His vision adjusted to the Sylvania light, and Laithe peered into the night toward the opposite side of the keep, patiently waiting for Veremund's signal.

Veremund had barely talked to Laithe since he defied him with Kez. They never discussed the woman living in the village of Fourteens, and Laithe was grateful Veremund had allowed her to remain so long without any fuss. They continued to have sex after their missions, thankfully, but it became increasingly rough, feral, and savage. Laithe wasn't sure if the Tal'Rach would ever forgive him, but he no longer cared; Veremund's behavior over the past weeks had soured Laithe's feelings towards him.

A pillar of bright blue flame erupted in the shadows from the far side of the keep, and the guards yelled in surprise. The azure fire quickly faded—Veremund's signal. The sentinel dashed across the parapets toward the inferno in a panic, leaving the gate empty save for the two wardens who stood directly before it. Both grizzled men gawked at the wall above in confusion; neither witnessed the blue flame.

It was the perfect opportunity to strike.

Leaping from the shadows, Laithe bolted out from underneath the root bridge. He lowered his center of gravity, both axes outstretched. The guards were preoccupied, but he was still forty paces out. Any sound would ruin his element of surprise.

Twenty paces.

He hurled an ax at the nearest warden. It narrowly missed him by a hair, and sunk into the wooden gate behind him with a crunch. The bewildered man directed his attention from the parapet to the ax.

It was all Laithe needed.

He descended upon the guard within a few heartbeats. Laithe's remaining ax slashed into the warden's exposed neck. It was a savage blow. Blood spurted onto Laithe's face, nearly blinding him. He wiped it from his brow, exposing his bright yellow eyes.

"Deviant!" the surviving guard exclaimed, charging at him with his sword raised. Laithe cursed. He should have been quicker; half of the keep had heard the alarm.

Pulling his ax from the gate, Laithe parried the warden's blow with the bloodied one. His opponent was strong, and his battle-worn appearance marked him as a skilled warden, undoubtedly called from the surrounding lands where Deviants were plentiful, as was violence. The warden was unrelenting in his barrage, and Laithe grunted as he blocked blow after blow. The enemy blade sliced his shoulder and his cheek, blood dripped from the stinging wounds.

Laithe was sure the warden had seen his fair share of battles; how he swung with deadly precision was a testament to that. He had undoubtedly murdered countless innocent Deviants.

Laithe used that to fuel his rage.

A carnal growl escaped his throat, and Laithe's vision blurred. Only the warden mattered. He ignored the sword that cut into his arm as he charged forward. Veremund would heal any flesh wound later, anyway. As long as he wasn't decapitated or impaled in the heart. The warden struck, cutting into Laithe, but now he was defenseless.

Laithe barreled ahead, crashing into the guard's sturdy frame. The guard cried out, losing balance, and fell into a heap, sword clattering to the side. Before he hit the ground, Laithe was already upon him, and his axes sunk into the man's flesh. Blood sprayed as Laithe struck the warden over and over, continuing his battle cry.

The heat of battle often consumed him, and Veremund regularly praised him for it.

An arrow sunk into the ground next to him, pulling Laithe from his violent trance. The warden below him was already a disfigured corpse. But the commotion of the attack had caught the attention of the keep. A few wardens had already returned to the parapets above, each armed with a bow. Laithe counted five in total. Another arrow struck the earth next to the warden's corpse.

Laithe swore.

The plan was simple but was already unraveling. The

warden strongholds had grown in number and power in the past few weeks, dealing a devastating blow to Tabulrossa's Deviant population and hindering Veremund's movements. The ram wanted them all destroyed, but they were well fortified and not easily burned from afar. Each of them housed scores of recently captured Deviants. The wardens interrogated and tortured their prisoners until they hung them outside the walls.

Veremund was supposed to create a diversion for Laithe to sneak in the rear gate, drawing the forces to him. While the Tal'Rach fought against the keep's forces, Laithe would locate and free the Deviant prisoners. Once they were rescued, Veremund could bathe the entire complex with his fire.

But now the element of surprise evaporated, and Laithe would have to fight his way into the keep. No matter. He dodged the deadly bolts, holstered his axes, and retrieved another weapon from his belt. It was a heavy grappling hook that Laithe had salvaged from a warehouse on a previous expedition. He tied it to the end of a long, heavy vine. Laithe twirled the cruel metal hook around, gaining momentum, releasing it at the apex of his swing. It hurtled toward the parapet. He smiled. A warden yelped when the hook hit her squarely in the chest. She lost her balance and fell backward off the wall. A sickening crunch punctuated her scream.

Laithe pulled the rope hard until the hook above was lodged firmly in the battlement. Not wasting a single, precious moment, he began to climb. Two arrows sunk into his flesh, but he ignored the stabbing pain and pulled himself upward. Laithe was an easier target, but soon he reached the top.

The keep beyond was a series of tall buildings grouped closely together. A courtyard formed beyond the gate Laithe had scaled. A larger yard lay beyond the central buildings, where Veremund assaulted the main entrance.

Two wardens waited for him, swords drawn. He flew over the merlon and onto the narrow walkway. He landed on his feet and dodged both of their attacks with ease. The poor bastard on the left lost his balance, over-committing to his swing. Laithe pushed him gruffly, sending him over the edge. He drew his axes, dodging a blow from the remaining warden and cutting his hand off at the wrist with a decisive strike.

The warden shrieked, blood flowing from the grisly stump, clutching at his wrist with his remaining hand. Laithe lashed out with his leg, kicking his foe in the chest, sending him over the edge to join his fallen brethren.

Another arrow burrowed into his shoulder.

Seven wardens to his left and eight to his right rushed across the parapet towards him. Another arrow sliced his cheek. A score of wardens seeped into the courtyard below, bows drawn. More sprinted up the stairs. Almost the entire battalion was rushing towards him. Why hadn't they stayed to fight Veremund?

But the other side of the keep was silent. There was no sign of the ram. Veremund hadn't adhered to the plan. And now Laithe would die.

Riddled with arrows and covered in blood, Laithe roared and sprinted down the walkway. If he finally met his end, he would at least make the wardens remember it.

He sunk his blades into the first warden, cleaving her head from her body. He kicked the corpse into her companion, burying an ax into his skull as he stumbled backward. Two more arrows collided into his thigh when he engaged the third.

Before he could end her life, an ear-splitting scream cut through the night. Every head swiveled to the source. It was a gigantic, dark form, hulking in the center of the keep. Veremund. The ram must have infiltrated the complex during the chaos.

Laithe had been the diversion, after all.

The Tal'Rach extended his arms outward, his entire form bathed in a hot, sapphire blaze. Laithe's heart flew into his throat when Veremund's words finally registered.

"LAITHE, JUMP!"

Before he could respond, the keep exploded. First, the wind surged inwards, pulling unlucky wardens off the parapet. The flames around Veremund erupted, almost white with heat. They consumed the nearest buildings within a few heartbeats, filling the Undergrowth with smoke and the smell of burned wood and flesh at their immediate incineration.

The orb of flame kept growing, and the tempest blew outward. Fortunately, Laithe heeded the ram's words and vaulted upward. The momentum of the blast enveloped him. But he hadn't jumped high enough. His feet struck the highest point of the wall, and he heard the sickening snap of both legs breaking.

His body spun head over heels into the dark. The blue flames consumed the stronghold's wall and the surrounding warehouses, incinerating as Laithe was flung into the Undergrowth.

Disoriented and stricken with immense pain, Laithe's vision blurred. He barely noticed his body breaking as he collided with something. He had finally landed.

Breathing in ragged breaths, feeling the warm rush of his lifeblood flowing from countless wounds, the world faded into oblivion.

# # #

"What the fuck, Veremund?" Laithe inquired angrily as he stared out the safe house's window. "I could have been burned alive!"

They hid in a tiny cottage halfway up an Aerial. The pair had started using the abandoned home since the wardens tightened their hold on the Undergrowth. He had awoken there, fully healed, grateful to be alive but fuming at Veremund's betrayal.

"You were far enough away from the blast," Veremund sat casually in the corner, legs sprawled, quite proud of himself. "I told you that I can heal any broken bone or cut. You were never in any real danger."

"I could have broken my neck, or been impaled by a branch, or bled to death."

"But you didn't. I don't understand why you're upset, little one. Look at what we accomplished in a single day."

The city below burned. The explosion mutated into a raging wildfire, consuming the mossy buildings indiscriminately, warden keeps, warehouses, and burial grounds. The ghostly blue blaze illuminated the city with a macabre light. By Laithe's best guess, almost a fifth of the Undergrowth was currently ablaze. The fires would burn for days unless the other Tal'Rach intervened.

"There were innocents in that keep." They had agreed on the plan. Save the Deviants, burn the keep. But Veremund deviated. And innocents died. Countless of them. "You were supposed to wait until I saved the prisoners before destroying the stronghold."

"I found a better way to defeat our enemies. Their sacrifices were necessary," Veremund scoffed and his expression became menacing. "The keep we attacked today wasn't the only one that burned. At least five more have fallen in a single strike."

"You used me as bait," Laithe spat, his rage building with every heartbeat. "I almost died."

"And you need to understand your place, little one," Veremund pressed Laithe against the wall. He could feel his bones strain against the pressure. "You are the one with the debt to repay. You are the one sworn to aid me. You are not the one to make decisions. You are only to follow and be grateful for my mercy."

"So this is your way of punishing me," the truth dawned on him. "For Kez. I felt every bone in my body break, Veremund. I felt every arrow pierce my skin. The inferno burned half of me, and the fall crushed the rest. And that was a lesson?"

"Yes. Now you understand the price of disobeying me. I recommend you don't do it again," Veremund growled. He released his grip and stalked out of the safe house without another word, leaving Laithe alone, angry and speechless.

Laithe remained in the small hut, staring at the fires below. He wasn't certain of the exact death toll, but it must have been catastrophic. And now those in the city that didn't already hate Veremund and his Fourteens would call for blood. Most people already considered the ram as the new Lucian, father of the Deviants and devil of Tabulrossa.

Laithe waited silently for a few hours until he decided to return to the Brazen Leaf. The way was clear; any warden not dead or guarding the Tal'Rach was below fighting against the fires. Laithe could have walked the entire way with his hood down, exposing his amber Roursche eyes, and not a single person would have noticed.

Despite Veremund's healing, Laithe's body ached when he arrived at the hidden village. To his delight, Isam sat near the main entrance. Someone constantly patrolled the village gate, and he was grateful that it was his friend. The village was quiet in the early morning hours, as it was too early for breakfast. Isam softly plucked his lute strings and smiled as Laithe approached.

Isam had warmed to him considerably after Laithe defied Veremund and returned with Kez. The villagers still avoided him like a plague, but the young musician began to talk with him frequently. It seemed that Isam was interested in a friendship now that he no longer blamed Laithe for Veremund's behavior.

It became Laithe's favorite part of the day. After a bloody mission with Veremund, he would return to the Brazen Leaf and watch Isam perform. Afterward, Isam would join him and chat late into the night. He was pleasant, kind-hearted, a great storyteller, and had a surprisingly sharp sense of humor.

They would discuss trivial topics like their favorite food. Isam loved fruit, especially raspberries, whereas Laithe preferred meat, especially boar. Sometimes, the conversation would evolve into deeper subjects such as their pasts, Isam would talk about his fathers, and occasionally, Laithe would tell him of different customs of the Roursche clan. Or they would sing into the night, with Isam strumming his lute.

Laithe finally understood what it was like to have a friend. And he immensely enjoyed the feeling.

"Seems like you had an eventful day. You look like shit," Isam smirked, appraising Laithe with a raised eyebrow. "Veremund must have worked you over last night."

"That is an understatement," Laithe sighed, slumping

against the railing beside Isam.

"You sound frighteningly ominous," Isam said flatly, apprehensive. He could already read Laithe like a book.

Sighing deeply, Laithe told Isam about everything that transpired: the plan, Veremund's betrayal, the fires, and the sheer extent of the ram's devastation. Isam remained silent during the story, face stony, grasping his lute tightly.

"If the people didn't want our heads before, they're sure to now," Isam said after an extended silence. "In one night, Veremund justified every cruel act and atrocity the wardens have ever committed. The public will probably beg for harsher treatment after this."

"I thought the same," Laithe admitted. He was frustrated at the Tal'Rach, at the situation, but mostly himself. He felt powerless; if he defied Veremund, his life would become short and painful.

"Something needs to change, Laithe," Isam breathed.

"I'm not sure," Laithe said pensively. He was relieved that someone else shared his anger, but it did not change their situation. They were both powerless. "Tell me a story, Isam. Or sing me a song. I need my spirits lifted."

"Sorry," Isam sighed, blushing and strumming his lute. "You almost died today, suffered unbelievable trauma, and here I go asking more of you."

"It's alright," Laithe replied. "I admire the passion. But I need to empty my mind before you and I go saving the world."

Isam chuckled. It was a bright and airy sound. His laughter always brought joy to Laithe's heart.

"When I was very young, my fathers used to take me to the burial grounds to visit my grandparents," Isam began, wistful. "It was before they opened the Brazen Leaf, when we lived in the Canopy. Many of their friends lived nearby; we would have these great big dinners almost once a week. My father, Alders, was an excellent cook and always baked a different pie: apple, peach, blueberry, cherry, and every exotic fruit. That's how I first tasted raspberries. Anything but the purple Tabul fruit. My dads hated the stuff. More often than not, he was forced to make a Tabul pie. They'd spend our savings in the markets to taste something different from the blasted purple fruit."

"I can't blame them," Laithe chuckled. The Tabul fruit was the city's most bountiful resource and a gift from the Tal'Rach. Tabulrossans incorporated it into almost every dish. After weeks of consuming it for nearly every meal and every drink, Laithe never wanted to see the fruit again.

"Neither can I," Isam giggled, strumming his lute with glee. "When my dads started saving to build the Brazen Leaf, we could only afford Tabul pies, so I decided to forage on my own. My other father, Nels, taught me to hunt for mushrooms, edible moss, and the like. So one day, when we went down to the Undergrowth, I snuck off while my dads paid their respects to our ancestors. I was discrete, so they didn't notice."

"You missed your calling as a spy or an assassin," Laithe jibed. Isam ignored him and carried on with a wry smile.

"It did not take me long to find a berry bush, like my dad showed me. It seemed barren, but I searched harder. Fallen berries covered the moss below. They were a deep purple, almost like blackberries, not bright like the Tabul fruit. It seemed they had fallen from the bush, so they were perfectly ripe. I gathered them in my pockets, staining my hands. But I was so proud of myself. I returned to the burial site before my dads suspected anything, hiding my stains. When we returned home, I took the berries to the local kitchen. In those days, fire was allowed in the city for cooking, but only in controlled, communal areas like kitchens, pubs, and restaurants. I wanted my pie to be a surprise, so I waited until night and crept out of my room, stealing my dads' cooking supplies. I was a pretty good cook, even at that age. My dads taught me well. The next morning, we all awoke to freshly baked pie."

"They must have loved the surprise." Laithe smiled. Hearing a wholesome story like this was precisely what he needed.

"They did. Until they tasted it," Isam said sheepishly. "They both vomited for hours. They asked me what stall I bought the berries from and what money I had used to pay for them. I told them I foraged them in the Undergrowth. They both paled when I described where I found them."

"Were they poisonous?" Laithe balked, stifling laughter.

"Worse," Isam's brow wrinkled oddly. "They weren't berries at all. Like I said, they were lying underneath a bush. Not on it. My dads told me they were rabbit droppings."

"You fed your parents shit pie?" Laithe roared with laughter. He slapped his thigh to contain himself. At first, he thought he offended Isam but the musician laughed along.

"They never let me cook or bake again," Isam was bright red. "Even when we opened the Brazen Leaf, they kept me as far from the kitchen as possible."

"I don't blame them," Laithe's chest heaved with excursion, his abs on fire. He hadn't laughed so hard in ages. "I needed that, Isam."

"Pleasure I could be of some assistance."

The pair allowed the laughter to subside, conversing light-heartedly until Laithe yawned.

"You should get some rest," Isam said, "The healing of a

Tal'Rach takes a lot of energy from both the healer and the patient."

"I do feel a bit drowsy," Laithe admitted, pushing himself from the floor. "I can't argue with you there. I'll see you later, Isam."

"Laithe?" Isam called after him. "Can you do me one favor?"

"What's that?"

"Could you finally speak to Kez?" Isam sighed, "You've been avoiding the poor woman for weeks. She's not going to break your bones like Veremund."

"Then you don't know her like I do," Laithe grunted, failing to disguise his horror. He was avoiding her for a good reason. "But yes, I'll visit her once I rest."

"Thanks, Laithe," Isam beamed brightly, his cheeks rosier than usual. Odd.

Laithe smiled and departed.

12

An Overdue Revelation

Laithe reluctantly entered the dim room, overpowered by the pungent smell of medicine. Calvin rose from his rickety chair in the corner, nodded curtly at the mercenary, and departed silently, leaving Laithe alone with Kez.

He had slept most of the day, recovering from the previous night's chaos. Awakened by the smell of dinner, Laithe remembered his promise to Isam. He needed to visit his old companion.

Kez was unconscious for days after Laithe rescued the Eight; her survival was uncertain until she woke a week later. The frail woman overcame the worst due to Calvin's diligence and a bit of luck. The wounds were extensive, however, and she was still recovering.

Isam visited regularly, and Calvin spent most days at her side; Kez and the healer had seemed to develop a close bond. Laithe, however, had avoided her and had not seen Kez since she had awoken. He did not want to answer too many questions, and she hadn't asked to see him either until now.

His avoidance of Kez visibly exasperated Isam, but that

did not change the frequency of the two men's nightly conversations. He had much more in common with Isam than he initially thought, and having some semblance of companionship was refreshing. Confronting her was another matter entirely.

Laithe sat in Calvin's chair next to Kez's bed. Her breathing was hoarse, and bandages covered half of her body, but otherwise, she seemed to be doing well. He braced himself for a stern lecture, understanding Kez possessed a tongue as sharp as her blades. She had every right to be angry at Laithe.

His conversations with Isam helped him understand how others thought and how his actions could impact their feelings. Emotions were unimportant in Laithe's previous life, and it was easier to ignore them altogether. But Isam insisted this was no way to live, so Laithe tried his best, though it was excruciatingly difficult.

Equipped with his fledgling grasp on empathy, Laithe assumed Kez was angry with him. He'd abandoned her and the others during the Calling. If he hadn't run off, Callandra might still be alive. By now, Calvin or Isam had undoubtedly informed her of Veremund's brutal raids. He was sure the stories revolted Kez. Laithe could hardly blame her. After all, he was disgusted with them himself. Since Laithe defied him, the ram escalated their attacks in frequency and ferocity, culminating in the explosion in the Undergrowth. They were only worsening the plight of the Deviants of Tabulrossa.

Veremund's attack burned swathes of the city, killing countless wardens, civilians, and Deviants alike.

Laithe was powerless to stop it.

"You should be ashamed of yourself," Kez finally broke the tense silence. Laithe gritted his teeth, preparing for the onslaught.

"I am sorry," Laithe said, listening to Isam's advice. He'd suggested leading with humility. He was usually right about such matters. "I should have stayed with you and the others; they might be alive now. And I am sorry for helping Veremund with his raids."

"Not for that, you idiot boy," Kez laughed. "Asking you to stop killing wardens would be akin to asking the sun not to rise every morning. I know your nature, boy. Kill every one of those bastards for all I care. I encourage it. But avoiding an old woman for weeks while she lays in bed, fighting for her life? Childish."

"Oh," Laithe said, stunned. Despite his nightly conversations with the empathetic Isam, emotions were still confusing and mysterious to him. Humans were strange creatures. "Well, I am sorry, Kez. I don't know what else to say."

"Well, that is the problem. Not afraid of death but afraid of facing an old woman," Kez tutted. "That lovely young man, Isam, told me you were afraid to see me. I don't know how he has the patience for a rock-skulled dolt like you. Though he seems to be rubbing off on you, I'd never thought I'd see the day you apologized for anything."

"Neither did I," Laithe admitted. "This place is strange. I think it's changing me somehow."

"Mostly for the better, I suspect. No thanks to Veremund," Kez dropped to a whisper. "Be careful with that one. The villagers grow wary of him. He has broken his promise, and they fear his wrath if they speak out of turn."

"I know," Laithe said. "At first, his plan made sense. Kill more wardens, save more Deviants. Now, there are more wardens than ever, and he's leaving Deviants defenseless.

There is nothing I can do."

"But that is where you are wrong, my boy. That is why I wanted to talk to you. You have Veremund's ear. Though you may not know it, you also have his heart," Kez said. "Isam is too scared to tell you, but Veremund wouldn't have allowed you to rescue me if he did not care for you. Use that knowledge, boy. Speak up more. You have the strongest will of anyone I've ever met. You may be even more stubborn than Veremund himself. He may listen, and you may be able to reign him in."

"Perhaps," Laithe replied dubiously. He didn't want to push his luck after the debacle with Kez, but maybe it was the perfect opportunity to assert himself. "It is worth a try."

It was odd to hear from someone else that Veremund had feelings for him. He would have been elated if he discovered that a month ago. But his emergent fear and disdain for Veremund had tainted his feelings. He no longer loved the ram as he did before.

Isam and Kez wanted Laithe to leverage his relationship with the ram spirit to manipulate him and convince him to return to his old ways and become the champion of all Deviants once more. It was too much to process, but something Kez mentioned perplexed Laithe.

"Why was Isam afraid to tell me this?" He asked. "He could have come to me. He didn't have to involve you in this."

"You're an idiot, boy," Kez scoffed. "Isam doesn't want to talk about your…relationship with Veremund because the boy has feelings for you, too. I'm not sure why, but he's fallen head over heels for you."

"What?"

Isam was a friend, a confidant, who had never once flirted

with him or given him any of the usual hints he experienced from previous lovers. He simply talked about his passions, feelings, and what he wanted from life. Plenty of men had fallen for Laithe in the past, including poor Benjin, but their affection was always apparent to him. He'd never once thought Isam felt this way. People were strange.

"You are such a fool," Kez said. "Be careful, boy. You have the heartstrings of two men; one is an all-powerful spirit, and the second is this village's leader. Tread lightly and make your next choices carefully. A lover's wrath is nothing to trifle with."

Laithe grunted. He was genuinely terrible at deciphering the thoughts and emotions of others. Both Veremund and Isam loved him. And now, one was asking him to seduce the other, to force him into their previous arrangement. It was too much to comprehend.

Kez sighed wearily, informing Laithe she needed to rest. He bade her farewell and exited. Calvin waited patiently outside the door. The healer gave him a wry smile. He had heard everything, that bastard. Though the entire village probably knew. They were all normal, unlike Laithe.

He trekked to the dining area, lost in thought. Kez's revelation forced him to analyze the last few weeks. His contemplation preoccupied him so much that he didn't realize Isam was performing, singing a sad song about long-lost lovers who died before they could reunite. Grabbing a bowl of stew from the cook, he sat off to the side and watched the rest of the show, struggling to understand what Kez had told him. Isam strummed the lute strings with long, delicate fingers and crooned forlornly.

Laithe recalled how he'd thought of Isam the first day they

met. He was cute and someone he would've pursued if it had not been for his desire for Veremund. But his feelings for the Tal'Rach soured after weeks of questionable behavior. As they receded, his affections had transferred to Isam. Laithe regarded him in a new light, knowing Isam fancied him. He realized that he might feel the same.

When the performance ended, Laithe and Isam were alone in the clearing, as usual.

"Good evening, Laithe," he said, strolling over and sitting beside him. "What was your favorite song tonight? I know you like the depressing ones, for some Lucian-forsaken reason, so I added more to my set tonight."

"I talked with Kez," Laithe blurted out. He never was one for tact. "She said you wanted me to seduce Veremund and convince him to return to your original pact."

"Oh," Isam replied flatly. Eyebrows raised in shock. "Did she?"

"She also told me why you didn't ask me yourself."

"I-I am not sure what you're talking about," Isam stuttered. His cheeks flushed bright crimson, eyes darting around the clearing, avoiding Laithe.

"Of course you do," Laithe said, his hand dangerously close to Isam's leg. "You have feelings for me."

"I-I," Isam said. "I never told her—"

Laithe smiled; he was cute when he was so flustered. He rubbed Isam's thigh, which stopped him from rambling.

"Don't be bashful about it," Laithe said. He wasn't one for words. Actions were more practical and his preferred method of communication.

He leaned in and kissed Isam.

Isam's lips were soft, his kisses delicate. Unlike the furious passion of Veremund, his was a slow, sensual burn. Laithe wrapped his arms around Isam's slight frame and pulled him close, feeling his body press against his. He gently caressed Isam's skin, causing him to let out a soft moan. Isam surrendered to Laithe's touch and melted into him, heart pulsating frantically.

Laithe enjoyed how easily he controlled Isam. He had always been the more dominant force in a relationship. After weeks of fucking the massive Tal'Rach, he had forgotten how much he enjoyed his typical role. His desire grew wildly, his tongue probed lustfully. To his disappointment, Isam pulled back.

"What about Veremund?" Isam breathed, filling with terror as he mentioned the ram spirit by name.

"I will try to convince him to change his ways for you."Laithe knew Isam was referring to his relationship with Veremund, but the ram was far from his mind. That was a conversation for later. "Come back to my room with me."

Isam protested but blushed at Laithe's bluntness. Now that Laithe had made the first move, the telltale signs of infatuation were apparent: lingering looks, coy smiles, and increased heart rate. Isam had shown remarkable restraint all these weeks. Perhaps not everyone was as forward as Laithe.

Isam jerked his head in approval, and Laithe lifted him from his chair and led him off. A few men were still awake, milling about the village. Their presence forced Laithe to keep himself in check as they rushed to his room. He didn't want others gossiping, though they all probably would regardless. It was hard to keep a secret in such a tight-knit village.

His bedroom door barely closed before Laithe pulled Isam by the waist and kissed him ferociously. The wiry man may have been taller, but Laithe, thick and muscular, outweighed him considerably. Isam grunted in pain, and Laithe eased his grip. He was so accustomed to the wild, rough sex with Veremund that he had forgotten his own strength.

Isam relaxed, and Laithe resumed with more care. He scooped Isam into his arms and carried him across the room before gently laying him on the bed. He crawled on top, making sure not to crush him. Isam's kisses were so sweet, so seductive, and his moans were so enticing that it took all of Laithe's self-control to restrain himself. Isam was human and fragile; Laithe could not release his passion in the animalistic way he had with Veremund.

Isam groped Laithe enthusiastically, exploring his body with a delicate caress. The pair became lost in the heavy, cloying kiss. Overcome with lust, Laithe grunted and pushed himself upwards, sitting on his knees and hovering above Isam. Big green eyes stared at him longingly, desperate for more. Begging. He would give Isam what he desired, what they both needed.

He clumsily released the latch on Isam's belt. With a savage tug, he tore his pants off, tossing them across the room. His shirt was next, and Isam's tunic ripped in the process. Laithe winced.

Now, Isam was entirely exposed. His naked, toned body was ready to be taken. To be worshiped.

Isam's chest heaved, and his face flushed. He gazed at Laithe with frenetic excitement, enjoying the display of carnal aggression. Good. Maybe Laithe did not need to repress himself as much as he first thought. Grabbing Isam's ankles, he threw his legs onto his shoulders, revealing his prize. He glanced back at those emerald orbs. Isam's lips curved in a coy smile. He was ready.

Laithe dove in and began the slow and sensual process of preparing his lover with his tongue, letting the soft moans guide him along his sacred duty. It had been a while since he rimmed an ass, but it was his specialty. He traced delicate circles with the tip of his tongue before plunging in, devouring the hole eagerly. He had forgotten how much he loved pleasuring a man like this; it was intoxicating. Laithe became lost in Isam. Finally, Isam could take no more.

"Please, Laithe," he begged, pulling Laithe out of his trance. "I'm ready. Please."

Obliging, Laithe eagerly undressed, joining Isam in his nakedness. He lay on top of Isam and positioned himself between his legs, savoring the sensation of his bare skin touching his. Rotating his hips, he aligned their bodies, feeling Isam's heartbeat quicken. He couldn't wait any longer.

He eased himself inside, and Isam's body accepted him readily. He massaged Isam's smooth skin, kissing those soft lips. Slowly, gently, he began to make love to the moaning Isam. Love. That's what this was. He stared into those green eyes and smiled broadly. Their connection was unlike the fierce lust with Veremund, which clouded his mind and changed his true nature.

On the contrary, his mind was lucid, and his heart light. Ever since he heard Isam sing that first night at the Brazen Leaf, the wall Laithe had built around his heart slowly eroded. Initially, he mistook his connection with Isam as friendship, but that was only one component of his feelings. He cared deeply for Isam, was eager to listen to stories of his past, and was keen to learn his desires, fears, and dreams. What Laithe felt at that very moment was love.

Isam moaned softly, clinging to Laithe as he fucked a gentle, sensual rhythm. The moans grew louder the faster he went, spurning him on. Isam whispered in his ear, begging him for more. He wanted it harder.

Pleasantly surprised that Isam wasn't as fragile as he had first assumed, Laithe released his raw passion onto his lover and allowed his enthusiasm to build. It wasn't rough and unfeeling like his experience with previous lovers. It was intense, strong, and powerful. They moved in tandem, their limbs intertwined, their lips embraced. Laithe never wanted to let go, but then Isam bucked faster and faster. Laithe grunted as he lost control, gripping the narrow shoulders of his lover. He reached down and stroked Isam, ensuring that his lover joined him in his climax.

Chest against the chest, lips against lips, skin rubbing against skin, Laithe accelerated his rhythm. Isam and Laithe's moans grew to a crescendo, their passions boiled over, and their bodies shuddered in unison as they rode the wave of pleasure together. It was unlike anything Laithe had experienced before. Once the aftershocks ceased, Laithe rolled over and lay next to Isam, who hummed contently.

He scooped Isam into his arms, holding him tightly. Laithe felt a growing desire to protect Isam, to cherish him, and to make it known that he was his. He stroked Isam's cheek, admiring the soft features. Laithe's hand meandered down his neck and stopped at his chest. He touched cool metal. Laithe almost choked. He had been so distracted that he hadn't noticed the necklace Isam wore. It was a simple chain link with a tear-shaped charm, a purple gemstone affixed inside the metal, exactly like the one Veremund wore but smaller.

"The deal you made with Veremund," Laithe said, the truth

falling into place like a puzzle. "He vowed to protect the village and help the Deviants, but what was your end of the bargain? What did he ask of you?"

"He wanted me," Isam fiddled with the necklace.

"In what way?"

"I promised Veremund I would be his avatar. In exchange for protection for the men here and any Deviant who journeyed to Tabulrossa."

"So is this…?" Laithe asked, holding the metal tear as if it were the deadliest weapon in existence.

"His vessel, where he resides when he isn't inside me."

"So could he hear…what we…?" Laithe was horrified. There was no telling how Veremund's jealousy would manifest. His instinct told him it wouldn't be pretty if the ram spirit caught him with someone else.

"Oh no," Isam said. "His consciousness is in a sort of higher plane. He calls it his 'mind palace'. He sends me there when he uses my body."

"So you have no idea what he does when he inhabits you?"

Both of Laithe's lovers shared the same body. It was a hard truth to grasp.

"No," Isam admitted. "We only interact with one another when he decides to enter the mind palace before relinquishing control. And he doesn't talk much. I've had to rely on you all these weeks."

Laithe began to ask about Veremund's mind palace, but Isam gasped in horror as the necklace glowed brightly. Violet mist poured out of the gemstone, filling the air around them. The purple vapor vaguely shaped like a ram then lurched downward onto Isam. It seeped into his nose and mouth, and he seized in Laithe's arms. Isam's body transformed.

Everything grew: arms, chest, feet, and legs. Muscles formed where they hadn't existed, his hair and irises darkened, and horns burst from his head, curling in a familiar formation. Veremund lay next to Laithe. First, his eyes were wide in shock, and then they narrowed as he glared at the naked Deviant next to him.

"Hello, little one," Veremund growled. "Looks like you've had some fun without me."

13

Feeding Time

Unbridled joy filled Sarina as the swarm of rach flew around her in intricate patterns. Almost two dozen rach answered her call, showering the study with ethereal light. The most prominent figure was a golden stag twice her size. Tavo was the smallest. Sarina had joined the temple of the peacock three months ago, and only one month had transpired since she began practicing her chants.

Alma stood at the edge of the room, observing Sarina's demonstration intently, the corners of her mouth upturned in a peculiar smile. The severe priestess had softened her edges ever since Sarina successfully called the rach. She no longer viewed Sarina as a burden but as an asset. Alma insisted that she regularly meet with Sarina personally to oversee her progress, instructing her more than any other senior priestess. Perplexingly, Alma said little during their lessons and merely watched, occasionally correcting, but only when necessary. She explained that Sarina did not need much guidance since she was a natural. It felt odd to receive such praise from Alma.

But it wasn't only due to innate talent; but also sheer

perseverance. Every night, Sarina pushed herself to the limit, sometimes to the point of fainting. She would have practiced more, but the senior priestesses discouraged novices from chanting outside the library.

The faster she progressed, the sooner Phymeria would grant her an audience and administer whatever test she had in store. Only then could Sarina begin her search for her friends. With each passing day, the chances of wardens finding Kez and Callandra increased.

She collapsed on her mat each night, exhausted. She dreamed of Kez and Callandra. She dreamed of her life before the Fifteenth Edit, of her family and friends. She dreamed of the great tree, the song of the Calling reverberating in her bones.

Sarina was intoxicated with power when directing the rach with her will. But making them dance was only the base of her emerging abilities. What she learned next would make her valuable to the persecuted Deviants around the world.

"Now lift the table," Alma prodded, gesturing to the sturdy oak desk in the library's center.

Sarina obliged, focusing on the table so intensely that everything else in the room faded. It became her candle, the focal point of her consciousness. Her lips were moving, and the gibberish Marikae had taught her fell out, but she did not hear the words. Only the table existed.

She imagined the table floating in the center of the room, six paces off the ground. Sarina held the image in her mind. Only the table existed. Above her, the stag's golden body shimmered, and a wave of energy washed over Sarina. The table shook, trembling back and forth until it rose into the air, lifted by an invisible force. The crimson swan to her right shone alongside the stag, and the table lifted faster. Sarina ignored the rach and focused on the table. It was hard work, keeping her entire consciousness fixed upon a single object, especially when she was surrounded by a beautiful display of otherworldly light. But still, she persisted.

The table reached Sarina's desired height, and the surrounding rach shimmered brightly, including Tavo. The table held fast. She could not celebrate her victory, however badly she wanted to. This swarm of rach was the greatest she had drawn upon since she began her training.

The nature of the rach was pretty straightforward. The older the rach, the larger it was. The more the rach grew, the more raw power it contained. The amount of rach a priestess could simultaneously harness determined the power at her disposal. The spirits never grew weary or wavered as long as the priestess maintained their concentration and resolve. Alone, a single rach had its limits, but their potential was nearly infinite when joined together.

"Well done," Alma said, satisfied. She was barely audible, a whisper on the edge of Sarina's consciousness. "Now set it down. Then create a flame for me."

Sarina swallowed. She had never conjured anything before. Her concentration faltered briefly, and so did the table. It shook violently, threatening to crash to the floor. Biting her lip, she willed the desk to descend onto the library floor, and its legs rattled gently on the wooden floorboards.

She released the oversized furniture from her focus and directed her mind to the space between her and Alma. Grinding her teeth, she imagined a ball of flame sprouting from nothingness, as Marikae demonstrated on her first day; for the high priestess, it appeared as easy as breathing. For

Sarina, it seemed almost impossible.

She thought of the candle and flame—Alma's teaching tool. Sarina envisioned a flickering orange flame filling the air before her. She held the image, allowing everything else to dematerialize. Now, it was only her and the fire. The rach radiated furiously, and a spark ignited in the center of the room. Air rushed past her, whipping her hair in a frenzy as the spark grew into a flame. Holding her attention on the fire, she willed it to grow until it was twice the size of her head. Holding it steady, she smiled, feeling the joy of accomplishing a feat she had previously thought unattainable.

"Very good, now extinguish it," Alma directed, and Sarina obeyed. The fire dispelled in a puff of smoke. "You continue to impress me, Sarina."

"Am I ready to meet Phymeria, then?" She asked the same question every night, and Alma always replied with a scoff. Regardless, she persisted.

"Yes," Alma said, jarring Sarina so much that the flock of rach escaped through the walls, floor, and ceiling. Tavo remained, lounging between her feet. "Consider yourself lucky I am in such a good mood. Don't pout. Yes, you are talented, too. I will speak to Marikae tonight and arrange your first meeting with Phymeria."

"When?" Sarina asked eagerly. She had been waiting for this moment for so long, working so hard to achieve it, that she could hardly believe it was finally occurring.

"Hopefully, tomorrow," Alma sighed, clenching her jaw in annoyance. "But it all depends on our mistress' wishes. Get some sleep tonight, girl. You will need it."

With that final foreboding message, the priestess exited the library. But Sarina was too excited to care. She couldn't help herself from nearly skipping down the hall with joy, Tavo on her heels.

She devoured her dinner and returned to the novice sleeping quarters. She would have undoubtedly spent the evening gushing with excitement if she had made friends with the other novices. But they were practically strangers to her, so she ignored them as always and allowed her mental exhaustion to weigh her into a pit of deep sleep.

# # #

Chores the next day were long and excruciating; she spent the morning scrubbing the entryway, looking every so often to see if Marikae or one of the senior priestesses had passed by. They did not. Then she ate her lunch, trembling with nervous energy, fixating on the door. But Marikae did not come. Sarina was practically hyperventilating during afternoon chores, tending to one of the abundant gardens. She hadn't seen a single senior priestess that day. Otherwise, she would have pestered them incessantly. Still, no one came. Sarina was nervous as she hurried to her lessons in the library. She could not wait another day. She had to meet Phymeria.

With a sigh, she entered the library. Marikae and Alma were already waiting, standing shoulder to shoulder. Her heart pulsated with excitement. Senior priestesses never oversaw a novice's lesson together. They must have news.

"Any word of Kez or Callandra?" Sarina blurted. It was always the first question she asked the high priestess whenever she encountered her.

She may have been cloistered in the temple with the other novices, but that did not prevent her from overhearing gossip. Veremund had burned half the Undergrowth the night before, and there was no telling the amount people who had lost their lives. Kez and Callandra could have been among that number.

Moreover, amid the chaos, the Tal'Rach failed to declare another Edict. It had been almost half a year since the Eighteenth, and it was only inevitable the next one would come soon. "I have not received any news, unfortunately," Marikae said. "Though I am surprised that is your first question, considering your conversation with Alma last night."

"My friends are all that matters since it seems I am the only one in this temple who cares," Sarina snapped, forgetting her station.

"You would be surprised by how much the women in this temple care," Marikae retorted. "Though I do bring good news."

Sarina couldn't help but smile despite her frustration. She had immediately liked Marikae upon their first meeting but resented the high priestess after she failed to find her friends. "So, do I get to meet Phymeria tonight?"

"Yes," Marikae said, jaw clenched hard. No one in the temple dared to address the regal woman in such a manner. Sarina did not care. Titles did not garner her respect. Only action. And Marikae had failed to earn her respect. "She will see you now. But before we go, there are some things we must tell you."

"Such as?" Sarina asked.

"Watch yourself with her," Alma interjected. "She is not as lenient as Marikae. If you speak to her as you do with our high priestess, you'll wish the wardens captured you. Do not look her in the eyes. Do not question her. Do not speak unless she commands it. You have seen the power of the rach, so imagine what a Tal'Rach is capable of."

Sarina shuddered, Alma's words finally hitting home. The temple's culture was relaxed compared to the others. But Phymeria was still a Tal'Rach. She was a force of nature. One simply did not sass a hurricane or question an earthquake. Sarina solemnly bowed her head in understanding.

"Excellent," Marikae said. "We should not keep her waiting any longer."

They escorted Sarina out of the library, and the trio ascended the grand stairs near the main entrance. She gaped with awe as they ventured into the temple's higher floors. The passages were narrower than the ones below, but intricate friezes and beautiful sculptures covered every inch of the walls.

Complex sceneries carved into the wood below her feet depicted stories Sarina remembered from childhood. Senior priestesses roamed these sacred passages, but the upper halls were vacant compared to the floors below. They wound through the labyrinth until Marikae stopped at a heavy door adorned with a colossal peacock, its body gilded in bright gold.

Without knocking, the high priestess opened the door and disappeared inside, Alma on her heels. Sarina breathed and entered Phymeria's private chamber. The room beyond was more like a cathedral than a bedroom. Lofted ceilings stretched upwards, high above the delicately carved wood floor. Several pools steamed in alcoves on either side, and a giant plush bed lay along the far wall. The room was vacant, however, without a sign of the Tal'Rach.

"Where is Phymeria?" Sarina whispered, afraid her words would echo in this grand chamber.

"She's right here," Alma explained, gliding over to a table

in the room's center. No, not a table. The elegant block of wood was more like an altar. A single silver chalice sat in its center, reflecting the light of the Sylvania flowers above. Alma gingerly held the cup aloft.

"What is that?" Sarina asked, eyeing the chalice cautiously. The light metal seemed to ripple and shift ominously.

"Phymeria's vessel," Marikae explained. "Maintaining their spirit form requires immense energy, so the Tal'Rach must inhabit a host. Only two substances in this world can contain a spirit's energy. A living human, who becomes an avatar or a metal object we call a vessel. Each Tal'Rach possesses one vessel in case something happens to their avatar."

"And Alma is her avatar?" Sarina asked.

"Alma, myself, and the other senior priestesses, yes," Marikae said. "Possession by a great spirit takes a serious toll on the body, so we alternate as our lady's avatars, distributing the burden. She finds it amusing. I've caught her bragging to other Tal'Rach about how many of her servants are willing to serve as her avatar."

The chalice rattled in Alma's hand, almost impatiently.

"Can she hear us now?" Sarina asked.

Alma nodded. "Our lady has complete control of her vessel, like her avatars. But she much prefers to reside within flesh rather than cold metal."

The silver chalice glowed. Amber mist poured out, arching gracefully. The sentient cloud swirled high above, taking the shape of a gigantic peacock. It flew triumphantly about the expansive chamber and descended upon Alma like a bird of prey diving onto a field mouse. The amber smoke poured into Alma's every orifice. She shook violently as the spirit invaded her. Her body changed. Alma's skin roiled like a stormy sea and expanded; her robe shifted colors and shape. Alma was gone and replaced by Phymeria.

The Tal'Rach stretched and yawned loudly once the transformation concluded. Ignoring her guests, she glided to her bed. She sat gracefully on its edge, lounging on the plush mattress like a throne. She spent a few minutes adjusting the pillows and changing positions, each one seemingly more unpleasant to her than the last. Finally, she settled herself, propped up by a mountain of pillows. Only then did her sharp gaze cut over to Marikae and Sarina, who hadn't moved an inch since the Tal'Rach's arrival. Sarina bowed and kept her head lowered, remembering Alma's warning.

"Tell me, Marikae," Phymeria said lazily. "What is the name of this new one?"

"Sarina, my lady," the high priestess replied, bowing deeply.

Alma wasn't the only one who had transformed. Gone was the self-confident leader who could make any woman jump at a single word. In Marikae's place was an eager servant, groveling at the feet of an all-powerful spirit. "She has remarkably improved these past few weeks. One of the most powerful priestesses I've witnessed in years. You will be pleased, my lady."

"Spare me the tedium, Marikae; I will assess her power myself," Phymeria said dismissively, her head snapped over to Sarina. "Summon them. Show me how many rach you can conjure."

Sarina realized this chamber was the only place in the temple utterly devoid of rach. Even Tavo, who was constantly by her side, had disappeared. Pushing that observation to the side, like every other thought in her mind, Sarina conjured the candle, composing herself. Due to months of practice, her desired serenity came immediately. She chanted. At first, no rach appeared, so she chanted louder, willing them with all her might. A full minute passed, and still no rach. Typically, the spirits would immediately flock to her when she began chanting. She focused fervently on the imaginary flame in her mind. She could not panic now.

She felt a slight tingle on her ankle, and her heart soared. She did not have to look to know it was Tavo. He was a faithful companion, but his presence wouldn't be enough to impress the Tal'Rach, so she continued.

A pair of ethereal jellyfish floated out of the floor. Then, a flock of birds soared through the far wall. She kept chanting. Ten more rach dropped from the ceiling, joining the ghostly whirlpool that enveloped her. Still, she persisted. Sarina wasn't content until four dozen rach joined the glowing torrent.

She would impress the Tal'Rach, achieve the freedom to leave the temple, find Kez and Callandra, and protect any Deviant she could. With the power of the rach, she could defend all of them.

"That's enough," Phymeria said. "No need to show off. I see your talents will be useful as one of my priestesses. Marikae, make sure to have a private room arranged for her."

"Thank you, my lady. I am honored." Sarina bowed deeply.

"I did not permit you to speak, girl," Phymeria barked. Sarina bowed, trembling at the Tal'Rach's force. "I am famished. Feed me."

To Sarina's horror, the Tal'Rach unhinged her jaw with a sickening pop. Her maw gaped wide, showing rows of cruel teeth. The peacock spirit sat on the bed expectantly, her massive mouth opened to the sky. She coughed in frustration, glaring at Sarina.

Feed her what? Sarina thought. There was no food in sight.

"She wants the rach," Marikae whispered gravely, so quietly that the new priestess barely heard it.

"Y-you want me to force the rach…inside…that?" Sarina asked.

"Yes," Marikae sighed, face downcast in shame. "Now, do it quickly before she becomes upset. She can be mercurial when she's hungry."

So that was the Tal'Rach's purpose for the priestesses. They weren't worshipers, guardians, or even counselors. They were mere servants, collecting her food and feeding it to her. And her diet was the rach.

Her stomach twisted as she willed the first jellyfish forward, guiding it towards Phymeria's great maw. The Tal'Rach inhaled; the jellyfish fought against the suction, but it was too great. The flailing rach contorted, dissolved into mist, and disappeared into the black hole that was the peacock spirit's gullet.

"More," Phymeria ordered, barely intelligible through her unhinged jaw.

Sarina closed her eyes and willed the rest towards her new mistress. The rach floated towards Phymeria one by one, who devoured them indiscriminately. She now understood why the rach resisted her call at first, even Tavo. They weren't standing in a bed chamber but a feeding ground. Her eyes opened in shock, and her heart raced furiously.

Tavo.

The blue cat floated at the end of the line, forced toward the peacock spirit by Sarina's will. His teeth were bared in horror, his back arched, and he thrashed against an invisible wall—

formed by Sarina. Only two rach separated her companion from the Tal'Rach's jaws.

She decided to act recklessly, foolishly. She must save Tavo.

In desperation, she maintained her laser focus on the other rach but split her consciousness in two. One part of her remained concentrated on feeding Phymeria, and the second was aimed at Tavo. It only lasted a few heartbeats, but the division in her mind sent tremors of pain through her skull and down her spine. The world spun violently.

But she persisted.

The fraction of her consciousness directed at Tavo willed him to flee. The cat spirit immediately bolted and dove into the intricately carved floor.

As soon as he disappeared behind the frieze, Sarina merged her disjointed mind, holding her aching head, and finished feeding the Tal'Rach. Once Phymeria absorbed the final rach, her features reverted to their human-like state, and she reclined on her pillows, resting with utter contentment.

Sarina felt a firm hand on her shoulder and turned to see Marikae.

The high priestess led Sarina silently out of the chamber and into the twisting halls of the upper temple.

"You could have warned me," Sarina said, still shaking.

"It is forbidden." Marikae's voice cracked. This behavior was unlike her. The typically self-assured high priestess was terrified of the Tal'Rach. "The great spirits want their true nature to be hidden from the public. Only their most trusted servants are allowed to know."

"By nature, you mean that they're monsters, feeding on poor rach to preserve their power," Sarina said. It was all beginning to make sense: how the Tal'Rach were so powerful and why they needed the priestesses. They couldn't control the common rach, so they used the women with the gift to deliver their prey. "Are all of the Tal'Rach like this?"

"Only the ancient ones, who must sustain their power," Marikae replied. "Which is everyone but Veremund. He still has a few centuries before he has to resort to such behavior."

"So the Calling is an annual dinner bell. And you're the ones who ring it."

"Yes," was all Marikae could manage to say.

Sarina balked, ready to vomit on the spot or scream in rage, whichever came first. "With all your knowledge and power, why don't you stop it?"

Marikae halted, whirling on Sarina, cheeks flush with anger. "Because we are their prisoners. Not just priestesses. Wardens. Deviants. Rach. Tabulrossans. All of us. You have not seen their wrath, what they are truly capable of. But I have. I do what I can in the dark, under her eye."

"What else are you hiding from me?" Sarina asked. Marikae had kept innumerable secrets these past months. It was difficult to trust her. "More importantly, what are you hiding from Phymeria? Besides your work with the other Deviants?"

Marikae's eyes narrowed, and the austere priestess glanced cautiously around the deserted temple corridor. The hour was late, and they were alone on the stairs. She led Sarina to the library, closing the doors.

She chanted softly, and the walls shimmered as if they were standing in the center of a bubble.

"There is a reason we forbid practice outside the library," Marikae whispered, gesturing to the luminescent walls around them. "It is the only place in the temple warded from Phymeria's gaze."

"Why would you hide our practice from her?" Sarina asked. The library returned to normal and she realized the ward had always been present, Marikae had simply allowed her to view it.

"Because to her knowledge and to all of the Tal'Rach's, our power only extends to herding the rach," she smiled devilishly. "Everything else you have accomplished remains hidden from them. From senior to novice, these abilities have been passed down throughout the centuries. We call them the secret arts. Feats and miracles that only the Tal'Rach are known to accomplish. But so can we. Few have the dedication to master them, fewer can be trusted to keep them hidden from the Tal'Rach. Less than half of the women in this temple are trained in the secret arts. Even fewer in the other temples, whereas some have lost the secret arts altogether."

"But you trusted me with this knowledge," Sarina furrowed her brow in confusion. "You revealed the secrets arts to me the day we met."

"I told you enough to test your abilities, but not enough to be dangerous. You will learn the rest, eventually," Marikae explained. "But yes, usually it requires years of training in the Call and assessment by the senior priestesses to determine whether a young woman is worthy to be trained. But the day we met I knew you had no love or loyalty to the Tal'Rach and there was something special about you."

Sarina felt her cheeks grow hot at the praise. She respected Marikae more than any person she had ever met, a kind word from her meant the world. Only then did she notice how close she was to the gorgeous woman. She could feel her breath, it smelled like cinnamon.

"So the Tal'Rach have no idea of your...our power," Sarina

said, trying to keep her focus from Marikae's lips.

"And they will only discover it when it is too late," Marikae said.

Sarina gasped. The wardens were never the true enemy; they were pawns of the Tal'Rach. And the priestesses weren't mere servants, at least not in the temple of the peacock. She had seen many other priestesses practice lifting objects or conjuring the elements. Marikae was training them to harness the power that could rival the Tal'Rach.

Marikae was building an army.

14

In the Mind Palace

Laithe lay naked beside Veremund, feeling vulnerable under the ram's icy stare. Words escaped him; Isam was the Tal'Rach's avatar. Now, he faced the most terrifying creature in Tabulrossa, caught in his infidelity.

Veremund and Isam. Tal'Rach and avatar. One wanted to burn the city to the ground in his campaign of revenge, while the other wanted to protect the haven his parents had built.

Moments ago, Laithe promised Isam he would support his goals and persuade Veremund to fall in line. But now he was in the Tal'Rach's arms, feeling the tight muscles around him. Smelling his musky odor, like burnt pine needles. His mind was muddled. He had forgotten the sheer magnitude of his attraction to Veremund. Laithe may have lost his respect for the ram spirit, but it did not quell his burning desire. It was utterly confusing.

"Oh," Laithe said flatly.

The emotional confrontation was foreign to him, so Laithe did what he felt was natural and departed. Without a word, he struggled out of the iron embrace, climbed out of bed, threw on his pants, ignored Veremund's protests, and escaped the bedroom. He didn't know how to handle the situation, so removing himself was the best option. He couldn't blame himself; he doubted anyone had ever discovered that both their lovers shared the same body.

Still in shock, he padded across the village floor. Half a dozen men were still milling about at the late hour, stealing glances at the half-naked mercenary. Laithe was too absorbed in his thoughts to care about the villagers' opinions. It was a small community, and word would spread whether or not he concealed it.

Laithe had placed himself in the most dangerous position possible. For all accounts, he belonged to Veremund. Not only did he cheat on the vengeful Tal'Rach, but he did so with the great spirit's avatar—the one closest to Veremund.

After lumbering about, engrossed in thought, Laithe arrived at the village entrance. Since the ram was currently naked in his bedchamber, he had nowhere else to go. He was probably about to be exiled from the village, so why not leave on his own accord? Laithe could find clothes elsewhere, but for now, he needed to be far away from this clusterfuck.

He only traveled thirty paces into the dark tunnel before he felt a firm grip on his arm. Laithe jumped. Veremund towered over him, fully naked, peering down with a fiery glare. Laithe braced himself to endure the wrath of the Tal'Rach.

"Do you think I am angry, little one?" Veremund's scowl softened and split into a heated grin. "I don't own your body, though I am quite fond of it. I'm lucky that you chose my avatar to fuck, though I wish you had told me you fancied each other sooner. We could have had more fun."

"I-It was our first time," Laithe stammered. "I wasn't aware he was your avatar."

He had not expected the Tal'Rach to act so casually about his infidelity. He was admittedly stung that Veremund hadn't been jealous. It meant the ram had never truly cared for Laithe. Their relationship was purely physical, after all.

The revelation slightly cleared Laithe's guilty conscience for sleeping with Isam. He loved Isam. He merely lusted after Veremund. He cursed all of these feelings. Life was so much simpler before this blasted city.

"Ah, and how was it?" Veremund inquired. Laithe blushed abashedly. He wasn't one to kiss and tell. "I see. It seems you have feelings for my Isam. That explains why he's been distant lately."

"He said the two of you barely speak," Laithe said. It would be challenging to converse often if they shared the same body.

"We do not have many opportunities to chat," Veremund explained. "Just like you, I believe actions are more fruitful than words. Especially with Isam."

"You fucked him?" Laithe furrowed his brow, a spark of jealousy ignited within him. Not only did Isam resent the Tal'Rach, but the logistics of sex between spirit and avatar were confusing. "How does that work?"

The Tal'Rach grasped the necklace around his neck and held the teardrop pendant in his massive palm. "My mind palace, would you like to see it?"

Veremund caressed Laithe's chest and wandered southward. Laithe nodded eagerly. Despite his jealousy, disdain, and confusion, he still yearned to please the Tal'Rach. The ram had sunk his hooks into him and could manipulate him with ease.

"Then follow me," Veremund said, leading him back into

the village.

Whispers trailed behind them as they walked through the haven. Veremund was utterly naked, while Laithe was shirtless. His skin felt hot; he was a private person, and now he was sure this incident would be the gossip of the Brazen Leaf for years to come.

He was relieved when Veremund finally returned to his room, leading him to bed. They lay beside each other, the bed frame groaning under their weight. He could feel the ram's hot breath on his skin. Laithe wanted the Tal'Rach to ravage him again.

"Now, all you have to do is touch it," Veremund beckoned, holding out his necklace.

Laithe obeyed and carefully clutched the Tal'Rach's hand, the amethyst wedged in between.

The world erupted in a blinding flash when his palm touched the cool stone. A whirlwind of light distorted his senses as he fell into an endless abyss. He cried out, but no words escaped. Did he even have a mouth?

The world materialized around him in an explosive instant. Laithe was no longer in bed but standing in the center of a grand room. Still half-naked. The surrounding walls were gray, smooth, geometric, and made of stone. Odd. He wasn't in Tabulrossa. He heard stories about formidable buildings of rock and mortar; people called them castles.

Alone in the majestic entryway, Laithe decided to explore the depths of the peculiar building. Oddly enough, he did not feel cold despite his near-nakedness. He climbed the wide staircase built along the far wall, which carried him to the second floor. Peering out the window, he saw rolling green planes surrounding the castle, sun-kissed and extending into infinity in every direction.

The grass outside remained perfectly still. There was no wind and no birds overhead. The sun was too bright, too intense. Ignoring the odd scene, Laithe climbed to the top of the stairs. He proceeded down a long hallway, delving deeper into the castle. Open doorways on either side led to lavish rooms with plush furniture; not even the Tal'Rach had enough wealth to afford such luxury. He was in Veremund's fantasy, however odd it was.

A single door remained shut, the one at the very end. The hall grew dim around it, shadows gathering menacingly. The wood was darker than the previous doorways, black metal hinges, and a doorknob shaped like a snarling ram. Naturally, Laithe was drawn to it, laying his palm on the ram skull.

"Not that door, little one. Unless you want to be lost in my consciousness forever." Laithe jumped at the voice over his shoulder; Veremund hovered over him. He retracted his hand immediately, as if the handle was a viper. He may not have fully understood the warning, but he was wary of the door, nevertheless. He shifted awkwardly on his feet, feeling foolish. "Snooping on your first visit. You make you a lousy house guest."

"I was looking for you," Laithe said. The gold embroidered silks draped over the Tal'Rach like a king. His mind palace, or whatever he called it, was indeed his private fantasy realm.

"Well, now you have me," Veremund smiled warmly, leaning in and kissing Laithe. It was unlike any kiss they had shared before. It was sensual, hot, and slow. Almost sweet. He wrapped himself around the ram spirit, unconcerned with his near nakedness, allowing this new sensation to consume him. This fantasy version of Veremund wasn't a lustful animal but a sensual and doting lover. The Tal'Rach grinned once more. "Let us find our Isam. Would you like that?"

Laithe gaped, confused. The man before him was not the same Veremund he had known these past months. He appeared and felt the same, but Laithe had never witnessed this softness. Realizing the Tal'Rach was waiting for his response, he grunted in affirmation.

Veremund lifted him and flew down the corridor. Their supernatural flight took them through the sprawling castle's gilded halls, up grand staircases, and past vast galleries of tapestries until they arrived at what seemed to be the highest chamber.

Veremund gently set Laithe on the plush carpet of a circular room, windows covering its walls from floor to ceiling. They were in the palace's tallest tower and could view leagues of incredible scenery in every direction. A steaming bath lay to the left, and an oversized canopy bed filled the chamber's center. Isam was sprawled upon it, wearing a soft woolen bathrobe, comfortably sandwiched between two pillows.

This lavish chamber must have been where Isam was kept while the Tal'Rach used his body. In Laithe's opinion, it was a fair exchange.

"What is he doing here?" Isam asked fearfully. He undoubtedly shared Laithe's initial alarm after the Tal'Rach caught them in bed together.

"Consider it a gift," Veremund said, leading Laithe toward the bed. "Both of you have been so distant with me lately. I realize now that I've been neglecting you, unable to give you what you deserve. I see now that you're both craving more, something I haven't been able to provide either of you. I am sorry I have been so focused on our mission to eradicate the wardens; I care deeply about you both. But we can change that. Now we can all be together. Fulfill ourselves in every way."

The ram spirit had never spoken so openly before and had rarely shown such vulnerability. Laithe and Isam exchanged a glance. Both were perplexed by the sudden outpouring of affection. Who was this new Veremund?

"What are you suggesting?" Isam asked the exact question on Laithe's mind. "That the three of us…become…?"

"Lovers," Veremund said.

"I can't," Laithe said, stepping backward.

Veremund's smile fell.

It was too much for Laithe to process. Earlier that day, he had unearthed his love for Isam and determined that the Tal'Rach never truly cared for him. On top of that, both men he cared for had a relationship long before his arrival. He had never had a serious partner before, much less two at once. Veremund had been so callous, so hellbent on the destruction of Alistair and the wardens. Laithe thought his feelings would have vanished by now, that his initial infatuation for the Tal'Rach had been fully replaced with disdain. He had been so sure what Veremund felt for him was purely physical, but something about the Tal'Rach's proposal excited him.

"Wait," Isam rose from the bed and joined Laithe, "I know Veremund is asking a lot. I should have told you everything much sooner. But he may have a point. I know that you two care for me deeply. And for one another. And I care for both of you. Why can't we all care for each other, together?"

"It is simple when you say it like that," Laithe said.

"I know you like simple things," Isam smirked, "What do you say?"

"Yes."

Laithe was surprised by his eagerness, unable to refuse both his lovers. When he awoke to Veremund, he had expected his entire life to explode in a fiery fit of revenge. He hadn't dreamed of this option. He lusted after Veremund; his initial feelings had never truly evaporated. He also wanted to explore his new connection with Isam. Now, they were giving him the option to pursue both. It was strange, but the more Laithe thought of it, the more he agreed with Isam. It was an ideal arrangement.

Veremund smiled, glancing at Laithe's physical excitement, and pulled him close. Isam blushed and looked away. The Tal'Rach placed his massive hand on Isam's chin, lifting his lips to meet his own. The two kissed passionately, and Laithe's desire grew. He traced his fingers along their backs as Isam melted into the mammoth Tal'Rach. Laithe moved behind Isam, pressing against his rear and delicately removing his robe. Veremund observed them, growing hot with lust. The mighty Tal'Rach snapped his fingers, and his silk clothes disappeared in a puff of smoke.

Veremund leaned around Isam and kissed Laithe. Both pawed at the thin musician in the middle. The three pressed inwards to form a huddle, trading kisses, stroking one another in a slow-building passion. Soon, Veremund led them both to the center of the plush bed.

He pushed Isam on all fours, who obeyed and arched his spine, waiting expectantly. Veremund seized Laithe by the waist and positioned him behind Isam, kissing his neck rigorously. Laithe pushed gingerly into Isam, who moaned softly as he entered him for the second time that day. Before he was fully inside, Veremund grunted in pleasure and pushed himself inside Laithe. All three groaned in unison.

The three lined up with Laithe in the middle, Veremund behind, and Isam in front. Fulfilled from both sides, Laithe let out a satisfied sigh. Isam curbed Veremund's aggression, and the Tal'Rach riled him in return. Laithe lost himself in the tides between them, torn between the dominant Veremund and the submissive Isam.

It was perfect.

The three fucked for an eternity, switching positions, oscillating between slow passion and rough intensity.

Making love with Isam earlier should have physically depleted Laithe; instead, a renewed strength coursed through him as the three fucked. He wasn't sure if it was the magic of this ethereal place, having all of his desires met at once, or a combination of the two.

Veremund was more generous than he ever had been in the outside world. He tended to both men equally, kissing them softly, and teasing them with his tongue, fingers, and cock. He overpowered Isam and Laithe, and they succumbed to his lust.

Laithe adored watching Veremund play with Isam, finding his sensitive spots and making him moan. He learned much about both his lovers' proclivities by observing them satisfy each other, and he was eager to discover more. He dove into them and lost himself in the rhythm of the sensual dance.

Though it lasted for hours, Laithe almost mourned when the session ended, and the three lay intertwined in a sweaty heap. Kissing Isam softly on the cheek, Laithe rolled over and brushed Veremund's hair with his fingers. The ram spirit smiled contently, catching his breath. They cuddled for a long while in silence. Veremund had never lain with Laithe like this after sex; he dressed and left before either grew soft.

Laithe couldn't believe what had transpired but couldn't be happier. Something about holding the two men close felt right. For the first time in his entire life, Laithe was utterly content.

"You seem happy, little one," Veremund said, chuckling when both Isam and Laithe perked up. "Perhaps I should call you both by your name. It will be less confusing that way."

"Call me whatever you want," Laithe smirked. "As long as you use that tongue like you did on Isam's ass."

The bed rocked violently as the Tal'Rach burst into vigorous laughter, shaking his two lovers.

"I've always appreciated your bluntness," Veremund said, turning to Isam and stroking his cheek. "And those moans of yours, littlest one. It looks like Laithe has plenty to teach me about pleasing you."

"You do just fine yourself, Veremund," Isam said. He blushed and nuzzled against the Tal'Rach's hulking chest.

"I know," Veremund chuckled and let out a deep sigh. "I should let you both go and rest; your minds have been here for quite some time."

The three said their goodbyes with a flurry of kisses. Laithe did not want to leave, but the Tal'Rach dismissed him regardless.

The world exploded in light, and Laithe flew into oblivion once more, his mind disconnected from his body, flung by an invisible force. Suddenly, he returned to his bed. Naked, holding the purple gemstone and lying next to Isam. Veremund had surrendered his avatar's body, remaining in his mind palace within his necklace and leaving Laithe and

Isam alone. Their bodies were in the same position as earlier as if they had merely fallen asleep. But where they had gone was better than any dream.

"That was unexpected," Laithe said, wheezing with exhaustion. It may have all happened in his mind, but his body felt every ache from the physical acrobatics he had performed.

"It certainly was," Isam said, though his brow furrowed, preoccupied in thought.

"It seemed like you enjoyed it," Laithe smirked, teasing his lover's hair with a flick of his finger. "Especially that part where we had you lifted between us."

"Would you like to go another round, Laithe?" Isam asked, "Your appetite is impressive. I've never seen you so happy."

"I am happy," Laithe said, "I was surprised you agreed with his proposal. You struck me as the monogamous type."

"Well, I am," Isam said.

"I don't understand," Laithe said, "Then why did you persuade me to join your relationship?"

"Because I can see right through Veremund's act."

"Well, I thought it was nice of him," Laithe said. "He brought us together. Right when you and I connected."

"Exactly. The timing is too perfect. Veremund reacted too calmly. Can't you see he was manipulating us? Have you ever seen him act like that before?" Isam waited until Laithe shook his head before continuing. "I have only known Veremund to be possessive, mercurial, and vindictive. But above all else, cunning. He admitted that he sensed us both slipping from his grasp. This new arrangement is the only way to retain both of us, to keep us docile and submissive to his will."

"So you don't want this relationship? With him or me?" Laithe asked, deflated. He had been overcome by lust again, blinded by his feelings for Veremund and Isam. Now, he desperately craved what the Tal'Rach offered. He wanted both of them simultaneously. And he thought Isam wanted the same. It was Isam who convinced him in the first place.

"Of course I want you," Isam leaned in and kissed him gently.

"But you don't want Veremund, too?"

"No," Isam admitted, "But playing along with his charade will work to our advantage."

"Advantage? For what?" Laithe sighed. The kind of deception that his two lovers seemed so adept at was perplexing—the pitfalls for falling in love with ambitious men.

"I still want him to keep his promise," Isam said, determinedly. "To stop these reckless attacks on the Undergrowth and protect what my fathers built."

"So you still want to manipulate him by seduction?" Such matters were outside of Laithe's realm of understanding. Too much was changing for his liking, and his head hurt from all the thinking.

"Yes, but now there will be two of us," Isam said. "Our will against his. We need to work together, convince him."

"What makes you think he will be more malleable now?" Laithe asked.

"Today was the first time he had spoken to me in weeks. He was the gentlest he has ever been in bed," Isam explained. "In the two years I've known him, we have never defined what we were. Veremund only implied I was his lover. His effort today shows me that he was afraid to lose me. And also to lose you. He cares about us, Laithe, and maybe we can use those feelings to bring him around."

"This is dangerous," Laithe said. "There is no telling what he would do if he discovered our intentions. No. I do know.

He will tear us limb from limb."

"That's why we do it the right way, gradually and cleverly," Isam said as he crawled out of bed and put on his pants.

"I am not clever," Laithe protested.

"That is why you have me," Isam said. "I'll leave you with the fucking and the fighting. He loves that. And I will locate stray Fourteens in the Undergrowth. All you have to do is rescue them as you did with Kez. They must be Fourteens; otherwise, Veremund won't help, though I'm unsure why. He's always been peculiar like that."

"Sounds like a good a plan as any, especially if I can focus on fucking and fighting," Laithe said. He rose and kissed Isam.

The slim man reciprocated, then yawned loudly. "I should retire to my room and let us both rest. Staying in the mind palace takes a toll on your body. The longer your visit, the more energy it takes."

"We would sleep the day away," Laithe said. "It must be nearly morning now."

"No," Isam said. "Veremund controls everything there, including the passage of time. What were hours in the mind palace could be minutes here, and vice versa. I'm sure only minutes have passed on the outside world."

"Then we should be getting our sleep." Laithe wrapped his burly arms around Isam. "And you're staying right here."

"Do I have a choice in the matter?" Isam's green eyes shone with mischief.

Laithe shook his head.

Isam sighed, snuggling close and resting his head on Laithe's chest. He listened to the petite man's steady heartbeat. A lot had transpired in one night. He had gained not one but two partners, though he suspected one love to be more authentic than the other. He studied Isam intently, whose skin glowed in the dim Sylvania light. He was beautiful.

What Laithe finally gained today was something he hadn't had for decades. Not since the Second Edict destroyed his family and his home. He had a true purpose—a reason to live.

15

A Short Tour

"How many of our allies reside in the other temples?" Sarina quietly asked as she and Marikae crossed the wide bridge from the Precipice into the Canopy. The pale morning light filtered by the thousands of leaves above her, casting a gentle green tint over the winding streets of Tabulrossa. She nervously adjusted her veil whenever they passed a warden. The sheer fabric marked her as a newly anointed priestess.

Phymeria's test had transpired two days before. Marikae and Alma had to practically restrain Sarina to prevent her from running into the city to find her friends. She would have spent those two precious days scouring Tabulrossa for Callandra and Kez if it were her decision. But Marikae was adamant that Sarina wait until they underwent the necessary preparations. It had been over a quarter of a year since the wardens chased her into the Precipice, but it was paramount that she was unrecognizable from her first days in the city. After all, Sarina killed a veteran warden, and the Sanctum spread her description throughout Tabulrossa. She was a wanted criminal, a fact she had long forgotten during her studies.

Her hair had grown considerably and now fell past her shoulders. To her dismay, the senior priestesses demanded she braid it into thick, ornate plaits. Sarina had always kept her hair short. Long hair was hard to maintain and a fatal distraction during battle. However, her weapon was no longer a quarterstaff, but the rach themselves. Hair was no longer a deterrent. Marikae gifted her a thin veil that new priestesses wore when they left the temple; most thought they were merely ceremonial, but they had a functional purpose—to hide her identity.

"That is a complicated question," The high priestess waited for a warden patrol to pass before she replied. She fell into a whisper. "Most temples know of the Fifteens hiding in their ranks and turn a blind eye. About half a dozen actively assist in maintaining the havens. Only those trained in the secret arts can be trusted and scarcely any outside of the peacock temple understand the true potential of the rach these days."

"Seems foolish to hide that from the others, especially if you trust those temples enough to harbor Deviants," Sarina pointed out.

"I can handpick the women who serve under me and dismiss the ones loyal to the Tal'Rach," Marikae explained. "Most priestesses understand the Tal'Rach can be lenient to Deviants under their care, which allows them to justify helping other Deviants. They understand that they are not monsters. But harnessing the rach to perform the secret arts previously reserved for the Tal'Rach? That is treasonous indeed."

"But wouldn't the reward outweigh the risk?" Sarina asked. "The great spirits would be powerless if every temple worked together."

"Quality will always overcome quantity," Alma interjected. She had insisted on joining Sarina and the high priestess on their journey into the city. It annoyed Sarina, who would have preferred to be alone with Marikae. She barely interacted with the high priestess outside of training, and she cherished those small moments with her.

Alma explained, however, that a pair of priestesses were conspicuous. Conversely, it was common for groups of three or more to venture into the city to shepherd the rach to the Precipice. To the ravenous Tal'Rach. Sarina shuddered at the thought.

Sarina fell silent, unable to argue with Alma's point, as they entered the busy streets of the Canopy. For the most part, the women remained unnoticed, a mundane sight to the citizens of Tabulrossa. Children, however, gawked as the trio of women glided by. Though Sarina hadn't quite mastered the graceful gait her seniors had.

Rach drifted about in tremendous numbers, though not as many as she remembered from the day of the Calling. She felt sick. It was why the priestesses replenished the population once a year. They were prey, lured in by the Calling.

Tavo padded softly next to her. The ghostly cat was unfazed by being nearly devoured by Phymeria. If only Sarina could have a short memory, like the rach. She would give anything to erase the horrors of her past. Maybe then she could finally have some restful sleep.

The trio traveled silently across the tree top, giving Sarina her first chance to enjoy the splendor of Tabulrossa. She was too preoccupied with surviving during her last trip in the Canopy to stop and gawk at the sights. Each house, regardless of size or shape, was beautifully crafted as if it had grown from the tree.

Marikae seemed to notice Sarina's expression of unmitigated awe. "It is quite marvelous. This city continues to inspire me, even after all these years."

The high priestess's words soothed Sarina's embarrassment and allowed her to appreciate the splendor around her. Alma walked a dozen paces ahead, out of earshot.

"So you never get used to it?" Sarina asked. "I would assume someone who grew up in the city would take it for granted."

"I lived in the country, actually," Marikae said wistfully. She paused, but Sarina remained silent, eager to hear more. "My parents were farmers. They were hardy people but kind. It wasn't a lavish life, but it was enough. When I was six, a pack of bandits sacked my village. Many of our men resisted. Most of them died, including my father. They burned our fields, burned our homes. There was nothing left. The following morning, the survivors packed what was left and headed to Tabulrossa, including my mother and I."

The high priestess's cheeks were wet, her chin trembling. This was clearly not a story she shared freely. Sarina suspected not even Alma knew. Marikae's trust in her must have been substantial to divulge this trauma.

"That is awful, Marikae," Sarina grasped the high priestess's hand and held it tightly. Marikae smiled warmly, wiping a tear from her eye. "So your mother raised you in the city?"

"The journey to Tabulrossa, as you know, is perilous, even for non-Deviants," Marikae clutched Sarina tighter, her voice breaking. "My mother did not make it. I arrived in Tabulrossa as an orphan at the age of eight. I spent years surviving in boarding houses; some can be dangerous places for a young girl. When I was ten, I ran away to the Precipice and found myself in the temple of the peacock."

Sarina's heart was in her throat as she suppressed tears of her own. She had never suspected the regal and composed woman had such a tragic and violent childhood. Sarina understood heartache, understood loss. A deeper sense of kinship with Marikae washed over her and she felt the urge to kiss her. To relieve the woman's pain. They locked eyes and for an instant Sarina thought Marikae was about to lean forward.

"We are almost there," Alma called from ahead. Sarina pulled away sheepishly and continued in silence.

They climbed high into the Canopy until they reached the edge of the great tree, where the branches narrowed and the crowds thinned. Only then did Alma stop. The quiet road ended abruptly in a compound of sorts. Tall structures grew on the branch's tip, situated in five clusters, each surrounding its own courtyard. Scores of people milled happily around each one, lounging on benches, grabbing water from the well, and enjoying each other's company.

These were some of the boarding houses Mags mentioned all those months ago, where migrants from all over the world would stay until they settled and created a life for themselves in the great city. According to Alma, each Tal'Rach patronized at least one boarding house to contribute to Tabulrossa. Judging by the peacocks carved above every door, Phymeria patronized these particular boarding houses. Marikae led them to the one at the end, where they would find Beriane. Sarina was adamant they see her first. She had to verify that her friend was alive and well.

"They seem so crowded," Sarina observed as they approached the entrance, doors half open. "Does it take that long for new migrants to clear out?"

"Longer than you would imagine," Alma sighed. "Only the foolhardy wish to live in the Undergrowth, and the rest of the city has grown overcrowded. A good number of our residents arrived half a dozen Callings ago."

"But it makes it easier to conceal that the residents don't want to leave," Marikae uttered in a hushed tone.

"How many live here?" Sarina asked as they entered the courtyard, gawking at the people around her. "How many have you saved?"

"In this complex, all of them," Marikae smiled brightly, relaxing as the doors to the courtyard closed. "The rest are normal boarding houses, but this one exclusively harbors Deviants."

Sarina froze, surveying the courtyard. There must have been hundreds of people in this complex alone. She had never seen more than fifty Deviants in the outside world at once. She didn't think a community of that size could survive. Her heart swelled as the inhabitants laughed and enjoyed the late morning sun. They were regular humans within these walls, living like the Edicts had never occurred. Their home was paid for by the very authority that determined them evil. It was brilliant. She studied Marikae and Alma, who both smiled in return. They were brilliant.

A high-pitched scream tore through the bustling courtyard. The full force of a crying woman collided with Sarina. Beriane flung her petite frame around her, wrapping her in a tight hug. Laughing, Sarina returned her friend's embrace. She was safe. Marikae had kept her promise on that front, at least.

She studied Beriane. The young woman's skin was clean, her cheeks full with proper nourishment, and she seemed well-rested. She had a better life here than Sarina had ever provided her. She was only missing Callandra, but Sarina would correct that soon. It was her primary goal.

"Your hair," Beriane stifled a laugh. Sarina bristled, tugging at her chunky braids abashedly.

"Don't start," Sarina warned but couldn't stop smiling. "It looks like they treat you well here; how have you been holding up?"

"Oh, Sarina, it's everything we imagined," Beriane said. "Three meals a day, my own room, and everyone here is so friendly. Did you know everyone here is like us? I couldn't believe it."

"Alma told me," Sarina gestured to her two companions. Beriane's eyes widened.

"Oh, Alma, I didn't notice you. I hope you and Floren aren't fighting anymore," Beriane hugged the older priestess, and Alma surprisingly smiled and returned the embrace heartily. She curtsied to Marikae. "Good to see you, my lady. Have you heard from Callandra? Or Kez?"

Sarina almost erupted with a belly laugh as the high priestess's lips tightened, but she suppressed it. Her friend shared her eagerness to find their companions. Together, their constant pestering must have driven Marikae crazy after all these months. It was encouraging to know that Beriane hadn't forgotten her wife or old companions despite her new, comfortable life.

Beriane truly loved Callandra, that much was certain. It still caused Sarina a bit of jealousy that she did not have someone who cared for her so fiercely. Three months apart couldn't shake what Beriane and Callandra had built together.

"She hasn't yet," Sarina hoped she sounded gracious to the

high priestess. "But with my help, we'll find them. I promise you."

"I'm happy you've passed your test," Beriane said. "Alma was a bit worried, but she said you were an absolute triumph."

"The two of you talk often?" Sarina raised an eyebrow at Alma, whose smile wavered ever so slightly. Even the stern taskmaster of a priestess held a soft spot for the bubbly Beriane. Sarina made a mental note to ask who this Floren was. She had no idea Alma had a partner.

"Oh, she comes by almost weekly and practically runs the place," Beriane gushed. "She and Marikae are always visiting with supplies and support. It seems like they bring a new Deviant whenever they visit. We've almost run out of beds."

"And Callandra and Kez will be next," Sarina said reassuringly.

Beriane's comment regarding the priestesses guiding strays to the safe house resonated with Sarina. She assumed Marikae neglected her promise to scour the city for Sarina's friends due to her responsibilities in the temple and the turmoil in the Undergrowth. According to Beriane, however, it seemed they spent ample time, energy, and resources locating lost Deviants. And if they spent three months scouring Tabulrossa for Kez and Callandra unsuccessfully, Sarina did not want to consider the unpleasant implications.

"I'm sure you will find them, Sarina," Beriane said, turning to the others. "She has always been a force of nature. There is no stopping her once she sets her mind to something."

"We are aware," Marikae said dryly. "But let us give you two a chance to reconnect. Alma and I must tend to some matters inside."

Beriane and Sarina sat on the nearest bench and chatted

while the other women bustled around the boarding house, conducting their business. Beriane did most of the talking, which was a relief. Sarina wasn't certain of how much Beriane knew about the temple and wasn't about to divulge any of its secrets, especially after Marikae stressed the importance of their secrecy earlier that morning.

Despite her delightful conversation with Beriane, Sarina felt a culminating dread. She had been so focused on leaving the temple that she did not fully understand the gravity of her next task. Marikae had spent years rescuing Deviants and knew the city better than anyone. If the high priestess of the temple of the peacock could not find them, how would Sarina? She had spent less than a day on the streets of Tabulrossa.

Soon, the senior priestesses returned, and Sarina bid her old companion farewell. Beriane gave her one last hug and bounded into the nearest building.

"Are you satisfied?" Marikae asked softly, watching the young woman disappear into the doorway.

"Thank you," Sarina said sincerely, taking one last glimpse at the Deviants going about their days in peace. "Both of you. I had no idea of the extent of what you were doing outside the temple. It's everything I could ever dream of."

"Would you like to see more?" Marikae asked.

"Yes, but what of Callandra and Kez?" Sarina said. She couldn't forget her promise to herself, Beriane, and her friends. She had to focus.

"Our other safe houses would be a good place to start," Alma said. "We have been using your descriptions to aid in locating your friends, but perhaps it would be more productive if you asked yourself."

Sarina now discerned that this was a lie; there was nothing

Sarina could do that the priestesses hadn't already. Nevertheless, she had to start somewhere. Their journey would help her understand the city's layout, so she agreed and allowed Marikae to lead her out of the boarding houses and into the Canopy.

They spent most of the day strolling about the lightly shaded streets, stopping periodically. The location varied: a home, a pub, a shop, an alleyway, or a storehouse. Their constant similarity, however, was a room or tiny hollow hidden underneath a trap door. Several Deviants lived in each. No group was more significant than the boarding house, but each stockpiled a myriad of essential supplies.

A vast, secret network of Deviants spider-webbed across the city. They descended the Aerials in the afternoon but avoided the Undergrowth altogether. It was still too dangerous to travel in such a diminutive group. Instead, they ventured to the Bole, climbing the wide stairs toward its apex at the Precipice.

It was more than Sarina could handle without becoming emotional. Hundreds of Deviants hid safely among the branches and roots of Tabulrossa, all under the nose of the Tal'Rach. And it was created and maintained by their most loyal servants.

When they entered the upper portion of the Bole, the hour was late, and Marikae guided them down the winding streets of one of the highest terraces. The dim light of Tabulrossa's Sylvania flowers illuminated the narrow alleys. The high priestess had one final stop before they returned home. Alma's expression grew sour as they moved closer to the trunk.

"This is a terrible idea, Marikae," Alma hissed as they

meandered down a narrow side street. "Imagine if anyone saw us here."

"Calm yourself, Alma," Marikae said. "We have searched under every rock in this city except this one. Perhaps we will finally find some luck."

"You have avoided this…rock for good reason," Alma spat. "Because I have begged you not to."

"Where are we going?" Sarina asked, her curiosity piqued. She had never seen the two at odds before. Ever.

"Hush, child. We're already here," Alma said.

Sure enough, Marikae halted outside a dingy pub built on the side of the great trunk. The faded letters above it spelled *The Brazen Leaf.*

The pub was cramped, dark, and dirty, more so than the other establishments she had visited today. The patrons were also older, grimier, and drunker. Alma pulled her towards the nearest empty table and sat her down. The old chair groaned at her weight, threatening to break. Luckily, the patrons around her were too intoxicated to notice three priestesses enter their bar. Only the graying barkeep behind the counter paid them any heed. He eyed the group warily as Marikae glided towards him, leaving the others at the table. The pair exchanged a few words, too quiet for Sarina to hear. Then, the bartender trundled through the back door and out of sight.

Marikae stood placidly between the two unconscious men slumped over the bar as gracefully as if she were in front of Phymeria herself. Alma tapped her foot nervously, periodically snapping her attention toward the door. Whatever this pub was, it frightened the older priestess.

Finally, the barkeep returned, although he wasn't alone. A young man accompanied him. He was tall and thin with delicate features, olive skin, green eyes, and thick locks of coal-black hair. His eyes widened when they fell upon Marikae, and he glanced at Alma and Sarina's table.

After the initial shock, he ushered the high priestess to a booth in the far corner, isolated enough that no one could overhear their conversation. Sarina waited impatiently as the pair spoke in hushed tones. The barboy was excited, gesturing enthusiastically. Marikae sat quietly and listened, intermittently interjecting. Sarina required every ounce of willpower to remain in her chair. She was about to stand and storm over when the young barboy abruptly dashed through the door behind the bar.

Marikae rose slowly with determination. Alma and Sarina were already on their feet. The trio silently exited the tavern and entered the busy streets. None spoke a word until they ascended the wide stairs leading to the Precipice.

"Must have gone well, then," Alma suggested. "Did you find what we were seeking?"

"In a way, yes," Marikae said, as stoic as ever. "And in another way, no, I'm afraid."

"Cut the cryptic talk," Sarina hissed, her patience withered and gone. "Who was that? Why are you both acting so strangely?"

The senior priestesses glanced at one another briefly, and finally, Marikae spoke. "His name is Isam. Owner of that pub. He used to be a valuable part of our network, and he is Veremund's avatar."

Sarina's shock prevented her from responding as fast as Alma. "That runt was talkative. Why would the ram's pup be so accommodating? We haven't heard anything from him since the Calling."

"Isam wants to help us," Marikae said. "He opposes his master's recent actions and plans to return the Brazen Leaf into the fold. We even discussed strategies; hopefully, he'll be a useful asset once more. He intends to reign in the ram."

"We'll see about that," Alma said wryly.

"Did he know Laithe?" Sarina blurted out. "You said Laithe, the mercenary I was traveling with, was with Veremund. Did you ask about him? He might know where our companions are."

"Yes, I did," Marikae said. "Laithe is in league with Isam and resides at the Brazen Leaf. As does your friend Kez."

Sarina halted at the mention of the older woman's name. She wheeled around, ready to sprint back to the dingy pub. She had been so close.

"No. You cannot see her now." Marikae gripped Sarina like a vice.

"Why not?" Sarina asked angrily. "Why did you wait until now to tell me when she was in that pub?"

"She wasn't," Marikae explained, her voice gentler than her grip. "There's a village below it, beyond a labyrinth of tunnels. Only Fourteens loyal to Veremund live there. If you went down running, it would throw suspicion on Isam and jeopardize everything we're working towards."

"And why can't she come out?" Sarina asked. "We could move her to the boarding house with Beriane, then all we need to do is find Callandra."

"The Fourteens rescued Kez from the Undergrowth months ago. The poor woman was near death. It will be months before she is well enough to walk. For now, she should heal under the Brazen Leaf. It's a miracle that Veremund allows her presence."

"What about Callandra?" Sarina asked carefully. "Does Isam know where she is?"

A tear fell from Marikae's cheek.

Sarina's knees shook uncontrollably.

"I am so sorry, Sarina. They found Callandra's body alongside Kez. She did not survive."

16

The More They Stay the Same

Laithe awoke to a slumbering Isam curled in his arms; he snored loudly, deeply asleep. Careful not to wake him, Laithe lay still, studying his lover's delicate features. Full lips, high cheekbones, and flawless skin. He savored these simple moments, though he couldn't believe how sentimental he had become. It had been three months since he discovered his feelings for the owner of the Brazen Leaf.

Every morning began like this, and they would end their days with a joint visit to Veremund's mind palace. Their consciousness left their bodies and traveled to the Tal'Rach's realm, where all three surrendered themselves to the throes of passion. Afterward, Veremund returned them to their bodies, where they fell asleep in an exhausted heap.

The arrangement took Laithe a while to acclimate to, as it was his first serious relationship. He had no experience living with one man, let alone two—Isam's disingenuous feelings for Veremund complicated matters. In turn, the Tal'Rach remained heavily guarded despite his gentler demeanor. Both saw through each other's facade but maintained the charade regardless. Both secretly struggled to manipulate the other. Laithe often wondered why Veremund hadn't confronted Isam. This indirect and conniving tactic was out of character for the Tal'Rach. But Laithe allowed the subterfuge to carry on, for he had nothing to gain from voicing the obvious.

The Tal'Rach's underlying jealousy became apparent fairly early on. It was evident the great spirit disliked his lovers consorting without him. Lingering animosity between Veremund and Isam was palpable after years of a dysfunctional relationship. Laithe was often tossed in the middle and used as a prop in their never-ending feud. After months of squabbles and passive-aggressive digs, he sorely regretted joining the throuple.

Laithe strove to avoid conflict and focused on the physical aspects of his new relationship, which were beyond euphoric. Sex was the perfect way to smooth over any argument. Laithe deployed this tactic often.

Lately, however, the evenings of pleasure ended in a conversation with the Tal'Rach. It was often superficial, but Isam's charm gradually eroded the ram's substantial armor. Laithe asked Isam why he had never attempted such a strategy before. Isam explained he had never considered it possible until he met Laithe, who provided him the confidence to do so. Yes, Laithe played a specific part in seducing the Tal'Rach, but he merely followed Isam's example.

The pair spent hours within the Tal'Rach's mind palace. Veremund allowed them to wander about the castle and its grounds as much as they pleased. Finding new places to fuck was fun, and Isam proved to be quite adventurous and flexible. The only area off limits was the strange door with the ram's skull knob that Laithe encountered on his first visit to the mind palace. He asked Isam why it was forbidden, but he had no answers. Veremund hadn't given an explicit reason but reacted menacingly. So Laithe avoided that floor altogether. No sense in angering the great spirit. Not again, anyway.

They would wake in Isam's room, which they now shared. Laithe had little use for his, and his partner's quarters were much nicer. They were plush, spacious, and on the ground floor of the cavern near the dining hall. It had only taken an afternoon for Laithe to transfer his meager possessions to Isam's bedchamber.

Finally, Isam stirred and opened his groggy eyes; he was notoriously slow in the mornings.

"Have you been awake for a while?" Isam groaned as he stretched his entire body. "You know I hate it when you watch me in the morning."

"And you know that I don't care," Laithe replied, kissing him on the cheek. The early morning was the only time his mind was sharper than Isam's, so he enjoyed taking advantage by teasing him as much as possible. "Some would call it romantic."

"I call it creepy," Isam yawned. "And you don't have a romantic bone in your body. I know what you've been waiting for."

Laithe smiled devilishly, pulling Isam close, his hands leisurely wandering down to the small of his back. Isam wasn't wrong; while his partner acted like a grump in the early hours of the day, Laithe was voracious. The dichotomy taught him a lot about patience. And the best ways to make Isam's heart race. "And what do you think I'm waiting for?"

"Something I can't give you now; I have much to accomplish this morning," Isam sighed, emerging from under the covers.

"Four newcomers in one week, and we still haven't made space for them yet. We may have to start double-bunking at this rate. I suppose I have you to thank."

Laithe leaned in close, teasing one of Isam's sweet spots with his thumb. "Don't punish me for doing my job. Stay a while longer. You won't regret it."

Isam was right; Laithe's success in the last month had put more pressure on him and the village. Every week, Laithe rescued more stray Fourteens from the Undergrowth. After months of complacency, the men had forgotten how to adapt to new arrivals.

"I have too much work, Laithe, and Veremund is patrolling this afternoon," Isam groaned, rolling from Laithe's embrace and out of bed. Laithe gawked at the man's slim body as he strolled to the closet to dress. "It takes discipline for two men to share one body. You should know by now."

Laithe sighed. He was generally satisfied with Isam and Veremund's situation, especially since they shared his body. However, this made timing tricky.

Abandoning hope for an early morning delight, Laithe pulled himself out of bed, dressed, and jogged after Isam into the village. Dozens of men were already eating breakfast; their laughter echoed across the cavern walls. The addition of the new arrivals brought excitement to the Brazen Leaf, as Laithe had been the only new face since the Calling. More couples had formed and late-night rendezvous became more common. The village atmosphere was buzzing and electric, all thanks to Isam.

It was a delicate matter, however, convincing Veremund to change his tactics; luckily, Isam managed the finer details, leaving Laithe with the more straightforward issues. Isam waited a week after they first fucked in the mind palace, allowing Veremund to become comfortable with their new relationship. Since the Tal'Rach was now conversational after sex, Isam promptly laid out his argument veiled in pillow talk.

Isam started slowly, making casual comments, complaining about the low morale in the village and his fears about the growing number of wardens in the city. None of it was a lie; they were all apparent issues Veremund could observe. Laithe's job was to keep Veremund's temper in check by continuing their regular cycle of fucking and fighting, which he did not mind at all. It was crucial to Isam's plan that the Tal'Rach believed he was still in total control. So Laithe remained his sex puppet at night and aided Veremund during the day to accomplish his ultimate goal—killing the archwarden. Their objectives were the same, but Veremund's path would end in ruin.

Their fortunes improved when a high priestess visited the Brazen Leaf. According to Isam, she cooperated with the Brazen Leaf before Laithe arrived in Tabulrossa. She was elated that Isam wanted to return to the fold and offered him intel on her network of havens in the Undergrowth. Unfortunately, Veremund's incessant raids had destroyed most of them, but there were still survivors who desperately needed saving.

After two weeks of laying the groundwork, they were finally prepared to enact their plan's first test. After their raid, Laithe led Veremund to an abandoned building for a post-battle romp. However, the dilapidated bakery was a hiding place for a Fourteen couple. The husbands begged the ram spirit to save them, terrified that the wardens would discover them soon. Laithe agreed with the men, and to his surprise, Veremund reluctantly consented. These men were Fourteens, after all, and he was still sworn to protect them.

They smuggled the men to the Brazen Leaf using the same strategy Laithe used when rescuing Kez, disguising himself as a harvester. The couple conveniently acquired two unused fruit baskets from a nearby warehouse. The high priestess' network smuggled the baskets to the abandoned building the night before. It was all part of a carefully crafted plan. If Veremund sensed any deception, he showed no indication. He carried the bigger man in his basket, masquerading as Laithe's companion. The Tal'Rach shifted his body into a burly, unrecognizable human to disguise himself. Again, the strategy paid off, and they successfully led the pair to safety.

The villagers were surprised yet excited when they arrived with the couple. They crowded the newcomers, pawing over them and asking countless questions. Laithe loudly credited Veremund with the idea. The Fourteens immediately lavished the Tal'Rach with praise and admiration. Positive attention was critical in persuading Veremund to return to the fold, and it worked wonders.

After settling into an empty room, the couple assimilated into the group seamlessly and proved to be quite talkative. Within days, every man underneath the Brazen Leaf heard of the couple's friends trapped in the Undergrowth. Isam and Laithe already knew every name and location, but Veremund did not. After tasting the men's adoration, Veremund declared publicly to focus their efforts on rescuing the stranded Fourteens.

Soon, half of their missions centered around a rescue instead of a savage raid. As the weeks went by, the chaos in the Undergrowth quelled. The constant pressure from

Veremund faded, and much of the Deviant population escaped to the safe houses in the Canopy. So the wardens steadily loosened their grip on the shadowy depths of Tabulrossa. The archwarden redeployed the reinforcements into the outlying lands, where the Deviant threat had festered without the presence of warden forces. Patrols were once more spread throughout the city, making it easier to operate between the gaps.

The dining area was filled with old and new villagers alike, enjoying their breakfast in high spirits. Laithe was surprised when Calvin and his burly boyfriend Lars gently ushered Kez toward a table. His old companion sat gingerly and ate sluggishly but seemed healthy. Her recovery had been slower than expected, primarily due to her age, but soon, she would be healthy enough to travel to a boarding house in the Canopy. Laithe had seldom visited her, though Isam checked in almost every day.

The elderly woman caused tension in their relationship with Veremund, whose resentment of the non-Fourteen living in his village grew daily. Laithe still did not fully understand what the Tal'Rach harbored against other Deviants or why he only held compassion for Fourteens.

Nevertheless, Kez would soon depart for the Canopy. Everyone was happy with that development, including Sarina. Laithe had not spoken to his former leader, but according to Isam, she was now a priestess and desperate to claim custody over the Eight. The sooner, the better, Laithe thought.

Laithe and Isam finished their breakfast hastily. After a quick kiss, Isam bounded off to complete his duties before the Tal'Rach inevitably decided to hijack his body for the afternoon's mission. When Isam disappeared behind the nearest building, Laithe sat up and left the village. He hurriedly traversed the labyrinth; navigating its twisting turns was now an afterthought.

He left the maze and entered the Brazen Leaf. Due to Isam and Pellum's diligence and guile, it was more crowded as of late. The room was brighter, cleaner, and rowdier. The patrons were younger but no less drunk.

Isam thought attracting more clients to the pub would ultimately aid their rescue missions. Though it was common for harvesters to deliver their wares to pubs occasionally, it would be conspicuous if they frequently visited a deserted bar. Two harvesters coming in and out four times a week would cause suspicion. So, Isam cleaned the place, lowered the prices, and advertised throughout the neighborhood. Soon, the Brazen Leaf was a bustling, lively establishment, giving Pellum more work and headaches.

The increased traffic was not without its complications, however. First, the pub was no longer as safe to loiter with so many unfamiliar patrons. They had to maintain appearances whenever they entered the pub, so Laithe avoided the main area and crept into a back room to take care of the second complication. Empty barrels filled the brightly lit workshop, along with piles of freshly delivered fruit and clunky brewing equipment. With more patrons, the Brazen Leaf needed enough alcohol to quench their thirst. They could not increase their regular orders from the actual harvesters. Not only did they masquerade as harvesters during each mission, but they became them.

Laithe and Veremund had to deliver fruit to the pub to meet the demand. They could draw too much attention if they only harvested in the Canopy, so the Tal'Rach used his powers to grow fruit-bearing branches in hidden hollows in the Undergrowth. Some of their missions were solely to harvest the fruit. Laithe was perplexed by the Tal'Rach's powers, and it seemed he discovered a new one each day. But luckily, this aided in the painstaking task of running a busy tavern.

It was also customary for pubs to brew wine, and the process was complex and tedious. Pellum was too busy at the bar, so he trained Laithe to take over the brewery. Where he used to have downtime between missions to recuperate, he now had a full-time occupation.

He spent the rest of the morning and the first part of the afternoon busy at work, mashing the fruit, moving barrels for fermentation, and cobbling new barrels together. It was monotonous work, but he loved every minute. Once he mastered the process, he enjoyed the meticulous labor.

Startled by a violent knock at the door, Laithe raised his fists instinctively. He relaxed when Veremund entered. The Tal'Rach hadn't bothered to disguise himself, his horns scraping the ceiling as he hunched over. He bent down and kissed Laithe on the cheek.

"It is nice to see you discover a new passion," Veremund noted softly. He smirked. Laithe still had his fists raised. He lowered them abashedly. "Though those hands have many other talents."

"Killing wardens, you mean?" Laithe asked wryly, gesturing to the worn axes the Tal'Rach gifted him half a year ago, leaning against his fruit basket.

"That too, but I was referring to what you do to my... " Veremund trailed off, grabbing Laithe by the wrist and guiding him toward his groin. The Tal'Rach had recently become more playful and more genuine. Laithe would have been ecstatic at such a change if it weren't for the constant pang of guilt. Lying and deception were out of his character, and he did not like manipulating his lover, no matter how noble the cause was.

The lust Veremund and Laithe shared had only been stoked in the past months. Now, the Tal'Rach seemed more comfortable and trusting with Laithe. The pair often had sex in the real world before and after missions. It felt no different than in the mind palace, but it was undoubtedly messier.

"Not in the brewery, Ver," Laithe breathed. "Our patrons drink this. Maybe we can sneak to Pellum's office."

Veremund relaxed his grip on Laithe's wrist and sighed deeply. "You are right, little one. We don't want to get too carried away. I know how loud you can get, and there are too many ears now. We should depart. Plenty of tasks to accomplish today."

Laithe sighed and disengaged, grabbing his cloak on the wall to prepare his harvester disguise. When he was ready, Veremund had transformed, replaced by a light-haired, blunt-faced man. The Tal'Rach's harvester persona was less aesthetically pleasing, but it was the only way the pair could travel together.

Laithe followed Veremund out of the bar and into the city. As always, no one paid them any attention as they conducted their business. They meandered into the Aerials, and to Laithe's delight, ascended into the Canopy above. The city's upper reaches were fantastic; the pair strolled along the winding roads and discussed mundane topics. Laithe savored every moment, for their journeys to the Canopy were quite rare. They occasionally harvested from the bountiful branches of the Canopy, filling their baskets halfway.

Their path led them down to the Aerials, their pace intentionally slow. Veremund coiled his body like a predator, waiting for the perfect opportunity to strike. Finally, the opportunity presented itself as two young wardens descended the stairs toward them. The drop root's platform was narrow and vacant. No witnesses. Veremund pounced when the soldiers stepped off the stairs. He was so fast they were unable to scream before he grabbed them both by their throats, followed by the gut-wrenching snap of their windpipes breaking. Veremund did not stop. With the momentum of his lunge, he pulled the two broken wardens into the alley between the staircase and the nearest building. He discarded the corpses and descended the stairs toward the Undergrowth. The attack lasted two heartbeats.

Veremund grinned wickedly, content. Laithe seldom used his axes these days; his joy of brewing sated his thirst for warden blood. But this was the way it had to be. It was essential for the attacks to be less ferocious, more random, and executed in parts of the city besides the Undergrowth. They were steadily reducing the wardens' great numbers. Not too much to draw the reinforcements back to Tabulrossa, but enough to lure more away from the Precipice. Veremund refrained from marking his attacks with his usual sigil to keep the killings random. Assassinating Archwarden Alistair was still Veremund's main objective, so Laithe and Isam's plan had to accommodate that goal. It all seemed to be working. Isam was a brilliant tactician.

"We are getting close," Veremund said excitedly as the pair left the Aerials and wound through the Undergrowth. They would fill their baskets at their hidden hollows and return to the Brazen Leaf. "I believe our opportunity to strike rapidly approaches. It is half a year from the next Calling; soon, Alistair will begin to prepare his forces. But thanks to you and Isam, he's more vulnerable now than ever."

"As long as I get to use my axes, Ver," Laithe said. He still felt naked without his weapons. "Though I might be out of practice."

"Maybe I'll let you have the next patrol," Veremund said. "To help you shake off the rust."

Laithe smiled, excited by the prospect.

The pair continued their way home, depositing their supplies in the Brazen Leaf's store room and traversing the labyrinth. Thankfully, Veremund reverted to his usual form as they walked through the gloomy dark. It was late when they returned to the village. Most had already retired for the evening. Calvin's boyfriend, the burly Lars, sat in Isam's place and played his lute. It was rather clumsy, but the drunken villagers paid no heed and enthusiastically clapped along to the tune. Laithe and Veremund passed by, ignoring the others, and slipped quietly into Isam's quarters.

They kissed and pawed at each other for a bit, riling one another up until Veremund pulled the pair into the mind palace. They wouldn't exclude Isam. For hours, the three played together on the enormous bed; they never seemed to grow tired in the magical realm within Veremund's mind.

Once they satiated their passions, the throuple chatted a bit—Veremund looped Isam into his plans to attack Alistair. In turn, Isam spoke of how he and the others decided to build a new house on the edge of the clearing for new arrivals. After a while, they all fell asleep in each other's arms.

An iron grip shook Laithe from his slumber. At first, he

thought it was Veremund seeking another late-night session, but he was alone in Isam's bed. He shot up and subdued his attacker, pinning him to the ground. The assailant yelped in pain. Laithe flipped the man around and immediately relaxed his grip when he recognized Calvin. The healer was shaking, his lip bloodied and his body bruised. But his injuries were clearly not caused by Laithe's overreaction.

"What happened?" Laithe asked, helping Calvin onto the bed. Isam was missing. "Where is Isam? Is the village under attack?"

"No," Calvin wheezed. "It's Veremund. He stormed into her room…I tried to stop him…but he was too strong."

"What has he done?" Laithe asked, horrified.

"Kez. He took her out into the labyrinth." Calvin said. "Said she's no longer welcome, and that she must find another haven. On her own. She can barely stand, Laithe. He's sending Kez out to die."

# # #

"Thank you, Derrara, you can send her in now," Alistair told his pale lieutenant. She saluted and exited his study hastily.

The archwarden cleared his throat and prepared himself for the impending negotiation, selecting his words carefully. One wrong move would end his life on the spot. His guest entered the study, ducking her head through the doorway. Though his private quarters in the Sanctum were spacious and grand, the Tal'Rach struggled to fit comfortably due to her size. It amused Alistair immensely. The great spirit strode in with the typical self-absorption of most Tal'Rach; she did not even possess the respect to look Alistair in the eye. The archwarden, however, stared back, unblinking.

He remained seated, forgoing the customary bow the

Tal'Rach required from humans, even the leader of the wardens. However, Alistair was unlike his predecessors and would not willingly bend. He understood that the Tal'Rach needed him as much as he relied on them for power, probably more so. Most archwardens bent the knee due to the Tal'Rach's promise. But Alistair was not so easily fooled. He would not wait to receive their gift but take it by force, which is why he summoned Phymeria to his chambers that evening.

The peacock spirit towered over him. His refusal to formally bow did not escape her. Phymeria's porcelain skin radiated in the flower light, her expression hardened with a quiet rage, and her lips pursed in disdain. Alistair enjoyed watching her squirm as he sat in silence. Phymeria expected a level of decorum from humans, but the archwarden gave her nothing. He would wait for her to speak, furthering the humiliation. Alistair had only interacted with the peacock on occasion. She was one of the more influential Tal'Rach. She and her allies were notoriously cunning, cruel, and vicious, which made her the perfect target.

"Why have you requested my presence, archwarden?" Phymeria asked, finally, exasperation apparent in her crystalline voice. "I hope this isn't about the Nineteenth Edict. We will notify you when we decide it best to announce, no sooner."

"It isn't about that," Alistair knew full well the Tal'Rach had no intention of declaring the next Edict anytime soon. The war against the ram was better for them than any Edict could ever hope to be.

"Then speak before I grow bored and decide to end your pitiful existence," Phymeria drawled.

"I have a question to ask of you, Phymeria," Alistair said calmly. He almost smiled as the Tal'Rach's visage contorted into rage.

"You dare drag me to your filthy study in the middle of the night for a favor?" Phymeria seethed, baring her teeth dangerously. "How could an insect ever imagine disrespecting their goddess in such a way."

"You misunderstand me," Alistair said, speaking rapidly. This next part was crucial if he wanted to keep his head attached to his shoulders. "I have already done you a great favor, Phymeria. All I am asking is for something in return."

The peacock bristled, but her rage ebbed into confused curiosity. Perfect. Alistair had caught her off guard.

"I know of no such favor," Phymeria said, "You must be mistaken."

"There is treachery within your house," Alistair explained, "My spies have uncovered quite the rebellion quelling under your nose. The other Tal'Rach would not appreciate such an oversight."

Phymeria's mouth snapped shut, a large vein bulging on her forehead. Finally, the Tal'Rach understood the reality of the situation. Alistair had leverage on her.

"Those are dangerous accusations, archwarden," Phymeria hissed, "Explain yourself immediately."

"My spies tailed your high priestess, Marikae, to a certain pub. One we suspect serves as a haven for Deviants. Not any ordinary safe house, but the very place Veremund is conducting his operations." Alistair said.

"If you knew where Veremund was hiding, why haven't you raided it? Such an omission of knowledge is treasonous," Phymeria retorted. Alistair almost winced. The stories of

Phymeria were true; she was cunning and above all else, ruthless. Bending her to his will wouldn't be as easy as he'd hoped. "You are grasping at straws, Alistair."

"On the contrary," he gestured to the dozens of letters and diagrams on his desk. "As archwarden, my primary duty is to rout out Deviant threats in my city. After discovering Marikae's treachery, I monitored every single one of your priestesses. I have compiled records of an extensive network your priestesses have operated for years. Smuggling and harboring Deviant refugees. I know that you certainly had nothing to do with such an insidious plot, but I'm wondering if your brethren would begin to question your loyalties if they ever caught wind of this."

"What do you want, Alistair?" Phymeria hissed. He smiled. His tactic had paid off. She was officially in his pocket. Now, he would claim his first prize.

"I told you, Phymeria, I simply want the answer to a simple question," Alistair lied. He wanted more and would squeeze out every last drop from the peacock and her allies. "Why does Veremund want me dead?"

17

The More Things Change

Sarina padded through the temple by the dim Sylvania flower light, careful not to wake the priestesses asleep in their rooms. She spent most of her day assisting Alma in the boarding house and the rest of the evening she was in someone else's bed. These late nights were an unexpected development and relatively new, but something she highly enjoyed. It had been years since she shared a bed with anyone and it was quite delightful, especially with the person she shared it with.

She arrived at her quaint yet simple bedchamber at the end of the hall and lay on her firm mattress, waiting for the day to begin. Sleep was of no concern, and time had ceased to carry meaning, but Alma informed her that over half a year had passed since the Calling, and much had changed. Sarina had changed, especially after learning of Callandra's fate.

Since arriving in Tabulrossa, Sarina had a singular goal: finding and protecting her friends. Sarina's mission had ended with Callandra dead, Beriane safe, and Kez held with Laithe and Veremund. She was listless for weeks, without drive or direction, but soon discovered a purpose among her sisters. Alma brought her to the boarding house, where Sarina could perform menial tasks with the rach's will. Mend minor wounds, thatch weakened roofs, and clean out the wells; it was the least she could do. Soon, the mundane chores bored her. She needed to do more to provide for the Deviants within the city.

Her life as a full-fledged priestess was much more flexible than she could have hoped, allowing her ample free time. Besides occasionally feeding the monstrous Phymeria, each priestess was responsible for her schedule, studies, and destiny. Sarina wanted her future to mimic Marikae's; it was the only viable option. She yearned to be a leader who protected hundreds of Deviants, not a handful. And not only those who resided within Tabulrossa but all of them.

The first hurdle was forgiving Marikae. Initially, she hated the high priestess for breaking her promise and allowing Callandra to die under her watch. However, the more Sarina's anger grew, the more she realized the high priestess was not the object of her resentment. Sarina hated herself for agreeing to train in the temple while she could have been searching for her friends.

Marikae was only one woman. Extremely powerful, but a mortal nevertheless. Moreover, she had hundreds of lives under her protection and scores more that entered the city each Calling. Callandra was one of the few under Sarina's protection. Marikae did not fail Callandra, Sarina did. If Sarina had decided to forgo training and rush into the city, she would be dead alongside Callandra. Unfortunately, she could not train fast enough to save Callandra. Marikae wasn't at fault.

So Sarina forgave the high priestess, though she had yet to

find the strength to forgive herself.

Once she resolved her internal resentments, Sarina threw herself under Marikae's tutelage, learning her vast network, the names of their informants, and the locations of each hiding place and storehouse. She became a student of strategy and how to evade detection by the Tal'Rach and the wardens. With her steely determination and innate talents for leadership, Sarina distinguished herself as an integral part of the underground network within weeks.

Her entire life, Sarina had responsibility thrust upon her. For the first time, she sought it out. And she'd never felt so fulfilled.

Moving about the Undergrowth had grown easier as each day passed. Veremund's avatar was cunning and brilliant. His plan to manipulate Veremund had succeeded better than anyone could have hoped. The archwarden sent most of his reinforcements out of the city and decreased the patrols around the Precipice and Undergrowth, making it much easier for the priestesses to go about their business unnoticed. Establishing new havens in the Undergrowth and restocking them with supplies was arduous, but labor was easy when one possessed the power of the rach.

The morning bell finally rang, and Sarina forced herself out of bed. She had hardly slept but learned to function without rest. Slipping on a fresh set of robes, she set out into the temple for breakfast. The priestesses dined on a pleasant terrace overlooking a manicured garden. Rach lazed about the lavish flowers and sculpted shrubberies, but the priestesses were too busy chatting to notice. Unlike novices, the women who obtained approval from Phymeria were friendly with one another, and their place in the temple was never in jeopardy.

However, the complex social dynamics were quite tedious to navigate. Most women resented the speed at which she gained Alma and Marikae's favor, preventing her from connecting with her new sisters. So she made her way toward the corner where her only two friends in the temple sat. Minora and Beriane.

Beriane joined the temple as a novice the day after she heard the news of Callandra. The death of her lover affected the young woman more than Sarina could have ever imagined. Gone was the petite, bubbly girl who could make light of any situation. In her place was a single-minded, serious woman who wanted nothing more than to learn the secrets of the rach. She reminded Sarina shockingly of herself. As far as she could tell, Beriane held no resentment towards her regarding the fate of her beloved. They spoke of it once, on Beriane's first day at the temple. All she said was. "It wasn't your sword that slit her throat. That sin belongs only to the wardens. You won't have to worry about my revenge. But they will." She progressed faster than any novice before her, including Sarina, and gained Phymeria's approval within weeks.

She joined Minora, who became a full-fledged priestess days before. They were the only two priestesses newer than Sarina. The unspoken laws of seniority and propriety branded all three as social outcasts. None of them cared, however, for they had more important matters to preoccupy themselves with than insipid gossip and temple politics. However, Sarina occasionally noticed Minora peering over her shoulder with a melancholy expression. She didn't blame her for wanting more friends, though she hoped Minora did not regret her choice of companions.

When Sarina was not at the boarding house, she was in the library, outside of Phymeria's detection, alongside like-minded priestesses: Minora, Beriane, and a handful of others. There, they trained themselves in the secret arts to harness the rach's more destructive powers—conjuring fire, lightning, and torrents of wind. There were numerous ways to kill a warden, and they were desperate for the chance.

"I heard you this morning," Beriane retorted as Sarina sat between her two friends. "You always breathed loudly at night, and the temple walls are surprisingly thin."

"You left the boarding house early yesterday, come to think of it. I wondered where you had gone. Have you found yourself a lover?" Minora teased. Sarina blushed and changed the topic.

"How goes the fortification of defenses in the boarding house?" Sarina asked.

Minora had decided to aid Alma at the safe house in the Canopy. She was meek and modest, so charity greatly suited her.

"I was going to ask the same, Minora," Beriane added. Sarina was grateful for the subject change. "There's something in the air; Alistair has held council with Phymeria half a dozen times in the last month. There's no telling what may happen."

Beriane was correct; although Veremund had ceased his attacks, an odd tension formed in the Precipice. The rach could sense it, too. Tavo would often shiver whenever he was inside the temple.

"The preparations are progressing nicely," Minora answered. "We have gathered enough rach for a single priestess to ward the entire complex. Though I hope we won't be forced to, I have heard a myriad of rumors lately. Should we be afraid?"

"We should prepare ourselves," Sarina replied. She did not want to alarm her friend but agreed with Beriane. She sensed the tension within the temple. Something was about to boil over.

"Right," Beriane smiled devilishly. Sarina suspected she desired an outright war with the wardens after Callandra's murder. She hoped nothing violent would ever come to fruition.

They were still drastically outnumbered by the wardens. And what if the temples loyal to the Tal'Rach banded together against them? No. Staying under the radar was essential. It would take years to prepare themselves properly. Perhaps they could even persuade Phymeria and the more lenient Tal'Rach to join them. Alert them to Alistair's scheming and let them dole out divine judgment.

The trio somberly ate their meal, the gravity of their musings weighing heavily on each of them. The supernatural intuition bestowed to women who communed with the rach was unsettling at best, but it was usually terrifying.

Every priestess sensed the same, even those who did not aid the Deviant cause. Apprehensive whispers and nervous glances filled the breakfast veranda. Something was coming.

Minora finished her meal first and bounded out of the terrace, undoubtedly on her way to fortify the boarding house. That left Beriane and Sarina alone, who finished their breakfast in an uneasy silence. Beriane reminded Sarina of her failings as a leader. She wasn't entirely convinced that the younger woman had truly forgiven her. How could she have when Sarina still hadn't forgiven herself?

"What does the day bring you, Sarina?" Beriane asked

cordially. Sarina thought carefully before answering. She did not want to upset her friend and had her own secrets to protect.

"Training in the library this morning," Sarina lied. "Then, heading down to the Undergrowth, a new storehouse is in desperate need of supplies."

"Care to join me for some training before you leave? It's never too late to learn defensive skills," Beriane asked.

Idiot. Sarina cursed herself. Her hastily contrived alibi had proven to be a poor one. Of course, Beriane would be training in the library, honing her destructive talents. She spent more time there than anyone else in the temple.

"Of course," Sarina replied. Her rendezvous would have to wait until after lunch. It was fine; she had left her only hours ago, and she could wait a few more.

"Excellent," Beriane smiled, almost a bit too pleased. That worried Sarina.

Her fears were soon justified, and within an hour, she sprawled on the library floor, her eyebrows singed. She had spent the better part of the morning training with Beriane and the others, almost four dozen in number. Not every woman within the temple knew the true power of the rach, but in recent weeks, their numbers increased. Marikae hoped that soon more than half of her temple would be sufficiently trained in the secret arts.

Given her status as a pariah, only her young companion would spar with Sarina. Beriane had grown powerful in the weeks since her ascension. She could only harness a meager amount of rach, but the energy she gleaned from each was immense. She could easily lift Sarina, holding her fast with a fist made of air.

Beriane used their sparring session to unleash her aggression on Sarina. Nursing a bruised arm, she only hoped Beriane would release everything out of her system today. She wasn't sure if she could survive another skirmish.

Lunchtime was Sarina's saving grace, allowing her to escape Beriane's wrath. She took the opportunity to sneak up the stairs to the higher floors of the temple. Careful to avoid prying eyes, she maneuvered the lavish hallways with Tavo on her heels. Most senior priestesses were busy at lunch, and anyone left in the temple was most likely busy feeding Phymeria. The peacock spirit desired to maintain the illusion of humanity and conducted her feeding times around the priestesses' mealtimes.

Sarina finally reached her destination but stopped abruptly when she touched the wooden doorknob. Three voices conversed beyond the door. One was Marikae's, which was no surprise, as this was the door leading to her private chambers. The other two were muffled but deep—one distinctively male and one female. Men seldom entered the temple unless they were Tal'Rach.

Why was Marikae hosting another Tal'Rach in private? Immediately, she summoned a few rach to her side and harnessed their energy. She wove a delicate veil of shimmering air around her, blocking any eyes from seeing her and ears from hearing her. It was the same ward Marikae used in the library. It was one of the arsenal of tricks the high priestess had taught her in the last few months. Sarina willed the rach to hide themselves; their figures faded into nothing. Sarina could still feel their presence, but they were completely invisible. It was a special bond priestesses shared with the rach that even Tal'Rach could not duplicate.

The door opened after the veil was secured, and Sarina almost choked when she saw who Marikae's guests were. The identity of the first was apparent when she ducked her massive head through the wooden frame, her peacock tail dragging behind her. Phymeria rarely left her chambers and never visited the private quarters of her servants. But her presence wasn't as shocking as the second guest.

He was not a Tal'Rach, like Sarina had presumed, but a human, wearing an emerald cloak and a set of armor more ornamental than functional. It took Sarina a bit to realize who he was, but she had heard too much about this man. Pride oozed from him like a rancid perfume, and he carried himself like a king. Alistair, the archwarden. The most dangerous and bloodthirsty man in the entire world. The reason for so much bloodshed and death.

"Thank you, archwarden, for being so accommodating. I know these are trying times, and you have the full gratitude of the temple of the peacock." Phymeria bowed graciously. It was odd seeing the deity so submissive to a human. Perhaps the Tal'Rach were frightened of the wardens. That would explain the liberal amount of Edicts they passed in the last few years.

"It is my pleasure, Phymeria," Alistair said as if speaking to an old friend. Not an ounce of respect. The Tal'Rach would cast out a priestess if they used a tone half as casual. "I will prepare a full contingent for you at dawn the day after next. There is no need to worry about you or your priestesses' safety, I can assure you."

"Wonderful," Phymeria said sweetly, then shifted her attention into the room and barked. "Marikae, make sure you alert the entire temple. I want every priestess in attendance."

"Yes, my lady," a soft voice responded from inside. "As you wish."

The pair glided down the hallway, chatting cordially; Phymeria ushered her guest to the door. How unusual. Sarina waited, barely able to breathe, thankful for the spirits' protection. Sarina slipped through the open doorway when the peacock feathers were finally out of sight. The room was sizable but cozy, with enough Sylvania light to bathe the entire space in a warm glow. Flowers of every sort grew on the windowsill, which overlooked the spectacular view of the Sanctum itself. Marikae waited pensively in the room's center, hesitating before closing the door. The walls shimmered slightly as the handle clicked shut, veiling the room from Phymeria, like the library. When the door was closed, Sarina dropped her ward mere paces from the high priestess.

"How long have you been eavesdropping on me?" Marikae asked coyly. Unfazed by Sarina's sudden appearance. "And is this the first occurrence?"

"You are too boring to spy on. I know most of your secrets already," Sarina said, sitting on the bed. It was much more comfortable than hers, so she preferred sleeping here over her quarters. The company was better as well. "I only heard the end. Is something happening the day after tomorrow? Should we be worried?"

"Nothing out of the usual," Marikae sat beside her. She smelled like warm nutmeg, and her skin almost sparkled in the soft light. It was difficult to leave her every morning.

"And what is so usual that requires the private audience of the archwarden himself?" Sarina asked, gently kissing Marikae's exposed shoulder. She wanted to reveal more, but she restrained herself. There was always a time and place for such a conversation, and now was the time for questions.

"Around this time of year, the Tal'Rach parade through the city individually," Marikae explained, relaxing a bit on the bed, regarding Sarina intently. It was difficult for either of them to focus when left alone together, but the high priestess carried on. "They visit the burial site of their former priestesses to pay their respects and to make an appearance in the city. Their true purpose is to gather more rach to the temple. We are now the furthest away from a Calling, and the supply of rach we summoned six months ago is beginning to diminish. Whoever can plan their procession first will secure the most spirits to sustain them for the rest of the year."

"But why is the archwarden involved?" Sarina asked.

"You are lucky that I find your curiosity so charming," Marikae chuckled. "Others find it most excruciating. This year is different; there are fewer rach than normal, and the Tal'Rach are still uneasy with everything that has transpired with Veremund. Usually, a contingent of wardens join us, but Phymeria requests an entire legion for her protection today. As well as every able priestess in her entourage."

"Seems excessive for one Tal'Rach," Sarina mused. "Will Alistair join?"

"No," Marikae said. "You've finally learned to ask the right questions."

"That will leave the Precipice exposed. Alistair exposed." Sarina mused. "We should alert Veremund immediately. This is exactly the opportunity he's been waiting for."

"We will later today," Marikae drew closer to Sarina. "But first, we have more sensitive matters to attend to."

Sarina smiled and kissed Marikae's soft lips, pulling her

onto the bed on top of her. Their relationship had progressed gradually, and neither understood their feelings until they made love for the first time. It started soon after Sarina forgave her; her anger towards Marikae receded, replaced by her initial respect for her. After that, they spent most days together, and she rapidly became the high priestess's most trusted confidant, even above Alma. Their conversations soon drifted from the serious to more private subjects. Of their childhood, past lovers, and women they considered attractive, what they had hoped to accomplish in their lives as children, and what they wanted now. Sarina had never met a woman who understood her so intimately, who shared her desires and her goals. They both put tremendous pressure on themselves, yearning to improve the world for people like them and women like them. They were leaders, inspirations, and survivors.

It was only a matter of time before Sarina recognized her feelings for Marikae. Sarina initiated the first kiss, for she couldn't contain her passion or feelings. It had been long before the Fifteenth Edict since another woman touched her.

She lay underneath her lover, exploring her soft skin and gazing deep into her dark eyes. The world faded, and she only focused on Marikae—her love.

18

Broken Promises

Laithe stood on the tunnel's entrance, overlooking the city far below from the side of the Bole. The corridor ended abruptly, spilling out into nothing but empty space high above the Undergrowth. The mercenary clutched his axes tightly, his brow dripping with sweat. He'd spent the better part of the day searching the labyrinth, and night had already fallen when he arrived.

Isam sat on the cliff's edge, legs hanging off the side, shoulders hunched, face downcast. He clutched the metal necklace, sobbing uncontrollably.

"So Veremund told you about Kez?" Laithe asked softly. Dropping his weapons, he sat beside Isam, legs hanging over the abyss.

He was surprised and relieved that Veremund had vacated his avatar's body. Laithe fully expected to confront the Tal'Rach once he found him. And with the rage flowing through his veins, blood would spill. But seeing the man he loved, miserable and distressed, broke Laithe's heart.

"We were fools to think we could change him," Isam

managed between sobs. Laithe wrapped his arms around him in his best attempt to console him, holding him tight. But that only caused the crying to escalate. "I was wrong. He knew our intentions from the start. He would never stop; death and destruction are in his nature. He will never protect. Only destroy."

"You did the best you could," Laithe said, running his fingertips through Isam's hair. Words weren't his strong suit, but he would try anything to soothe his love. "Think about the lives you saved in the last months alone."

"But I couldn't save Kez," Isam whimpered. "If only I were more cunning, I could have seen this coming. I could have prevented this."

"Where is she?" Laithe asked softly. His partner's feelings were important, but almost a full day had passed since Veremund expelled the older woman from the Brazen Leaf. He needed to find her. And fast. "Did he tell you where he left her?"

"No," Isam's voice cracked, trembling uncontrollably. "Kez could be anywhere by now. She could be dead. Do you know what he told me? That her blood is on my hands. This my punishment for deceiving him, for breaking my promise."

"You may have pushed him a little, coaxed him a bit here and there, but you never lied to him," Laithe said adamantly. "He was the one who lied to us. For months."

"Well, I'm glad to have you on my side," Isam's expression brightened slightly, and Laithe's heart soared, elated that his words had a positive effect. But Isam held the necklace somberly. "But it doesn't matter anymore. I severed my contract with Veremund; I am no longer his avatar. He can rot in his mind palace for eternity."

"You were able to escape? I didn't know that was possible," Laithe asked.

"I forced him out. His mind palace isn't in the necklace, or at least not always. It's an extension of him, whether he inhabits his vessel or avatar, it follows," Isam said, pointing to his forehead. "When he possesses me, it's in here. He uses my mind and imagination to create it, to latch his consciousness to mine. It took all my strength, but it's my mind, not his. And he no longer had access to it. I'm done."

With that final statement, he spat on the necklace and hurled it into the air. The metal chain fell into the darkness and out of sight.

"Well, I hope that felt good," Laithe said flatly.

"You must hate me now," Isam lamented, dripping with shame and regret. "I know you loved Veremund, but you must understand what he wants to accomplish. It's not about protecting us. It's never been about that. It's about revenge."

"I don't care," Laithe said, wiping the tears from Isam's cheek. "I had a connection with Veremund, yes, but it was a sexual heat. Purely physical. I admit that I believed it to be love. But it will never be that. Especially after what he did to Kez. But you gave me a reason to live, Isam, and made me a better man. I love you."

"Big ole sap." Isam chuckled, kissing Laithe sweetly. "You used to be so stoic. Look at you now. And I love you, too. No one has ever made me feel safe as you have."

"Well, that's settled," Laithe said. "We are better off without the ram. But what is next?"

"We find Kez," Isam said. "And then we have to make sure—"

The words escaped him, his mouth hanging in horror as he peered down toward the Undergrowth. Laithe followed his gaze and nearly choked. An imposing purple mist rose from the forest floor below, roiling angrily, culminating in a sizable violet knot. The shape of the ram became more evident as it hurtled upwards along the great trunk. Tendrils of purple smoke curled toward them. Isam scrambled to his feet and fled. Laithe retrieved his axes, and hurtled down the tunnel after him.

But Veremund was faster.

The ghostly form of the Tal'Rach poured into the tunnel, right on their heels. They only advanced a hundred paces until it overcame them. The purple mist blinded Laithe. He almost swung his axes, but he refrained for fear of hitting Isam.

Isam screamed.

His body seized violently, and the mist poured down his throat. He choked and flailed his arms, but nothing would stop the purple cloud's progression. Isam's eyes widened in pure horror. Laithe grabbed his convulsing frame and held him tight. He yelled in vain, powerless to prevent Veremund from taking hold of his partner.

Isam's body shifted, grew, and transformed into Veremund once more. The ram spirit towered over Laithe, leering down with a bitter smile barely visible in the dank tunnel.

"So it seems you have made your choice, after all," Veremund said. "Isam has corrupted you."

"He ended your contract, Veremund. He is no longer your avatar," Laithe said, his entire body shaking with rage. With hatred. "Now release him."

"I am sorry, little one, I cannot do that," Veremund replied, equally upset. "He BROKE our contract. He betrayed me and will now fulfill his promise whether or not he cooperates."

"He did everything you ever asked of him," Laithe roared, voice echoing down the winding corridor. "He only desired you to fulfill your end of the bargain. Alistair is losing; you almost have your opening. Don't be angry at him that he tried to manipulate you, just as you manipulated us."

"Oh, I wasn't mad about the two of you conspiring against me," Veremund chuckled dryly. "I knew what you were doing from the start. But I admit, my initial plan was failing, and Isam's seemed the better option. And the nights we spent in my mind palace were worth the sacrifice. But no. I punish Isam because of what he hid from me."

"I don't care. Release Isam now," Laithe growled.

"Aren't you curious about what he withheld from us?" Veremund asked. "Don't you want to know what Isam concealed from me? Concealed from you?"

"No," Laithe said, grasping his ax handle tight. "Release him."

"I WILL NOT RELEASE HIM. HE IS MINE TO COMMAND," the Tal'Rach bellowed. The sheer force of the sound shook the tunnel walls. "He broke our contract, Laithe. He withheld a crucial piece of information from me. The priestesses came to him yesterday. Today, the peacock spirit embarks on a special pilgrimage to the Undergrowth, accompanied by a huge force of wardens to guard her. In only a few hours, Alistair will be vulnerable. It is the perfect opportunity to strike. Isam intended to let it pass by and allow Alistair to live. Unfortunately for him, I can sense his every thought and feeling. He cannot hide anything from me. So, he must atone for his insubordination."

"You desire to slay the archwarden more than anything. Why?" Laithe asked.

"That doesn't concern you. All that matters is that I am going to the Precipice to end it. It's what we've been working towards. Come on now."

"No," Laithe remained defiant.

"Don't you care about me, little one?" Veremund softened. He leaned forward until their noses almost touched. He was seducing him, as always. It was how he controlled him. Laithe understood that now. "Haven't you wanted to make me happy? Nothing will make me happier than this."

"No. I cannot love someone who does not care for anything but himself," Laithe said. "I have Isam, and he has me. Now find another body to use, get your revenge, and leave us alone."

"Well, that puts us in a precarious predicament," Veremund retorted icily. "Here is what will happen. I will go to the Precipice. I will kill Alistair. Then, I will leave Isam's body. You can either join me to carry Isam to safety afterward or remain here and allow him to die when I abandon him. The choice is yours to make."

"Why are you so cruel?" Laithe breathed.

"BECAUSE LIFE IS CRUEL!" Veremund exclaimed. "LOVE IS CRUEL! Give Isam a chance, and he'll break your heart. They all do it in the end. Love makes you weak and vulnerable. Now shut the fuck up and follow me."

Without waiting for a response, the Tal'Rach stalked down the tunnel, leaving Laithe speechless, clutching his axes. Veremund was right; the ram spirit would survive regardless of his mission's outcome. The Tal'Rach would move on to another host whether he succeeded or not.

It was Isam's life that hung in the balance.

Laithe had no choice. Alistair must die today, and Laithe had to help make that happen. Six months ago, he would have been happy to rush to his death for Veremund's whim, but now all he cared about was saving Isam.

The labyrinth was pitch dark; Laithe abandoned his Sylvania lantern on the ledge during the commotion, so he stumbled forward blindly until he collided with Veremund's hulking frame. The Tal'Rach did not require light to see, but a miniature ball of blue fire flickered into existence once he noticed Laithe was following. Veremund's satisfied grin stoked Laithe's rage into a wildfire. Laithe would have lodged his ax deep into the monster's skull if Veremund wasn't actively possessing Isam. He resisted his urges, reminding himself that Isam's safety was the only reason he joined this mission.

The pair crept through the labyrinth silently, climbing upwards with renewed vigor. Dawn, the most advantageous time to strike, was approaching fast. Laithe was exhausted after a full day and night of searching the tunnels; his vision blurred with fatigue. Regardless, he mimicked the Tal'Rach's breakneck pace. Nothing would stop him from following, not even his tired body.

They arrived at a tight bend in the labyrinth that Laithe recognized well. Turning left would lead them to the village, and the path on the right would lead them to the Brazen Leaf. Instead, Veremund continued straight, choosing a tunnel that gradually slanted upwards. They climbed higher in the Bole than Laithe had ever dared venture.

It finally dawned on him. The labyrinth spanned the entirety of the Bole and contained a direct path to the heart of the enemy. "This tunnel leads to the Precipice," Laithe said flatly.

"To the basement of the Sanctum itself," Veremund said.

"Seems like the wardens would have discovered a network as extensive as this, especially one built into the base of their operations." Laithe pointed out.

"This labyrinth isn't naturally occurring," Veremund rebuffed. "Only the village hollow and the tunnel that leads to the Brazen Leaf. I created the rest. And I wouldn't be so foolish to complete the tunnel to the Sanctum."

Of course. The tunnels were too smooth, too neat to be natural. The Tal'Rach built this tree themselves. They would have known of a vast network of tunnels beneath their feet. Not only did the labyrinth act as a line of defense and a means for escape from the village, but it gave Veremund direct access to his ultimate prize—killing the archwarden. He had been incredibly single-minded. Every battle, every lie, every action led them to this moment.

Soon, they reached a dead end. Laithe assumed they were high in the Bole. Veremund extinguished his flame, leaving them in pure darkness. There was a strange groaning sound in front of them, and Laithe imagined the wood parting in front of them like water.

A tiny circle of light appeared a dozen paces before him, and he could see once more. The hole expanded until it was wide enough for Veremund to pass through, which he did. Laithe shuffled through the portal into a compact storeroom filled with swords, green helmets, shields, bows, and arrows, all expertly crafted and in perfect condition. They indeed were in the Sanctum.

Laithe tensed. Footsteps echoed beyond the storeroom door. He drew his axes, ready for battle. Veremund lay a giant hand on his shoulder, urging him to relax. The footsteps grew louder, and shadows passed underneath the door. Laithe waited for the rusting handle to turn. Instead, the feet disappeared, and the footsteps faded.

"Good, we arrived in time," Veremund whispered when the footsteps disappeared. "We have two minutes to reach the private study before the next cycle of guards. Follow close."

Veremund appeared gleeful, like a child given a new toy. He had been waiting for this, ever since Laithe tackled him off the bridge during the Calling. Probably longer. The Tal'Rach opened the door softly and paused for Laithe to follow before closing it silently. Like a great cat, he stalked through the vast, ornate hallway.

Laithe followed silently, gripping his axes, attempting to ignore the majestic structure. He had never seen anything so intricate, so beautiful. The Tal'Rach had constructed almost every building in this city, but they must have spent years crafting this tower. Veremund crept through the halls briskly, not hesitating at any stair or junction. The Tal'Rach knew precisely where to go, obviously familiar with the Sanctum. It was foolish to question Veremund's familiarity with the building. It was the wardens' stronghold and the center of the Tal'Rach's power, and he was a Tal'Rach. Something Laithe always forgot. The great spirits were supposed to be benevolent, nonpartisan, calm, and loving. Veremund possessed none of these traits.

They climbed ever further upwards, nearing the apex of the Sanctum, Laithe's legs begging for mercy. They narrowly avoided half a dozen guards, the sound of metal-booted footsteps echoing in their wake. Veremund knew the patrols by heart and avoided them with ease. He had planned every footstep like an intricate, deadly dance.

Finally, they came across the door to the archwarden's

chamber. Laithe recognized it due to its grandeur. For a military leader, Alistair was not modest. An intricate frieze was carved on the door. It depicted noble wardens defeating grotesquely shaped humans that could only be Deviants. It was enough to make Laithe's stomach turn.

Veremund inhaled deeply and rotated the door handle slowly, careful not to make a sound, revealing a great hall beyond. Grand steps led upwards to an additional floor. It wasn't a chamber but an entire mansion built on the top of the Sanctum. Two guards lounged lazily at the foot of the stairs, chatting among themselves quietly.

A swift death fell upon them both. Veremund closed the distance between the door and the guards in three heartbeats, slashing their throats in unison. He caught their corpses before they hit the ground and set them down gently.

The Tal'Rach didn't hesitate before climbing the stairs, no doubt towards Alistair's study. Laithe hoped the archwarden was there; otherwise, he had climbed thousands of steps for naught. He followed the Tal'Rach upwards and down the hall, barely catching up before Veremund burst through the door at the end of the hallway.

To both of their relief, the archwarden sat behind his mahogany desk on the far side of the study. Illustrious tapestries hung on each wall, and an enormous plush rug covered the floor. The archwarden glanced up as the broken door landed in the middle of the room. He looked older up close, without his armor, tired.

"Veremund, so nice to see you," Alistair crooned. He wasn't surprised by their intrusion. Laithe did not detect a hint of fear in him. No one could be that arrogant in the face of an assault. Not unless...

"It's a trap!" Before the words left his lips, the air shimmered around them, revealing a dozen armored wardens on either side of the room. Swords drawn. Four figures stood directly behind Alistair who caused Laithe's blood to turn to ice.

A broad-shouldered, stately man with a lion's head. Lykos.

A sneering woman with a snake's tail. Ducarix.

A muscular man with short bull horns. Behemoth.

A woman with the ears of a wolf and vicious claws. Ylvara.

They were Tal'Rach. Ancient. Powerful. Every human in existence knew their names. Any one of them could be a match for Veremund on their own. But there were four of them.

"You have been quite the thorn in our side, Veremund," the lion, Lykos, said. His words rumbled like distant thunder. "And after such a gift we bestowed upon you."

"Quite a foolish way to conduct yourself," the serpentine Ducarix chimed in, her tone deep and rich. "Besmirching the name of the Tal'Rach is something we do not take lightly."

Veremund paid them no heed, focusing on the archwarden before him, blue flames forming in his palms. They had planned this, expecting Veremund to arrive at this very moment. They were prepared for him. Alistair's calculating eyes glinted with victory.

The ram spirit bellowed and unleashed two columns of hot blue fire, bathing the room in flame. Wardens shrieked as their skin melted, running in horror. Veremund ignored the dying soldiers and leaped at Alistair, but a violent torrent of wind flung the ram backward. The giant Tal'Rach collided with Laithe, and the pair flew out into the hallway beyond in a heap.

Laithe's head bounced against the floor, and darkness

overtook him.

239

19

Mourning the Dead

Burial grounds were common in the Undergrowth; there were more corpses than living humans on the foundation of Tabulrossa. The morbid complexes were an excellent place to hide Deviants, especially the older tombs near the north. The dead who rested here were ancient, their names lost to the ages, too worn to be legible. Scarcely any mourners visited the decrepit northern mounds, so they sat in disrepair, covered in moss and steadily decaying.

The grave sites on the city's western edge were ancient but had been properly maintained. The structures here were built of stone, surrounded by lavish gardens, and high root walls shielded the entire complex from the public. These tombs were the resting place of the Tal'Rach's most faithful servants: priestesses, wardens, and notable citizens who gained the favor of the great spirits throughout the centuries. They were all commemorated and immortalized in stone. It was a sacred place, heavily guarded and avoided by anyone with common sense. Even priestesses circumvented this place, save for an annual trip arranged by their Tal'Rach.

Sarina glided through the ancient tombs alongside her sisters, over a hundred strong. Wardens flanked them on either side, double their number. The procession spent the better part of the morning leisurely descending the Bole and winding through the Undergrowth, a painstaking process with such a great host. Phymeria led the column, regal as ever, smiling at every citizen who gawked at her splendor and beauty. Marikae followed the Tal'Rach alongside a small contingent of wardens and the senior priestesses. Alma was notably absent from the procession, and Sarina could only assume she was serving as Phymeria's avatar.

The remaining priestesses trailed behind silently in the dim light; even the novices joined, wide-eyed at the rear. Rach flew above, but the peacock spirit instructed the women to refrain from gathering rach as they normally would and to wait until their journey home. Sarina willed Tavo to conceal himself, though she could sense him scurrying between her feet. She also sensed additional rach floating invisibly about their ranks.

It dawned on Sarina that she wasn't the only priestess with a companion similar to Tavo, though she had never witnessed such a connection.

Minora and Beriane strode beside her, both tense with apprehension. The newly ascended priestesses were situated near the parade's rear, directly ahead of the novices. Sarina's initial assumption that the temple lacked a strict hierarchy proved false. Phymeria regarded seniority above all else, which was never more apparent than during this procession.

The priestess ahead of Sarina halted, and she nearly collided with her. A murmur washed through the procession, and the formation broke apart. They had arrived at their destination:

a giant tomb marked by hundreds of peacock statues. The priestesses gathered close at the foot of the steps of the ancient monument.

Phymeria had already climbed the stairs and overlooked her servants with a kind smile. The senior priestesses flanked the imposing Tal'Rach. The surrounding priestesses jostled Sarina as the crowd tightened, each woman desperate to reach the stairs to hear their mistress more clearly. The wardens were positioned towards the rear, standing guard over the sacred ceremony.

"We come to this place to remember," Phymeria said, her melodic voice carrying across the burial ground, bouncing off the stone. Her priestesses stared upwards in wonder. "We journey to this hallowed ground to pay our respects to those who have come before. We thank them for their service. Most importantly, I thank you, my precious daughters. The glory of this city would not be possible if it weren't for you. So, I am here today to recognize your work. And your treachery."

Before she finished her monologue, Phymeria spread her arms wide, and the six senior priestesses behind her choked, violently thrust into the air by their necks. Several women gasped. Sarina was one of them. She elbowed her way to the front, focused on Marikae, whose face was pale, struggling against her invisible bonds.

"Some of you have arrogantly presumed you could act without my authority. My most trusted attendants foolishly thought they knew better than me and conspired in secret to undermine my divinity," the Tal'Rach hissed, her pretty features twisted into a hideous mask of rage. She addressed the half dozen women hanging behind her. "You miserable wretches thought you could hide this from me? A Tal'Rach?

No one's thoughts can escape me, especially my own avatars, in whose minds I dwell. Yes, there are many secrets that I have kept from you, for you are nothing more than my playthings. And you will soon see how disposable you are."

She flicked her wrist.

The head of a senior priestess, Grizelda, twisted violently. Her body crumpled lifelessly to the floor. The crowd erupted in horror, and novices attempted to flee, but the wardens had closed ranks. A wall of shields surrounded them on three sides—the steps where Phymeria leered at them, the fourth. The wardens corralled the women in a tight knot, and the shield wall receded. A second row of soldiers marched forward, bows drawn and aimed at the priestesses. The wardens were not here to guard Phymeria but to trap her treacherous priestesses.

"The time has come for you to repent for your sins or pay with your lives," Phymeria announced. "If you kneel before me now, I will spare your pitiful lives, and you shall earn my forgiveness. I do not fault lambs who follow a twisted shepherd. Now kneel before your goddess."

Sarina locked her knees, glaring hatefully at Phymeria. The women around her held fast. A few novices knelt, but the rest stood in unison, defying their mistress. The peacock spirit's delicate lips twisted in a snarl. Despite the Tal'Rach's power and gravitas, the priestesses understood that she depended on them. She could dispose of a handful but couldn't afford to lose her entire host of servants. The other Tal'Rach wouldn't aid her with such a significant loss; without her source of sustenance spoon-fed to her daily, she would wither and die. Despite their deification, the Tal'Rach were not truly immortal, and their longevity came at a cost. The older a great spirit was, the more they must consume to survive. Marikae had told each woman this, and Phymeria's wild expression confirmed it.

"Very well, then," Phymeria gestured to the senior priestesses floating behind her. "Kneel, or they all die."

Not a soul moved. No one bent the knee.

Phymeria snarled viciously and flicked her wrist again.

Sarina smiled.

Nothing happened.

The Tal'Rach swung around with a guttural scream. The five remaining senior priestesses hung in midair, unharmed and chanting softly. They dropped to their feet one by one, forming a tight formation behind the Tal'Rach. Phymeria lashed out, but a shimmering ward enveloped them, blocking the peacock's blows. Marikae calmly led the women past the great spirit, who flailed at the magical barrier, and down the steps to join their sisters below. A flock of rach materialized above the senior priestesses. They had prepared for this outcome.

"KILL THEM ALL," Phymeria exclaimed, and the wardens obediently loosed their arrows at the crowd of priestesses below.

The deadly bolts flew at them with a violent fury. But the arrows halted paces from the group, and the air shimmered, holding them in place.

"Ready yourselves, sisters!" Marikae cried. The ward now hung over the entire host of priestesses. A thunderbolt flew from Phymeria's talons, crashing harmlessly against the shimmering shield. "Show them the true power of the rach!"

Sarina summoned the candle in her mind, allowing Tavo to appear. Dozens of rach materialized as the women chanted.

An otherworldly glow illuminated the burial grounds. A host of rach flew towards them, answering their call.

The wardens fired their arrows relentlessly, but each one halted harmlessly amidst the shimmering air, joining the dozens of projectiles trapped within the priestess's ward.

The arrows shined softly and rotated until they pointed in the direction they had come. Towards the wardens.

Sarina summoned a ball of fire, as did Minora and Beriane. The balls of light floating in their hands.

Marikae shouted, "Release."

The arrows unleashed.

The wardens screamed. Dozens fell to the brilliant volley, mowed down by their own attack. Some fled in fear, but most charged at the priestesses.

But the women were ready. Those who were trained in the secret arts situated themselves on the edges. They protected the untrained, who cowered in the center of their ranks. Almost half of their number had been successfully instructed by Marikae and the senior priestesses. And the unfortunate wardens were about to feel their wrath.

Balls of fire, bolts of thunder, and gusts of wind buffeted the charging wardens while hundreds of rach glowed majestically over the battlefield, blissfully unaware of the carnage below.

Sarina hurled her fireball toward the nearest warden. His screams of terror were extinguished as flames consumed him. She pivoted and pushed through the fray, attempting to reach the stairs and Marikae. The high priestess challenged the peacock proudly, arms outstretched, keeping Phymeria at bay with a shimmering ward. The Tal'Rach howled in fury, unable to descend the steps.

The remaining senior priestesses were preoccupied with

the surging wardens around them, abandoning Marikae to subdue the Tal'Rach alone. Sarina's heart sank as Phymeria took a beleaguered step forward and pushed against the magical barrier. It was withering rapidly. She was too powerful for one priestess to contain.

Sarina fought a warden off with a brutal barrage of punches. She hadn't forgotten her combat skills from her previous life. She had to reach Marikae before Phymeria could.

The high priestess sank to her knees. Her shield shattered.

The Tal'Rach barreled down the steps, summoning deadly lightning, fingers curved into sharp talons.

Sarina bellowed and called upon Tavo. He shimmered, and a fireball exploded against the Tal'Rach's sturdy frame. The peacock spirit screeched in pain as the attack sent her sprawling on the stairs. Sarina joined Marikae and readied another fireball.

"Stop!" Marikae pulled Sarina's arm. The fireball sputtered and vanished. "You will kill or injure Alma with attacks like that."

"How do you propose we defeat Phymeria without attacking her?" Sarina yelled over the deafening sounds of battle.

"She is like any common rach, Sarina," Marikae said. "Only older and stronger."

Sarina furrowed her brow at the cryptic response but did not have the luxury to question her. The Tal'Rach clambered to her feet, shrieking with rage. Phymeria had already doused the blaze, her skin and clothes unfazed by the flames. She lunged forward with a battle cry.

Before Sarina could respond, Marikae lashed out, chanting loudly. Phymeria drew closer, talons ready to strike. The great Tal'Rach dropped to her knees and clutched her throat.

She coughed violently, and tendrils of smoke flowed from her maw.

Sarina gasped. She finally understood.

Marikae was forcing the Tal'Rach to vacate her avatar as if she were an ordinary rach.

Phymeria was still incredibly powerful, clashing against the high priestess's will. The monster thrashed and lashed out with her talons, catching Marikae in the shoulder. Horrified, Sarina chanted fervently. Focusing on the glowing mist gathered around Phymeria's chin, she forced it upward from Alma's body. The peacock spirit howled in horror as more amber smoke poured out.

It was working.

Still, the Tal'Rach resisted, fighting until the bitter end. Fortunately, nearby priestesses took notice of the battle and encircled the monstrous spirit. Over a dozen women chanted in unison, combining their will to force the spirit out of Alma's body. Together, they were more powerful. Phymeria knew that. She flailed savagely, slaying the advancing women with her terrible talons. For every fallen priestess, two more took her place.

The Tal'Rach howled; her body became limp, the mist poured out of her violently, and a petite figure collapsed in the aftermath. Sarina attempted to restrain the amber mist with her mind, but it was too fast for her. The great mist formed into a peacock and flew toward the Canopy.

Sarina cursed as she watched Phymeria's escape. They could defeat her. With their combined forces, they could command her like a common rach. But how? She was a force of nature, a deity. How could priestesses harness a Tal'Rach like a common spirit?

A sword cut Sarina's dress, glancing off her shoulder. She cried out in pain, whirling to confront her attacker. But Marikae was quicker. The high priestess lashed out with a thunderbolt, sending the armored man flying. He slammed against the stone wall of the tomb and crumpled to the ground, lifeless. Sarina smiled at her lover and directed her attention to the battle surrounding them.

She sighed. The fighting had already ended. The warden Marikae had just dispatched was the last remaining enemy. The rest were either smoking piles on the ground or escaping into the Undergrowth. Against the full might of the temple of the peacock, even a few hundred wardens did not stand a chance. The women cheered.

Following Marikae, Sarina examined the battle, searching for survivors. Despite their victory, the ambush took its toll on the priestesses. If it weren't for the high priestess's intervention, none would have survived.

It took a brief moment to assess the situation fully. Almost a quarter of the priestesses had lost their lives during the skirmish, and half of the survivors were wounded. Sarina gazed upon the corpses of her sisters, tears of anger flowing freely. Glaring up into the Canopy where Phymeria fled, she silently swore revenge.

Marikae ordered the survivors to aid the gravely injured up the steps, and the remaining senior priestesses healed the more benign wounds. Sarina accompanied Marikae up to the top of the stairs, where Alma lay in a heap alongside half a dozen badly injured women.

The senior priestess was stirring and seemingly unharmed but white as a sheet. Sarina's heart dropped. Minora lay in a pool of blood next to Alma, her torso covered in deep wounds, four gashes caused by Phymeria's talons. Sarina knelt on the ground next to her friend and willed the rach to heal her, but nothing happened. Tears streamed forth as Minora gasped for air. Sarina cradled her head in her lap and rocked it sweetly. She tried to heal her once more, but it was in vain. She pulled Marikae over, but the high priestess shook her head.

"It is too late for her, I'm afraid," Marikae said quietly. "Poor thing, I didn't even see her near Phymeria."

"She is too young," Sarina sobbed. Minora shuddered and fell still. "She did not deserve this."

"None of them did." Marikae wavered momentarily but was strong as iron as she gestured at the other fallen priestesses. Besides Alma, the survivors were only able to save two gravely injured women. Sarina felt the urge to vomit. "Reserve your grieving for later. Quiet your mind. I'm about to reveal the final secret of the rach. Something that only the oldest priestesses and the Tal'Rach themselves know. Watch Minora closely."

Confused, Sarina obeyed and calmed her mind, focused solely on Minora. The young woman's eyes were closed, skin already paling with death, chest still. It was too much for Sarina. Her focus wavered, sorrow threatening to swallow her whole.

Then it happened.

It started slowly, and it was so subtle that Sarina almost missed it. But Minora's skin shone. A faint light covered her entire body, then it shifted, gathering at her chest. The light grew brighter still as a translucent red orb emerged from Minora. The ball of energy floated an inch above her pale skin for a heartbeat. Then it shuddered and changed. Two wings formed from a tiny cylindrical body. It was a butterfly. The ghostly insect fluttered its wings before landing on Sarina's finger.

"She…how…rach?" Thousands of questions bubbled out of her in an incoherent stream. Marikae did not need to answer any of them, for she understood the truth. "The rach are the spirits of the dead."

"Precisely," Marikae said. "A spirit is a human's soul once their body has failed."

"How did I not notice sooner? I have seen plenty of people die," Sarina asked.

"That was before your training," Marikae said. "And death is rare in the Precipice. Only priestesses old enough to experience it firsthand know the truth. Until today."

Sarina studied the battlefield; scores of newly formed rach floated from the bodies of priestesses and wardens alike. The surviving women gawked at them with a strange mix of shock, wonder, and horror.

"Does that mean the Tal'Rach…" Sarina said, finally understanding the full horror of Tabulrossa. How had she missed it?

"Are simply old rach who prey on weaker spirits," Marikae said. "Like all spirits, they were once human. They were never gods."

"And the Edicts?" Sarina asked. The Tal'Rach never really cared about enforcing them with their priestesses, so there was only one reason why they created them in the first place.

"They fabricated the great lie of Deviants to create new rach. Nature was not fast enough to keep up with their appetite," Marikae said grimly. "The Tal'Rach manipulated people's fear to persuade them to massacre innocents by the thousands."

Sarina bent over and vomited. It had always been the

Tal'Rach pulling the strings. They butchered countless to maintain their immortality. She heaved again, emptying her stomach, her eyes watering and tongue sour. Marikae held her hair until her heaving ceased.

Sarina regarded the high priestess with newfound respect. This was why Marikae had trained these women. This is why she created an entire network to help the Deviants of Tabulrossa. And she had kept this terrible secret for all of these years.

Marikae rose to her feet and finally addressed the others, all in similar shock and grief.

"Hear me, sisters! Look around at the dead. See what Phymeria and the Tal'Rach have hidden from you," Marikae called. "They are not gods. They are human. Flawed. Greedy. Ambitious. Weak. This world we live in is for their benefit and theirs alone. The Edicts. The wardens. This city. But together, they are no match for our might. You witnessed that yourselves. Together, we can defeat them."

The women cheered, and the rach above glowed brightly. Sarina cried along with them, glaring at the Precipice towards the cause of all of her pain and suffering. Alongside her sisters, she would end it.

20

A Lover Scorned

Laithe lay in a plush bed, pleasantly surprised that he was neither dead nor trapped in a Sanctum cell. However, his relief did not last long. He recognized this expansive bed situated in the center of a circular room. Giant windows on every wall overlooked an overly perfect landscape.

He was in Veremund's mind palace.

"Isam!" Laithe yelled. He willed himself out of bed and into the castle halls, searching for his lover.

The ethereal palace was empty, and Laithe was alone within its heavy stone walls. No Isam, no Veremund. He froze, the reality of the situation dawning on him. The mind palace either existed within the mind of the Tal'Rach's avatar or in the vessel itself. Veremund's necklace was lying far below in the Undergrowth. If Isam wasn't in the mind palace, Veremund was not currently possessing him. If Isam had complete autonomy over his body, he could not have pulled Laithe here. No. Veremund no longer possessed Isam because the Tal'Rach had found a new host. Laithe.

The memories of the Sanctum flooded forth. Laithe was

in a study filled with wardens. The archwarden hid behind his desk, protected by four Tal'Rach. The room was on fire, bathed in Veremund's blue flames. The ram was flung backward, crashing into Laithe and throwing them both into the hall. Laithe could remember the excruciating snapping as the impact broke his ribs and legs. His arms twisted under him, leaving him broken and powerless. Veremund paid him no mind, lunging into the room.

Sounds of battle ensued, but Laithe could not see anything. The ram spirit bellowed in agony. Laithe recalled a heavy mist covering his vision, pouring into his nose and mouth, suffocating him—Veremund's spirit.

The ram had possessed him against his will. Veremund was probably using Laithe's body to continue the battle against the archwarden. He paled with a sudden realization. There was only one reason why Veremund left his avatar and jumped into Laithe. Isam was dead.

He angrily called for Veremund. The monster had to answer for what he had done. The castle walls rumbled, and Laithe bellowed louder. This was his mind, not Veremund's. He could expel the Tal'Rach like Isam had done, though that wouldn't stop Veremund from possessing him again, as he had done to the poor musician. But Laithe's only thought was on Veremund, commanding him into the mind palace. To make him answer for his crimes. For taking Isam's life.

The walls around him crumbled, but the mystical prison entrapped him. He did not care. He relentlessly called Veremund towards him. Seeking vengeance against the ram spirit consumed his every thought.

Unseen hands pulled his body into the air. The invisible force flung him forward, hopefully towards wherever the

Tal'Rach hid. Instead, it led him to the last place in the mind palace he expected. The mysterious door he had almost opened on his first visit—the forbidden chamber.

Without hesitating, he opened the door. A furious light immediately shrouded him. The invisible vortex ripped him from the corridor.

Then, he was in a gloomy hallway. The floors, walls, and ceilings were all made of wood instead of stone. He instantly recognized where he was: the Sanctum.

The door was an escape route.

This must have been how Isam broke free of the Tal'Rach before. And why Veremund guarded it so fiercely. It wasn't dangerous, after all. Yet another deception. He inspected his hands, which appeared normal; he had regained his body. But the ram spirit was nowhere to be seen, same for the archwarden and the other Tal'Rach. He was no longer in the study; the battle must have carried him further into the tower. He didn't care. He wanted to locate Veremund and enact justice for Isam.

The sound of footsteps caused Laithe to jump in surprise. A warden hurried toward him. There were no doors, intersections, or stairs between him and the approaching man. There was nowhere to hide. His axes had been lost in the shuffle, rendering him defenseless. The warden had not noticed him yet, so he seized the element of surprise and rushed the man. The poor fool was too distracted to see him as Laithe collided with the guard at full force.

Instead of crashing into the man, Laithe phased through him as if he were a ghost. The warden appeared unfazed and unfettered by the odd interaction. Puzzled, Laithe shouted, but the warden did not hear him. He examined his hands once more. There was nothing strange about them. The warden disappeared around a corner, and Laithe bolted in the opposite direction. He held little interest for the odd, ghostly warden. He needed to find Veremund.

But when the warden exited the hallway, the world fell away, and Laithe lurched into the void. He landed after a few disoriented moments.

Laithe was still in the Sanctum corridor, directly behind the strange warden. He acted as if Laithe did not exist; Laithe disregarded the odd behavior and escaped into the stairwell ahead. He bolted past the phantom and quickly descended the stairs. He only traveled one flight before the void enveloped him. He materialized beside the warden once again.

This place could not be the real world.

Was this part of the mind palace, or was Laithe now a spirit himself? Is this what the door's purpose was?

He decided to follow the guard, for he had no better choice. The unknown force transported Laithe to the warden's side whenever he lost sight of the man. The warden was a bit younger than Laithe, with short raven hair and a dull expression. Mundane and uninteresting. Nevertheless, Laithe followed him through the Sanctum. They passed more wardens, who greeted the man cordially but completely disregarded Laithe.

The warden departed the busier passages into a barracks of some sort. Young men and women lounged in common areas, entering and exiting scores of compact bedrooms. Finally, the young warden stopped at a random door. Instead of entering, he paused until the hallway was empty before knocking. A tall and thin man with wispy hair opened the door and greeted him with a wry smile. The door closed in Laithe's face. But suddenly, he was whisked inside the room beyond.

It was a tidy bedroom with plush beds on either side of each wall. It was much nicer than the bunks Laithe had seen crammed in the living quarters he passed. A handsome man nearing his middle years lounged on one of the cots, he stirred slightly when the guest entered.

"I have news from the archwarden, captain," Laithe's new companion said, addressing the warden on the cot.

"Oh?" The man, apparently an officer, sat up and smiled wryly at both men. "I am anxious to hear it. Aren't you, Luxo?"

His tall, wiry roommate loitered near the door, busying himself with his armor. "My stomach is rumbling. I better go to the mess for some grub. I'll be on patrol tonight, so I won't return until morning. Have fun, you two."

"Bye, Luxo," the captain said, rising from his cot. He barely waited for the door to close behind Luxo before kissing the younger warden.

The warden gave in to the kiss. The two men were quite familiar with one another. Then he pulled back, and his eyes darted frantically at the door. "Luxo knows about us? But we've been so careful. What if he tells my captain? He'll surely expel me from the order if he discovers our relationship."

Laithe wrinkled his brow. Curious as to why this man only feared mere expulsion as a consequence of his torrid affair rather than death.

"Don't worry, Martin," the captain chuckled. "Luxo is a good friend, and he's had his share of affairs with recruits. It's not as uncommon as you may think."

"So this is merely a fling, then?" Martin asked, raising an eyebrow. "Well, if that's the case, I may see if Luxo is interested in dinner in the Canopy tomorrow."

"You fool," the captain pulled Martin on the bed beside him and kissed him sweetly. "You are much more than a quick fuck, my love. And if I catch you with Luxo, I'll have to castrate the both of you."

"So romantic," Martin said sarcastically. However, his cheeks flushed with excitement. "I'm glad you're so protective of me, Alistair."

Alistair. Laithe was frozen with shock. The hair, the jaw, and even the smug air of superiority were unmistakable. He was the archwarden, only much younger. Where did the odd door in Veremund's mind palace take him? Not only was the archwarden younger, but he was a Fourteen.

It finally clicked for Laithe. Alistair's age, Martin's relatively cavalier attitude toward their relationship, and how no one could see or hear Laithe. This must be a dream of some sort. Or even a memory, of a time before the Fourteenth Edict.

"Of course, you are my one and only, Martin," Alistair said. He was not much older than the young warden but oozed confidence and charisma. Martin was powerless against his spell and succumbed to his lust.

Laithe hunched awkwardly next to the bed as Martin and Alistair peeled their clothes off, his cheeks flushed as they made love right before him. He faced the wall out of respect but stole a glance or two. He was only human.

Hours passed, and the pair finally subsided. Laithe was impressed by their stamina and took mental notes for his repertoire. He now had an arsenal of new tricks to perform on Isam.

Isam was dead.

Laithe was immediately overcome with sorrow, remembering the stark truth.

Finally, the two lovers lay intertwined, and Martin drifted to sleep. The world faded, and Laithe was thrown into the abyss once again.

He landed on his feet on a balcony overlooking the Bole, standing in the center of a dining area on the side of a pub. It was fancier than any establishment Laithe had ever visited. There was even cloth on the table. A bard sang spiritedly from a small stage in the corner, and couples sat together alongside the railing. Martin and Alistair occupied the table at the far end. Both had aged years in a single instant. The two spoke in hushed tones, both brimming with excitement.

"I wanted to deliver you the news myself," Alistair said. "Your promotion is already in process, but you'll be a captain by the end of the year."

"Does that mean what I think?" Martin asked pensively.

"That we no longer have to hide our love?" Alistair asked in return. "Yes, Martin, and I want your hand in marriage as soon as it is official. I cannot wait any longer."

"Captains may be able to marry, but I hear old Mags is retiring as archwarden," Martin said. "No doubt you will be next in line for the title. You will still be my superior even if I am a captain."

"If I am archwarden, then the rules will no longer apply," Alistair smirked. "Just our love. What do you say? Will you marry me?"

The captain pulled a tiny black box from his pocket and set it on the table. He opened it, revealing a beautiful necklace inside. It was a metal chain with a tear-shaped pendant inlaid with a violet gemstone. It appeared identical to the one Isam and Veremund carried.

What was this odd dream?

Tears welled in Martin's eyes. He reached to hold the captain's hand but recoiled sharply, remembering they were in public. "I love you, Alistair. More than I ever thought I would love anyone. Of course, I will marry you."

The world faded again.

Thousands of wardens surrounded him in a spacious arena, wedged between Martin and another warden grunt. The warden hadn't aged since the last vision. Laithe scanned the magnificent room; every warden in the city must have been in attendance. He suspected the theater was in the center of the Sanctum, the apex of the Tal'Rach and warden's power.

A group of figures stepped onto the stage before the crowd. The Tal'Rach. All of them. Laithe recognized four from the ambush in the archwarden's study earlier that day. Or had that been years ago? Or years from now? Time did not make sense anymore.

The group gathered around a giant pole in the middle of the stage, and Laithe's heart skipped when he realized what it was—the Edicts. A wooden column made of thirteen disks sat on top of one another, like the ones built across the world. Only this one was massive. The Tal'Rach sang, and the pole grew again; a new, fresh cylinder of unmarked and unblemished wood sat at the top. A more diminutive form stood on the stage among the Tal'Rach, who gazed upon the magic with the rest of the wardens. Laithe squinted and recognized Alistair, now wearing the cape and ornate armor of an archwarden. He'd achieved the highest office in the order since the last vision, even before Martin obtained the rank of captain.

The Tal'Rach continued to sing, and the side of the column burned, carving deep canyons into the pillar. When the smoke settled, Laithe recognized the words too well. Men who loved men. The Fourteenth Edict. This vision was no dream at all. He was witnessing history unfold before him. These were memories. Martin's memories.

"The Fourteenth Edict," Alistair called, staring at the freshly carved column. "The first under my watch. Each man and woman here shall uphold it and find those who the darkness corrupted."

The archwarden faltered as he read the Edict.

"Men who love men."

Alistair was supposed to be the most powerful man in the city, in the world. And he was discovering the Edict alongside the rest. The wardens had nothing to do with the Edicts, only the Tal'Rach.

The world faded once more. Laithe was almost accustomed to the jarring flights through time and space. He fell on his knees when he landed in a chaotic scene. Martin screamed, fighting off three wardens who pinned him down next to his cot. His roommates remained still, soberly watching the struggle unfold. No one moved to help him. Tears streamed down the warden's face, begging for some aid, crying out for Alistair. But no one listened. Once he stopped fighting, a fourth warden entered and tied his wrists behind him.

The room around them spun, and Laithe felt dragged alongside Martin as the wardens carried him down the Sanctum's halls. The young warden's body became limp, despondent. Finally, his captors brought him into the vast stadium at the heart of the Sanctum. The room was empty, save for the stage. A gallows loomed next to the Edict totem, and a dozen wardens milled about.

Two nooses hung from the gallows. One man already

occupied the first noose, staring at the stage floor, completely dejected. The second noose was empty.

It was for Martin.

Alistair grimly watched from the platform's edge as the warden thugs dragged Martin to the empty rope. Laithe's stomach dropped once he recognized the first prisoner on the gallows. Luxo. The archwarden's old roommate. The wiry captain was gagged with a dirty rag, devoid of emotion.

"Alistair, what is happening?" Martin pleaded as his captors forced him into the noose. A swift kick to the stomach cut his words short.

"Do not dare address the archwarden, Deviant scum," the warden beside him spat.

"Deviant?" Martin scoffed.

"Multiple witnesses reported accounts of you and former captain Luxo engaging in activities forbidden by the Fourteenth Edict," the warden responded. "You have been sentenced to death to free the world of the Ae'Rach that now inhabits your body."

"This is ludicrous. Under whose authority?" Martin asked. "I haven't done anything with Luxo. Who claimed they witnessed us?"

"Me," Alistair said, emotionless. "The Archwarden of Tabulrossa. First of the Wardens and protector of the Tal'Rach."

Martin stared at the archwarden, and his expression twisted from fear to pain to absolute consuming rage. Laithe felt every bit of it as he hovered above the gallows like a ghost, unable to intervene. Even if he tried, there was no use. These events had already transpired.

"Luxo wasn't my lover. It was—" Martin would never

finish the sentence. The platform under his feet opened. The fall snapped Luxo's neck immediately, but poor Martin's remained intact. His declaration was replaced by choking as he dangled from the noose, staring at Alistair until the world faded.

Laithe was not spirited away but remained in pitch darkness. Martin's memories still rolled around in his mind, and Laithe finally understood. The world erupted as a ghostly violet specter sparked into being. It was hooved with curved horns—a ram. The void dissolved and Laithe and the ram returned to the Sanctum next to Martin's corpse. The gallows were vacant; Alistair, the wardens, and Luxo were all gone. But fourteen robed figures encircled the body—the Tal'Rach. Two dozen priestesses made their own circle around them, and the air above shone bright with hundreds of rach. The priestesses chanted loudly, and the rach above descended on the ram all at once. They dissolved as they touched the spirit. Martin's spirit. Now a rach. The purple ram grew as the waterfall of spirits fell upon him.

"Welcome, Brother," a Tal'Rach with a lion's head said. Lykos. "Your torment has granted you our sacred favor, and we have bestowed our most precious gift upon you. May the world be introduced to Veremund, the ram spirit. Long may he live."

The other Tal'Rach and priestesses chanted in unison, repeating Lykos' last words. The ram spirit howled and possessed the nearest priestess. Her body shifted, grew muscles and horns, and transformed into a form Laithe was familiar with. He looked a bit like Martin, but each attribute was larger and more perfect as if he were the ideal version of the young warden. But Veremund did not smile. Instead, his eyes bore into Laithe, causing him to jump. It was the first time anyone had noticed his presence since he opened the forbidden door.

The world faded away and Laithe's body threatened to tear apart as he rocketed through the void. Suddenly, he was standing in front of the door in the mind palace, next to Veremund. He gazed at Laithe mournfully.

"So what do you think, little one," Veremund said, "now that you know the truth? Do you understand me, finally?"

"Where is Isam?" Laithe bellowed. Regardless of what he had witnessed, he cared little for the nuances of the ram's past.

"In the archwarden's study, I suppose," Veremund said, jaw clenched. Laithe's apathy appeared to sting him. The Tal'Rach assumed his tragic memories would elicit Laithe's sympathy. He was mistaken.

"You abandoned him," Laithe growled. The castle walls shook with his fury. "Left him to die. Kept me from saving him."

"The Tal'Rach broke your body during their ambush; both you and Isam would have died," Veremund stepped closer and gently held Laithe by the shoulders. "And I chose to save you, my Laithe."

"Do not start this, Veremund," Laithe yelled, twisting out of his clutches. "It was between a trapped avatar and a broken one. You chose the easier of two options, not because you love me more."

"Fair," Veremund sighed. "But we have escaped because of my decision."

"Where are we, then?" Laithe asked.

"Back in the labyrinth, waiting for our next opportunity to

strike Alistair," Veremund said.

"How did you get past the wardens and Tal'Rach so easily?" Laithe asked.

"The wardens were preoccupied," Veremund explained. "The priestesses have attacked the Canopy. The Tal'Rach are at war with their servants."

21

The Nature of Spirits

Phymeria's boarding house was engulfed with flame. Black smoke billowed out of the windows, blocking the sun. Armed wardens scurried about the grounds, chasing Deviants out of the building and into the courtyard. Scores of poor souls already lay dead among pools of blood. Sarina could see perfectly fine without the sun, for hundreds of rach surrounded her and her sisters as they sprinted down the avenue toward the burning safe house. She called upon the rach, summoning balls of fire and loosing them upon the nearest wardens. Sarina would not allow the death of a single additional Deviant. Not if she could help it.

After the battle at the tomb, the priestesses regrouped under Marikae's command. They were vulnerable in the burial grounds; speed was essential for survival. Phymeria would undoubtedly alert the Sanctum, and within an hour, the holy ground would be swarming in the collective might of the Tal'Rach and wardens. The battle-ridden priestesses wouldn't stand a chance against such a force, and the peacock's temple was no longer safe. So, Marikae dispersed their number into small groups, allowing them to efficiently maneuver the city streets and gather themselves in various safe houses in her vast network.

Marikae sent Sarina to Phymeria's boarding house along with Alma, Beriane, and two dozen priestesses. She divided the rest and sent them on their way, one by one. However, she did not assign herself to a group and refused to accompany Sarina. The high priestess would not listen to Sarina's pleas or answer her questions. She alluded to a task she had to fulfill alone, leaving Sarina in the Undergrowth with a worried heart.

Sarina obeyed her lover, however, and escorted Alma to the Canopy. To their horror, they soon witnessed the extent of Phymeria's ambush. The Tal'Rach had targeted not only the priestesses but each of their safe houses. Their group encountered half a dozen patrols setting fires to compromised havens. Phymeria's mental connection with the senior priestesses had proven to be catastrophic. Within the day, the wardens would destroy the entirety of Marikae's network and massacre every Deviant in Tabulrossa.

They saved who they could, slaughtering the patrols of wardens and leaving priestesses behind at the larger safe houses to heal and defend the casualties. Those untrained in the secret arts were tasked with gathering rach so those who were trained could channel their power. Before today, Sarina had been worried about the priestesses Marikae hadn't already recruited for her cause. Their devotion to the Tal'Rach could have proven a liability. But Phymeria's betrayal destroyed that trust. Sarina was surprised at how quickly her sisters adapted, though she could sense their palpable fear and trepidation.

Their destination was Phymeria's boarding house, home to the most significant number of Deviants in all of Tabulrossa. Sarina gritted her teeth when she approached the burning complex. If only a single priestess had been present, they could have easily warded the haven against such an attack.

Alma dashed into the blazing courtyard without a word, arms outstretched, Beriane on her heels. Sarina swiftly dispatched the remaining wardens on the street. When she entered the chaotic courtyard, hundreds of dormant rach materialized and glowed violently. A rush of wind filled the square, whipping Sarina's hair into a frenzy. Water fell from the sky and doused the blaze. Wardens poured in from every doorway, drawn by the blinding light.

While Sarina hesitated in bewilderment, Beriane ran past her and summoned half a dozen lightning bolts, blasting the nearest wardens. The green-clad survivors rushed at the priestess with bloodied swords drawn. They had no idea what they were about to endure. The robed women chanted, and another volley of brilliant, deadly bolts of light filled the courtyard. Within a heartbeat, dozens of steaming corpses and broken armor littered the ground.

"Gather up the ward," Alma called. "There is no telling if—"

A vicious tempest ripped the front gate from its hinges, cutting the senior priestess's sentence short and sending the women, corpses, and surviving Deviants flying. Sarina crashed into the well at the courtyard's center. Dazed and gasping for breath, she climbed to her feet as another blast of violent wind berated her once more. She held onto the well, using it to steady herself. Most others in the courtyard weren't as lucky, lying in bloodied heaps near the far wall. Sarina's attention, however, was directed to the gate and the street beyond.

Two figures strolled down the boulevard toward the boarding house, a man and a woman. Their size alone betrayed their identities, but Sarina had seen both Tal'Rach often in the temple of the peacock as personal guests of Phymeria. Behemoth and Ylvara. The bull and the wolf. Behemoth relaxed his body as if recovering from a blow. It was evident that it was he who had summoned the destructive gails. Ylvara stepped forward, and red flames danced in her hands. She must have been the one to set fire to the building. They'd waited for the priestesses to enter before making their presence known. When it was too late to run.

It was another trap.

Fire erupted from Ylvara's claws, two flaming serpents dancing toward the courtyard. The attack would incinerate the entire complex instantly. Sarina focused on her internal flame, emptying her mind of everything but Ylvara's blaze. With a loud chant, she called out to the rach—not just a few but every single one within reach.

Almost blinded by the brilliant light surrounding her, she harnessed its power and imagined a ward surrounding the safe house. The air around the gate shimmered, and Ylvara's flames evaporated when they struck it. Behemoth bellowed and unleashed another tempest, but it, too, was negated by Sarina's ward.

The pair of Tal'Rach snarled and launched a bevy of elemental assaults at Sarina, but the ward held fast. She focused on the shining air and chanted, hearing several voices nearby: Beriane, Alma, and a handful of others. She dropped her concentration and glanced behind her. More priestesses, over a dozen in number, joined the chanting circle.

The rest evacuated the survivors farther into the safety of the complex, tending to the wounded, and eradicating the remaining wardens.

The Tal'Rach were mere paces from the ward when Alma ceased her chanting. She gestured to a pair of young women no older than Minora.

"The two of you stay and keep the ward raised. Such a task typically requires a single priestess, so it shouldn't be much trouble." The girls nodded grimly, their initial apprehension soothed by Alma's matter-of-fact reasoning. The senior priestess beckoned the rest as she approached the open gate. "Everyone else, with me."

Alma strutted across the destroyed courtyard with a flock of rach in tow; stretching out her arms, she summoned a ball of fire in each. Beriane followed closely, her hands brimming with lightning. Sarina chased after, and Tavo leaped onto her shoulder. He glowed brightly as she summoned her fire. They stepped through the ward unfazed and unleashed their fury upon the Tal'Rach.

Ylvara roared as her skin melted, and she slashed at the nearest priestess. The raven-haired woman fell with a screech, replaced by two more. It was fourteen against two, but the rach floating behind the priestesses numbered in the hundreds. Two more priestesses fell to the violent frenzy, but the women successfully repelled the Tal'Rach.

Alma outstretched her arms, and a glowing rope materialized, lashing itself around Behemoth's right wrist. Its other end fastened to the ground next to him, holding his arm in place. He grunted and pawed at the ghostly bond, but a second rope appeared and captured his free hand. His muscles bulged as he pulled at both ropes, crying out in frustration and pain. The bonds frayed, threatening to break, but Sarina joined alongside Alma, summoning more ropes to bind the bull. Beriane and the others replicated the same bondage, fastening the wolf spirit before she retreated. Eleven priestesses remained standing, six around Behemoth, five around Ylvara. It was slim margins, and the ropes flickered against the Tal'Rach's desperate thrashing, but they managed to hold them fast.

Less than a dozen priestesses subdued two Tal'Rach at once. It was preposterous, but soon, the world would realize the sheer power hidden within the priestesses.

The ropes continued to fray. A woman to Sarina's left collapsed in exhaustion. Their power was not enough.

"Sisters! We need your assistance!" Alma called, turning to the boarding house. Agonizing moments passed, and the remaining priestesses strained under enormous pressure. Finally, four more women emerged from behind the ward. Alma tutted. "We will have to make due. Pull them out, as we did with Phymeria. Slow and steady; we don't want them escaping. Start with Behemoth."

The four newcomers chanted, and Behemoth choked and seized, like Phymeria had. Sarina did not recognize a single one of the new priestesses, they must have been untrained. They may not have been able to summon fire or wind, but they could command the rach with their chants. Puffs of emerald smoke expelled from Behemoth's maw, but the Tal'Rach resisted. It wasn't enough. Alma dropped her reins and joined the newcomers. Sarina groaned at the added pressure. Focusing, she called upon more rach, strengthening the bonds. More smoke billowed out, but Behemoth remained whole.

"Beriane, I need you," Alma ordered. The petite priestess

dropped her reins and began to chant. Behemoth bucked against the onslaught, but Alma progressively pulled the bull spirit from his avatar.

A flurry of motion jarred Sarina's focus. Ylvara broke from her newly weakened bonds and lunged directly towards her; fingers transformed into nasty claws. If she released her bonds, Behemoth would surely break free and join the onslaught. Her body tense, Sarina accepted her fate. The claws were a few paces from her when she heard someone scream. Beriane cast a powerful squall directly at Ylvara. The lupine Tal'Rach was flung into the air, caught up in the torrent. The wolf grunted as the blast of wind pushed her sideways. Beriane held her arms aloft, and the gust changed directions, dragging the screaming Ylvara between two clusters of buildings and off the edge of the branch road. The Tal'Rach plummeted to the Undergrowth below. Her howls grew faint as she disappeared into the darkness.

"Quickly, before she returns," Alma barked, and the priestesses who once chained Ylvara joined her, Beriane, and the others around Behemoth. The Tal'Rach had regained his spirit during the distraction caused by the wolf. But now, he was powerless against the priestesses. He groaned and bucked in terror. Nevertheless, the priestesses pulled out his true form like a weed from the soil. Slowly, the green mist pooled above Behemoth's head, growing larger and larger. Alma expertly directed it upward, gathering it in a messy bundle of emerald smoke. The last bit of mist leaked from Behemoth, and his form reverted to a mousy priestess. "Hold him! Release the avatar!"

Sarina obeyed and shifted her focus upward to the orb of mist, which shuddered violently, struggling to break free.

But Alma was too quick. She warded the air around the Tal'Rach, now a formless blob, trapping him in place. Once Alma formed the ward, the priestesses relaxed. The barrier needed only one woman to maintain it. Alma displayed talents Sarina never knew existed. What was the actual limit of the rach?

"What now?" Sarina remained calm, staring in awe at the senior priestess's craftsmanship.

"We destroy him," Alma said calmly.

"And how do we accomplish that, exactly?" Beriane asked, catching her breath.

"His power, like every Tal'Rach, comes from the poor rach they consume. Their power adds to theirs, increasing their lifespan and strength," Alma said somberly. "But it takes years for their prey to assimilate fully. Examine the orb, push past his form, and you will see."

Sarina obliged. The Tal'Rach was one spirit, but she could feel hundreds, no thousands trapped inside. The surrounding priestesses gasped. They also sensed it.

She focused on one, a golden crow. It was scared, weak, trying to flee. Sarina connected with it to harness its power but could not find any. The Tal'Rach had absorbed it completely. She called upon Tavo and willed him to pull the poor crow from the emerald quagmire. The crow struggled and floated to the surface, but an emerald tentacle dragged it back into the depths.

Behemoth was resisting.

Clenching her jaw, Sarina harnessed every free rach within her range and pulled on the crow. The green mist roiled in a rage, but Sarina was more determined. In a fury of blinding lights, the crow burst free and flew into the swarm of rach above.

"Excellent, Sarina," Alma said. She turned to the women. "Follow her lead, free the rest. Rid the Tal'Rach of his stolen power."

The priestesses chanted in unison, mimicking Sarina. They pulled rach after rach from the Tal'Rach: a silverfish, a flamingo, a rhino, a gorilla, and dozens of shapeless and nameless creatures. After each rescue, the green mist howled and receded. What was once the size of the boarding house was now no larger than Sarina herself, now the shape of a young bull. The more rach freed from its belly, the calmer it became.

Alma dropped her arms, and Behemoth floated to the ground. The priestesses gasped and summoned defensive elements, but the senior priestess raised a calming hand.

"There is no need, sisters," Alma said. "Our task is complete. This spirit is no longer Behemoth, the bull titan, but an ordinary rach."

"Where is Behemoth's spirit, then?" Sarina asked, eyeing the bull cautiously. The spirit was no more significant than Tavo and pranced around the women gleefully.

"That is his spirit," Alma explained. "All Tal'Rach begin as ordinary rach until the great spirits select them to join their ranks. By our power, of course. Common rach have no memory of their human lives. No part of their original self remains unless they transform into Tal'Rach. Only then do they become human once more, the thoughts, memories, and emotions of a human, with the power of a thousand rach they consume."

"So now he is harmless, like the rest of them?" Beriane asked.

"Yes," Alma said, clearing her throat. "But we have no time for a lesson. We must retreat into the boarding house before Ylvara seeks revenge. Or dispatches the entire Sanctum in her stead."

The priestesses obediently hurried behind the safety of the ward. The courtyard beyond buzzed with survivors. Many eagerly helped the wounded, recovering from the invasion. Alma promptly set to work, barking orders and sending the uninjured priestesses to various tasks around the safe house. The priestesses had lost almost a fourth of their number during the battle but arrived in time to save the majority of the boarding house's residents. Sarina estimated that more wardens lay dead than the other two groups combined.

She spent the following hours tending the wounded and re-pairing doors. Ylvara never returned, nor did any warden, for that matter. Regardless, the boarding house was constantly guarded by two trained priestesses. The day drew on, and finally, Sarina mustered the courage to ask Alma a question that had been on her mind since later that morning.

The senior priestess was near the well, lifting debris from the water with rach-powered air. Sarina joined in the effort, pulling the remaining shards of wood from the well. She pulled Alma aside when the task was complete and waited until the others were out of earshot.

"May I ask you something?" Sarina asked.

"Leave it to you to ask questions during a crisis, girl," Alma said but then sighed and leaned against the waist-high wall. "Go ahead; what answers do you seek?"

"So Behemoth could have been anyone before the others claimed him? A harvester, a beekeeper, a soldier?" Sarina asked.

"Yes, we all become rach one day, floating along in the world until eternity," Alma said.

"But how do we know that?" Sarina pressed. "Can you know who a rach used to be by looking at it?"

"Yes," Alma replied. "If you focus on them hard enough, you can access their memories to see who they were. We've withheld this skill from you for obvious reasons. It is a breach of privacy with the rach. They are the dead, after all, and we must respect them. However, their memories may be the key to explaining the special connections some of us possess with certain rach."

Sarina followed the senior priestess's gaze to her feet. To Tavo. Alma's explanation confirmed her steadily evolving theory. She had always felt familiar with the cat, as if she had known him since the first he led her to safety. If Alma's claim was correct, then Tavo must be someone she had known in his previous life.

She peered at the blue cat and into his big, sweet eyes. Sarina pressed her consciousness forward, focusing only on Tavo. The world melted into a blur of obscure images, floating around her like a swarm of bees. She focused on one image.

She was sprawled on the ground, clutching her throat. It was not her, of course. This was the memory of whoever Tavo had been before.

She wasn't shocked to see her own face looking down at her. Dirt smudged her cheeks, and her hair was in a tight, nappy braid. She crouched, eyes wide with horror and sadness. Beriane huddled next to her, and Callandra shrieked in terror. Behind them loomed colossal circular gates carved from an imposing root wall. It was the day they arrived in Tabulrossa. The day of the Calling. She did not have to witness anymore to comprehend whose memory this was. Who Tavo was during his life.

Benjin.

The young, naive man had been so lively in the face of such turmoil and tragedy. He had died due to her poor leadership. Despite all of that, he saved her life. Somehow, he had garnered the strength to find and guide her to the temple of the peacock. She had spent months searching for her old companions, and one of them had been beside her all along. Tears threatened to fall, and she wished she could scoop up the small rach and comfort him.

"You said they can't remember who they were," Sarina said, concentrating on Tavo. "But how do you explain him."

"There is much we do not know about the rach," Alma replied. "But in my experience, the stronger the priestess, the stronger her bond with her departed loved ones. And you are one of the most powerful women in the gift I have ever seen. Your sheer will allows him to hold onto some part of his old self.

Sarina began to reply, but the priestesses by the front gate shouted alarmingly. The two women raced toward the ward, ready for battle. But the intruder by the entrance was neither Tal'Rach nor warden. Instead, it was a young novice covered in sweat and blood. Sarina did not recognize her, and she had spent quite a bit of time with the fledgling priestesses these past months. The girl was also a stranger to Alma, who stared at her warily.

"Who are you?" Alma ordered. "Speak quickly, girl. More pressing matters require my attention."

"Y-Yasmine," the girl whimpered. She was terrified and exhausted. "Novice from the temple of the spider."

"Explain yourself, child," Alma snapped.

"Marikae sent me to send you a message," the young priestess said, panting. "She gathered us, any priestess who would listen, to the temple of the peacock. Marikae showed us the true nature of the rach. My master, Archades the spider, attacked, and she revealed to us who he truly is, a cannibalistic common rach. The remaining Tal'Rach discovered us and are laying siege on your temple. I barely escaped. The Tal'Rach are so strong. She sent me to fetch you, to bring back as many as I could find."

So, the high priestess's mission was to galvanize the sisters and strengthen their numbers. They would need them after Phymeria's priestesses had been divided and depleted.

"How many of you are there?" Alma inquired.

"Hundreds from every temple," Yasmine replied. "But few of us know how to perform the miracles Marikae displayed."

"Very well," Alma said, standing up and brushing the dirt off her robe. "Beriane, accompany this girl to our hiding places; they were sure to be ambushed like we were. Aid them and send any survivors you find to the Sanctum. For the rest of you, prepare yourselves. Who is prepared for a third battle?"

<h1 style="text-align:center">22</h1>

<h1 style="text-align:center">A New Defense</h1>

The castle wall crumbled and fell as Veremund tackled Laithe through it. Such a blow would have been fatal in the outside world, but this was not reality. This was Laithe's mind. Both Tal'Rach and avatar were equals.

Tossing the Tal'Rach aside, he punched the ram with all of his might. His fist connected with Veremund's jaw, sending him flying. He crashed into a nearby tower. It shook and groaned as it collapsed.

Their battle lasted an eternity—or a series of heartbeats. Time had lost meaning in the mind palace. Most of the castle was already in ruins. Veremund roared and descended from above, unfazed by the latest attack. He pounced on Laithe, and the pair tumbled around the stones. Neither felt fatigued, and neither felt pain. But Laithe had to overpower the great spirit somehow. It was the only way to regain his body, punish the ram, and find Isam. If the poor man was even still alive. He shoved the likelihood of Isam's death from his mind and focused on the task—defeating the ram spirit.

The pair brutally struggled amid the ruins. Veremund

smiled, displaying his enjoyment of the savage dance. Only months ago, Laithe would have succumbed to lust, and the battle would have devolved into passionate sex. But that was before he met Isam, who had changed his life forever.

Isam.

Laithe shoved Veremund and regarded his opponent carefully. Somehow, Isam had overcome the Tal'Rach, dispelling the ram spirit from his body. But it wasn't by force. That was not in Isam's nature. He likely used his wits to outsmart the Tal'Rach. Laithe did not possess that sort of cunning or intelligence. But his usual method of brute force was proving ineffective. He would attempt the unthinkable and talk his way out of this situation.

"Have you finally given up?" Veremund goaded Laithe back into the fray. "I see that you're thinking. It's not your strong suit."

"You asked me if I understand you. After witnessing your memories," Laithe replied. "But I don't. You're pathetic."

The Tal'Rach bristled, and the sky above them grew dark with thunderclouds. It was working. Laithe had never seen such a fury in his ex-lover before. He had struck a nerve. Excellent.

"You witnessed my true love betraying me. I was sent to the gallows by his order, and you think I am pathetic?" Veremund asked, deathly quiet. "I thought if anyone would understand me, comprehend my pain, it would be you, Laithe. I foolishly thought you would appreciate my desire to make Alistair suffer."

Laithe's ploy had achieved the desired results, and the Tal'Rach was succumbing to his emotions. Now for the next move. Talking was similar to a battle, only with words.

Though inexperienced with such discourse, Laithe would use any tool available to him.

"I don't understand why you care more about a man who tossed you aside like trash for his ambition than two men who truly loved you," Laithe said.

"Care more about Alistair?" Veremund scoffed. "I gave the two of you everything, and all I wanted was to end that bastard's life. You were never really intelligent, but I never thought you to be this stupid."

"It is more than that; revenge has consumed you, Martin," Laithe said, enjoying the sting on the Tal'Rach's face when he used his human name. "If that doesn't prove that you are still madly in love with him, I don't know what will. It's why you could never fully give yourself to Isam or me. It is why you abandoned Isam to die."

"You two never really loved me, not the way Alistair did," Veremund said, choking back tears. It was working. "Isam only used me to protect his little village. The brat wouldn't have looked at me twice if it weren't for my power. And speaking of power, that was all that attracted you. Do you think you would have loved me as Martin? As a young, foolish warden?"

"No, I do not know this, Martin. But I do know who you have become. And I loved you for it," Laithe said honestly. "I have never seen someone so ferocious, determined, or captivating. I loved you from the moment I saw you. No one has ever understood me like you. Or so I thought."

Laithe caught himself, realizing he was divulging more than he intended. He wasn't sure if he'd ever been this vulnerable with Veremund. Expressing his innermost feelings felt unnatural. His cheeks flushed bashfully.

"But then you fucked Isam," Veremund growled. "And he twisted you against me."

"He wanted to use our connection to convince you to fulfill your promise," Laithe admitted. "But that doesn't mean he ever loved you any less. He said he had never met anyone who made him feel safer, more alive. That's why he gave half his life to you. You were the one who betrayed him, and you understand what a lover's betrayal can do to a man."

"I never knew you felt that way," Veremund said, tears cascading. He stepped closer, but Laithe withdrew.

"It is because you were too focused on your hatred for Alistair," Laithe said. He had begun to cry, too. "We could have had everything together, the three of us, but you chose your vengeance instead."

"What would you have me do, little one?" Veremund asked, and Laithe's heart fluttered. Was the ram serious? He must start using his words more often.

"Get out of my body so I can rescue Isam or recover his remains," Laithe said adamantly. "You can take revenge, but please leave us alone."

"No, I will not take another avatar," Veremund stated. Laithe's fists tightened, ready to continue the battle. But the Tal'Rach's expression softened once more. "However, I will help you recover our Isam. It is the least I can do."

"I do not want you inside of me anymore, Veremund," Laithe objected. He still did not trust the Tal'Rach. For all he knew, this was a bluff, another ruse for the ram to achieve his ultimate goal.

"I won't need to possess you to help. I will need a vessel," Veremund said; the sky above the mind palace cleared, and the fake sun shone upon them.

"Isam cast your necklace deep into the Undergrowth. It would take days to find it," Laithe pointed out.

"I don't require that, anything metal will do," Veremund said. "Like your axes."

"Alright," Laithe said, not wholly understanding the ram's plan. "But our only goal is to find Isam and bring him home. If you see Alistair, you can do what you will, but I will not help you further."

"Very well, little one," Veremund said. Without warning, he leaned in and kissed him, soft, sweet, and intimate. Laithe almost succumbed to the kiss, but he restrained himself. "Thank you, Laithe. For showing me a glimpse of true love. You and Isam deserve happiness."

Laithe gawked at him, stunned. He was flung into the void before he could respond. One moment, he was in the mind palace facing Veremund; the next, he was alone in pitch darkness. He took a step forward and grunted as he collided with something; pain lanced across his forehead. The sound of his cursing echoed against solid walls. It was a tunnel. And he felt pain.

Laithe had returned to his body.

He carefully inspected himself, assessing his current physical state, and was relieved to discover his body fully healed. The Tal'Rach's power mended the broken bones, torn skin, and bruised flesh. It was limited to mortal wounds, which Laithe was thankful that he did not suffer such an injury. As a consolation, both axes lay safely secured to his belt.

Laithe squinted as a brilliant light illuminated the tunnel. His vision adjusted, and he saw a ghostly purple ram floating before him. The ram motioned to his weapons. Remembering what Veremund mentioned about metal, Laithe drew the ax on his right and held it out for Veremund.

The purple mist swirled and descended on the ax, consuming the metal blade until no smoke remained, leaving Laithe in pitch darkness. He waited impatiently in utter silence. He could not navigate the labyrinth without a lantern or Veremund's fire. He hadn't fully thought this plan through.

The ax shone brightly, and Laithe jumped, almost dropping it. He stared in awe as the metal roiled and bubbled as if made of liquid. The ax blade grew and shifted its shape, the wooden handle popped off, and Laithe caught the falling ax head before it clattered to the floor. He yelped in surprise as the metal grabbed his hand, consuming it. He clawed at the silver liquid to free himself of the flowing alloy.

But to his horror, the metal seeped up his arm to his shoulder and sunk into his skin. His arm itched, but he felt no pain. He examined his flesh and saw an intricate tattoo in the place of the liquid metal—one of a ram leaping over a field of Sylvania flowers. Inspecting the glowing ink closely, Laithe furrowed his brow. How was a tattoo more valuable than an ax? The tattoo transformed again, the liquid metal pouring from his arm and forming in his palm. Then the metal moved again, shaping itself into a hefty battle ax. He felt its power brimming, though he wished the handle was longer. He gave a start when the ax complied and lengthened its shaft.

"How do you like my gift, little one?" a voice asked. Laithe looked around. He was alone. It was in his head. "Do not worry. You're in total control."

Veremund was still inside the ax, but after forming into that strange tattoo, the Tal'Rach could feel Laithe's will, and Laithe could sense him in return. He practiced his newfound ability, reshaping the ax head, turning it into a scythe, a mace, a broadsword, and any shape he could imagine. Although the ax was his weapon of choice, changing its form in the middle of combat could be quite useful.

Footsteps echoed against the tunnel walls, and Laithe and his ax moved as one into a defensive position. Laithe gripped the metal handle tightly as the light from half a dozen lanterns spilled into the dim corridor.

A flash of green armor entered Laithe's vision. He lunged forward, swinging the impossibly enormous ax in the tight space. The metal shifted as it arced against the tunnel wall, avoiding the wood altogether. The warden screeched in surprise as the giant ax cleaved her in half. Her torso slammed into the floor with a loud clang.

Grunting, Laithe lifted the ax and willed the shaft in the middle forward, forming it into a spear. The spearhead shot out like a viper and impaled the next warden in the eye. As he withdrew the spear, the two moons of the ax head roiled of their own volition, forming themselves into malleable, serpentine blades. The swords arched violently, stabbing the remaining four wardens, their screams cut short by the terrifying blades.

"Seems like you have some control, after all," Laithe said as he stepped over the bodies, raising an eyebrow.

"Only to aid you, little one," Veremund responded. "Now, we must leave before reinforcements arrive."

"They must have pursued you into the tunnel during your escape," Laithe observed. "They were ready for a fight."

"No, we are further down than that," Veremund said. "This is the path between the Brazen Leaf and the village. The priestesses' attack must have prompted the entire Sanctum to assault every safe house along the Deviant's network. Nothing escapes the Tal'Rach's knowledge, not even our village."

"How far are we?" Laithe whispered as footsteps echoed through the labyrinth.

"Forget them," Veremund said. "We must find Isam as soon as possible. We won't be able to save both."

"Isam loves that village," Laithe said, following the sounds of footsteps. "He would never forgive me if I allowed it to fall, even to save him. I can't fail him."

"You will fail him either way," Veremund pleaded. "At least he will be alive to forgive you eventually."

"And what if he's already dead?" Laithe asked, approaching the sound of footsteps. "No, we stay and defend. It is what Isam would want. It was all he ever wanted."

He waited for the Tal'Rach to interject or to force his body in the opposite direction. But nothing happened. The ax merely lay dormant, emitting a soft glow. Laithe soon recognized where they were, only two turns from the village's secret tunnel. He heard screams.

Rushing forward, he veered around a corner and collided with an unsuspecting warden. The armored man was quicker and scrambled to his feet, slashing downward at Laithe with a growl. Veremund's metal twisted and parried the warden's blow at the last second. Laithe clambered to his feet. The warden wasn't alone. Six more soldiers in green sprung from behind, swords drawn.

The warden at the rear grunted and fell in a heap. Laithe wrinkled his brow in confusion; he hadn't used the ax, and neither had Veremund. A knife sprouted from the forehead of the nearest warden; she fell silently, dead before she hit the ground. Laithe urged the ax blades forward, and they sank into the remaining wardens. Within a few heartbeats, half a dozen bodies littered the murky tunnel.

A woman materialized out of the shadows, brandishing a pair of knives.

"Good to see you, Kez," Laithe said, smiling. "I thought you were dead by now."

"It'll take more than a temperamental spirit to end me," Kez scoffed. Laithe knelt and collected her knives from the corpses. "The dolt left me at the pub entrance and didn't even bother finishing me off. Been wandering this maze ever since."

"Tell your friend to watch her words," Veremund hissed. The ax roiled and shifted, but Laithe chuckled and ignored it.

"Looks like you've done well for yourself," Laithe said, handing the knives to the elderly woman. She somehow managed to keep an arsenal of weapons within her cloak when Veremund threw her out. There was a reason she had survived as a Deviant for all these years.

"No time for small talk, boy," Kez snapped. "I've been following this squad for an hour now since the green scum infested the tunnels. I overheard them discussing the village. There's a Tal'Rach with them."

A screeching sound assaulted Laithe's ears, and the great tree rumbled around them. Laithe inhaled sharply and hurried down the hall, not waiting for the limping woman to follow. If they did not reach the village soon, no one would be left to save. He turned the final corner, and his heart sank. The secret door lay in pieces, and the last wardens disappeared into the portal. He lifted his ax high and sprinted into the village.

The men huddled in a tight group amid the overturned dining tables. They gaped in horror at the dozens of wardens pouring down the stairs. A monster with a woman's torso and a snake's body slithered down the steps, deadly fire dancing in her hands. Ducarix.

Kez dashed past him, knives drawn, grappling the nearest warden to the ground with ease. She stabbed him violently and repeatedly. Laithe would have marveled at Kez's speed, but he was too busy barreling through the remaining rear guard to notice. He slayed the first three with little resistance. The ax fulfilled his desires, cleaving warden after warden until he reached the stairs. The snake Tal'Rach was advancing on the dining hall, flanked by half a dozen wardens. The remaining soldiers were packed tightly on the stairs. Laithe stepped over the bodies of a few poor villagers along the balconies. He would avenge them swiftly and savagely.

Kez dispatched the soldiers that he missed, slaying them mercilessly with her knives.

"Toss the swords off the railing. Give the villagers something to defend themselves," Laithe roared.

Instead of waiting for her response, Laithe threw himself down the stairs, willing the metal tendrils to shoot out before him. He allowed Veremund to maneuver the blades, killing every warden on the stairs. His chaotic descent was enough to draw the attention of Ducarix, who wheeled around to confront him, her lips parted to reveal frightening fangs. With a flick of her wrist, she dispatched her surviving wardens toward the villagers.

The green-clad soldiers disappeared around the houses. Laithe heard the satisfying sound of metal ringing against metal. Kez had done her duty and had armed the Fourteens. At least the men weren't utterly defenseless.

Ducarix lunged with sharp claws dripping in venom. Laithe

dug in his heels and willed the great ax forward, shaping the metal into three scythes. Veremund's power rotated the deadly blades, and Laithe lifted the weapon to meet the Tal'Rach. She shrieked as the ax sliced off both claws. She recoiled but remained within Laithe's striking radius. Laithe shaped the metal into a spear once more and stabbed Ducarix repeatedly in the torso.

Howling, the Tal'Rach spit venom at Laithe, but Veremund reformed his vessel into a shield, repelling the projectile poison with ease. They had always been a perfect team on the battlefield, and this new arrangement, however strange, was no different.

A pair of knives sank into Ducarix's backside, and she whirled on Kez, who had slipped down to the cavern floor and behind the Tal'Rach. Before the monster could strike his ally, Laithe took his opportunity and swung the ax with all his strength. With a sickening snap, the magical blade sliced into the Tal'Rach's neck, cleaving her head from her shoulders in one fluid motion. The body crumbled to the ground, spasming in its death throes.

"Be careful. The snake is still alive," Veremund warned.

Sure enough, a sapphire mist shot from the corpse's bloody neck towards Laithe. Again, Veremund shielded the mercenary, and the fog shuddered as it touched the metal vessel. The smoke recoiled and reshaped into a formidably sized serpent, hissing ominously, wary of this strange new weapon. Then it sprung, not at Laithe or Kez, but for the ceiling above. She was escaping.

"Cut her open," Veremund directed.

Laithe obeyed, shaping his weapon into a scythe. He lashed out, slicing into the spirit. To his surprise, the metal connected and tore into Ducarix, who screeched in pain. A sea of rach poured out of the ethereal wound, floating through the floor and walls. Ducarix, now significantly smaller, flitted into the flock, nearly indistinguishable from the common rach.

"What was that?" Laithe asked as the snake rach faded.

"We rid Ducarix of her power," Veremund responded. "It takes thousands of rach to create a great spirit. But their power fades after centuries. The older Tal'Rach prey on common rach to maintain their strength. I, however, do not require to feed to sustain myself."

"Oh," Laithe muttered absentmindedly, directing his attention to the skirmish beyond the houses.

When he arrived, the Fourteens had already dispatched most of the wardens, using the swords Kez had thrown from above. The elderly woman followed him, wielding a pair of knives. Laithe and Kez joined the fray and slayed the remaining attackers with animalistic savagery.

Without a Tal'Rach to defend them, the wardens soon fell to the combined force of the Deviant defenders. Soon, the village was quiet once more; Laithe could only hear the groans of the dying. The invasion was over.

Luckily, Calvin survived the attack, partly due to his boyfriend Lars, who proved skilled with a sword. The healer treated the casualties while his lover and a group of stronger men reinforced the broken village gate. Laithe helped a bit, but he soon grew anxious. The longer he stayed, the greater the opportunity the archwarden had to kill Isam. He could only hope that Alistair had held his lover hostage, but after seeing his ruthlessness in Veremund's memories, he highly doubted it.

"Where are you going?" Calvin asked, noticing Laithe

climbing the stairs toward the exit. "I wanted to thank you for saving Kez. Are Isam and Veremund out patrolling?"

"No," Laithe said. "Veremund is with me. And Isam is in the Sanctum."

"Oh," Calvin said, wide-eyed with fear and confusion. "Well, you will need help. Everyone in this clearing is alive because of Isam. Take them with you."

The healer trundled off and returned with not only Lars but almost a score of Fourteens brandishing their newly acquired swords. These men had proven themselves in battle and had likely faced similar danger before their lives in the village. Laithe grunted his approval.

"Don't slow me down," he muttered. He wasn't surprised to see Kez join the ranks of his reinforcements, and he didn't mind. They would need every advantage in the impending battle, for they were headed straight for the lion's den. Most would never return.

23

Under Siege

It was barely dusk. The Canopy was eerily quiet, the streets abandoned, homes vacant and boarded. Sarina expected to encounter at least one warden patrol, but not a single green-clad soldier appeared as the priestesses raced forward. As they passed, she noticed scared faces behind apartment windows; the citizens were hiding. They should be frightened. Their world was about to crash around them.

Alma led the procession of priestesses and Deviants toward the Sanctum. A single novice remained at the boarding house to maintain the protective ward and guard the injured and elderly. Everyone else joined the assault on the Sanctum. Sarina wasn't surprised by the sheer number of Deviants who took up arms. They had experienced pain and heartache at the hands of the Tal'Rach as much as she had.

A score of priestesses and three times that number of Deviants followed Alma. But a force that size wouldn't be strong enough to aid Marikae. By Sarina's calculations, there were about a dozen Tal'Rach remaining. Behemoth, the bull, and Archades, the spider, were the only two, by her knowledge, that were defeated. But there was no telling how successful her sisters had been in their battles throughout Tabulrossa.

She accompanied Alma through the Canopy, pausing at every safe house they passed. Sarina was relieved to discover each outpost survived the onslaught. The wardens' citywide campaign targeted Marikae's entire network, but the Deviants repelled the wardens with relative ease due to the assistance of the priestesses. Remarkably few safe houses suffered substantial casualties. The wardens had underestimated their powers and suffered the consequences. According to the Deviants' accounts, they hadn't seen any Tal'Rach besides Behemoth and Ylvara. Reports stated that the wolf retreated to the Sanctum. She assumed the surviving great spirits remained safely within the Precipice.

At each stop, their numbers grew, though Alma always ordered one priestess to stay behind to ward the wounded. They often came across groups sent by Beriane and the young Yasmine. The pair of younger priestesses could move swiftly, alerting more safe houses than Alma's lumbering company. When they neared the Precipice, their numbers were in the hundreds, priestesses and Deviants marching together. The rach pooled above them in a ghostly stream, dancing among the leaves.

Sarina only hoped that their forces would be enough to aid Marikae. Maybe half of the priestesses of the peacock were proficient in channeling the true power of the rach, and a great number had been slain or left behind. Imitating the Deviants, the untrained women armed themselves with pitchforks, kitchen knives, or swords scavenged from fallen wardens. They would be effectively useless in a fight, but their skills of calling the rach would prove useful. Especially when facing the remaining Tal'Rach.

Every moment wasted in the Canopy was another that the Tal'Rach could breach the peacock's temple. The high priestess achieved an incredible feat, galvanizing the other temples to their cause in mere hours. She was the leader Sarina always wished to be.

Sarina was not confident, however, that Marikae could survive with only untrained women at her side.

They reached the final bridge, and there still was no sign of a single warden. That was not a good omen, for it implied the Tal'Rach had recalled every soldier in Tabulrossa to the Precipice.

On the bridge's crest, the entire Precipice, temples, and Sanctum became visible. Dangerous flashes of light tore through the glade, fireballs exploding against shimmering wards. Sarina halted, her heart filling with dread as she surveyed the scene below. Her worst fears became reality in a single heartbeat. A horde of wardens swarmed around the temple of the peacock, led by several Tal'Rach. Fire and lightning streaked across the Precipice, colliding into a thin veil protecting the temple. The magical barrier wavered at each attack, threatening to break. Sarina noticed a single figure standing on the temple's steps, arms outstretched, desperately holding the ward in place.

Marikae.

Unfamiliar priestesses cowered in the doorway behind her, while a handful of the more courageous women stood beside her. None, however, could aid in the defenses without proper training. Marikae withstood the might of an entire army, holding them at bay. Sarina had never loved her more.

A giant fireball crashed into the high priestess's ward, and the shimmering shield faltered, allowing a second flaming sphere to slam into the temple. The structure shook violently, and flames licked the elaborate walls. After hours of defending, Marikae was wavering. The next attack would surely break the ward altogether.

Sarina rushed forward, reaching out and connecting to the entire swarm of rach above her. Her head split in agony, struggling against the torrent of energy. She had never attempted to harness so many at once before. But she was no longer concerned with caution or restraint. Marikae was about to be overtaken by the enemy. Sarina would not allow that to happen.

Calling upon the rach, she unleashed havoc upon the army before her. A lightning bolt crashed into the center of the armed legion, tossing wardens about in a flurry of screams, metal and flesh. She unleashed another, then another.

She would not stop until Marikae was safe, and she crushed every warden and Tal'Rach in her path.

A dozen thunderbolts wracked the warden's army until she relented, relinquishing her hold on the rach above. She wavered, her body almost entirely spent, dizzy with exhaustion. Only then did she realize that Alma was standing beside her, ordering the others forward.

Sarina's assault left the warden formation in disarray, scattered between the temples. Scores lay dead on the road, and more fled into the safety of the Sanctum, though the majority surged forth to challenge Sarina and Alma's forces. A pair of imposing Tal'Rach led the assault, their teeth and talons flashing dangerously. The Deviants around Sarina swarmed forth, screaming in defiance, flanked by priestesses who hurled fire and lightning at the green tide.

Sarina barely noticed the two forces colliding. She was fixated on the temple of the peacock. On Marikae, who defended the stairs, fists raised in defiance. The diversion allowed the high priestess to regain control of her ward. Even more women crowded the doorway behind her; the terrified priestesses gradually regained their courage. A few joined Marikae's chant, strengthening the ethereal shield with their fledgling power. But Phymeria and her cohort remained at the bottom of the temple's steps, launching projectiles at the magical barrier. Sarina charged through the battle, fixated on her love.

Sarina ignored the brutality of the melee. She focused solely on reaching Marikae. If she encountered a warden, she ended their life. Her rage propelled her onward, leaving carnage in her wake. She did not care that the charging forces included two Tal'Rach and relied on her sisters to defeat them. From the corner of her eye, Sarina saw a Tal'Rach, the ocelot spirit, disintegrated by a large group of women. The sky above danced with shimmering rach, granting power to the priestesses below. Sarina had never seen such a host in one place. The Precipice was brighter than the noonday sun on the plains.

Sarina and her forces steadily rebuffed the attack, pushing the enemy towards the temple of the peacock, handily destroying both the ocelot and crane Tal'Rach. The priestesses and Deviants were only a hundred paces from the peacock temple when Marikae's ward wavered and fell. Sarina screamed in panic.

Half a dozen tiny fireballs sputtered toward the wardens below. A handful of women stood behind Marikae, struggling to concentrate and call upon the rach. Out of the dozens of women the high priestess managed to gather, only these few could learn the basics of harnessing so quickly. It was a miraculous feat. The attacks were pathetic, but it had taken Sarina months to conjure fire. Moreover, Marikae had less than a day to train these priestesses; Sarina was beyond impressed. If the rest of the priestesses had a month or two of training under their belts, there was no telling what they could be capable of. It was inspiring and terrifying.

The high priestess gracefully and determinedly descended the steps, unleashing torrents of bright white fire on her foes. Sarina smiled and pressed forward. The wardens were now pressed on two sides, about to be crushed in a newly created pincer.

A screech split the air. Phymeria, a head taller than her army, sprinted towards the Sanctum. The remaining warden's force quickly broke rank and withdrew to the sacred tower. The streets of the Precipice exploded in pandemonium as hundreds of wardens retreated to the Sanctum steps, following their Tal'Rach, fending off the Deviants and priestesses at their heels. The air shimmered above as Phymeria wove her own protective ward around the Sanctum.

Sarina gaped in awe. The siege had flipped on its head, and the defenders had become the assailants. The priestesses' might was entirely on display.

A heavily-armed regiment of wardens formed along the Sanctum's front steps, periodically discharging waves of soldiers beyond the safety of their failing shield. Freshly spawned rach floated from the battlefield to join their brethren above. Three Tal'Rach perched at the top of the

Sanctum's steps, holding their hands above their heads, keeping the ward in place. They were mighty beings with the power of thousands of rach within them, but they were no match against a host of priestesses. Phymeria stood in the middle, flanked by Ylvara and Lykos. Their brows were furrowed in immense concentration. Were they all that remained of the glorious Tal'Rach?

Sarina pushed through the Deviant forces towards the Sanctum, locating Marikae at the forefront of the assault. Scores of newly trained priestesses surrounded the high priestess. These women were no longer terrified but empowered and unified, their arms outstretched, chanting loudly. Sarina could not help but smile with pride. The high priestess had accomplished more in one day than any thought was possible in a lifetime. Sarina ignored them and headed straight for the Sanctum, weaving through groups of chanting priestesses, avoiding fireballs, and taking her place at Marikae's side. The tall woman smiled when she noticed Sarina's presence.

"So this was the task that only you could accomplish," Sarina said, arching an eyebrow as a lightning bolt streaked above her head. "You could have taken me with you."

"I wanted to ensure you were safe in case I failed," Marikae explained. "But that is neither of our concerns now. Ready to topple a dynasty?"

Sarina nodded and focused on the Tal'Rach ahead, chanting loudly and harnessing the infinite power of the thousands of rach above her. The great spirits were never gods, never guardians. They were merely leeches, scared men and women who preyed on the helpless to live for eternity. It disgusted her.

The ward wavered; fireballs snuck between the gaps, exploding on the delicately carved facade of the Sanctum, igniting a ravenous blaze. The lion Tal'Rach, Lykos, roared and leaped into the air. The moment he cleared the ward, he unleashed tongues of flame on the priestesses below. Marikae and others raised their shields, but the lion's attack incinerated the slower women. Lykos landed on a priestess behind Sarina, crushing her with his claws. Another swipe and three others flew into the air. He snarled ferociously at the high priestess. Alma and the priestesses around him summoned heavy glowing ropes to bind him, but he slashed them to pieces. He was more ancient than Behemoth and infinitely more dangerous.

Sarina whipped around at the sound of a battle cry. A wave of wardens charged through the barrier, taking advantage of their master's distraction. Fireballs felled a few, but the women within range were too busy dealing with Lykos.

"Take care of them," Marikae instructed. "I will dispose of Lykos."

Sarina relished her lover's firmness but strove to stay on task. Only Marikae could disrupt her normally laser-like focus. Regardless, the wave of wardens was only thirty paces away and was about to crash into the defenseless priestesses.

But she would become their defense.

She summoned flames and scorched the ground between her and the attacking force, creating a solid wall of fire. Brave soldiers dared to approach the blaze, and she slew each one with a lightning bolt.

A small group of priestesses from either side of the circle joined her, driving the wardens back before they could strike. She manipulated the firewall, pushing it forward, burning anyone slow enough to be overtaken until it crashed against the failing ward.

Marikae cried out in pain.

Whirling around, Sarina exclaimed in horror as Lykos loomed above the high priestess triumphantly, claws raised, ready for the kill. Marikae lay bloodied on the ground in a daze. Alma lay dead next to her side, her throat torn open. Every priestess in range was either dead or unconscious.

Sarina howled with rage and flung her focus into the ground around the Tal'Rach. She would crush him into dust for hurting Marikae and for killing Alma. The wood from the tree around him shifted like sand; Sarina controlled the great tree itself. She formed the wood into two immense hands on either side of the lion spirit in two heartbeats, then willed them to clap. There was a sickening crunch as the two wooden hands crushed Lykos. The Tal'Rach screeched, and Sarina focused on his spirit, forcing it out of his avatar. Lykos was ancient and powerful, but Sarina connected to each rach above her, her body shuddering, the sheer power of the spirits threatening to tear her apart. The lion's body gave way before hers, and a golden cloud expelled from Lykos. He was attempting an escape.

But his spirit struck an invisible wall. Marikae had climbed to her knees, chanting quietly, forming a prison around Lykos as Alma had with Behemoth.

Alma. Sparing her a glance, Sarina focused her attention from the senior priestess's corpse to the newly trapped Lykos. She ripped rach after rach from his ghostly form, freeing dozens of spirits trapped beneath the surface. More priestesses joined, and within five heartbeats, the Tal'Rach was no more than one of the thousands of rach floating above them.

She helped Marikae to her feet and beheld the gristly wooden statue she had created to crush Lykos. The broken body of the Tal'Rach's avatar was barely visible through the wood. Sarina paled. Any physical harm they unleashed against the Tal'Rach would only harm their human host. She may have defeated one of the most powerful of their foes, but she murdered an innocent in the process.

Then her eyes fell on Alma, who lay sightless beside the grotesque sculpture. Her stomach emptied. Alma was strong, kind, and powerful, one of the best people Sarina had ever known. A glowing tiger rach had already emerged, staring at her intently. Tavo approached it eagerly and rubbed his body against its legs. She would mourn her friend and others, but she had to focus on the task at hand—defeating Phymeria and the remaining Tal'Rach.

Someone shrieked behind her. A ferocious battle raged on the top of the stairs. Deviants had poured from within the Sanctum and fought against the wolf and the peacock. How did they get into the Sanctum? Sarina recognized the man swinging a giant ax at Ylvara. Laithe.

She grabbed Marikae by the forearm and darted towards the Sanctum; the ward had already fallen. Most of the surviving wardens had climbed the steps to defend their mistresses. The charging priestesses dispatched the stragglers and climbed the stairs, dozens of priestesses in tow.

They reached the top as Laithe cut into Ylvara's chest. She yelped, and a black cloud of mist poured from her wound. The women behind her caught the Tal'Rach and began dissolving her, but Sarina did not care; her focus rested solely on Phymeria. The peacock had her back to the stairs, slashing at the attacking Deviants behind her. Sarina flung a fireball in her direction. The peacock cried out as it exploded against her sturdy frame. Phymeria contorted in pain, and she twisted around, summoning her own fire, but the flames fizzled out when she saw the forces of Deviants and priestesses alike ascending the stairs. Sarina threw another fireball at the gigantic woman, who was already gone, fleeing into the Sanctum. Sarina bolted forward, ready to slay the monstrous spirit.

"Wait," Marikae said, holding her back with a strong arm. Sarina resisted, but the taller woman held fast. "Listen to me. It is foolish to run in alone. Wait until we've regrouped. Then we will confront her together."

Sarina reluctantly agreed, focusing on the wardens around them; most had retreated with Phymeria. It only took a minute to clear the stairs fully and flood the entire entry with priestesses and Deviants. Marikae prevented their charge from progressing into the Sanctum; the high priestess blocked the entrance, keeping her army at bay. Sarina stood between Marikae and Laithe, who hoisted his strangely giant ax and glared intently into the Sanctum beyond the high priestess.

"It is nice to see you are taking some action for a change," Sarina said. "But where is your master, Veremund? I would have thought he would want to be here for this."

"Good to see you, Sarina," Laithe said. His sincerity surprised Sarina. She had never thought she would see any emotion from the cold-hearted man. The city must have changed him as much as it had her. "And Veremund is here, with me. In this ax."

"This reunion can wait. There are gods to destroy," a familiar voice said from behind. It was Kez, bruised and bloodied, standing tall, wielding a pair of bloody knives.

Sarina flung herself on her friend, ignoring the scrapes. "Get off me, girl."

"I like this one. She reminds me of what you'll be like when you age and wrinkle," Marikae said, smirking. She turned to the masses. "Sisters! Friends! Comrades! We have pushed the imposter gods into their stronghold. We have returned half of them to their rightful place among the rach. But do not grow careless in our victory, for the war isn't over. The ones who remain inside are the most ancient and powerful, guarded by a legion of servants. Be cautious, but show them your fury!"

Sarina heartily joined the battle cry and accompanied her love into the depths of the Sanctum. She had never been inside the heart of Tabulrossa and marveled at the lofty ceilings and grand staircases. The temple of the peacock seemed like an outhouse in comparison to the Sanctum's splendor. She followed Marikae under another archway and into an enormous stadium. The stands were empty, but the stage brimmed with heavily armed wardens. Alistair and his warden officers gathered near an immense Edict pillar. In front of him were seven Tal'Rach, the surviving great spirits. Phymeria was among them, illuminated by the light of thousands of rach floating into the vast space.

Fireballs descended upon the dais, but a solid rach-powered shield repelled them. Sarina sensed the Tal'Rach on the stage were as powerful as Marikae suggested. But still, she flung herself forward, leaping onto the platform alongside the high priestess, Kez, Laithe, and the faster priestesses and Deviants.

She attempted to harness the rach to fling fire at Phymeria, but nothing happened. A vice gripped her body, immobilized by an invisible force. She heard a chorus of gasps, assuming a similar stranglehold trapped the rest of Marikae's army. There was a low chanting. A chill ran down her spine.

Alistair and his warden officers were chanting.

They could harness the rach as well. Of course, they knew the true nature of the spirits. How could she have been so blind?

Combined with the eldest Tal'Rach, their power was enough to subdue Marikae's forces. A whirlpool of light above the Tal'Rach pulled thousands of rach into itself.

"Thank you, Marikae and Veremund," Phymeria shouted for the whole theater to hear. "For bringing us the biggest meal we have ever had the pleasure of indulging. And for giving us the gift of having fewer mouths to share it."

"You revel in the death of your brethren," Marikae spat. "You are more pathetic than I ever imagined."

"That is no way to speak to your mistress, Marikae," Phymeria tutted.

"You control me no longer, you are nothing but a cannibalistic rach," Marikae spat.

"Oh, I am so much more than that, my dear," the peacock's eyes gleamed dangerously. "Do you think a handful of priestesses created what you call 'the secret arts'?"

"That's not possible," Marikae whispered.

"It used to be referred to as magic, thousands of years ago. I was called a magician before I died, a powerful one at that," Phymeria explained, gesturing to the Tal'Rach behind her. "We all were. Harnessing the power of souls to accomplish miracles a mortal like you couldn't begin to imagine. But despite our power, death eventually came for us all. A human body will always fade, but the rach can live on forever. But the spirit lacks a personality or memory. Then we discovered that if a rach consumes another rach, that person regains a sense of self. Lykos was the first to attempt it. He regained his memories, his personality, even his ability to perform magic, using the rach he recently devoured. Unfortunately, he was unable to control the rach with the Call. Once we ascended to Tal'Rach, we culled our order and left only those loyal to us to become our priestesses. Then we reshaped the world in our image."

"Lykos, Behemoth, and the others were your brethren for a thousand years, yet you don't mourn for them," Marikae pointed out. She was incredibly calm, considering Phymeria's revelation.

"They proved themselves weak. Falling to insects like you," Phymeria said. "In the world we created, only the strong can live forever. They wouldn't have allowed a pitiful contingent of servants to defeat them if they were worthy of their title. And their deaths leave more food for the rest of us."

"Then why create more Tal'Rach?" Sarina asked, still struggling against her restraints. "If you want to hoard power for yourselves, why take the trouble in making more of you, like Veremund."

"They all served their purpose," Phymeria said. "Behemoth and the others offered protection, and Veremund provided…a distraction. People tend to direct their grievances to the top when their lives become stagnant and complacent. We needed a villain, so we created Veremund. It worked for us once before, thousands of years ago, when the public grew restless. Lucian was the perfect diversion, absorbing the people's hatred like a sponge."

"The father of Deviants?" Marikae gasped. The truth finally dawned on her. The devil of Tabulrossa, the Ae'Rach,

Deviants, and the Edicts were all lies. They were all tools for the Tal'Rach to maintain their power.

"Lucian was a scapegoat," Phymeria explained, brimming with hatred. She enjoyed this game as if she were toying with her food. "And an effective one at that. Exactly like our Veremund, who created countless rach for us with his wrath. How many wardens did you slay, ram? Hundreds? Thousands? And how many innocents died in your wake? Maybe more? Our Edicts were no longer generating enough sustenance, and you were the perfect replacement."

"And the wardens were so willing to sacrifice themselves for you? That's hard to believe," Laithe said flatly.

"The Tal'Rach gave us assurances," Alistair said, ceasing his chants and stepping forward.

"They promised you immortality, didn't they?" Marikae asked. "You are a fool, Alistair. They will never give you the power you truly desire. And if they do, it will be for their gain, not yours."

"You would be surprised at the generosity of the great spirits," Alistair mused.

"Where is Isam?" Laithe yelled.

"Oh, he is long dead, my boy," the peacock crooned. "You and your dear ram spirit shouldn't have abandoned him."

"Enough with the dramatics, Phymeria," the raven spirit called from behind. "It is time we feast."

"Oh, you won't be joining us. There will only be enough for two," Alistair said, taking Phymeria by the hand.

Red hot chains materialized, binding every Tal'Rach apart from Phymeria; they shrieked in pain as their skin burned. Two great spirits left their avatars in an attempt to escape, but the warden officers dissolved their ethereal bodies. More rach joined the whirlpool, descending upon the archwarden and Phymeria. Alistair pulled a dagger from his belt.

Laithe's ax boiled and shifted, flowing like water. The metal reformed into two spears, striking out savagely. The attack was too fast to negate, and the spears took both Phymeria and Alistair in the heart. The archwarden gasped and fell, his dagger clattering to the floor. Phymeria coughed, and her spirit flowed out of her wound.

The wardens lost concentration for a split second, which was enough for the priestesses and Tal'Rach to break from their bonds. There wasn't enough power to contain both groups. Pandemonium exploded on the dais as wardens, Tal'Rach and priestesses broke loose and fought in a frenzy.

"You fool," Phymeria cried, her maw opening wide.

Her spirit floated out of her body into the torrent above, leaving her avatar, who slumped to the ground, gasping for air. He was a young man, tall with tan skin and coarse hair.

"Isam!" Laithe exclaimed, dropping his ax to the ground, and rushed over to the man with a hole in his chest.

24

The Last Tal'Rach

Laithe sprinted across the dais, ignoring the flying fireballs and clashing soldiers, focused solely on Isam. The bastard Alistair lay dead, sightlessly staring above at the storm of gleaming rach. Veremund's attack had caught the archwarden in the heart, killing him instantly. The ram finally enacted his vengeance.

Isam, however, was not awarded a swift death. He lay on the ground, coughing up blood, a sizable wound on his shoulder pouring out crimson liquid, pooling around him. Laithe knelt and cradled Isam in his arms. His skin was pale and cold, and his breath shallow. Laithe held him tightly, wishing he could stop the lifeblood streaming from the gaping wound in Isam's chest. He called for help from the nearby priestesses; Veremund once mentioned their healing powers to him. None of the women paid him heed.

Sarina and Marikae were too preoccupied with the chanting wardens and the giant peacock spirit above. The ghostly bird flew into the storming rach, devouring any in her path. The Tal'Rach grew larger, her body glowing brighter.

But Laithe didn't care about any of that. He ignored the battle raging around him, holding Isam, tears streaming down his face. He'd thought his lover died earlier that day in Alistair's study. Then one moment, Isam was still alive, captured and possessed by the peacock, and the next, he was dying in his arms. Life's cruelty never ceased to amaze him.

There was so much he wanted to tell Isam. He had given Laithe a purpose and had shown him what true love was. He'd never fully expressed his feelings for Isam—maybe in actions, but not words. And there he was, fading away. Laithe always thought he would protect him, but today he failed. They all failed him.

He screamed for Veremund, but he had dropped his ax. It wouldn't have mattered anyway, this wound was clearly beyond the Tal'Rach's power. Laithe could see the dais through the grisly hole in Isam's chest.

Isam spasmed, spitting up blood.

This was not how it was supposed to happen; this is not how the stories ended, even the tragedies. Laithe was supposed to get one last word before his lover died. But life was cruel. Love was cruel. Isam let out one final breath and became still.

"I am sorry, little one. I didn't know." A strong hand softly grasped Laithe's shoulder. He did not have to turn to recognize Veremund's deep timbre.

"You could have healed him." Laithe was hollow, fixated on Isam. He didn't believe his own words, but he needed someone to blame. "Whose body did you steal?"

"A warden, but that doesn't matter now," Veremund answered. "We need to get you to safety, before Alistair—"

"Alistair is dead!" Laithe roared, leaping to his feet and pushing the ram spirit away. His agony evolved into pure fury. "You had your revenge. You have accomplished what you've always wanted. Now leave us alone!"

"I don't think your boy toy understands the current situation, Martin," a gravelly voice drawled behind them. Laithe turned. His blood ran cold.

Veremund summoned blue flames and tensed like a viper, ready to strike. Alistair appeared before them, grinning fiendishly.

Laithe wrinkled his forehead, gazing at the archwarden's corpse, then back to the creature before him. It was similar in appearance to Alistair but much larger, a head taller than Veremund himself. Bright red scales covered his body, a powerful tail swished behind him, and his smile revealed murderous fangs.

Alistair had become a Tal'Rach.

The wardens behind him must have aided in his ascension, as they had in Veremund's memories. Laithe recalled the archwarden drawing a dagger before he was impaled. It wasn't for defense. It was to use on himself. Alistair had meant to take his own life and transform into one of those monsters. And Veremund had simply done the deed for him.

"Oh yes, I knew it was you, Martin," Alistair said. "The Tal'Rach discovered I was gaining power and used you as a pawn to stop me. But not even a newly formed great spirit could hinder my ascension."

"This is what you always wanted." Sorrow and rage dripped from Veremund. "You were promised a place among them, like every archwarden before you."

"Yes," Alistair said. "Every officer knows the rach's true nature and is told that only the most powerful, faithful, and competent archwarden will join them at the end of their life.

In the history of Tabulrossa, only one archwarden has ever received this blessing. Behemoth. Every archwarden since yearned and toiled for that honor. Instead, they chose you—a sniveling runt who wouldn't have made it out of basic training without my help. The first Tal'Rach created in a hundred years was a lowly warden with no ambition, no talent. They meant to hinder my ascent. At that point, I knew the Tal'Rach never meant to share their power with me, or any archwarden after the bull, for that matter. They used him as an example to keep future archwardens compliant and obedient, but I have always known the truth. So I decided to take it for myself."

"That was why they made the Fourteenth Edict, in an attempt to stop you after you ascended to archwarden," Veremund said. "Instead, you framed Luxo and betrayed me."

"A small sacrifice for eternal life. Besides, I will have millennia filled with new lovers who will adore me as much as you did. Maybe more so," Alistair said.

Veremund roared and shot tongues of blue flames at the scaly Tal'Rach. The monster laughed, unaffected. The ram howled in rage and launched toward his former lover. The two Tal'Rach collided, exchanging blows and throwing themselves across the stage, toppling the great Edict pole and crushing anyone unfortunate enough to stand in their path.

Laithe knelt beside Isam's body, covering it with his own, feeling powerless. Sarina, Marikae, and the remaining priestesses gathered on the far end of the platform, surrounding a group of subdued wardens. Ethereal bonds ensnared the green-clad survivors.

The priestesses joined together, chanting in unison. Without the Tal'Rach to protect them, the wardens didn't stand a chance against the ferocious women. Laithe was surprised to see Beriane in their midst; he wasn't aware she had joined the order.

A sickening screech compelled him to cover his ears. High above the dais, the peacock devoured a pink whale almost half her size. The aquatic creature exploded, and thousands of rach disappeared inside the peacock's maw. Laithe recognized the whale as Leviathan, one of the last remaining great spirits. Laithe glanced at the captured Tal'Rach and discovered that only three remained, each thrashing against their mystical bonds.

The priestesses struggled to hold their prisoners. Most were preoccupied with subduing the great peacock and warding their party from the destructive battle that raged between Veremund and Alistair.

The more the peacock devoured, the fewer rach the priestesses could harness. Soon, the Tal'Rach would be unstoppable.

Laithe had an idea.

He dashed towards the priestesses, reaching a dozen paces before glowing vines ensnared him. Luckily, Sarina recognized him and ordered the women to release him; he hobbled the remaining distance. She glared at him like a petulant child.

"Laithe," Sarina said distractedly. "Now is not the—"

"Use them," Laithe interrupted, pointing at the three remaining Tal'Rach. "Veremund used his spirit against Ducarix when he possessed my ax. It sliced the snake spirit like a knife."

"He may be right," Marikae said, turning to Sarina. "I saw the weapon your friend mentioned. I've never seen a vessel manipulated like that. I never thought it possible. But if we combine the power of a Tal'Rach and metal, we might secure a chance to free the rach from within Phymeria. Beriane, grab three swords. Hurry."

The younger priestess scrambled to gather three discarded swords. She returned shortly, giving one to Sarina and Marikae, keeping the third for herself. The trio rushed over to the captive Tal'Rach, laying the swords at their feet.

Priestesses began to chant. The odd, ethereal sound filled the chaotic theater, sending shivers down Laithe's spine. The glowing ropes that bound the Tal'Rach disappeared, and Laithe tensed. However, the great spirits convulsed, mist pouring out of them. One by one, the priestesses pulled the great spirits from their avatars, collecting the mist in three tight balls and forcing them into each of the three swords.

Once the spirits settled in their new vessel, the metal roiled grew, and some tendrils shot out at the women, but the priestesses held the attacks at bay. After a short minute, three glowing swords lay before Marikae, Sarina, and Beriane.

"Don't touch them!" Laithe called out, recalling the odd tattoo that bonded him to Veremund. "That will give them more power!"

Heeding his warning, Marikae willed her sword off the ground, pointing it upward. It faltered. The peacock spirit had consumed most of the rach above. They were running out of time.

The high priestess cried out and hurled the huge sword upwards, sending the glowing projectile toward the peacock's heart. Phymeria was too preoccupied with her overindulgence to notice, and the blade struck home. It pierced the peacock as Veremund's ax did Ducarix. The sword cleaved the outer veil, freeing thousands of rach as it tore the ghostly body. But as it neared the center, Laithe could see rach pouring from the sword itself. Before it pierced her ghostly heart, the sword fell to the ground, clattering lifelessly on the dais. The Tal'Rach inside lost as much power as Phymeria, but the peacock was stronger. The great gash created by Marikae already healed and reformed. Her ghostly maw was agape, ready to feast upon the cloud of rach recently released from her body. If she reached them, the first attack would be rendered pointless.

"Beriane!" Marikae cried, and the petite woman threw her sword at the great beast. The blade cleaved thousands of rach from the peacock before falling lifeless to the floor to join the first. Phymeria healed herself again, devouring the fleeing rach indiscriminately. The first two strikes would be in vain if they did not defeat her soon. Would the third sword be any different?

"Don't stab her," Laithe called, realizing the difference between their attacks and Veremund's. "Slice her down the belly!"

Sarina struggled against the sword, the Tal'Rach inside desperately attempted to escape after witnessing the fate of the previous two. But more rach were free, so Sarina had more power to harness. She shaped her weapon like a scythe and struck. Laithe smiled as the peacock shrieked in pain, the scythe tearing into her. More rach poured out than the first two strikes combined, and Phymeria finally directed her attention to the priestesses below. The Tal'Rach roared and dove upon them. The remaining women extended their arms upwards, forming a glimmering ward for protection. As Phymeria descended, Sarina's scythe cut deeper. The peacock was a tenth of her original size when she neared the mystical shield. The women chanted as she collided with the ward, wrapping the shimmering air around her. The priestesses removed the final rach from the peacock as the scythe fell to the ground.

In minutes, the priestesses defeated the most powerful Tal'Rach in living memory. And now there were only two remaining.

With the peacock spirit flying listlessly overhead as a normal rach, all attention fell upon Veremund and Alistair, whose battle had taken them to the vacant benches of the theater. Veremund was faster, but Alistair benefited from the energy of the rach he had recently absorbed. The ram breathed heavily and bled from multiple wounds, whereas Alistair looked as if he had recently woken, refreshed, and unfazed. A savage blow sent Veremund flying, and he landed on the dais near Laithe and the priestesses.

"I would like to thank you all for disposing of the others," Alistair said. "It saves me the work of betraying Phymeria. Power like this cannot be shared."

The lizard unhinged his jaw and breathed in, catching the floating rach above in his terrible maw.

"We must rid the archwarden of his prey," Sarina said. "Sisters, with me!"

"No," Marikae warned. "The rach used to create him are gone now. There is only one rach inhabiting that body. It takes decades for the Tal'Rach to rely on others to survive. Alistair and Veremund can't be destroyed the same way as the others."

"So, how do you suggest we accomplish that?" Sarina inquired, gesturing to the fallen swords, lifeless and dim.

"Veremund," Marikae snapped. "You are the last Tal'Rach. Your spirit. Only you can stop the young Tal'Rach before he devours this entire city. It may destroy you, but you will succeed in your vengeance."

"Very well," Veremund breathed. "I have one request."

The Tal'Rach beckoned the high priestess, and she left the ward's safety, kneeling next to the ram. He whispered in her ear, and she cocked back her head, shaking it.

"Those are my terms, priestess," Veremund said. "Disagree, and I leave you all to Alistair's mercy."

"As you wish, Tal'Rach," Marikae said, though she did not seem pleased. "Let us begin."

Veremund rose, regarding Laithe. "I love you, little one. Please accept this as my apology for everything that I've done."

With that, he opened his mouth and released his avatar, who fell to the ground dazed. In the form of a ghostly, violet ram, Veremund thundered full force toward Alistair. But the lizard was ready. After devouring a score of rach, he leaped on the dais and charged the ram, hands filled with a blue flame. But instead of attacking, Veremund stopped, allowing Alistair to draw near. The priestesses chanted.

The women around Laithe spoke in unison, hands reaching out toward the newly formed Tal'Rach. Alistair stopped in his tracks, coughing up mist. He resisted, but their powers were too strong. They tore Alistair out of his avatar and ripped the freshly consumed rach from his form. Alistair howled and descended upon Veremund in the shape of a monstrous salamander. The two enormous beasts battled, their spirits thrashing violently; each blow diminished their mass. Alistair was stronger, but Veremund was faster; the ram slashed savagely with horns, striking twice as much as the salamander.

The priestesses chanted again.

The two forms, now diminished, roiled and lost their shapes. Both Tal'Rach were powerless against the power of the priestesses. Both veils of mist swirled around and collided with one another in a bright flash. Laithe covered his eyes until it was all over.

Neither ram nor salamander remained, but the battlefield wasn't empty. A third creature sat amid the wreckage, glowing blue. It was a mammal with a serpentine body and padded paws. Laithe had seen the beast in the rivers by his childhood home—an otter.

The priestesses around him ceased chanting and set about healing the wounded and hauling the captive wardens off the dais. For them, the battle was over. But Laithe was fascinated by the new creature.

"What is that?" Laithe breathed, realizing only Marikae and Sarina remained beside him, gazing at the beautiful figure.

"It was Veremund's stipulation," Marikae said flatly. "Behold the final Tal'Rach, born from the energies of two before him. The otter spirit. You know him as Isam."

"He didn't," Laithe said, stunned. The Tal'Rach collided exactly where the otter was now floating—above Isam's body.

"Yes," Marikae said. "Veremund was adamant that his spirit would restore Isam. And none here would dare make another Tal'Rach using defenseless rach. But it was a sacrifice I was willing to make."

"He'll need an avatar, Laithe," Sarina said gently, but Laithe hadn't heard either of the women. He was too busy running headlong at the otter.

The blue mist formed around him, and he inhaled deeply, accepting it inside him. His vision blurred, and his consciousness entered the void. It was a familiar sensation for him now, so he barely stumbled when he materialized in a meadow, a bright sun beating down on him. A young man with perfect skin and sharp, kind eyes sat upon a mossy rock. Laithe dashed across the meadow and gathered him in a tight embrace.

"Put me down, you big oaf," Isam chuckled, playfully hitting Laithe's shoulder. "I'm fragile now."

"Nonsense," Laithe said, though he still set Isam down with a sweet kiss. "You are the most powerful being in the world."

"Well then, maybe you should show me some respect," Isam said, his expression troubled. "What do you mean most powerful? Where is Veremund? Aren't we in his mind palace?"

"No, my love," Laithe said slowly, realizing Isam wasn't conscious during the last battle. "What do you remember?"

"I was in a study, surrounded by four Tal'Rach and Alistair," Isam trembled. "They…questioned me…for a while…then there was smoke, and I was possessed again. I was in a mind palace. But it wasn't Veremund's. Then everything went cold. And dark. What happened, Laithe?"

Laithe motioned for Isam to sit on the grass with him, and the pair sat for a long while as they discussed the previous day's events. Of Veremund's escape, the revelations found within the ram's memories, the strange weapon, their fight against the Tal'Rach, defending the village with Kez, the final battle, and Isam's death. His lover sat silently, taking it all in, asking no questions, and simply nodding. It was only when he fully understood his new condition, a newly formed Tal'Rach, that he cried. Laithe pulled him close and held him tight.

"I did not ask for this," Isam sobbed. "Why would Veremund do this to me? I didn't want any of this. I simply wanted to protect my friends. Protect people like me."

"He did it because he loved you," Laithe said. "Because he loved both of us. I think I talked some sense into him when I realized why he wanted revenge on Alistair."

"You used words to convince him of something?" Isam scoffed, raising an eyebrow. "I find that hard to believe."

"I'm telling the truth, you dolt," Laithe said, pushing him playfully. "I think in the end, Veremund wanted to give us what we desired most. For you, he provided a way to protect those you love. As a Tal'Rach."

"And what did he give you?' Isam asked.

"A reason worth living," Laithe said. "He brought you back to me."

He leaned in and passionately kissed the new Tal'Rach. They rolled on the ground, enjoying themselves with fervor, until Isam sat up.

"But does that mean I need to possess someone to walk in the real world?" Isam asked. "I don't think I could do that to anyone."

"You already have my body, wholly and completely," Laithe beamed. "And I don't mind it here alone. You are all the company that I need."

"But if you are my avatar, then I'll never touch you again," Isam sighed.

"And this isn't real now?" Laithe asked, gesturing to the idyllic meadow. "We spent most of our nights in a mind palace since we met. And you can make this place anything you want to be."

"Are you certain?" Isam asked cautiously. "Is this what you want?"

"Definitely," Laithe answered without hesitation. "I

wouldn't want it any other way. But please don't make a castle. I feel like I can't breathe in halls made of stone."

"If that's your only request, then I think we can manage," Isam said. "I love you, you idiot."

"And here I thought you were only using me for my body," Laithe chuckled, ducking to avoid a playful slap.

The pair rose as Isam changed the landscape around them, creating an oasis filled with trees, warm pools of water, and birds—a place for them to be together for as long as they lived. In the mind palace, separated from the worries and strife of the world outside, Laithe held his hand, feeling like he was finally somewhere he had been searching for most of his life. Home.

25

The Final Choice

The meadow was quiet, save for the gentle rushing of the waterfall spilling into the otherwise tranquil pond. Songbirds chirped lazily in the trees above. The brilliant sun shone through the motionless leaves, untouched by wind. The grass pricked Laithe's exposed skin. He ignored the itching sensation, and his eyes rolled back.

Isam straddled him, soft hands holding his chest tight as he bucked his hips greedily. The light bounced off his flawless skin; his toned muscles strained with effort. His tongue lolled to the side, loud moans escaping his soft lips. He was beautiful.

Isam kept riding, changing the rhythm from slow and sensual to fast and heated. Laithe grunted, grabbing him by the hips and thrusting upwards. He enjoyed it when Isam took control, but only for so long. It was his turn now.

Isam cried out, begging for more. So Laithe obliged. Planting his feet into the grassy earth for leverage, Laithe gripped his hips and fucked with powerful, determined strokes. The slaps of skin against skin echoed across the clearing, along with Isam's loud moans of pleasure. Grinning savagely, Laithe shifted his weight. In one fluid motion, remaining inside Isam, he rotated his lover onto his backside, legs in the air over his shoulders.

His muscles tightened as he slammed into Isam, who lay on the grass, green eyes locked with his. With better leverage, Laithe accelerated his pace, thrusting harder and faster. The louder Isam moaned, the harder Laithe fucked. He persisted for a while, allowing intense lust to overtake him.

But he wasn't done yet.

Using the immense strength granted to him by the mind palace, Laithe scooped up Isam, wrapping his arms around his shoulders, and lifted him in the air. Isam curled around him, clinging on tightly, kissing his neck, and bouncing on his cock. Laithe groaned, allowing Isam to have his way before pressing him into the nearest tree. Isam dug his fingers into Laithe's broad back, legs wrapped around his thick waist. The pair kissed, their tongues dancing together expertly. Laithe pounded into Isam, knowing there was nothing he could do to harm his lover in the mind palace, no matter how fragile he seemed. His thrusts were deeper, longer, and more passionate. He was getting close.

"I love you, Laithe," Isam said, words muffled by the second tongue in his mouth.

The words worked like magic. Laithe's entire body tensed, then shook as he climaxed. Isam went limp, allowing his lover to fill him. After an intense spasm, Laithe let out a great sigh, grinning. He gazed into those dazzling green orbs and held Isam tight.

"Beriane is probably waiting," Isam spoke between heaving breaths, resting his chin on Laithe's shoulder. "You know how she gets when we keep her waiting before a patrol."

"I'm not done with you yet," Laithe sighed, pulling Isam off the tree, effortlessly supporting his entire weight. "That woman can wait a little while longer."

"But—" Isam began.

"It's not my fault that you haven't mastered the time here," Laithe jibed, laughing at his lover's scowl. Isam still hadn't figured out how Veremund manipulated time within the mind palace, which irritated him to no end. And Laithe loved ruffling his feathers. One heartbeat within the palace was one heartbeat without, so the couple had to manage their schedules more carefully than before.

"There aren't exactly written instructions for these things," Isam complained. Laithe chuckled and carried his partner across the meadow. "And there aren't any Tal'Rach left to teach me, either. You know that."

When Isam uttered the word Tal'Rach, Laithe knew what he implied. The pair never discussed Veremund explicitly, but the ram had left his mark on both of them, for better or worse. He was like a ghost, leaving behind memories both painful and pleasant.

"You will get the hang of it soon, my love. And we can fuck for hours on end, like we used to," Laithe reassured him, kissing him gently on the cheek. He hadn't meant to rile him up like this, at least in this way. "But we are not leaving until you are satisfied."

Laithe's inflection was stern like iron, and Isam did not argue as they crossed the meadow to their home. It was more of a pavilion than a cottage since weather was not an issue, and there was no need for a kitchen. Great wooden beams held up an intricate dome roof over a mossy floor. A great bed sat in the middle, overlooking the pond and the picturesque landscape.

Laithe flopped Isam onto the bed, staring down with intent. Isam preferred sex in the comforts of the sheets, but every once in a while, he indulged his lover with a romp outside. Laithe loved fucking in nature—it reminded him of his days in the Undergrowth—but he knew he needed to thank his partner before they began their patrol with Beriane.

Kneeling next to the bed, Laithe clutched Isam's smooth thighs and took him in his mouth. He swirled his tongue around the head, getting it wet before taking it all in. Isam exhaled in delight while Laithe began working. He knew exactly how he liked it. He proceeded at a leisurely pace, relishing the taste. Only when Isam begged did he start to suck with intent. Isam cried out, and Laithe was filled with his warmth.

"That's better," Laithe said, wiping his lips clean. "We can depart when you're ready."

"Let us lay here a while," Isam sighed, patting the mattress beside him. Laithe eagerly climbed into the bed and pulled Isam into his arms.

The pair lay in silence for a while, listening to each other's heartbeats. They rested together each night, but these moments of solace were rare. At first, they were often apart, one spirit in the mind palace, one without. It was a miserable existence, so they soon discovered a new way of living.

They could inhabit Laithe's body simultaneously.

At first, it was disorienting, like being drunk. They could maintain it for long periods, otherwise Laithe would vomit out of nausea. But they persisted, determined to spend as much time together as they could glean. They could communicate using their thoughts as speech, which proved useful during battle. Two minds were better than one while fighting, and Laithe was pleasantly surprised by this new dynamic.

Veremund and Laithe were a pair of tempests, raging together and destroying anything within their path. Isam and Laithe were two pieces of a whole. Laithe was the smoldering inferno of violence, whereas Isam was the cooling breeze, tempering him, bringing logic and prudence. Laithe was the hammer, and Isam the shield. It was a perfect partnership.

"Are you ready, my love?" Isam asked, stretching lazily.

"I suppose, little one," Laithe replied, kissing Isam gently on the forehead. "Let's not keep our people waiting."

They intertwined themselves in a fervent embrace and kissed as the world around them fell away. Together, they flew into the world to protect their fellow Deviants.

# # #

Sarina crouched on the grassy knoll beneath the Dragon's Teeth, overlooking the once-great city of Tabulrossa. Three months had passed since the Deviants and priestesses defeated the Tal'Rach. The once illustrious green canopy had faded to brown with decay. The great tree was withering without the great spirits' power and, by her estimate, would be uninhabitable within the year. The vast power of the great spirits sustained the enormous tree, and after that fateful day in the Sanctum, only one Tal'Rach remained. And he wasn't concerned with the health of the tree. Without the power of the rach, the city would wither and die. Good riddance.

To her dismay, Tabulrossan's hatred for Deviants did not die with the Tal'Rach. Very few who were not present in the Precipice during the siege believed the true nature of the rach. Even with the great Edicts destroyed, the prejudice they created endured. If anything, the destruction of the Tal'Rach inflamed the tension between ordinary people and the Deviants. In their minds, the Ae'Rach and their leader, Veremund, succeeded in their nefarious plot to murder their protectors and destroy the world.

The days following the siege were nothing but chaos. Thousands fled the city in droves, unable to accept the priestesses at their word. Regardless of identity, anyone who took up arms against their deities was no better than the Deviant scum they had grown to fear. And now their fear was realized. Incidents often devolved into violence, especially when the remaining wardens returned from across the world to find their leader and their gods slain by the servants sworn to protect them.

Marikae reasoned with the green-clad order, but most wardens who witnessed the battle refused to believe the truth. Belief was a powerful agent of delusion. Untangling years of propaganda would take more work than a single day. Such hatred became unmanageable, and the city was no longer safe for anyone involved in the Tal'Rach's destruction. Sarina assessed the sprawling encampment built at the bottom of the knoll; it had served as their home while they gathered their numbers from across the city and the surrounding lands. Marikae ordered three deep trenches dug on the exposed sides of the camp. The Dragon's Teeth on the fourth side proved to be as effective a defense as rach-powered wards, but it did not deter the wardens from attacking almost daily.

The camp's defenses handily negated the assaults; each passing day was another where the newly awakened priestesses grew stronger. Sarina, Marikae and the priestesses of the peacock transferred their knowledge to the other temples, though they deconstructed those distinctions after they left the city. Almost every priestess, regardless of whether they joined the siege, accompanied Marikae to their new encampment and resided in the central tents. They were the easiest to convince of the Tal'Rach's true nature since they spent years serving the monsters. A small number remained to support the wardens, but most were powerless. The thousands of rach that floated between the encampment tents were a testament to that. Almost no spirit dwelled in Tabulrossa; the priestesses within the encampment drew them all with their song.

Tavo rested on the ground next to Sarina's feet, gazing lazily at the bustling masses in the encampment below. He never left her side, and she wondered how much of Benjin was still inside him. He reminded her of the countless who sacrificed their lives to make this future a reality. And of what she had lost along the way. Benjin. Loving, energetic, and kind. Callandra. Positive, stalwart, and calming. Minora. Shy, mysterious, and eager to learn. And Alma. Severe, powerful, and the greatest leader she had ever known. The four of them and countless others were now gone, roaming freely as rach. But they would live on in the memory of those who remained. Sarina vowed to ensure that the world would never forget their sacrifices, and by doing so, she could immortalize their memory.

The priestesses and Deviants of Tabulrossa were not the only inhabitants now. Word spread throughout the land of what happened in the city. Every day, new migrants journeyed from their homes to join them, drawn by tales of an actual haven for Deviants with solid defenses. Their numbers grew tenfold in the first weeks, bringing dozens of challenges to the encampment. It filled Sarina with hope when non-Deviants joined the camp. At first, she suspected it was a plot by the wardens to plant spies in their midst, to destroy them from the inside. But these new arrivals were simply family or friends of Deviants from around the known world. Unlike the masses, these few hid their Deviant loved ones from the wrath of the wardens, disbelieving someone they knew so intimately could be an evil spirit.

Sarina was surprised by the legion gathered at the encampment. Sometimes, she wondered what her life would have been if her village had supported her. She shook the thought out of her mind. Although her new life presented challenges, Sarina couldn't change the past and was more than happy with her present. Housing such a host in a limited space was impossible; daily warden raids made farming unfeasible, and supply runs became dangerous once their enemy reclaimed the city.

The mountainous man standing near her on the hill, however, offered a considerable amount of protection. The newly created Tal'Rach volunteered to guard any Deviant who made their pilgrimage across the plains and lead the weekly missions to supply the encampment with food, water, and necessities. He was tall, with brown hair, an intense disposition, and heavily muscled. Unlike the great spirits before him, he bore no animalistic signs. When he spoke, two voices harmonized, speaking in unison. Marikae mentioned she had never witnessed an avatar and Tal'Rach commune in such a way, but the mercenary and his great spirit became one. Conversing with two people in one body was unsettling, but Sarina was grateful for their help. They neither went by Laithe nor Isam and like all Tal'Rach, they chose a new name to call themselves, distinguishing themselves from their old lives. Isemelith.

Their new visage appeared remarkably like Veremund, though Sarina would never comprehend how the two men could still love the ram spirit after everything they suffered at his hands. Yes, his final gift granted them a new life together, but it was Veremund's fault they were in that situation.

Each night, they would return to what they called a mind palace, a dreamlike place within their consciousness, according to Marikae. The avatar's relationship with the spirit was too complex for Sarina to fully understand. Since the priestesses weren't interested in creating another Tal'Rach anytime soon, she wouldn't have to worry about the intricacies of the partnership.

One thing was certain: dozens of Fourteens always trailed Isemelith, most of them marked with a strange tattoo on their forearm. The men fawned over him like a deity, for they considered him their champion, above all others, despite his adamant claims that his purpose was to protect all Deviants. She hoped the men's devotion to the new Tal'Rach wouldn't lead to problems in the future. Beriane would see to that. She always knew how to humble the Tal'Rach and keep him in his place.

The new priestess spent the most time with Isemelith, joining him on his patrols along the camp's perimeter and into the city. She proved to be one of the most powerful priestesses in the land, more adept in battle than even Marikae. Beriane's skills and ingenuity with the rach knew no equal. She could replicate the odd phenomena they witnessed during the final battle at the Precipice when the priestesses forced the Tal'Rach to possess metal weapons. Beriane eased common rach into swords, and half the Deviant fighters now fought with one. Since they were common rach, they could not communicate with their host as Laithe described Veremund had during the battle. It was a bit unsettling to Sarina, who worried about the ethics of such an art, as a rach could not consent. But her pragmatism was stronger than her altruism. They needed protection and these new weapons were essential.

Sarina was sure that Beriane would one day replace her lover as high priestess. And the order would be in excellent hands.

But today, their entire future rested fully on Sarina's shoulders.

Marikae climbed up the hill, smiling brightly. Beriane, Kez, and a handful of priestesses joined Sarina and Isemelith on the hillside. The blind woman bonded with the high priestess in the days after the Tal'Rach's defeat. Few in the encampment would speak to its leader so frankly and forthrightly, and Marikae valued that relationship. Sarina blushed, and the tall woman took her hand and led her off to the side of the group. There was only one relationship the high priestess cherished more than the rest. Sarina was proud that it was with her.

The pair spent every night together, and Sarina became Marikae's most trusted advisor. She had earned this respect, but Sarina initially thought it preposterous. She was a failed leader, in her opinion, allowing everyone in her care to perish, save three. All of whom were alive because of Marikae. She was the strongest person Sarina had ever met. Sarina felt safe in her arms, encouraged by her presence, and truly seen. Sarina couldn't imagine how she survived so long without her. If she had any say, there would never be a day they would spend apart ever again.

"All of the preparations are ready," Marikae gestured to the thousands milling between freshly dismantled tents. Hundreds were already climbing the hill towards them. "But the real question is, are you prepared?"

"I stood here nine months ago, presented with the same decision," Sarina said. "For all this time, I believed it was the wrong one, that I could have saved Benjin and Callandra by abandoning these lands. But now I stand here with every Deviant within a thousand leagues. I stand here with you by my side. And now I know I made the right decision."

Holding hands, the pair turned to the winding road that led into the Dragon's Teeth, high into the mountains, passing east into an unknown world. A world where they weren't Deviants, weren't labeled as evil Ae'Rach. They were merely human.

Two weeks ago, a galvanized force of wardens assaulted the camp, confronting the Deviants with the reality of their situation. It seemed the wardens' numbers were only growing after the death of the Tal'Rach, and their priority was to destroy those who murdered their deities. Only two options remained. For the priestesses to crush their enemies, killing every warden and becoming the monsters the people feared them to be. Or to take the voyage across the Dragon's Teeth to a new world beyond. One without daily threats, where they could settle in peace and start afresh.

Marikae presented the second option one night after the wardens almost breached their defenses. It was a simple choice. Fighting the foe who they knew or gambling on an unknown. There could be nothing on the far side of the mountains or more formidable enemies than the Tal'Rach and their wardens. It was the same decision Sarina faced all those months ago. At first, most of Marikae's advisors laughed at the second choice. But then Sarina processed it. There was no viable future for them here, only death, destruction, and pain. With the power of the rach, the mountain pass would be more than manageable. And with a leader like Marikae, they would surely flourish in this new world.

"I am ready, my love," Sarina said. "None of this would have been possible without you. I have never been more sure of any decision I've ever made."

"Do you know what your most infuriating quality is?" Marikae asked softly. Sarina cocked her head at the odd question. "It is that you are the only person alive who doesn't see how wonderful you are. You inspire me, Sarina, guide me, and make me want to improve myself. You always think of me as this perfect, stalwart bastion of hope. But I was close to giving up before you entered my life. I have never met a more focused, dedicated, and unwavering soul in all my years. Do you think these people are here today for me? It's you, Sarina. They are following you."

Sarina's heart swelled with pride. Marikae was always free with her words and quick to compliment, but she had never expressed her appreciation in this way before. Sarina never knew Marikae thought the same way she thought of her, and she respected and appreciated her so thoroughly. She always knew there was love there, but simply hearing how much she impacted the high priestess's life in a few short months filled her with energy and gave her a purpose.

She would live up to Marikae's expectations and be the woman she thought she was. Sarina gripped her hand and headed towards the mountain pass, towards the unknown.

"I will take the compliments. Know that I think of you in

the same light, my love," Sarina said. "But you are wrong on one account. They will follow us."

The priestess motioned to her former companions, Beriane, Kez, and Laithe, now in the form of Isemelith. To the priestesses gathered on the hillside below, to the dozens of Deviant leaders who protected their people outside Tabulrossa for years. Finally, to the rach. The spirits of those before them who died for their sake. Each one would be honored, revered, and protected. Never again would a spirit be destroyed for another's immortality.

As they entered the mountain pass together, away from a world that despised them, they were one group, unified by fire. They would never again use the slur "Deviant," but they used their name in the ancient tongue, the Ae'Rach. A new people for a new land, and may the gods protect anyone who tried to stop them.

9 798989 026029